Epiphany

Epiphany

The Acolyte

Patrick Totman

Library of Congress Control Number:		2018910235
ISBN:	Hardcover	978-1-9845-4964-8
	Softcover	978-1-9845-4963-1
	eBook	978-1-9845-4969-3

Print information available on the last page.

Rev. date: 10/21/2019

**To order copies of the
Epiphany Series contact:**
EpiphanyNovels.com

Or Call:
Xlibris
1-888-795-4274

784124

For Edward Stackpoole, S.J. and for Peggy McDow and Zita Murphy, two strong women of the 20th century.

EPIPHANY

AN EPIPHANY CAN be simply defined as a flash of insight flowing from an unusual, sometimes terrifying, experience. Epiphanies often are associated with the appearance of supernatural beings, either good or evil. Perhaps the best known epiphany is that of Saul of Tarsus on the road to Damascus. Saul is knocked senseless to the ground and blinded by an appearance of God. Saul, a pharisee and a persecutor of Christians, becomes Paul, the author of nearly half the books of the New Testament and the greatest proselytizer on behalf of the nascent Christian religion. His epiphany was clear and complete and he knew precisely how to respond. By contrast, most epiphanies are subtle and ambiguous, difficult to decipher and easy to ignore.

ACOLYTE

AN ACOLYTE IS one who attends, waits upon and serves someone viewed as superior to the acolyte. The acolyte seeks not only to serve and to be directed by the superior, but also to learn from and be enlightened by him or her.

CHAPTER 1

Wednesday, May 27, 1987 10:00 a.m. San Francisco, California

"JESUS." A STRONG oath for any who knew the priest.

"What have I done? Abomination."

The priest knelt but could not lift his eyes, could not find his voice to call on God. Finally, the priest rose and began to dress himself.

+ + +

"Great day for a stroll across the bridge, Father."

What the hell? I purposely wore no collar or cross, nothing to identify me as a priest. How could this cabbie know?

"What do you mean, 'Father'?" he asked in a level tone.

"You gave the sermon up on the hill a couple weeks ago and I happened to be there. Wish I could say I made it every Sunday."

"You must be mistaken. I'm not a priest."

"Whatever you say, Father. . . I mean Mister," said the cabbie with a glance in the mirror. "Anyway, it is a great day.

Want me to pick you up on the other side?" he asked, with another glance in the rear-view.

"No, no, I'm...meeting someone over there."

It *was* a great day, a veritable feast for the senses, the kind of spring day for which San Francisco was rightly famous. Soon enough the malaise of summer, with its seemingly endless fog and chill, would descend on the City. The priest began to admire God's handiwork. He always had seen God in His creations and now he was tempted to surrender again to this reverie. The view from the bridge was marvelous. Ahead, Marin County and its headlands stretched westward toward the Pacific. To the right, looking past Angel Island and Alcatraz, lay the East Bay. Behind, seen while walking backward on the bridge, the San Francisco coastline from the Cliff House to Coit Tower and Fisherman's Wharf. Beyond lay Treasure Island anchoring each span of the Bay Bridge. With an effort, he pulled himself back to the present. The time for reflection or analysis, indeed for thought of any kind, was over. All had been considered, all available words parsed in search of an acceptable solution. Now there was no escape from the inescapable except death, and with it, if he were fortunate, blessed oblivion. He knew in his heart, however, that his faith in the existence of the immortal soul was justified and that mere oblivion was not his fate.

Even in his tortured state, he'd known it would come to this, and had researched it with care. Adam Thelen was a priest and a member of the Society of Jesus. He also was, notwithstanding his relative youth, a noted teacher and writer in the areas of law and psychology, and the increasingly prevalent interaction of the two disciplines. He was a Jesuit and a lawyer, admittedly somewhat of a redundancy, and a product of Jesuit training. His life, therefore, was governed by the seemingly contradictory tenets of reason and faith. What he'd done, what he'd facilitated by his actions and inactions, truly was an abomination, anathema to the very core of his being. He'd had the opportunity to intercede, albeit at great personal cost, and he had foregone it. Even as he'd tried to rationalize his actions, to live through them, he'd known he could not do so. Now, all that remained was the bridge.

As Adam Thelen had exited the taxi in the parking area adjoining the bridge's south anchorage, an anonymous black Buick pulled into a parking slot fifty yards away. Its driver remained in the vehicle, apparently taking in the view to the east.

The Golden Gate Bridge had opened May 27, 1937 and today was the bridge's fiftieth anniversary. The bridge deck is just under 9,000 feet long and is about 250 feet above the water at its center, which also serves as the boundary between San Francisco on the south and Marin County to the north. For reasons of aesthetics, Adam Thelen did not wish to dash himself upon the southern footing of the bridge. This had occurred all too often in the past and been duly described in grisly detail in the morning *Chronicle*. Also, even with the terrible recent events, the priest felt a residual fondness for San Francisco or, as he thought of it, "The City." He wished to die within its confines rather than inside the legal boundaries of Marin County, which is comprised of scattered cities and towns of no particular distinction. Mindful of this, the priest proceeded beyond the south tower of the bridge, past several crisis phones ("There is hope—make the call"), but well short of the bridge's midpoint. Thus, he would insure that he hit the water on the City side. Also, to further assure his final resting place within San Francisco, he had consulted a tide table and chosen an incoming tide which, God willing, should deposit his mortal remains somewhere on the seabed off Fisherman's Wharf. Now, as he walked along the eastern promenade of the bridge adjoining the northbound traffic, the priest was able to avoid conscious thought, allowing his stunning surroundings to fill, almost to anesthetize, his senses. When he was well past the south tower, he came into view of the midpoint sign perhaps three hundred yards ahead, announcing Marin County. Without hesitation he mounted the rail and leapt out and away from the bridge.

"Mistake," uttered aloud, before his feet actually left the rail. He had thought his sins unforgivable, even unredeemable. Now he knew he was a fool and a knave, doubly so given his priestly status. His actions and failures to act were heinous, bestial— precisely the stuff of forgiveness and redemption. What he now was doing was the unforgivable, the hubris of one who defined right and wrong for others but was unable to chart his own path. Also, it was the ultimate cowardice allowing, as it did, the evil of others to proceed unchecked and unconfronted. All of these thoughts occurred in less than a second or two, leaving, he knew, only two or three more until the end. There was nothing for it now but a stylish entry and a stylish exit. "Oh my God I am heartily sorry..."

While at Fordham Prep and Fordham University in the Bronx, New York, Adam Thelen had been a varsity swimmer and diver. In 1976, as a University sophomore, he had been good enough to compete in the U.S. Olympic diving trials but had failed to qualify. When the 1980 Olympics rolled around, he was attending Fordham Law School at Lincoln Center in Manhattan, and his competitive diving days were behind him. Nonetheless, he had stayed in shape since then with a regular regimen of swimming, weights, and lately, martial arts. So it was not mere coincidence that he entered the water feet first and virtually vertical, with his hands cupping his groin. Also, as a youth in upstate New York, he had fallen from a good-sized tree and ruptured his spleen; it had been removed on an emergency basis shortly thereafter. Thus, when he entered the water at just under ninety miles per hour, he did not die on impact as would have been likely with any other entry position. And, he was not susceptible to the most common cause of death post-impact, a ruptured spleen and the accompanying internal hemorrhage. Notwithstanding these two propitious events, he was unconscious from the moment of impact until perhaps two minutes later. He entered the water at approximately 11:20 a.m. just as the inward flood tide was reaching its zenith at 3.5 knots flowing east/southeast in the general direction of Fisherman's Wharf.

+ + +

As soon as Adam Thelen had ascended the steps onto the deck of the bridge, the Buick's driver departed the parking area and turned left. This road led rather steeply downward to Fort Point, located right on the water, just east of the bridge. The driver parked and now exited the car. In his hands he held a pair of eight power wide angle binoculars with which he began to scan the east railing of the bridge. When, approximately fourteen minutes later, he saw a figure leap from the bridge and strike the water, he smiled slightly, reentered his car and drove off.

+ + +

"...for having offended thee, and I detest all my sins..."

His first thought was *why am I not dead?*

This was followed by an enormous rush of gratitude to God for sparing him. Then, unbidden, came a spontaneous but solemn vow to use this second chance to atone for what he had done and to cause the others also to atone or to pay a very dear price if they chose not to do so. All these ruminations occurred before consciousness fully returned; when it did, he found himself floating on his back with San Francisco on his left. He saw a helicopter lift off and fly directly toward him. Instinctively, he lay motionless as the helicopter passed overhead and continued toward the bridge. Apparently, his jump had been witnessed and reported. Without much conscious thought, he turned onto his stomach and stripped down to shorts and a tee and began pulling for shore. For reasons he did not comprehend, he removed his wallet before discarding his trousers and stuffed it into his shorts. He could see what he knew to be Crissy Field and the masts of St. Francis Yacht Harbor. He knew the tide was incoming and could feel it pushing him along the Marina.

A thought formed: *I could survive this.*

A myriad of other thoughts ensued, all begging the same questions. *What should I do if I do survive? How best to do whatever that might be?*

Finally he forced these intrusions aside and concentrated on the single task at hand which was, simply, survival. Already, Crissy Field was mostly behind him and the yacht club was coming up on his right. And the water was so cold. The tide and his feeble attempts at swimming had taken him a little closer to shore. Suddenly, he remembered Aquatic Park, where he had swum two or three times a week until the twin burdens of teaching and writing conspired to allow only laps in the pool on campus. If he could reach the municipal pier and pull himself into the Aquatic Park lagoon, he knew he could survive. The water felt less cold. Just for a moment, he turned onto his back and allowed himself the luxury of watching the bridge, the cerulean sky and the Marin headlands; soon all three began to merge in his consciousness. It no longer seemed cold at all.

+ + +

S.F. Chronicle, May 28, 1987, page 6
UNKNOWN PERSON JUMPS FROM GOLDEN GATE
Sometime prior to 11:30 a.m. yesterday, an unknown person was seen jumping from the Golden Gate Bridge. Witnesses described him only as a white male. Search and rescue efforts from the nearby Coast Guard station were launched immediately, but no trace of the man was found. Search efforts were suspended at nightfall.

CHAPTER 2

Thursday, May 28, 1987 10:30 am. Inner Richmond District, San Francisco, California

"VERY STRANGE," SAID Mike Burke, muttering to himself while reading the Sunday *Chronicle* across the breakfast table from his wife, Maria.

"What's that?"

"Ah, just talking to myself again. Yesterday morning I had a fare to the Golden Gate and now I read that someone jumped."

"Michael, that's a terrible thing. You don't think….."

"No, of course not, it was a beautiful morning and there must have been hundreds of people on the bridge. It's just that I thought I recognized this guy. He looked like the priest who gave the sermon week before last."

"Michael, you should be thankful that God doesn't strike you dead this instant for even thinking that a priest might commit suicide."

"Maria, you are correct as always and I am nothing but an Irish ass."

+ + +

The driver of the anonymous Buick perused the same page 6 article from the Sunday *Chronicle.* He is Father Damian Kung and he is seated in the dining room of the campus rectory with another man. This man spoke first. "It's got to be him. You saw him jump."

"I saw *someone* jump."

"Come on. What are the chances that you follow Adam Thelen's taxi out to the bridge, watch him start across and then see someone else jump. Besides, why did he take a taxi unless he knew it was a one way trip? He could have taken one of the cars if he were simply out for a stroll."

"I grant you all of that. Plus, he never came back last night and he still isn't here. What bothers me is that they haven't found a body. I want to see that son of a bitch on a slab and the sooner the better. I want his family grieving rather than crawling up my ass. And I think everyone else agrees, although they're such pussies they'd never say so out loud."

"For a priest, you have a mouth like a sailor."

"Listen you little prick, don't give me any holier than thou bullshit. Your ass is hanging out further than mine. We'll give it a few days to see if he washes up somewhere. But if by some miracle, and I hope God isn't that puckish, he shows up alive, then you're going to finish the job."

CHAPTER 3

Friday, May 29, 1987 10:00 a.m. Marina District, San Francisco, California

"YO, MIKE BURKE, where are you?" asked the dispatcher.

"I just dropped a fare from SFO at the Mark Hopkins."

"I've got a pick-up for you over at the Travelodge in the Marina. Can you take it?"

"Hey man, I'm a block away from the place. I'll take the call," said another cab driver.

"Sorry my man, this fare asked for Mike by name."

"OK, I'll head over there," answered Mike, "but it's gonna take me ten minutes or so. Who is the fare anyway?"

"No idea. Just a guy who says you've hauled him before. You must have made quite an impression."

"Probably some fairy that liked your looks, Mikey," interrupted the other driver."

"All right, we'll have none of that," said Mike. "You know I'm not that way even though I do count several of them as friends."

It was another fine day, crystalline up on Nob Hill, although there had been fog that morning when Mike Burke set out from his home in the Richmond District.

"Better get used to it." said Mike to himself. "The summer is almost upon us."

Since the guy apparently was willing to wait, Mike decided to head down Taylor toward Columbus rather than taking California to Van Ness. The view across the Bay was wondrous and he felt his spirits rise. Also, he was curious about this call. It wasn't often that a fare requested him by name. He took a left on Columbus and then another on Bay to make his way around. There was no one in sight other than passers-by who obviously weren't looking for a cab. He parked near the office and went inside.

The women at the desk saw him coming and said, "He's in #7 and he can't be gone soon enough for me."

"Really. What's wrong with him?" Mike had experienced his share of strange fares and was prepared to just drive away if the guy sounded too weird.

"Well, he had no luggage when he showed up yesterday and he was barely dressed. What clothes he had didn't come close to fitting him and no shoes at all! He had a wild look about him. But he was polite enough and he had cash for two days so I let him in. The other funny thing was his money was wet."

"Any trouble since then?"

"Didn't hear a peep from him until he called this morning asking for a cab. And not just any cab. He had to have Mike Burke. Are you him?"

"Yes, I am," said Mike. And then, after a pause, "When did he get here?"

"He arrived about 1:30 on Wednesday afternoon. And that's another thing; I don't think he's been out of the room since then.

I checked with the night man and he wouldn't let housekeeping in either. Weird. Please just take him somewhere else."

Mike walked outside and stood thinking as he looked across at #7.

Maybe I should just walk away from this.

But, he was curious as to how this person knew his name. Plus, there was something else he could not yet name. Reaching a decision, he walked across the lot and knocked on #7. The door opened immediately, as if the man inside had watched Mike approach the door.

"You," said Mike Burke.

"Yes it is," said Adam Thelen. "Thank you for coming. Will you step inside for a moment?"

"You're kidding. I'm not coming in there with you."

"Please. I understand your hesitance, but I need your help. Just come in and listen to me for a moment. If you want to leave then, I won't stand in your way."

Something about the man and a dawning realization of who he was and what he'd done two days before caused Mike to overcome his hesitance and enter the room. The man was clad in a sweatshirt at least two sizes smaller than needed and a pair of cutoff jeans. He looked even worse than the office manager had indicated, with two days of no food or grooming added to the equation.

"I am Adam Thelen and I am a priest, as you guessed on Wednesday."

"How did you get my name?"

"I saw it on your license in the cab. I remember items like that, especially regarding people who make an impression on me and I can assure you that you did make an impression. The last thing I wanted on Wednesday was to be recognized by someone, especially a parishioner, even though ours is not technically a parish church."

"All right, Father. Where can I take you?"

"I don't want to go anywhere just yet. What I need is your help."

"Father, I'm a taxi driver..."

"I know, and I'll pay you for your time."

"For God's sake. You know it's not about money. You're a priest who has tried to commit suicide and I'm just a cabbie. How can I possibly help you?"

"For now, I need food and some decent clothes. I have money and you can assure the lady in the office that you know me and that I'm harmless and will be out of here by 2:00. Tell her I'll pay her extra. Then, if you're still willing, I'll tell you where you can take me."

After a long moment of thought, Mike Burke said, "All right Father. I know a good sandwich joint close by. I'll bring back a couple and go out for clothes while you're eating. I should be back by 1:30."

+ + +

Ah, ambrosia! It's got to be Freddy's.

Mike Burke had not mentioned where he had bought the sandwiches, but in fact Adam Thelen's conjecture was correct. Freddy's was a San Francisco institution, seemingly known to everyone with even a passing familiarity with the City.

The bread, my God the bread! I think it's still warm. They could put lawn clippings between slices of this bread and it would be a great sandwich.

The bread in fact was extremely fresh, having been delivered to Freddy's earlier that morning, but the residual warmth was only in Adam Thelen's imagination. The bread was San

Francisco sourdough beloved the world over and air freighted to many parts of it. The innards of the sandwiches were not, however, lawn clippings. There were thin pungent slices of Mortadella, Jack cheese, shredded lettuce, coarsely chopped tomato, and pepperoncini with just the right amount of Freddy's mayo and sweet mustard spread.

Adam Thelen wolfed the first sandwich, paused and began to eat the second more slowly, the better to savor each bite, relishing the momentary bliss of food—great food! After fully forty-eight hours of fast, his mind returned to the present reality. On Wednesday morning, he had lapsed into unconsciousness with St. Francis Yacht Club and the Marina Green coming up on his left. That would have been the end of him, but for the incoming tide, which continued to push him, floating on his back, in a generally easterly direction. He had been jarred back to consciousness when the current drove him head first into one of the concrete supports of the Municipal Pier which, along with the Hyde St. Pier, encloses the lagoon which is Aquatic Park. His first inclination was simply to float into oblivion. Then he remembered his vow to God, made only a short time earlier, to atone for his sins and to cause others to atone. With a groan he turned to his left and began a feeble side stroke under the pier and toward the shore. He swam a course parallel with the inner edge of the pier. Soon he could hear the desultory words of the day fishermen casting from the pier above him. He became aware that he was in sight of others and began to gather himself into a semblance of normalcy. He knew that other swimmers would be out. Suddenly he was aware that his formless floundering side strokes made him look like a swimmer in extremis, which he was. He quickly took a bearing on the shore, turned onto his back and with energy born of desperation began a passable back stroke. Soon he could feel the gentle shore swell and knew he was close.

But what the hell am I going to do when I get there?

In the event, he simply sat on the sand about ten feet from the water. He looked around and noted with relief that no one was staring at him. He recalled from his earlier days swimming here that the few hardy souls who braved the chill waters of the bay were thought to be somewhat deranged. This was good in his present circumstances. Still, he couldn't sit here forever. Looking about, he noticed a pile of clothing some way up the beach. With a great effort, he found that he could stand and then very slowly walk to the clothes. He could see three swimmers out on the lagoon, but no other clothing on the beach. The clothes consisted of a sweatshirt, cut-off jeans, a towel and a pair of sneakers. He sat down, checked that the swimmers continued their rhythmic progress back and forth and pulled the zip front sweatshirt around his shoulders.

Way too small, but it will have to do.

The jeans were better because the waistband was elastic. The shoes however, were not going to work—at least three sizes too small. He stood and used the towel to dry his legs and arms and brush off the sand. With a last look at the three swimmers, he turned and began to trudge up Van Ness toward Bay. He made a right on Bay and after about three blocks saw the Travelodge a couple of blocks to his left.

He had collapsed on the bed as soon as he entered the room. When he awoke, it was dark. The bedside clock said 4:30. He was very thirsty. He tried to arise but fell back into bed.

My God, I feel like Marvin Hagler after going twelve rounds with Sugar Ray Leonard.

In a way though, he was relieved to be suffused with physical rather than psychic suffering. After a bit, he struggled to his feet and made his way to the bathroom. He drank three glasses of water—Bless you Hetch Hetchy Dam for the pure mountain water enjoyed by San Franciscans.

He awoke again at noon feeling physically refreshed. Almost immediately, however, he began again to contemplate that which had driven him to the bridge. The passage of time had made it no less real and no less abominable. The same feelings of anger, frustration, and despair began to overtake him. Now, however, instead of succumbing, he suppressed them and turned his thoughts toward God. He spent the next twelve hours in prayer to God. He contemplated God's strange and wondrous ways. Finally, he considered at length the eternal mystery of God's perfect goodness juxtaposed with the evil which suffused this world. By midnight, his feelings of frustration and despair had passed away, but his anger burned brighter than ever. He fell into a fitful sleep until he awoke on Friday morning. His anger had not abated.

+ + +

"I got you a t-shirt, jeans, shorts, and the hooded sweatshirt you asked for. Also socks and a pair of Nikes, size eleven."

"Michael, you are helpful indeed. Those sandwiches have given me a new lease on life. Let me change into the clothes and we can be out of here. Do I owe the lady any more money?"

"No. After the story I told her about you, she's just happy to see you go."

"Ah. Thank you for that also, I guess."

"All right then Father. Where to?"

"To the rectory please."

"What kind of reception do you think you'll receive back there?"

"Rather frosty I imagine. Perhaps worse than that."

After a minute or so of silence, the cabbie turned briefly toward Adam Thelen.

"Look Father, you obviously are in some kind of serious situation. Is there something else I can do to help?"

"You've already done much more than I could reasonably expect. I have no right to ask for more."

"You're right there, Father! But, I am offering even though I can't rightly explain why."

"Are you absolutely certain you wish to become more involved? The situation could become even more dire."

Mike Burke looked at Adam Thelen in the rear-view mirror before responding, "Yes I am."

"OK, when we get to the rectory, drop me just around the corner. I'll show you where. Then give me time to go in the back door, shower and shave and change into my own clothes. Precisely twenty minutes after you see me enter, I'll pay a visit to another priest. If he's in, I'll talk to him for only two or three minutes. After I leave him, I strongly suspect he'll be in his car, which is a black Buick. I'll also show you the garage area. I'd very much like to know where he goes. If you can follow him and find out, I'll be more than thankful."

"OK, I can do that."

"Just drop your flag as soon as he leaves, and I'll be your phantom fare. I gave you my last cash for the clothes, so I'll have to owe you for the fare up here and then to wherever he goes."

"Father, I know you're good for the money..."

"OK. If you don't see him leave within forty minutes after I go inside, just forget about it. Either way, I'll get in contact with you and pay what I owe. Don't call here. I'll find a way to contact you."

"Let me give you my address. It's not far."

"No, I don't want to be seen anywhere near your home. Do you work tomorrow?"

"Yes, I take off Sundays and Wednesdays. Those are slow days to and from SFO. I was working last Wednesday because someone asked me to switch days."

"What time do you leave for work?"

"8:30 am. I try to keep regular hours."

"OK, I'll be in front of the market at the southwest corner of Fulton and Masonic at 8:35 or earlier. What will you be driving?"

"Father, I own this cab."

"Great, I'll hail you down."

Precisely thirty-one minutes after Adam Thelen entered the rectory, a black Buick flew from the garage, turned to the left and proceeded briskly to the end of the block. Even though he was watching from the car, its instantaneous appearance took him by surprise. He started his engine and was preparing to pull out when the Buick swerved to the curb and stopped. The driver's window came down and it was apparent that the driver of the Buick was watching the garage. A full two minutes elapsed before the window was raised and the Buick turned away from the curb. This time it moved away sedately, taking another left toward the center of the City. Mike Burke followed the Buick.

The Buick proceeded eastward on Fulton matching the speed of the moderate traffic. For Mike, it was as if the years separating him from his earlier life melted away. He was driving a yellow cab which was by definition anonymous—part of the landscape. His earlier persona came back in a wave and he once again was tailing, if not a perp then at least a priest in a

Buick who was suspected of something by a man he trusted, if for no definable reason. The driver of the Buick no longer seemed concerned with the possibility of followers and drove leisurely, complying scrupulously with all traffic laws. Mike was even able, with the Buick stopped at a red light, to pull to the curb as if stopping to converse with his dispatcher. As the Buick approached City Hall and the rest of Civic Center, it made a left on Franklin St. which was one-way traveling north. Mike stayed in the center lane about a block behind. After about twelve blocks, the Buick signaled for a right turn onto California and Mike easily was able to make a smooth lane change and follow. Now traffic was heavier, but much of it was buses, cable cars, and taxis heading over Nob Hill and down toward the foot of Market Street. As he approached the top of Nob Hill, the Buick's driver turned left into the Pacific Union Club.

Shit. What now?

Mike Burke thought that his profane past was gone forever. But just as his skills at tailing another car had seamlessly returned, so too had his earlier manner of articulating his thoughts. He continued past the Pacific Union Club taking the next left, proceeding around the block and back to the entrance to the Club.

Too late for lunch and too early for dinner. Probably in the main reading rooms just past the entry desk.

As it happened, the desk attendant was away from his desk at the far side of the adjoining reading room. This gave Mike Burke the opportunity to move past the desk and look around the reading room, which contained only three men reading newspapers and two other men talking softly in one corner. One of the men in the corner wore a priest's collar. Mike Burke looked closely at the man seated with the priest, as the desk attendant hurried over to deal with the obvious outsider.

"How may I help you sir?"

"Got a call for a pick-up at the Pacific Union Club. I'm parked outside."

"The last taxi pick-up we had was at least ten minutes ago…"

"Ah, some opportunist beat me to it. Thanks anyway," said Mike Burke as he headed for the door. He got in his cab and drove away.

CHAPTER 4

Saturday May 30, 1987 Masonic & Fulton, San Francisco, California

THE CHANGE IN Adam Thelen as he entered the taxi was dramatic. He was perfectly groomed and dressed in full, if understated, priestly regalia. More notable to Mike Burke was his change in demeanor. He looked fully in control of himself, yet his focus. . . a word not common to Mike Burke's lexicon came unbidden to his mind. *Maniacal.* He had heard it used by one of the shrinks in connection with a long-ago case, an especially brutal crime.

"Well Father, you look particularly purposeful this morning."

Adam Thelen looked sharply at the cabbie.

Not much escapes this guy.

Adam Thelen smiled. "Well yes. You might say I'm in the Devil's grasp," he said with a small chuckle. "Anyway, here's the money I owe you from yesterday."

Mike took the money saying, "This is way too much."

"You don't realize how much you've helped. Besides," said Adam Thelen almost as an afterthought, "I come from money."

Mike Burke had driven about five blocks since picking up the priest. Now he turned onto a side street and parked the cab.

"Did you discover anything yesterday afternoon after I left you?" asked Adam.

Mike Burke related the tailing of the Buick and what he had seen at the Pacific Union Club.

"The man talking to the priest was seated, but I can tell you that he was a small man, perhaps 5'6" or 5'7". He was extremely well groomed and well dressed. His suit was at least $800 and his shoes maybe half that. I could tell that his wrist watch was a diamond Rolex. He had cuff links worth more than my best suit."

"Excellent. Truly excellent. I owe you much more than I just gave you."

"Father, I won't accept any more money..."

"Did you notice anything else? What did this guy look like?"

"Well, Father, he looked like a ferret. Eyes very close together, a round nose and a moist pink mouth. And the other thing I noticed was that your priest friend seemed to be doing most of the talking and he didn't seem to be happy."

"No, I expect not. And he's definitely not my friend."

Here the maniacal look seemed to reappear and for a moment, Adam Thelen appeared to Mike Burke not to be fully in control. But the look passed as quickly as it had appeared, and full composure returned.

"I think I've seen this man you describe once before up at the rectory. And I think you've given me all I need to put a name to him."

"I thought about waiting around until he left the PU Club..."

"No, no. No matter. I know Father Kung is not a member of this club, which means that his associate is. And I happen to know another member quite well. I think I can discover who this guy is."

"Father, what else can I do to help?"

"Mike, your help already has been invaluable. It may well get messy, or even worse. Starting now, I can't ask you to be part of this going forward."

CHAPTER 5

"A CALL FROM your son, sir."
"Brave Bradley, leader of our East Coast outpost? Put him through."

"No sir. It's Adam."

Got to be something serious for him to call. And not good news.

"Put him through then."

"Dad? How are you?"

"I'm fine Adam. And you?"

"I'm OK Dad."

"So, what causes you to call?"

"I need to talk to you Dad. In person."

As anticipated, a serious problem. But what?

"All right. Why don't you come by the office tomorrow."

"Can we meet today, Dad? Are you free for lunch?"

"Actually not. I'm meeting Gisele for lunch."

"Oh . . . Well, say hello from me."

"No Adam. I shall cancel lunch with Gisele and you will join me for lunch. It will be that rare instance when she is easily mollified. You know you're the apple of her eye."

Probably because she was so successful in turning you away from my plans for you.

"Dad?"

"Yes Adam. What else?"

"Can we meet at the Pacific Union Club?"

"What?" Now he was genuinely baffled. "You of all people want to go to the Pacific Union Club? I believe you advised me not that long ago that evil was to be found inside those doors."

"Evil is everywhere, Dad."

"Ah, progress! Meet me there at 12:45."

Charles (Chaz) Langley Thelen was Adam Thelen's father. He was seventy-two years old, more than forty years his son's senior. He was and had been for many years the managing partner of Stein Brothers, Singer and Thelen, which had its roots in the nineteenth century. The father of Joseph and Isaac Stein had started it as a merchant banking house in Philadelphia and his sons had moved the bank to New York just as Prohibition became the law of the land. Chaz had joined Stein Brothers immediately after receiving his degree from Columbia in 1931. Chaz Thelen did well through the thirties, but he likely would have moved on from the sleepy, relatively small firm had not WWII intervened. Some of his Columbia classmates had joined the Roosevelt administration and one of them aided his entry into the Navy following Pearl Harbor. He never left the Pentagon for three years and when he emerged in 1945 as a Commander, Stein Brothers welcomed him back as a partner and added his name to the letterhead, along with that of his colleague, Joe Singer. It was at this point that wags in the banking industry began calling Stein Brothers, Singer and

Thelen, "The Judeo-Christian Firm." Both Stein brothers died in the fifties and Joe Singer left the firm in 1962 with enough money to pursue his real calling as a rabbinical scholar. Chaz Thelen had been managing partner for twenty-five years and had long since moved his office to San Francisco, while keeping the east coast office in midtown Manhattan. The firm now was comprised of eleven partners and 160 other associates of varying rank.

"Gisele. Hi."

"Hello Charles."

"I'm afraid I have to cancel lunch today."

"Not acceptable Charles. We need to talk. Those clowns on our trading floors seem to have had their heads up their asses more than usual during the last quarter."

When Gisele divorced Chaz Thelen in 1955, while the firm was still located exclusively in Manhattan, her terms had been simple. She asked for no money or support and she took only selected items of personal property, mostly art. She did require that she be made a partner in the firm with full and unfettered authority over its then nascent trading operations. She also retook her maiden name, Gisele Mellon. She remained a partner in 1987 albeit much less active on a day-to-day basis. Trading operations had accounted for just over 60% of the firm's net income in 1986.

"As it happens, Gisele, I agree with you and, in any event, nothing normally could persuade me to forego a lovely lunch with you."

"Cut the crap Charles. What's up?"

"It's Adam. He called just now and asked urgently to meet with me. He even suggested the Pacific Union Club."

"Adam? Called you? And is willing to set foot in the Pacific Union Club? I'll see you at lunch tomorrow then. And I wish to know all that Adam had to say."

"As you wish, my dear."

Gisele was not Adam Thelen's mother. In fact, she and Adam's mother, Emily, both were employees of the firm in 1955 when Chaz and Emily had been caught *in flagrante*. The divorce ensued along with an extraordinary development. The two women, who had been acquaintances, became close friends. After Emily's marriage to Chaz Thelen, Emily stayed in the firm and became a pivotal part of the investment banking business. After Adam Thelen's birth in 1957, Emily continued to work in the firm and Gisele became like an aunt to Adam. Emily was twenty-four and Chaz Thelen forty when they married in 1955. She now was fifty-six years old, and a partner in the firm.

"Adam, I see you've opted for mufti this afternoon. Curiouser and curiouser. Usually you wish to impress me with your priestly presence. Just like your sainted half-brother."

Adam's half-brother, Theodore, was twenty-two years older than he and also a Jesuit priest. He had been a professor at Fordham University, as well as Dean of Men during Adam's time there. He now was Father-President of that university.

Notwithstanding his preoccupation and his unease at being within the Pacific Union Club, Adam could not resist the opening, "How is Theo, Dad? Has he persuaded you yet of God's existence and of His overarching beneficence?"

"I indeed am convinced that God exists. Of His beneficence I am less certain. He mocks me every day now that not one but two of my sons are priests. And Jesuits to boot—the most devious of God's servants."

And the other son gay. No grandchildren likely from that source either.

"Ah, Dad. Age is not softening you one bit."

"Nor will it."

At this point the waiter made his presence known and the next few minutes were occupied with conversation about other family members. Adam's focus was on his father, but he also casually but carefully surveyed the other occupants of the room. Finally, the first course was served, and the two men drew closer together.

"All right Adam. What is the problem?"

"It's complicated and evil."

"There's an ominous preface. Let's hear it."

"I have a girlfriend. . . a lover. Actually, she's more than that. I love her."

Excellent! Maybe one of my gelding sons is returning to the world of men.

"Her name is Lorena Montes. She comes from a wealthy Catholic family in Seville. She's in the doctoral program in clinical psychology at the University."

"Don't you teach in that program?"

"Yes I do, in addition to some undergraduate classes."

"Go on."

"I've been seeing her since last summer. In December, I asked not to teach this semester, supposedly to write. I have done some writing but the real plan was that we would stay apart and not see each other again. She's finishing her program and should receive her Psy.D. next month. Then she was going to return to Spain."

"But…"

"Yes, we started meeting again in late February. Then early this month we learned that she was pregnant. It was a shock.

She had been on the pill at all times. We still don't know how it happened."

Hallelujah! A grandchild at last and from a most unexpected quarter.

"Don't look happy Dad. There's nothing happy in this story. More like grotesque. Lorena was devastated. She said she would never be able to return to Spain, let alone face her family and friends there. I offered to leave the priesthood and marry her, but she was inconsolable."

The waiter came with the entrees at this point and the conversation stopped. Adam again scanned the room while his father sat pensively. When the waiter had gone, Chaz Thelen simply looked at his son, saying nothing.

"Now comes the evil part. About a week ago, Father Kung approached me. He's a theology professor and the acting Dean of Women. I really don't know him well. He came here less than a year ago from a posting somewhere in Africa. No one seems to know anything about him. He suggested we have a private dinner out, which was unusual. He doesn't seem to mix much with any of the priests or other faculty."

"Where was he in Africa?"

"I don't know and I don't know anyone who does. He's very unforthcoming. Anyway, at dinner, he came right to the point. He said that Lorena had come to him and told him the whole story. She wanted to finish her degree and then enroll in the post-doctoral program at the University of Chicago. She indicated she was going to deal with the pregnancy over the summer. He said she wanted his help with enrollment at the university and with an internship or other cover story she could deliver to her parents to explain her decision to stay in the United States through the summer. He said he had done all Lorena asked, concluding it was best for the University and for me. I believed him."

"Why not? His account seems credible."

"It sounded reasonable to me too. But an abortion? I knew she had strong feelings about that, so I asked him. He said it was true that her plans for dealing with the pregnancy were a little unclear. He said he helped her with the decision to have an abortion and even went so far as to refer her to a doctor. It couldn't happen at St. Mary's but he knew someone up at UCSF Hospital. He said his own view of abortion was—evolving. I remember his words. He said, 'I believe the church's teachings also will change to give weight to all the costs and benefits of a particular situation. In this case, it was a no-brainer.'"

"Sounds rather like an investment banker."

"That's exactly what I thought at the time. But I was weak. I was troubled. I didn't object. I thought that would be the end of it but then he said, 'This is best for the University and also a good outcome for you, frankly a better outcome than you deserve. Perhaps you could by way of thanks do something for me.'"

"What did he want?"

"An introduction on behalf of an associate of his to mother."

"What? Your mother?"

"Yes."

"Why?"

"I don't know. All he would say was that it would help on some kind of a transaction and that given the circumstances, she should have no difficulty cooperating."

"Who was this associate he mentioned?"

"I didn't know then, but I think I do now. All he said was that he would give me the details the next day."

"And what did you say?"

"I said I would see him the next day."

"So you agreed to his proposal."

"I thought I could. But that night I prayed. I prayed as I never prayed before. And I realized the horror of what I was about to do. I was going to sanction the taking of a human life and I was going sentence Lorena to a lifetime of guilt and regret. The next day he came to my rooms directly after the lunch hour. He began to talk about the introduction, but I stopped him. I recall our exchanges very clearly."

"I cannot do what you propose, Father Kung. An abortion, especially in these circumstances, is monstrous. Thank you for your efforts. However, I am going to go to Lorena and help her through this time. I will make a full confession to our provincial and accept whatever discipline is prescribed, even expulsion from the Order and the priesthood"

"Do not play the fool, Father Thelen. This is the real world we inhabit and one bastard more or less is of no consequence whatever. Besides, the die was cast yesterday evening when you agreed to our proposal. The abortion now is a fait accompli, as are your obligations regarding the introduction."

"No, this cannot be. I will confess everything to the provincial."

"That was last Tuesday. I left my rooms with Father Kung still there, I was stunned, devoid of hope or direction. I went up to the campus and into the library and sat in one of the carrels. I could think of nothing except the desolation I had created. I don't know how long I was there, but it was dark when I returned to my rooms. I have a small bar there for visitors and I started to drink."

"You, drink? I've never seen you take more than a glass of wine."

"True. But that night I drank until I achieved oblivion. I awoke at 10:00 the next morning and called a cab."

"A taxi? What for?"

"Do you still read the *Chronicle* each morning?"

"Yes, along with the Wall Street Journal, the New York Times and excerpts from a dozen other papers prepared by a clipping service. I start at 7:00 and I'm finished at 8:15 every day, maybe earlier on weekends without the Journal."

"Then you saw the short article about the Golden Gate Bridge jumper."

"Yes, I did. What about him? Apparently he hasn't been found."

"That was me, Dad."

At this, his father stood up abruptly, drawing a few stares from around the room. With an effort, he composed himself and sat down.

"I warn you Adam, do not toy with me. Do not try me with this long fable. People, even you, do not waste my time and do not make me the butt of their jokes. I suggest you leave immediately."

"It's no joke Dad. I wish it were."

Adam Thelen spent the next fifteen minutes relating everything which had occurred since Wednesday morning. When he finished, the dining room was empty. Chaz Thelen sat with eyes downcast. Finally, he raised his head.

"So it's true about Lorena and the abortion?"

"Apparently it is, Dad. I tried to contact her yesterday on some bogus academic matter I created out of whole cloth. I reached her faculty advisor who told me she had left last Tuesday to begin an internship — two days after her discussion with Father Kung. All of her coursework was completed so she'll miss only the formal graduation ceremony. I also tried UCSF, but no luck there either. Abortion these days is an outpatient procedure, so she could have been in and out in a few hours."

"What a tragedy. A life — our life — simply extracted and thrown away."

My grandchild. Conceived and then discarded.

Adam Thelen watched a rage begin to overtake his father. He'd seen it happen before but only rarely and never to this extent. He thought his father might attack him physically. But when he spoke, Chaz Thelen was fully composed and soft spoken.

"I know this man your Father Kung was speaking with on Friday. Your cabbie's description is very accurate indeed, although the man is more weasel than ferret. His name, at least the name he uses, is Ezra Casque. He is a bad man, but he is merely an underling, albeit an effective one, of a man I consider to be truly evil. That man's name is Maxim Spektor and what he does is despicable. I also begin to see a possible connection with something your mother has been pursuing for some time, but I'll need to research all of this further. In the meantime, you must be very careful. And stay away from Father Kung or whoever he is. I believe you may be in serious danger. Will the Order allow you to travel, perhaps in connection with your writing?"

"I think I could arrange that."

"Good. Why don't you start work on such a trip right now? I will pursue the research I mentioned. Can you meet with me tomorrow afternoon at the office?"

"Yes."

"Let's say 2:30."

When Chaz Thelen returned to his office, he first called Gisele and then Adam's mother, Emily. He arranged for all three of them to meet for lunch the following day.

+ + +

When Adam Thelen arrived back at the rectory, it was nearly 4:00. As he approached the entrance to his rooms, he saw an envelope taped to his door. His name was handwritten on the envelope. He removed it as he unlocked the door. The note inside the envelope was cryptic.

"Father Thelen, please see me urgently concerning Ms. Montes. I will be here all afternoon. Father Kung."

Mindful of his father's warning, he considered his options. But in reality what option did he have other than to listen to whatever Father Kung had to say about Lorena. He went directly to Father Kung's room and knocked on the door.

"Ah. Thank you for coming, Father."

"Let's dispense with the niceties. What information do you have regarding Lorena?"

"As you wish. Ms. Montes advised her faculty advisor she has left the University to take an internship which unexpectedly opened. If you do precisely as I instruct you, she will complete this summer internship and will begin her post-doctoral studies at the University of Chicago in the fall. You will become a memory, a fond memory if you are fortunate. Her summer of love with you and her now departed love child will become a footnote in her life. If you decline to cooperate Ms. Montes will encounter an accident, a fatal accident as it happens. Her parents will be bereaved."

"What is it you require?"

"It is now 4:30. Be at Point Lobos by the USS San Francisco Memorial at 9:00 this evening. Do you know the place?"

"Yes. I'll be arriving by taxi."

"Fine. Have the driver drop you at the foot of Geary. Tell him you wish to walk the rest of the way down to the Cliff House Restaurant. Then walk out to the Memorial. Bring with you all the information necessary to begin discussions with your mother."

"I'll be there at 9:00."

+ + +

Adam Thelen waited until 7:00 p.m. before calling Mike Burke. Maria Burke answered the phone.

"Good evening Mrs. Burke. I'm calling for your husband Michael. Is he at home?"

"He is. May I tell him who is calling?"

"My name is Ed Bradley. Your husband dropped me at the Pacific Union Club yesterday and said I could call if I needed his services while I'm in town. I need him tonight for an hour if he's free."

"Just a moment. I'll get him for you."

"Ah, Mr. Bradley. Good to hear from you Sir," said Mike Burke.

"Can you pick me up about 8:30? I need a ride down to Point Lobos for a meeting. I'll be waiting down at the corner of Fulton."

"A strange place for a night time meeting."

"So I thought. Perhaps you'll have some advice for me."

"See you at 8:30."

At 8:25, Adam Thelen departed his rooms and the door closed behind him. He had taken three or four steps down the hall when he stopped, turned, and retraced his steps. He reopened his door and went to his dresser in the bedroom. He reached into the rear of the second drawer and extracted a twenty-two caliber revolver from between two sweaters. He checked the cylinder, and then felt around in the drawer for the box of ammunition. He grabbed a handful of cartridges and walked over to the window. The lights in his second floor bedroom were off. He placed the cartridges on the windowsill and methodically loaded the gun. When he was finished, he checked the cylinder, closed it, and placed the pistol in the right hand pocket of his jacket. Three shells remained on the windowsill. He scooped them up and dropped them into the pocket of his jeans.

+ + +

"Father, my advice is this," said Mike Burke. "Don't go."

"I have no choice. Father Kung said they had Lorena and that she would have an accident if I failed to cooperate."

"And who is Lorena?"

"Oh that's right. You . . . don't know about her."

"No, I don't."

"She's… my girlfriend. I…"

"I don't need to know any more right now," said Mike Burke as he examined Adam Thelen in his rear view mirror. "Did you confirm that he has her?"

"I confirmed that she's gone to take an internship, just as he said. I have no choice but to believe the rest."

"You said he used the word 'they' when he said who had Lorena."

"Yes, he did."

"Father, this looks like a classic set up. At least let me drive in there with you and check it out."

"No. He was very specific about coming alone and walking the last quarter mile. Just drop me at the bottom of Geary and then double back and park. You'll be able to see everyone who goes toward or leaves the San Francisco Memorial. There's only one entrance."

"OK, Father. But at least stay in the trees and shadows as you walk back there, don't just walk down the middle of the road like a slow moving target."

Adam Thelen heeded Mike Burke's advice as he made his way along El Camino del Mar, which was an extension from the northern terminus of 48th Avenue. The San Francisco summer fog was making an early but light appearance and visibility was only moderate. He skirted the inland side of the road, staying near the plentiful trees and shrubs. He saw the black Buick. It had made a U-turn and was parked immediately adjacent the Memorial of the U.S.S. San Francisco, which is a part of the bridge of that ship set onto a concrete base with the usual plaque. He moved deeper into the trees and was able to circle around and emerge into the parking area directly behind the Buick. He stepped quickly to the driver's side and rapped on the window. Father Kung had been watching the road in front of the car and turned his head with a noticeable start. He rolled down the window and looked at Adam Thelen with naked disdain.

"Get in the passenger side."

"All right," he said, moving around the front of the car and scanning the parking area.

Nothing there. Maybe this will work out OK.

"I've got what you requested. I can guarantee you that my mother will see your associate and cooperate with any reasonable request."

"You simple dupe. I can't believe they let you in the Order. Tonight is going to be a pleasure. The time for cooperation of you and your mother and her do-gooder firm passed you by last week. We've found another way to get what we want and your mommy won't know what hit her. Now it's time for you to die. And by the way, your girlfriend never approached me. I contacted her and told her we knew all about her affair and the baby. Now that little accident we talked about is going to befall her. Just another piece of collateral damage in the calamity which has been your life to date."

As he spoke, Father Kung looked to one side of Adam Thelen, who turned his head in the same direction. Emerging from behind the bridge of the U.S.S. San Francisco was the man his father had described as a weasel rather than a ferret. The description was apt. His moist pink mouth was slightly open and he was smiling. In his left hand was a large revolver fitted with a suppressor. He was about twenty-five feet away and moving quickly. Adam Thelen turned back to Father Kung and saw him smiling openly. With one motion, he pulled his .22 from the right pocket of his jacket and reached his left arm behind Father Kung's head. Adam Thelen pulled Father Kung's head toward his own so that his face was no more than three inches away. "You evil bastard! May God damn your soul into eternity. You'll be in hell before me." He pressed the muzzle of the gun hard against Father Kung's right temple and fired once. Then he sat back to await his own similar fate. He heard the shot, but it was at once louder than he expected and somewhat farther away. He looked to his right and saw the Weasel laying face up with a ragged hole emerging from his left cheek just below his eye. As usual, the Weasel's attire was exquisite; his right hand lay upon his chest and Adam could see the diamond Rolex. Moving toward Adam from the trees to the left of the Memorial was Mike Burke.

"My God, Mike! What have you done?"

"I know what I have done. The question is, what have you done?"

He had a large flashlight with him and he quickly shone it on Father Kung and on the .22 pistol still in Adam Thelen's hand.

"Quickly now. Tell me what you've done," said Mike Burke.

"I shot him. We have to call the police."

"I can see that you shot him. As for calling the police, let's hold off on that until we figure out what we have here. Now listen to me. I need you to tell me in exact detail everything you did after you pulled the gun. Also give the gun to me."

Adam told him everything, in as much detail as he could recall. As ordered, he also handed the pistol to Mike, who had returned his own weapon to a holster he wore under his jacket.

"Show me the angle at which the bullet entered his head. Use your finger and point to your own head."

Again, Adam did as requested. Mike Burke walked quickly around the car, opened the driver's door and examined Father Kung's head carefully with his flashlight. There was no exit wound. He also checked his neck for any pulse. There was none.

"Good," he grunted. "OK, tell me about the popgun."

"I stole it really, when I was ten years old. It belonged to my uncle and I took it from his dresser after he died. No one knew I had it."

"Was it ever registered?"

"Not that I know about."

"Do you have any more bullets?"

"Yes," he said, while reaching into his pocket.

"All right, get out of the car and give me one shell. Do you have any more ammunition back at the rectory?"

"Yes, about half a box."

He did as directed and Mike Burke came back around the car and sat in the passenger seat where Adam had been seated. He used his handkerchief to meticulously remove all fingerprints from the gun. The keys were in the ignition and he turned them to the right two notches. He shone the flashlight on the ignition and noted that two car keys were on the ring along with one additional key. He then reached across Father Kung's body and lowered the driver's power window. Next he pushed the body into an upright position and raised its head into a caricature of a live human being. Finally, while holding the body upright with his left arm, he placed the gun in Father Kung's right hand, aimed it out of the window in an upward trajectory, and fired a second round. He allowed the body to slump. He reached over and returned the key to the 'off' position. Mike Burke emptied all the shells from the pistol including the two expended casings. He placed one of the casings in his pocket and replaced it with the extra bullet Adam had given him. With his handkerchief, he carefully wiped all fingerprints from the bullets, the one expended casing and the gun itself. With the handkerchief he opened the cylinder and placed the gun in Father Kung's left hand as if he were loading it. With the handkerchief, he reloaded the cylinder, making sure that the expended casing was in the proper chamber. With Father Kung's right thumb, he pressed each cartridge into its chamber. With his handkerchief, he took the pistol, closed the cylinder, and replaced it in Father Kung's right hand. About two minutes had elapsed since the initial shots.

"O.K., what did you touch?"

"Only the door handles, I think."

Mike Burke quickly and carefully cleaned all possible prints from the exterior and interior door handles and all other nearby surfaces.

Finally he took the keys from the ignition and removed the single key which was not marked with the "GM" emblem of General Motors. Then he replaced the keys in the ignition, closed the door and looked at the man on the ground.

"Help me move him. We'll take him about fifty yards back toward the cab."

When this was done, Mike Burke returned to the Buick. Using his flashlight, he examined the pavement where the

Weasel had been laying and found nothing. Next he shone the light on the pavement nearby.

"Come here and help me look for the slug. It's a .357 and it will be kind of beat up from bouncing around inside his head and then exiting his face."

After about ninety seconds Adam said, "I think I've got it."

Mike took it from him and, after a brief examination said, "OK we're out of here. I'm going to make sure he left nothing where he was hiding on the Memorial. I want you to return the same way you came in here. You'll find the cab parked a little way up Clement. It's open. I'll meet you there."

Again, Adam Thelen did as Mike Burke directed. When he got to the cab, Mike was not yet there. He entered the passenger side of the front seat and sat numbly. Mike arrived a moment later.

"Get in the back. I want you to look like a fare. What we're going to do, if we're lucky, is drive back in there and load the body into the trunk. I have a tarp in there along with a number of other things."

"OK," said Adam without inflection.

"I need you to hold it together. Can you do this?"

"Yes."

He started the engine and drove slowly back toward the Memorial. When they reached the area where they'd laid the body about twenty feet off the pavement, with the gun on top, he cut the engine and turned off the lights. He looked in all directions and saw no one. They got out of the car and opened the trunk. Mike Burke took the tarp to the body and rolled it up along with the gun. They carried the tarp back to the car and placed it in the trunk. They saw no one as they drove away.

After a moment or two, Adam Thelen asked, "What do we do now?"

"Well, the first order of business is to get you back to the rectory. And then the dear departed Weasel will have his final ride, in this case out to Hunter's Point."

"What are you going to do with him?"

"Let me worry about that. All you need to know is that I'll be driving very carefully indeed, almost befitting a funeral procession. The last thing I need with a stiff in the trunk is some kind of accident or a cop pulling me over for speeding. For now, let's talk about you and the rectory. If we're lucky, the first team of cops to respond to the scene will buy off on suicide as the cause of death and won't even call in homicide. But because of who he was, there will be much greater interest by the media and, therefore, a more thorough police investigation. There's going to be a circus at the rectory as soon as the body is discovered."

"What should I do?"

"First thing is the box of ammunition."

Mike Burke reached into his pocket and extracted the key from Father Kung's ring.

"I believe this is the key to Father Kung's door. Do you think you can take the box of ammunition over to his rooms without being seen?"

"Yes I should be able to do that at this hour."

"Fine. Then take the box and if the key opens the door, place it in a not too difficult hiding place. Maybe at the back of a drawer. Leave the key out in the open as if Father Kung had left it there. If for any reason you can't get into his rooms, then get rid of both the ammunition box and the key so that they won't be found and linked to you."

"OK. I can do that. Anything else?"

"The police will want to interview all the priests. They'll be asking if you spoke to him recently, whether you noticed any change in his state of mind, that sort of thing."

"I think I can handle that. No one saw me talking to him today, but I had dinner with him a week ago at a little place over in the Richmond District. That's where he first approached me about Lorena."

"You have to assume that you were seen with Father Kung and that it is possible, no matter how unlikely, that the police will hear about it."

"Yes, I guess that's true. I'll have to think through what I should say."

"All right Father. That's all I can think of right now. I'm going to drop you off a couple of blocks away so that you can claim you were out for a walk if anyone saw you coming or going."

"Thank you, Michael. I know that's wholly insufficient after all you've done, but my gratitude is all I have to offer."

"Your thanks is quite enough Father. However, we should meet again tomorrow. I'll need to know what went on at the rectory. And another thing, Father."

"Yes?"

"I'll need to know more about Lorena."

"And so you shall Michael. I have an appointment tomorrow at 2:30 with my father at his office in the TransAmerica Tower. Can you pick me up at 2:00 at the usual place?"

"I'll be there Father."

After dropping Adam Thelen, Mike Burke continued east to Masonic and turned right. After a few blocks, he turned left onto Oak St. and followed it about twelve blocks until it merged onto Highway 101 South. He stayed on 101 about three miles and exited onto Army St., and then right onto Evans toward India

Basin and Hunter's Point. Traffic was light at this time of night, but stopping out here, especially in a cab, was problematic. After a recent series of robberies, most cabbies wouldn't respond to calls in the Hunter's Point area and also would refuse requests by fares to go there. He pulled into a parking lot in an industrial area and parked near a dumpster. He scanned the area carefully to insure it was deserted. He exited the cab, opened the trunk and removed the tarp, placing it on the pavement. Quickly he unrolled it and was about to place the weasel's body in the dumpster when the diamond Rolex caught his eye.

Such a waste.

He removed the Rolex from the Weasel's wrist and placed it in a baggie which he retrieved from the trunk. Then he heaved the body up and into the dumpster, covering it with assorted trash. Quickly he refolded the tarp and replaced it in the trunk. He reentered the car and departed the way he had come. The Rolex in its baggie was on the passenger seat next to him. Only when he was back on the freeway did he allow himself to relax somewhat.

Jesus, Mary & Joseph! What have I gotten myself into?

Mike Burke did not return directly home. He stayed on 101 North until it terminated on Turk Street near Jefferson Square. From there he continued a short distance to St. Mary's Church, which was the cathedral of the archdiocese of San Francisco. He parked about a block away and took the Rolex out of the baggie. He wiped all fingerprints from it and, holding it in his handkerchief, walked to the side entrance to the church. He slipped the Rolex into the slot of the locked steel donation box bolted to the concrete wall of the church. He chuckled at the thought of the Archbishop's reaction when this donation was brought to his attention. Mike Burke's final stop before returning home was another dumpster, this one behind a nearby seafood restaurant located just off Van Ness Avenue. The food at the restaurant was quite good, but the dumpster's contents were nauseating. He took the tarp from his trunk and inserted it beneath the top layer of offal.

When Adam Thelen reached the rectory, all was quiet. It was just after ten o'clock. The events of that last hour were beginning to crowd back into his consciousness, replacing the numbness. With an effort, he cleansed his mind. Entering the rear of the building, he made his way to his rooms without encountering anyone. He retrieved the half full box of bullets from his dresser. Following Mike Burke's example, he wiped down the box and each of the cartridges, including the two from his pocket, even though he could not remember touching any of the shells from the box. After replacing them in the box, he took it and re-entered the hallway outside his rooms. Quietly he walked to Father Kung's rooms and used the key to open the door. He had been fairly certain that the key would work, since it looked just like his own. Without turning on any lights, he entered the bedroom and, using his own handkerchief, opened the second drawer and felt inside. Underwear and socks. He placed the box of ammunition at the rear of the drawer and covered it with a pair of socks. He left the key, wiped clean, on a table near the door and exited, leaving the door unlocked. When he got back to his room, he removed his shoes and jacket and collapsed onto his bed.

CHAPTER 6

Tuesday, June 2, 1987 San Francisco, California

AT 7:15 A.M., the phone rang in Adam Thelen's room. He answered somewhat groggily on the fourth ring. It was the rector, Father Smythe, saying that an unfortunate event had occurred and that all the priests were requested to meet in the dining room at 8:00.

"OK, Father, I'll be there. Can you tell me what has happened?"

"It's a very unhappy situation best covered when we're all together."

"All right Father, I'll see you shortly."

Adam Thelen wore the same clothing as the night before. Quickly he stripped it off and stepped into the shower. As he showered and then shaved, he tried to bring himself to think clearly.

God, help me to act and speak appropriately . . . But, really, why should You after all that I have done?

He entered the dining room shortly before 8:00 to find at least half his fellow priests already there. The rest filed in behind him and all were present by 8:00. The group was almost silent, probably due to the presence of two strangers standing at the front of the room with Father Smythe.

"It looks as if everyone is present, so let me come to the point. Father Kung was found this morning by the driver of a street sweeper in the parking area near Point Lobos. I regret to inform you that he is dead, apparently of a gunshot wound," said Father Smythe.

Gesturing toward the two men standing with him, he continued. "These men are Sergeant Edward Gallica and Detective Kenneth MacMurry of the SFPD. They will provide more details and try to answer your questions. Then, I'm sure they'll have some questions for you. Sergeant?"

"Thank you, Father," said Sergeant Gallica. "As Father Smythe indicated, Father Kung was discovered about 5:00 am. He was seated in one of the rectory cars with a gunshot wound to his right temple. Apparently he had been dead approximately six to eight hours. A small caliber pistol was found in his right hand. The gun was fully loaded with one shell expended. Thus far, we have found no further evidence at the scene, although a forensics team is there now. Also, two of our colleagues are examining Father Kung's rooms. The media was not at the scene when we left there about 6:45 but I'm sure that's changed by now. I also suspect that they'll be here shortly seeking interviews with any of you who will talk to them. That's about all we have now, except to offer our sincere condolences regarding this tragedy. If you have any questions, we'll try to answer them now. Then, we and our colleagues will wish to speak with each of you. Any questions?"

"My God, you think this is a suicide?" asked one of the priests.

"That is a possibility which is consistent with the evidence found thus far. However, our investigation is incomplete and we've reached no firm conclusions."

After a few more desultory questions, the room began to buzz as priests talked among themselves expressing shock and sadness. Sergeant Gallica was about to interject himself into the emerging conversations when two other officers entered the room. The four men spoke together briefly with the two newcomers appearing to answer questions directed to them by Sergeant Gallica.

"All right, Fathers. These two men are detectives James and Davies who just now have completed the preliminary examination of Father Kung's apartment. Now we'd like to speak separately with each of you. It shouldn't take long with four of us conducting interviews. I ask that you simply remain seated and we'll call on each of you over the next few minutes."

Out of a long habit, Adam Thelen had seated himself near the rear of the room close to an exit. Thus he would be among the last of the priests to be interviewed. He watched as the police officers invited the first four priests into the adjoining common area where four sets of two chairs had been set up in each corner of the room. Adam Thelen's first thought was that the setup looked somewhat like four confessionals.

Better banish that thought lest I actually volunteer a confession.

The priest seated next to him, Father Bertram, tried to start up a conversation with Adam. Adam answered tersely and looked away, affecting what he hoped was a somewhat stunned and sorrowful expression. He watched carefully as each priest emerged from his interview. Without exception, the interviews were brief and after less than fifteen minutes, it was his time.

"Hello Father. My name is Robert Davies and I'd like to ask you a few questions."

"All right, detective," he said as they walked together toward the chairs at one corner of the adjoining room.

As they took their seats, Detective Davies picked up a notebook from a side table. Adam noticed that the entry for each preceding interview was brief, only about four or five lines each.

"Did you know Father Kung well?"

"Not really. He seemed a quiet man."

"Have you spoken to him recently?"

"His rooms are fairly close to mine, so we would greet each other in the hallway."

"Nothing else?"

"Well, yes there was and it was somewhat unusual."

"Please tell me what happened," said the detective, his pen poised over his notepad.

"Well, about a week ago . . ."

"Can you recall the date, Father?"

"Let me see," said Adam, seeming to ponder the question. "I believe it was a week ago yesterday. That would be the Monday before last. Father Kung approached me and invited me to dine with him that evening."

"Did he want to eat here in the rectory?"

"No he didn't. He suggested a small restaurant in the Richmond district, Vince's, out on Geary about 20th. A standard Italian place with booths and checkered tablecloths."

"Please tell me what transpired."

"Well, that's just it. Not much really happened. We drove out there together in one of the cars . . ."

"He drove?"

"Yes, I rarely use one of the cars. In fact, I can't remember the last time."

"Tell me about the conversation. What did you discuss?"

"Again, nothing substantial. Father Kung seemed pensive but not really troubled. He started by saying that he really hadn't gotten to know any of his fellow priests and had resolved to change that. Then he talked about his classes and other small talk. I tried to draw him out on a couple of occasions, but each time he just shook his head slightly and continued on with the small talk."

"Anything else you recall?"

"No that's it. We split a pizza and half a pitcher of beer and then drove back."

"Nothing else of interest?"

"No. He thanked me rather profusely for joining him and then he returned to his rooms."

"All right, Father. Thank you. If you remember anything else, please call me. Here's my card."

Adam Thelen returned directly to his rooms. He closed and locked the door and then sat in one of the armchairs. He began to shake as the full import of his actions over the past week finally began to sink into his consciousness. Abruptly he stood, threw off his clothes, and stepped into the shower once again. It was as if he hoped the physical act of washing his body could cleanse all sin from his soul. After ten minutes, he emerged, dried himself and began to dress. Once again, when this process was complete he sat down and began to think coldly and clearly. He realized that he had no remorse whatever regarding the deaths of Father Kung or his associate, the Weasel. In fact, if it were possible to rewind the hands of time he would do it again purposefully and thoughtfully.

Yes God, I would do it again without a moment's hesitation and without a trace of sorrow or remorse.

By now it was eleven o'clock and he had eaten nothing since lunch with his father the day before. He left the rectory and walked down the hill for a solitary lunch. After he had eaten, he sat staring sightlessly out the window, his mind awash with thoughts of Lorena and the lost infant.

Unbidden, the memory of his first dinner with Lorena came back to him.

Their first dinner together, he conveniently in casual clothes sans Roman collar, again to discuss "academic" issues. He remembered everything with a clarity born of pain. She had a car and she had driven them to a small intimate restaurant. It was only about a mile from campus but it was a neighborhood place catering to residents of the Inner Richmond as well as military personnel from the nearby Presidio. She obviously frequented the place and was known to the owners, husband in the kitchen and wife out front.

"Ah, Ms. Montes. So very good to see you again."

"Thank you Ilsa. It's good to see you also."

"Your usual table this evening for you and your friend?"

"No thank you. We're studying together. May we have a booth in the rear?"

"As you wish."

He had known the danger in their conduct and the risks they were taking, the titillation of being Lorena's "friend" and the blurred boundaries implicit in "studying together." He also knew that his attraction to her already was strong and he sensed her reciprocation. Nonetheless, he forged ahead confident, perhaps arrogant, in his ability to maintain control and call a halt before anything truly untoward occurred. Seated in the booth, they had laughed together at the need for anonymity.

"Of course our dinner together is innocent, but Ilsa and her husband might be scandalized if they knew you were a priest. They're both of Basque origin and I come here because some of their food reminds me of home."

"Ah. So we must pretend to be a beautiful young woman and her older friend studying together. Very intriguing."

"You're not that much older. I'll be twenty-three next year. How old are you?" –

"Thirty."

"You don't look a day over twenty-eight," she said, laughing. And you certainly don't act like an ancient thirty-year-old. Besides, I'm sure you've been through all of this before. I can't be the first moderately attractive student with whom you've had professional interaction."

Lorena was just over 5'7" with medium length brown hair and skin about the shade of the best mid-summer tan Adam Thelen ever had achieved. She had high cheekbones and lovely full lips which always seemed to wear an expression of slight amusement. Her eyes, however, were her most striking feature. They were slightly wide set and were piercingly blue, as is not uncommon among Spaniards of Castilian descent. Like her mouth, her eyes reflected amusement, as well as a seemingly bottomless clarity. Adam Thelen gazed at Lorena before responding.

"That's true," he finally answered. "But you do yourself a large disservice by describing yourself as 'moderately attractive'."

"Really? What would you say?"

Looking at her he smiled. "I would have to say stupendously attractive. But even that doesn't cover it. I'd be forced to append 'smart, vivacious, funny and talented.' And that would be only the initial catalogue of virtues."

And what about flirtatious, incredibly sexy and an off-the-chart body?

Lorena blushed slightly, the first time he had seen this. "You're very gracious, Father. And I appreciate your very subtle segue to one of the areas we're studying."

Ironically, they were studying professional ethics and lately had been discussing the distance which must be maintained between client and therapist and the dangers of self-disclosure and transference. Laughing together Adam and Lorena then pursued this train of thought for a few minutes as if to create a veneer of propriety for being together on this night. Then Ilsa reappeared. She placed a carafe of red wine on the table between them.

"I took the liberty of bringing your favorite wine. I hope that will be acceptable."

"Absolutely, Ilsa. Thank you."

"Are you ready to order?"

"Yes, I believe so," said Lorena. "Do you know what you want... Adam?"

"I think I will let you order for both of us," said Adam, causing Ilsa to beam. Lorena also smiled.

"All right Ilsa, I think we'd each like your porrusalda followed by your wonderful lamb stew. We'll decide later whether we want dessert."

"Thank you, Ms. Montes. Those are excellent choices."

When Ilsa had left, Adam poured each of them a glass of wine. He tasted it and smiled.

"To avoidance of self-disclosure," he said as he raised his glass. Lorena laughed and raised her glass to join the toast.

"And may we not impose too much distance between us due to the porrusalda."

"Is it really that pungent?"

"You shall see. Here it is now."

The soup was smooth and not at all pungent. In addition to a full head of garlic first baked and then sautéed in olive oil, it contained leeks, potatoes and onions cooked in a mild vegetable broth and then blended into a silken texture. It was delightful, as was the lamb stew. Lorena and Adam proceeded through dinner laughing and each enjoying the other's company. They talked of many things, including their childhoods in New York and Spain, but there was no further discussion of academic issues. When the lamb stew had been cleared away, Ilsa returned and inquired about dessert.

"I think not, Ilsa. The soup and lamb stew both were superb, and we're sated. Maybe we'll share something later in the evening," said Lorena with an amused expression as she glanced at Adam.

Back in the car Adam said, "Thank you Lorena. That was a wonderful meal and I enjoyed being with you and hearing of your life in Spain."

"I enjoyed it too… Adam. But a Basque meal is not complete without a dessert of fruit and cheese which I have back at my apartment. Please join me and then you can walk home."

"Lorena…"

"Adam, you must. I had this cheese shipped from home. You need only sample it and then be on your way."

Lorena's apartment was four blocks from campus. The kitchen, living area, a small dining room and two bedrooms were on the second floor above a two-car garage. Lorena opened the garage door as they approached the apartment and drove straight into the garage. As soon as the car came to a stop, she closed the door behind them. Interior stairs from the garage led to the apartment above. It was spacious and extremely well appointed with what appeared to be original art work on the walls. The front window of the living room looked up the hill toward campus. The opposite wall opened directly into the kitchen. Lorena flicked a switch and a gas fireplace came to life.

"Please excuse me for a moment. There's another bottle of wine in the bar over there which you can open. It's the same tempranillo we had at the restaurant and it's a perfect accompaniment to the cheese."

Lorena then disappeared into one of the bedrooms. Adam stood uncertainly for a moment looking out the window toward campus.

If I simply left right now. . . Oh for heaven's sake, we're just two people who have enjoyed dinner together and now we're going to share a piece of cheese.

Adam walked over to the bar and found the bottle of tempranillo in a small refrigerator chilled to 55 degrees. He took it out and opened it. He found wine glasses in a cabinet above the bar and took out two of them. He walked over and stood in front of the fire. After a moment, he heard Lorena emerge from the bedroom. She went into the kitchen.

"Bring the wine in here while I slice the cheese."

He carried the bottle and two glasses into the kitchen and poured a glass for each of them. Lorena had changed into a silk dressing gown approximately two shades lighter than the blue of her eyes. The long-sleeved gown covered her neck to ankle with a simple sash around the waist and a concealed zipper at the throat. It should have been extremely demure and proper, yet it was not. There appeared to be nothing under the gown and her breasts moved under the fabric as she padded about the kitchen on bare feet. She opened the refrigerator and as she bent down to remove the cheese from one of the lower drawers, the gown molded itself to her bottom. She brought the cheese to a cutting board on the counter and took a sip from the wine.

"Yum," she said. "The taste of home. But it needs to warm a bit. Why don't you warm it up in your hands while I slice the cheese?"

She brought out a cheese slicer and began to cut very thin slices. She then sliced an apple into eight pieces. She arranged the cheese and fruit on a small platter and took it and the wine bottle into the living room where she placed everything on a small table located between the fireplace and a large sofa. She sat down and motioned to a spot next to her on the sofa. As Adam sat down, she took one of the glasses from him and tasted it again.

"Perfect! Your hands are little heaters. Here, try some of the cheese."

He took a slice and tasted it. "This is excellent! Mild and smooth, almost sensuous."

"Sensuous, eh? You're a romantic. It's called Roncal and it's made of sheep's milk, usually from fairly high up in the Pyrenees."

Adam took a sip of wine and said, "Thank you. Thank you for the whole evening, in fact, it's been extremely enjoyable, not to mention educational."

"There's another cheese that's really the signature Basque cheese. It's called Idia Zabol but it's not available in the United States, for an obvious reason."

"Why would that be?"

She smiled at Adam mischievously. "It's made from the breast milk of mothers. Human mothers. U.S. consumers are far too proper for such a thing."

Lorena set her glass on the table and looked at Adam. Her smile showed the tip of her tongue between her teeth. She continued to gaze at Adam but said nothing.

Adam said, "Lorena, I think it's time for me to go," and began to rise from the sofa.

"Adam, look at me," she said.

He sat down and looked at her. Still smiling, she reached up to the zipper at her throat and slowly pulled it down to her navel. She shrugged her shoulders and removed her arms from the sleeves, lowering the gown to her waist. As Adam had surmised, she wore nothing beneath the gown. With the long elegant fingernail of her left index finger, she flicked her right nipple lightly once, and again. She then took the nipple between her thumb and index finger and began kneading it with a slight twisting motion. In the firelight, Adam could see it harden and come to a point.

"Lorena, I'm a priest…"

Without taking her hand from her breast, Lorena moved closer to him and slid her right hand down his stomach under his belt and inside his shorts. She held him softly in her hand.

"This doesn't feel too priestly."

"Lorena…"

"Adam, I want you to make love to me. I want you inside me."

Looking deeply into Lorena's eyes, Adam Thelen pulled her lips toward his and reached across his body with his right hand and slid it under the sash of the gown and between her legs. She wore nothing there either.

At 12:45, he decided to walk down Masonic to the Panhandle of Golden Gate Park and take a stroll before meeting Mike Burke, as agreed, at 2:00 o'clock. But as he approached their meeting place on his way to the Panhandle, he saw a Yellow Cab parked at the curb. As he came closer he saw Mike Burke seated inside scanning the Chronicle. He opened the door and got in the back seat.

"Ah, Father Thelen! I trust you had a fine night's sleep and a pleasant morning."

"You have a mordant sense of humor. Are you always this jolly after a double murder?"

"Definitely not a double murder if we were successful in proving what actually occurred. My killing of the Weasel clearly was justified. The sad demise of Father Kung is somewhat more questionable, but a good lawyer likely could gain an acquittal for you. An 'irresistible impulse' defense or some such trendy nonsense. All in all, though, much neater if the simple suicide scenario holds up. How did it go this morning?"

Adam told him everything that had occurred that morning, including the names of all the police officers. He also described his success in relocating the box of ammunition the night before.

"Excellent work on the bullets. There's no doubt that they were found during the initial toss of Father Kung's rooms this morning. And, as it happens I know Ed Gallica, at least slightly. He was a patrolman with some involvement in one of my last cases. I would rate him as good, but not excellent."

"Anything in the papers?"

"No, but the Examiner will have it tonight. It's already on the radio."

"What are they saying?"

"Priest from University found dead. Investigation proceeding but incomplete. Stay tuned."

"What about the Weasel."

"Nothing, and if we're lucky he may find his eternal rest in a landfill. That part went uneventfully last night, thank the Lord. I did do one thing which was not strictly advisable. I simply couldn't resist."

"What would that be?"

Mike Burke recounted to Adam the story of the Rolex and the donation box. The part about the likely reaction of the Archbishop brought a smile to Adam's face.

"Good for you. The wages of sin are death and it's appropriate to redirect the fruits of evil to the less fortunate among us."

"I'm glad you approve Father. Now, will you hear my confession?"

"You are jolly indeed this afternoon."

"OK Father, it's a tasteless joke. But now I do need a confession from you... regarding Lorena."

The mention of Lorena caused Adam instantly to banish all of the momentary lightness and frivolity. He realized that all the remorse, sadness and guilt he harbored centered on Lorena, and on the infant.

Dear Lord, if I could hold her one more time and see our child, I happily would sacrifice myself.

He told Mike Burke the entire story of his relationship with Lorena Montes, withholding nothing other than the intimate details. As he spoke, he realized that the story was almost a parody of the conventional teacher/student affair. The questions from her in the classroom, exuding admiration for the brilliant teacher. The ensuing meetings ostensibly to discuss classroom matters, but really an extended flirtation on both sides. Their first dinner together, the subject of his reverie at lunch just a few minutes ago, culminating in their first lovemaking. In retrospect, it was clear that she had seduced him. But it was just as clear that he had placed himself in a position to be seduced and in fact had encouraged it. And that could have been the end of it, a one-night stand with Lorena validating her ability to have the older and more accomplished priest and to take him away, for one night at least, from his devotion to God. Adam had been willing to let that happen. At their next class together, he took pains to act as if nothing had happened between them. And at first so did Lorena. In the end, however, he could not forget the intimacy, the authenticity of their lovemaking; it haunted him daily notwithstanding his and his confessor's efforts to banish it. After ten days, he approached Lorena after class.

"Lorena, I want to see you again, if you're willing."

"Yes. Come tonight."

Thus had begun the first of many dinners and overnight stays in Lorena's apartment. The intensity, instead of waning, only increased with each liaison, and so it continued until the recent events. Mike Burke listened to all of this, saying nothing, asking no questions. Finally Adam Thelen was finished with his "confession" to Mike Burke.

"Father, I understand. Truly, the wisdom of requiring chastity among priests always has escaped me. But the church has spoken."

"Yes it has. And it was not up to me to change the rules."

"I don't know, Father. I'll leave those decisions to my betters. I do know that it's time to go if you're to keep your appointment with your father."

They drove toward the Transamerica Tower in silence, each lost in his own thoughts. As they approached the pyramid, however, Adam Thelen spoke.

"Michael, I think you should come with me to the meeting."

"Whatever for, Father? You can tell me all about it."

"I can't say why, Michael. But suddenly I know that this isn't over and that I'm going to need your help going forward. Please come up with me."

"All right, Father."

Mike Burke parked the cab in a public garage near the tower and they walked over together. They took the elevator to the 38th floor and announced themselves at the desk in the elevator lobby. After a short delay, they were directed to a separate door off the lobby which in turn led to stairs up to the 39th floor. The entire 38th floor housed Stein Brothers, Singer and Thelen's west coast trading operations. The New York office had a similar but larger trading floor plus the offices of the investment banking and private banking operations and of a new entity which was called "Emerging Markets." Here in San Francisco, there was just the trading floor plus a very few offices on the 39th floor. As they walked up the stairs, Adam Thelen turned toward Mike Burke.

"I suggest you prepare yourself. This is a bit… unusual, and unnerving."

Mike Burke looked at Adam quizzically but said nothing. At the top of the stairs was another door. Opening it they stepped into what appeared to be an anteroom about twelve feet square. It was devoid of furnishings save for artwork hanging on three walls. The fourth wall, on their left, contained a large door about eight feet wide and the same height. It was formidable in appearance and seemed more suited to a castle of another age. Moving further into the room Mike Burke saw that it was not perfectly square. To their left and to the left of the massive door was an alcove with a single counter at a height of about three and a half feet. A large man stood behind the counter. He looked quite presentable in a dark suit with white shirt and tie. Mike Burke knew instantly that he was armed and would have been willing to bet that a light weight Kevlar vest was beneath the man's rather loosely fitted shirt.

"Good afternoon Father Thelen. It's good to see you."

"And you Morris. It's been awhile. You look fit."

"Thank you, Father. I try."

Morris looked better than merely fit to Mike Burke. The man was perhaps ten years younger than Mike and looked to be about an even six feet tall and two hundred pounds.

Maybe ex-law enforcement but more likely retired military.

"Your father was expecting only you," said Morris.

"Yes. I'm sorry. I should have called ahead. This is Michael Burke who is… an associate of mine. He is a retired police officer."

"A pleasure to meet you Mr. Burke," said Morris, extending his hand. "I actually am ex-military."

"As am I," said Mike Burke "although a long time ago. Early Vietnam."

"I was there also, but quite a bit later."

"Whereabouts were you? And when?"

Morris looked steadily at Mike Burke before answering and Mike returned his level gaze.

"We were there from early '68 through the end of '69. 3rd Marines. We were in a number of places, but Conthein and the A-Shau Valley usually come to mind first."

"Yes. I read about the A-Shau Valley quite a while after the war."

"How about you, Mr. Burke?"

"Please call me Mike. I was there quite early, in '61 and '62. We were Army. At least that's what they called us. Our role was purely advisory at that time," Mike said, smiling.

"Ah yes. Advisors," said Morris, his eyes seeming to look back through the years.

Finally, with a small smile he returned to the present. "I'll have to pat you down in any event but, are you carrying any weapons?"

"No. None today," said Mike raising his arms.

Morris performed a quick but thorough search and then returned behind the counter. He pressed a concealed button and the mammoth door began to slide open. The door itself made no noise. All that could be heard was the slight whirring of the electric motors.

"Quite impressive," said Mike Burke.

"Yes it is. It also can be opened manually from within in the event of a power loss. Do you recall the way, Father?"

"I do, Morris. Thank you."

They passed by a conference room with seating for twelve and a spectacular view of Coit Tower and the north bay. At the end of the hall Adam knocked on a closed door. They heard footsteps approaching and Chaz Thelen opened the door.

"Come in Adam. They told me you had a companion."

"Yes, Dad, this is Michael Burke. He retired from the SFPD three years ago as a detective lieutenant and now is a cab driver. He's the one who took me to the bridge last weekend, having no knowledge of my intentions. He's also the one I called to pick me up from the motel on Friday morning. He knows everything, Dad."

"Does he now?"

"Yes he does. Plus he saved my life last night."

"Ah. There's nothing in this morning's papers but the radio stations are all talking about the priest out at Point Lobos. No identification. I was concerned enough to call the rectory this morning after the story broke. They assured me that you were among the living."

"Dad, I'm sorry. I should have called."

"Not to worry. But please do sit down and tell me all about it now."

Chaz Thelen sat on a sofa along one wall of the office and his two visitors took the two arm chairs across a coffee table from the sofa. It would be difficult to imagine an office with a superior view. To the right of the sofa as you faced it and to the left of the desk, a very large window afforded a view across the bay encompassing the entire Golden Gate Bridge. Beyond the bridge lay the Marin headlands and then the vast expanse of the Pacific Ocean.

"A sublime view," said Adam.

"Yes. One never tires of it. Now please begin."

Adam recounted to his father all the events of the previous evening as well as those at the rectory that morning. He also mentioned his reflections earlier in the day relative to the deaths and his complete lack of remorse or regret at having killed Father Kung.

"And what of the Weasel, the man who went by the name Ezra Casque?"

At this Adam nodded to Mike Burke, who proceeded to tell the story of the disposal of the Weasel's body as well as the diamond Rolex and the tarpaulin. Chaz Thelen rose from the sofa and stood looking out the window seemingly lost in thought. After a few moments he returned to the sofa.

"Mr. Burke, I owe you an enormous debt of gratitude. Without your intervention the radio reports and the newspaper stories this evening and tomorrow morning would have been speaking of the death of my son. Thank you, Sir."

"You're very gracious Mr. Thelen."

"I and the firm wish to hire you," said Chaz Thelen. Holding up his hand as Mike Burke began to protest, he continued. "Our desire to employ you has nothing to do with my gratitude. Simply put, we need your services, as I believe will become clear when I tell you of my discussions over lunch. I mention the employment offer now so that you can be considering it as we continue our conversation."

"Well…thank you, Mr. Thelen. I will do that."

"Adam, I had lunch today with both Gisele and your mother Emily. I brought them up to date on all you had told me, as well as the radio report regarding the dead priest. They know you're OK, but they agree with me that there may be continuing danger."

"I agree that there's danger in that the police may discover that the suicide of Father Kung was staged," said Adam.

"That's not the danger we see. The mention of the Weasel and his boss, Maxim Spektor triggered a strong reaction in your mother."

Chaz Thelen described his wife's recent activity in what the firm had dubbed "Emerging Markets." This was a relatively new venture in which the firm had carried out extensive internal analyses of Third World countries coupled, about two years ago, with on-site discussions in a few of them. After narrowing the number of candidates to four, the country of Ghana had been chosen as the site of the firm's first banking foray.

"Emily calls it 'Doing well while doing good,' which you should appreciate, Adam. It's rather a Jesuitical conceit. She believes we can make money while improving lives. Emily finally chose Ghana because it has natural resources, some trading partners in southern Europe and the Far East, notably India, and access to the South Atlantic. Its capital, Accra, is located right on the coast of the Gulf of Guinea. Most important, it has enjoyed political stability, although that's a relative term in West Africa. The leader of the country, Rawlins, took over in a bloodless coup in 1981 and since 1984 has moved the country in the direction of a true democracy. He also has been pushing to expand the country's nascent industrial base. That's where we have been helping."

He went on to describe how Emily and her associates in the firm had developed personal relationships with Jerry John Rawlins and others in the government. They had gained a degree of trust by, among other things, active participation in the National Commission on Democracy.

"There's a so called Blue Book coming out later this year which will set forth a constitution largely patterned after ours and other western countries. Emily has been active in the NCD since shortly after its creation in 1984. Just as importantly, she and others in the firm have helped them to reset the exchange rate of the cedi and to install fiscal and monetary controls. The net result to date is a dramatic lowering of the inflation rate and the expansion of the country's industrial base. They were able to eliminate price controls earlier this year. Your mother is very excited because, even though we have yet to do well, she feels that we have done good for the people of Ghana."

"I'm even more proud of Mom than before. But how does all this relate to the recent events here?"

"In two ways. First, eight months ago, the firm took the Republic of Ghana to market with an $80 million bond issue, the proceeds of which are being used to modernize gold and bauxite mining facilities, two lumber mills and a tuna processing plant. These are the major engines of foreign exchange and, at present all of these facilities are state owned. The plan over time is to make them private enterprises. Secondly, and here Gisele and her trading operations have been working closely with Emily, our analysts have been publishing reports of the progress in Ghana and opining on the growing stability of the cedi."

"All of that sounds good. . ."

"It is good, and we've been making a little money on it. The problem is we have far more exposure in Ghana, in fact in all of West Africa, than any other firm. We've been facilitating markets for the trading of the cedi and then there is the bond issue. We knew it would be a tough sell initially and it was. Thirty million dollars of the issue is still owned by the firm although we've been selling four or five million dollars per month."

"So how do you think this man Spektor is involved?"

"Simply put, we think that he's going to try to destabilize the government and that through you he was seeking our cooperation. It would be an easy matter for our analysts to publish negative opinions and for the firm to withdraw from any support of the bonds and stop trading the cedi, especially if something were to happen."

"Like what?"

"Therein lies the problem. We don't know. Emily is flying to New York this evening to try to find out through the firm's sources there. Then she's threatening to fly to Accra, even though I've tried to dissuade her. If something is going to happen, she could be in danger."

"But she wouldn't listen..."

"You know your mother. Of course she wouldn't listen and that's where you come in, Mr. Burke. We have a two-man security department—Morris, whom you've met, here in San Francisco, and his associate in New York. I want Morris to accompany Emily wherever she goes. I'd like you to be briefed by him before he leaves and then start to take over his duties here. More importantly, I want you to continue to work with Adam to ensure that this whole Father Kung nightmare plays out as planned. Finally, I want to know, and I'm sure Adam does too, where Lorena Montes is and whether she's safe. What have you been making as a taxi driver?"

Mike Burke told him what he usually cleared per week after paying the daily medallion rental.

"But really, that's just some extra cash. We live on my police department pension."

"Your salary here would be twice that number plus the usual benefits. What do you say?"

"I say yes. But it's not about money. This is something I want to do. And please call me Mike."

"Excellent, Michael," said Chaz Thelen as he stepped around the table to shake Mike Burke's hand. "Let's go talk to Morris right now. Adam, please wait here. I'll return shortly." When his father had gone, Adam stood and walked to the window. He gazed across the bay to the Golden Gate Bridge. Only five days ago he had sought to destroy his earthly existence by hurling himself from that very bridge. Yet he had lived.

Why? Why, against all odds, was his life spared?

Adam continued to gaze out the window, but his eyes were sightless. Earlier he had mentioned to his father rather gratuitously his lack of remorse at having killed Father Kung. Yet it was more than that. He could feel viscerally some greater purpose growing deep inside himself. He did not notice his father's return to the office.

"Adam, you look spectral. I'm not certain I wish to know your thoughts."

"Oh, Dad," said Adam with a start. "Yes. Spectral is apt." After a moment he continued. "Did you get Mike squared away? I must say, by the way, that you never fail to amaze me."

"How so, Adam? I merely hired a man who seemed well suited to fill a rather pressing need."

"Dad, you've scarcely met the man. You know nothing about him. Nor do I for that matter."

"Do you doubt that he saved your life last night or that his motive for doing so was pure, with no hint of self-interest?"

"No, but . . ."

"Adam, I have no doubts either nor do I doubt that his background check will come back clean as the driven snow."

"But you're still having a background check done?"

"Yes, of course, and it will be thorough. That's how it works in this business. But it always starts with what I see in a person and how a person has conducted himself with me or those close to me. For instance, a person like Maxim Spektor could show up with the most glowing c.v. and it would make no difference. We'd never deal with him."

CHAPTER 7

June, 1942

IN TRUTH, MAXIM was not his given name nor was Spektor his true surname. Nor was his birthplace located in Ukraine as was publicly reported with no dissent from him or his people. In fact, his actual birth place was well south of Ukraine and the last two people with knowledge of his true name, his father and older brother, were long dead. His mother had been one of those executed in 1942 by the Nazis as reprisal for the activities of his father and brother as part of the resistance effort. Thereafter Maxim had denounced his father and brother to the Nazis, resulting in their deaths along with eleven of their comrades. He had been twelve years old at the time. As his reward, he had been allowed to live. Had he remained in his birthplace, he would have died at the hands of the other members of the resistance. But the Germans put him on a truck which was part of a convoy bound for a town located on the Danube. Still, he should have died. But he had not. He had survived and become Maxim Spektor. When the convoy reached the Danube, it off loaded its cargo onto several barges which were to be hauled to Budapest by three tugboats. The wife of one of the tugboat captains, and in truth the captain's first mate on the boat, took pity on the twelve-year-old boy and allowed him to accompany them.

"What is your name?" the captain had asked.

"My name is Max," the boy had replied, using the name of one of the German truck drivers.

"Ah, Maxim!" shouted the captain. "If you come on this boat, you shall work and work hard."

"Yes, I will," replied Max.

"Come aboard then."

Thus did Max make the acquaintance of Captain Giorgei Spektor and his wife, Elena. When the tugboats reached Budapest, a trip of four days, the cargo was unloaded. During the four-day voyage, Max had shown himself to be a quick study and a willing hand. Max remained on the boat until late in 1943 and he learned the ways of the Danube and of those who traveled upon it.

The Spektors' tugboat was just that—a single, very old boat which they owned and which was available for charter. They were not part of any larger company or consortium, nor did they have an agent to arrange loads. In practice this meant that as soon as the Spektors reached a port and tied up the barges which they had under tow at the unloading docks, one or the other of them would be out on the wharves looking for their next load. Given the age of their boat, they could tow up to three barges but two was preferable, especially if the cargo was heavy. It was this task of finding new loads which devolved to Max and he proved to be remarkably adept. The instant the tug touched the dock, Max would leap ashore and head for the office which was a feature common to all but the smallest of wharves. There he would quickly determine whether new loads were available either that day or the next. If not, he would so advise the captain and they would move up or downriver to a likely port and the process would be repeated. At first, whenever a load was located, Max would race down to the boat to fetch the captain so that he could negotiate terms of passage. However, by means of watching and listening, Max quickly learned the trade. He was a natural negotiator, able to cajole and bargain, either for a better price or more advantageous timing of pickup or delivery. He had learned the capabilities of the tugboat and more importantly, the intimate knowledge possessed by the captain and his wife of the currents and depths of the river and the intricacies of traveling each lock. Thus, if a load's delivery date was time sensitive, he could judge whether a day or two could be made up, for a higher fee of course. Both the captain and his wife were pleased with the new arrangement.

"Maxim, you are a wonder!" the captain would boom. "I think you are able to negotiate a better deal than even I could manage. And now, I'm able to patch up this old tub while you're out finding work. Keep it up and I may start to pay you more than room and board."

The captain's wife would smile at this because she rather than he ultimately had been responsible for the negotiated terms of their loads. In addition, she was very fond of little Max and was secretly pleased to have plucked him from an almost certain death on that first day in Budapest. They had returned to Budapest several times since then and the orphaned children wandering the wharf area always were a new crop. Rarely did she recognize a child she had seen on an earlier trip. Soon, with encouragement from his wife, the captain did begin to pay Max a stipend, barely more than a pittance. Max was grateful for this and it caused him to redouble his efforts. He now saw the connection between his efforts, which he enjoyed anyway, and personal rewards.

"Maxim, you're doing an even better job now that I'm paying. But please don't expect more money. I can't afford any more."

"Thank you, Captain, for what you are paying me," answered Max. "I will do my very best."

Max also learned other things. He learned, for instance, that not all employers were alike. In many cases their employer was a branch of the German army. In others the loads were private carriage. Even in wartime foodstuffs and other necessities of daily life moved up and down the river. Occasionally, however, there was a third type of entity seeking to move goods from one part of the river to another. These entities went by various names, but they shared a common characteristic—resistance against Germany, which controlled the river from its headwaters in the Fatherland most of the way to its terminus in the Black Sea. Caution and self-preservation would seem to dictate that employment by such entities be rejected. Yet, the temptation could be great, and not simply in terms of the money to be gotten. Max knew that these opportunities were to be taken to the captain and his wife for consideration and discussion. Usually they would decline the business and Max would go out again in search of a less risky cargo. Occasionally, however, the captain and his wife would decide to take the risk. Perhaps the payment was very good or the distance to be traveled was short and the papers accompanying the cargo appeared good or the customs officers along the proposed segment of river were well-known and friendly. The reasoning of the captain and his wife was not always predictable or consistent. Max suspected that the partisanship of the couple might play a role. He had learned that both of them were born in Kiev. In those cases where the risk was undertaken, it was the captain who went ashore and completed negotiations. During Max's time with the captain and his wife, these types of cargo had been accepted only twice. In the second instance, Max had been allowed to accompany the captain and observe the final negotiations. Now a third such opportunity had arisen. They were near the port of Paks in southern Hungary and Max was hurrying back to the tugboat.

"Boy. Come here." The speaker was an Oberscharfuhrer, the equivalent of an American Army First Sergeant.

"Yes, sir?" said Max, walking over to him.

"Come with me."

Max followed the sergeant on a circuitous route covering perhaps four hundred yards. Finally, they came upon a German staff car parked in the deep shadows of an alley.

"Get in"

This is the end, then.

Inside the car Max was directed to sit across from another man, this one a sturmbannfuhrer of the German SS. The sturmbannfuhrer offered no introduction.

"You are mate on the tugboat *Princess Elena*. You have been offered a cargo of illicit goods. We wish you to accept this cargo and to tell us the times and places of your planned departure and arrival."

"Yes sir. I will do as you ask."

"Of course you will"

"But . . ."

"But?" said the sturmbannfuhrer with raised eyebrows.

"But when it is over, I want the Princess Elena for myself."

"You would betray the captain and his wife so easily?"

"I do not betray them. They will cause their own betrayal by accepting this illicit cargo."

CHAPTER 8

<u>Wednesday, June 3, 1987</u>

MAX SPEKTOR HAD traveled far since the tugboat. He had arrived in the United States in 1947, a seventeen-year-old refugee of World War II. Through the good offices of his benefactor, a wealthy U.S. family, he had been admitted to Columbia University and had graduated with a degree in economics in 1952. He had become a U.S. citizen that same year at the age of twenty-three. Thirty-five years later, his primary office was in New York and he was there now.

"I understand that Father Damien Kung is dead. Frankly, I am unconcerned. I never was comfortable with the idea he and Casque hatched. The cooperation of Thelen and his pious wife would have been useful in our undertaking in Ghana, but it would have cost us money—money we didn't need to spend. Now we can do it my way. Instead of paying for the Thelen's cooperation, we can achieve the same goal and hurt Thelen's firm in the bargain." This was Max Spektor addressing one of his lieutenants, Leon Knoss.

"It will cost money to do it your way," said Knoss.

"Yes, and it will be money well spent with a reliable return on investment. I don't give a damn about Kung but I am concerned about Casque. He went missing at the same time as the death of Kung and we've heard nothing since. Are we overlooking something here—some connection with the death?"

"We don't know. Our sources say the police are satisfied that Kung was a suicide. There's no information at all about Casque. He's simply disappeared."

"All right. Keep me informed of any developments in San Francisco. Now, 'it is "time to move forward with plans in Ghana."

+ + +

San Francisco Chronicle Saturday, June 6, 1987, page 9.

Death Ruled Suicide

The death of Father Damien Kung on Monday, June 1, 1987 now officially has been ruled a suicide by the SFPD. Father Kung was a Jesuit priest at the University and had resided at the rectory on campus. He is survived by his mother, Rina, of Prague, Czechoslovakia. Sergeant Edward Gallica stated during a brief press conference yesterday afternoon that the police investigation was complete. "This was a terrible tragedy. We don't know what motivated Father Kung to take his own life, but the physical and forensic evidence clearly shows that this is what occurred. His fellow priests are grief stricken as is the Archbishop." A memorial Mass will be held at the church on campus on Monday, June 8, 1987.

CHAPTER 9

Monday, June 8, 1987

ADAM THELEN WALKED with a heavy heart toward the church. He knew that this memorial service was a farce and wished that his attendance was not required. But he knew that it was. His absence would be noted, especially since he had no good reason to be elsewhere. As he entered the church, he saw Mike Burke. Neither showed any sign of recognition and they took separate seats. The crowd present in the church was small and the memorial could have been held in one of the side chapels. Since the Archbishop would be in attendance and was scheduled to speak, Father Gleeson, the president of the University, had decided that the main altar would be used. Father Gleeson would say Mass and both he and the Archbishop would give a brief homily. Both no doubt would tread lightly or simply ignore Father Kung's suicide, given the Church's stance on that topic. In fact, Father Kung's body was being flown back to Prague for interment there. Let them deal with the question of priestly suicide. The Mass proceeded uneventfully as did Father President's remarks. Then the Archbishop ascended the pulpit and began his own insipid sermon which was endured silently by those present. For Adam Thelen and Mike Burke, the only noteworthy occurrence came when the Archbishop raised his arms rather theatrically. Clearly visible on his left wrist was a fine diamond Rolex.

✝ ✝ ✝

"Can you believe that guy?" asked Mike Burke.

"Straight from the donation box onto His Excellency's wrist."

They were in Mike Burke's private car en route to a meeting with Chaz Thelen.

"Maybe it's not the same one. Maybe he's had one all along."

"No, it's the same one all right. It had a very distinctive adjustable link to fit the Weasel's skinny wrist. I had a hard time removing it and I saw it clearly in church today."

"Maybe he's just wearing it for a few days before he converts it into alms for the poor," said Adam.

"You priests all support one another right or wrong, just like doctors and lawyers. And the Archbishop isn't even a Jesuit," said Mike, laughing.

"No, not a Jesuit. Not even a priest primarily. Just another politician, except this one has his eye on the red hat of a Cardinal of the Church. Like most of the Church hierarchy, I guess."

"I doubt that most of them are like that, Father. And certainly not our current Pope. I think the Holy Father is a good man."

"Funny you should mention John Paul II," said Adam. "I've been thinking of him a lot of late. I think he has the potential to become a great Pope, maybe even an historic one."

They drove in silence toward the Transamerica pyramid.

What is happening to me? Am I becoming a cynic or an idealist? But what difference does it make either way, given the ghastly news Mike has uncovered about Lorena?

+ + +

In Morris's absence, Mike Burke was the guardian of the gates on the 39th floor and they did not have to repeat the ritual of a few days earlier. They simply announced themselves on the 38th floor and proceeded up the stairs. Mike then used his key to unlock the standard size door behind the entry desk. Chaz Thelen was waiting for them by the door to his office and ushered them inside.

"How was the memorial service? No second thoughts by anyone about Father Kung's suicide I hope," said Chaz Thelen.

"No, I think that's a fait accompli. I was thinking about that on the way over and, in a way, Father Kung did cause his own death by turning his back on God," said Adam.

"How did you two get here, anyway, now that Michael has retired his cab?"

"I drove over with Adam in my private car. And by the way, I want to mention that I'm renting the taxi to my brother-in-law for $35 per day. So Mr. Thelen, if you wish to lower my salary by that amount..."

"Michael, don't be absurd. You've already saved my son's life and now you've saved him from charges of manslaughter or worse, not to mention God knows what difficulties may have arisen within his order. Plus, you've gained information about Lorena. Please tell us about that."

"Well, I've already told Adam what I learned, which was sad news indeed. It was easy enough to obtain the facts. I simply contacted the Montes family by telephone in Spain and held myself out truthfully enough as an employee of the firm. I told them that Adam had taught Lorena and was concerned about her sudden departure from campus. I also explained that my employer was Adam's father."

"And what was the response?" asked Chaz Thelen.

"I explained all of this to a representative of the family who advised that he would review everything with Mr. & Mrs. Montes and call me back within twenty-four hours."

"When did all of this occur?" asked Chaz Thelen.

"I made contact with the family's representative on Tuesday and as promised, they called back on Wednesday morning our time. The news was not good. I was told that Lorena had died in a single car accident and that the family was in mourning. She was found in her car after the crash. The car and body inside were burned severely and identification was made via dental records. All of this happened in central Nevada. Both the Winnemuca and Reno papers carried brief stories of the accident. The body was flown home to Spain and burial was yesterday."

Adam and his father sat in silence for some time after hearing this account of Lorena's death. Adam felt nothing but a continuation of the simmering rage and self-loathing which had begun immediately after the death of Father Kung. Chaz Thelen experienced a rare feeling of helplessness as he watched what he perceived as recrimination, guilt and grief settle upon his son. He also felt a deep sense of sadness at the loss of the grandchild he never would know. After a moment, he was surprised to hear his son break the silence.

"What of this Maxim Spektor? What has Mother learned of his activities?"

"Not a great deal, I'm afraid," responded his Father. "Emily is in New York as is Max Spektor. His principal office is there and he also has a small office in London. There's been no indication that he has plans to travel anywhere in West Africa."

"No doubt he has operatives there to act on his behalf," said Adam.

"That's true, and so do we, in Accra, the capital of Ghana. None of our people have heard anything. Michael, I understand you've heard something concerning our friend the Weasel."

"Yes. An acquaintance of mine in the department told me that a representative of Mr. Spektor, one Leon Knoss, has made inquiries regarding the disappearance of Mr. Casque. My contact with my friend was to advise him that I now was working in security for the firm, which was considering business dealings with Mr. Spektor. I told him we had heard some rumor of shady activities by Mr. Spektor's firm and that I was checking into it. I said I had never heard of Mr. Casque and was surprised to hear of his disappearance. Apparently Mr. Casque's trip to the landfill went unnoticed and unlamented and he now rests there under another week's worth of garbage. Very fitting, I say."

"Fitting indeed. Dust to dust, garbage to garbage," said Chaz Thelen. "So, the only Weasel artifact remaining among us is his Rolex."

This remark caused Mike Burke to recount the story of the Rolex at the morning memorial service. Chaz Thelen listened intently with a growing smile on his face. Adam Thelen said nothing and seemed not to be involved in the conversation.

"I've met the Archbishop on several occasions, and somehow I'm not surprised," said Chaz Thelen. "What do you think, Adam?"

"What? Oh, as I said to Michael, I'm not surprised either. Just another politician going for the red hat."

"That seems a little harsh, Adam. He may be a little full of himself but he seemed generally a good man."

"Yes, I suppose you're right," said Adam distractedly. "I hardly know him."

After a moment's pause, Chaz Thelen said, "Adam, what are you going to do?"

"Dad, if you had asked me five minutes ago, I couldn't have answered, other than to say that I had to get away from San Francisco. Now, I'm not sure how, but I know what I'm going to do."

"And, what is that Adam?"

"I'm going to Poland—Krakow actually."

"Once again you astound me, Adam. What do you propose to do in Krakow?"

"Well, you know the Order is there..."

"Adam, as nearly as I can tell, the Order is everywhere. What is it that you will be doing?"

"Officially, I believe I will be studying and doing very limited teaching at the University there. I think most of my time will be spent writing and defending a thesis concerning the survivors of World War II death camps. Auschwitz-Birkenau is only fifty kilometers from Krakow. Also, I'll be learning the Polish language in order to do research in original texts and speak to survivors in their own tongue."

"You say 'believe' and 'I think.' Is this real or something which just now occurred to you?"

"I've had some preliminary discussions and I know I can get the required approvals. The last piece of the puzzle came to me only in the past few minutes—an epiphany if you will."

"What kind of an epiphany, Adam?"

"I know in my heart that our Pope, John Paul II is a good man, without reservation or qualification of any kind. I believe he was called by God to do good and this he has done, first in Poland culminating in his time as Archbishop and then Cardinal in Krakow and now in Rome as the Vicar of Christ. I am going to devote myself in whatever small ways I am capable to his causes."

"Adam, that all sounds good, but. . ."

"Dad, right now I am full of anger and hatred. If Maxim Spektor were here with us this moment, I swear to you and to God almighty that I would kill him where he stood. I am going to immerse myself in Poland in the hope that it is possible to purge this anger and hate."

Chaz Thelen and Mike Burke simply stared at him in wonder.

CHAPTER 10

Wednesday, June 17, 1987

ACROSS THE COUNTRY, in Manhattan, Max Spektor addressed the managing directors of the Spektor Fund. The London managing director took part via conference call.

"Gentlemen, it is time to implement Operation Ghana. Let us move forward immediately as planned."

+ + +

April---June, 1987---Nigeria

During its initial phases, nothing whatever relating to Operation Ghana occurred within the boundaries of the Republic of Ghana. Thus neither Emily Thelen nor any other member of the firm heard anything untoward from operatives inside Ghana.

Two countries, Togo and Benin, lie between Ghana and Nigeria. The capitals of Ghana and Nigeria, Accra and Abuja respectively, are five hundred miles apart. At first glance, the Federal Republic of Nigeria would seem an unlikely place to stage a campaign aimed at Ghana. But there were other factors to be considered beyond common borders and distance. Nigeria is a large country, significantly larger than the state of Texas. It also is a populous country, in fact the most populous of any African country and the most populous black majority country in the entire world. Lagos, a major port located, like Accra to the west, on the Gulf of Guinea, had a population approaching eight million. Nigeria's geography is extremely diverse, ranging from the coastal plains and mountains to the tropical rainforests of the Niger and Benue River valleys dominating the south central part of the country to the savannahs farther north and finally the near desert conditions of the far north Sahel. Perhaps most importantly, the government of Nigeria was fragmented, due largely to the wide variety of tribes and factions residing in the country. Nigeria was divided into thirty-six states and almost eight hundred "local government areas" or LGAs, most governed by ex-members of the military. The economy was growing and corruption was rife.

After extensive deliberation, Max Spektor chose the state of Sokoto located in the extreme northwest corner of Nigeria. The center of government there was the city of Sokoto situated at the confluence of the Sokoto and Rima Rivers, but Max Spektor settled upon the LGA of Saban Birni, a town of about 100,000 on the northern border of Nigeria. This region was part of the Sahel savannah, a hot dry area where temperatures regularly exceeded 112 degrees Fahrenheit in summer and where the Harmathan winds out of the north blew dust from the vast Sahara Desert into the tiniest crevasses. The town had limited infrastructure but it did possess a rudimentary airfield. And whatever assets the town possessed were available to the highest bidder.

+ + +

Two months prior to the meeting in Manhattan putting Operation Ghana into motion, three men had flown into the airfield at Sabon Birni. One of the men was white and the other two were black; all three were U.S. Citizens. All three also had served at least three tours in Vietnam in the U.S. Military. The leader of the small group, one of the black men, had been a U.S. Army major and the commander of what euphemistically had been called a "special op" battalion. This battalion had not been attached to any brigade or division headquarters. It was a rather small battalion of about three hundred men organized into three companies. Each company's commander was a first lieutenant or captain. In practice, the unit was highly mobile and autonomous, with missions focused on the death or destruction of specific personnel or materiel throughout Vietnam and, later, Laos and Cambodia. In simplest terms, it was a death squad expanded to battalion strength and this was precisely the mission of the three men in this northernmost outpost of Nigeria. The three men arrived in a two engine Cessna and were picked up by another man in a Range Rover and taken to a hotel in the town of Sabon Birni. Arrangements already were in place with the local governor and the major, known universally as "Major Vickers", began the recruiting process. The other two men, who had served in Vietnam as senior non-commissioned officers under Major Vickers, traveled each day to an area near the airfield and supervised the construction of what they called "Battalion HQ". This was comprised of large tents and the requisite furnishings, including a field kitchen, all of which was flown in or purchased locally. The personnel recruited by Major Vickers served as construction labor. These recruits were mostly Ghanian nationals who had fled Ghana in the severe economic dislocations of the late '70's and now wished to return to the relative political stability and economic upswing brought about by the Rawlins regime. They also knew that, sooner or later, they would be deported by Nigeria, as had more than a million of their fellow refugees from Ghana. Thus, Major Vickers' recruitment task was relatively easy. But a relatively easy task became virtually effortless when Major Vickers made three representations to each recruit:

1) Your total service will be 120 days or less during which time we will feed, house, equip and train you for a single mission.
2) You will be transported to Ghana at our expense.
3) Each of you will be issued a new AK-47 "Kalashnikov" which will be yours to keep at the conclusion of the mission.

Major Vickers had three hundred seventy-five suitable recruits at the end of four days. Training began immediately thereafter. During the first week, training consisted of four hours of stringent physical exercise followed by a meal and another four hours of labor completing Battalion HQ. Then there was an evening meal and one or two hours of lectures on military tactics by one of the three leaders. The physical exercise weeded out a few unfit recruits for whom replacements were brought in. During this time the three leaders began to organize squads, platoons and companies and to identify potential leaders of each unit. The men were treated fairly but discipline was strict. One of the disciplinary techniques was an announcement made very early on that Sharia Law would be enforced within the camp. Many of the men were at least titular Christians but they were familiar with Sharia Law since virtually all permanent residents of the state of Sokoto were Muslims. The City of Sokoto was the seat of the Sokoto Caliphate, the Sultan of which led the millions of Muslims living throughout Nigeria and comprising more than one half the population. Each man had seen Sharia Law invoked and applied against transgressors. Thus, thievery and other infractions within the camp were rare. After two weeks of training, no weaponry had been issued nor had any reached the camp. Publicly the three leaders showed no concern; in private their sentiments were much less sanguine.

Back in New York, Max Spektor met with one of his associates, just returned from China.

"Did you get them?"

"Yes, but it wasn't easy… or cheap."

"How much?"

"$240 each plus $30,000 for 800,000 rounds of ammunition. All together about $240,000 when the grenade launchers, transport, and other extras are included."

"Robbing bastards. They must have known our timeframe was short. When will they deliver?"

"Should be day after tomorrow. I've advised our friends in Nigeria."

"What about transport to Ghana?"

"I've arranged a charter of an old DC-8. Used to be a United plane but flies mostly in Egypt and Sudan now. It's a big plane and we're having to do runway repair in Ghana. But it can take everyone along with all the extra equipment in one load, although about fifty men will be standing or sitting in the aisle. That won't be a major problem for a flight of six hundred miles. Total of two days with two pilots, $45,000."

"And we're all set with the airfield and refueling in Ghana?"

"Yes. Another $20,000."

"OK. That's just over $400,000 for weapons and transport. It's over budget but our return on our investment still should be excellent if we get enough bodies."

+ + +

Emily Thelen's operatives in Ghana had been instructed to listen carefully for any event out of the ordinary. News of unusual activity at a disused airfield outside the city of Kumasi reached them and was transmitted to Emily Thelen. In San Francisco, she was in her husband's office.

"Are you sure it's Spektor?" asked Chaz.

"No. We're getting all sorts of reports, including one about basketball shirts, but this is one of the few that can't be discounted," replied Emily.

"What did we hear?"

"Only that the airfield will be used for one or two days sometime in the next forty-five days. Also refueling arrangements are being made, which suggests a flight from some distance away. We don't know the size of the plane or how many arrivals or departures are planned."

"How big a plane can the airfield handle?" asked Chaz.

"It's long enough for anything but a jumbo jet but it's in disrepair. If they bring in anything heavy, they'll have to do some patching and some kind of temporary runway lighting."

"What's close to the airfield?"

"That's just it. The answer is not much. It's about twenty miles from the outskirts of Kumasi. There was some mining nearby but not anymore. Now there are just villages of people, mostly farmers."

"Should we tell the Rawlins people?"

"I don't think we really have anything to report. We're going to keep checking but right now my emphasis is on preparing all of our people within the firm. Something is going to happen and we know it won't be a good thing."

The AK-47's arrived in Nigeria two days later. The mood of the recruits, who now were beginning to think of themselves as part of a unified force, brightened perceptibly. Tens of millions of AK-47s, commonly called "Kalashnikovs" in its multitudinous iterations were in use around the world by military forces and less formal entities such as this one in Nigeria, and it possessed enormous cachet. No less than four African nations including Burkina, Nigeria's neighbor to the northwest, featured a depiction of the actual weapon on their flags or coats of arms. The model purchased by Max Spektor's associate was known as the 'Type 56' in the Peoples' Republic of China, where it was manufactured. In fact, Max Spektor could have purchased a version of the weapon being manufactured in Nigeria, and likely for a lower price than he paid for the Chinese type 56. He had chosen to purchase in China for several reasons, including the fact that African arms merchants were notoriously loose lipped. The AK-47 used 7.62 x 39mm ammunition and a variety of magazines were available. The three leaders of the battalion in Nigeria had specified 20 round magazines for training purposes. Before departing for Ghana, each recruit would be issued forty magazines holding forty rounds each. They would load these magazines and carry them on the flight to Ghana. Each man would carry sixteen hundred rounds into Ghana.

+ + +

At the outset of training, no uniforms were issued. The men did their initial physical training in whatever clothes they brought to camp. Typical garb was shorts and a t-shirt with a variety of footwear. Some men were shoeless. When the AK-47s arrived, they were distributed and the men were schooled in disassembly, maintenance and cleaning. Each man was allowed to personalize his weapon with a small carving of his own choice. The carvings had to be the same size and had to be located in the same spot on the wooden stocks of the weapons. This was a time of excellent morale as the men reveled in the ownership of something with far greater monetary value, not to mention cachet, than anything they ever had possessed.

The AK-47 has a maximum effective range of just over four hundred yards when fired in semi-automatic mode and perhaps three hundred yards in full auto setting. In the interest of conserving ammunition and improving marksmanship, the men were trained with their weapons set on semi-automatic operation. Curiously, their instruction focused almost exclusively on frontal assaults with little mention of defensive tactics or flank protection. Some of the men had military experience and a few asked about this through their squad, platoon or company leaders. These men, now called "sergeants", "lieutenants" and "captains" respectively had been chosen in part because of their perceived leadership skills. But each of them also possessed at least rudimentary English, and the ability to translate these questions. The three main leaders treated all of these questions respectfully, knowing that if one or two men actively asked a question, many more were interested in the answer. The men were told that they were part of a much larger operation involving multiple camps such as theirs and that these other units would provide flanking protection, ongoing supply, field medical treatment, and many other services. Always it was emphasized that all things would be made more clear upon arrival in Ghana.

+ + +

In San Francisco, Emily and Chaz Thelen once again were meeting, this time in Emily's office adjacent to the 38th floor trading room.

"Anything more about our friend Max Spektor?" asked Chaz.

"Basketball shirts."

"What?..."

"Basketball shirts. We've learned that he bought five hundred Houston Rockets t-shirts."

"What possible connection could that have to Ghana?"

"None that we can imagine. Maybe he just can't pass up a bargain. These shirts are emblazoned with a logo that proclaims the Rockets as 1986 NBA champions. As you know they lost in six to the Celtics and the shirts never were used. I'm sure he got a great deal on them."

"But Max Spektor is a huge Knicks fan. He's always showing up in news clips and sports pages sitting at courtside right behind the Knicks' bench."

"All true," said Emily. "This is just an example of the chaff we're hearing. You know how it is when you tap into the rumor mill."

The men grew restive in the heat and dust and the normal irritations of being confined in close quarters with three hundred other men. There were several instances of women being smuggled into camp and some of them were discovered. The reaction of the three leaders was swift and severe although no one actually was stoned to death as prescribed by Sharia Law. The leaders conferred. The consensus was that only two or three weeks remained until they would be directed to proceed to Ghana. Instead of redoubling their training efforts, they determined to cut back somewhat on the length and rigor of each session. The men thus had more free time. However, rather than allowing them to relax at loose ends, the leaders introduced a new and potent distraction: basketball.

+ + +

Akeem Olajuwon was born in 1963 in Lagos, Nigeria. In 1980, he traveled to the United States for a walk-on tryout with the University of Houston Cougars. At the time he had little basketball experience, having played only soccer until the age of fifteen. By 1982 Olajuwan was starting for the Cougars and he led them to the national championship game where they narrowly lost to North Carolina. The next year the Cougars again went to the championship game, losing to the Georgetown team led by Patrick Ewing. In 1984, the Houston Rockets made Olajuwon the first pick of the NBA draft. In his second season with the Rockets, they shocked the Lakers in the Western Conference final and then lost in six games to the Boston Celtics. In 1987, Akeem Olajuwon was a living legend in his home country of Nigeria and basketball rivaled soccer as the national sport of choice. It was no surprise therefore that the introduction of recreational basketball into their daily regimen was cheered by the men.

+ + +

With the departure to Ghana now scheduled to occur in three days, Major Vickers convened a meeting in the mess tent. The men were instructed to gather with their respective squads, platoons and companies. The major stood at the front of the tent with Company B in front of him and Companies A and C to his left and right. Standing in front of Companies A and C were the other two U.S. leaders. Major Vickers stood behind two long tables on which were stacked baseball hats, black tee shirts and twelve grenade launchers designed for use with the Kalashnikovs. At the end of the table on his right was a small metal box. Stacked behind the table were a large number of cardboard boxes labeled "Meals — Ready to Eat." Major Vickers spoke slowly and paused so that each company commander could translate. The major and his two associates watched carefully to insure that every man understood what was being said.

"Men, we will be departing by plane for Ghana in three days' time. A four engine jet airplane large enough to carry all of us will arrive here early the day after tomorrow and we will load all of our equipment and depart very early the next morning. Each of you will carry your Kalashnikov and forty clips of ammunition with you on the plane. About two hundred fifty of you will have seats and the remaining one hundred or so will sit or stand in the aisles. It doesn't matter who has seats at the beginning of the flight since you will rotate twice so that every man will have a seat for most of the flight. The flight will be only about two hours so the crowded conditions will not matter anyway. Are there any questions so far?"

One of the men asked how they would get in such a large airplane. Another asked about the items on the table. Knowing that most of the men had never flown in an airplane, Major Vickers treated the first question very respectfully.

"We will board the airplane at the front and rear doors with wooden ladders which we will build later today. The plane has two levels, one for passengers and one on the bottom for freight. We also will build ladders to allow us to load equipment on the lower level."

"The items on the table are for you. First, we have shirts for each of you. There also are hats for the company, platoon and squad leaders to wear. The gold colored ones are for company commanders and the white and black are for platoon and squad leaders. Next, we have twelve grenade launchers which attach to your Kalashnikovs. There will be one for each platoon and the company commanders will designate the man to carry it. He and two other men from the platoon will also carry twelve grenades each. You will be trained in the use of these launchers today and tomorrow. Finally, this metal box contains money. Each company commander will receive $100. The platoon leaders will receive $50, the squad leaders $20 and all the rest of you will receive $10 each. Any other questions?"

The men had begun to talk excitedly among themselves but there were no further questions.

"All right then. In addition to all the items I mentioned you each will receive eight ready to eat meals and a pack to carry all your equipment. You will be shown how to eat these meals. Now, first platoon, Company A line up over here at the end of the tables. We want you to put on the hats and shirts now and keep them on. We'll have more announcements during the flight to Ghana."

As the first platoon picked up the equipment, word began to spread among the men. The shirts were Houston Rocket Championship t-shirts. The fact that Houston really wasn't the '86 champion didn't seem to faze the men at all. They began to chant, "Akeem! Akeem! Akeem the Dream."

+ + +

Back in San Francisco Emily and Chaz Thelen were at lunch. Gisele had joined them at a small restaurant in North Beach.

"Our people have been watching the airfield we identified earlier outside Kumasi in Ghana," said Emily.

There's been some activity recently. They've patched up the field and built some makeshift rolling steps. From the height of the steps our observers think they're expecting something fairly big, maybe a 707 or something about that size."

"What do you think may be happening?" asked Gisele.

"Well it could be nothing to do with Spektor at all. In fact, that's probably the case. But we have developed a possible scenario."

"What is it?" said Chaz.

"There have been persistent rumors that Spektor and his people have made money in the past, sometimes a fairly sizable chunk of money, by manipulating third world economies."

"What kind of money are we talking about?" said Chaz.

"Nobody can really pin that down or even be very specific regarding the countries which may have been involved. But the speculation has centered on a couple of small South American countries and also some areas of Southeast Asia. The dollar amounts which are bandied about aren't large. Never more than $10 million and usually quite a bit less. And all of the information is nebulous, with no real verification."

Gisele was nodding her head. "So you think he may be planning something that may somehow affect a country's trading patterns. Maybe something like commodities?"

"We're thinking maybe trading manipulation, but commodities don't seem to fit the bill. Ghana mines some gold and bauxite and there's also some developing export of agricultural products and a small tuna fishery, but there are really no futures markets. Ghana simply sells into the world market and their production isn't that high yet."

"I think I see where you're going," said Chaz. "When you factor in the attempted approach to you through Adam, you're thinking Spektor may be trying something in areas we've been developing."

"Exactly." said Emily. "And that would seem to narrow it down to trading in the recent bond issue, where we effectively are the market makers. The other possibility is trading in the Ghanaian cedi. We've also been active in that currency futures market. Finally, our people have been by far the most active in publishing analyses of the Ghanaian economy."

"How badly could we be hurt?" asked Chaz.

"Well, our exposure in the country is high right now, clearly higher than any other trading house. We could take a fairly sizable hit. And, we have been noticing some potentially troubling short selling. We can't tie it to Spektor though. It seems to be small contracts from all over the place but all of them shorting both the bonds and the currency. There's no single large contract, but in the aggregate it's pretty significant."

"Anything we can do?" asked Gisele.

"Yes, and we're doing it. The problem is that it's tough not knowing if the threat is real and, if it is, not knowing the timing. But, we've worked out a plan which can be implemented on very short notice if something occurs."

The three principals in the firm continued their lunch and conversed on lighter matters for a time. When coffee had been served Gisele spoke.

"What do we hear from Adam?"

Chaz related his last discussion with Adam and Mike Burke. He also briefly brought both Gisele and Emily up to date regarding the hiring of the latter. Gisele smiled when she heard Adam's plans.

"Poland," she mused. "There is a lot going on there right now. All over Eastern Europe for that matter. There's the Solidarity Movement which the Catholic Church has supported quite successfully thus far. That was Cardinal Wojtyla, now John Paul II. Now he's standing up against the communists. Talk about trading opportunities, the entire Eastern Bloc could change dramatically."

"Leave it to Adam," said Emily. "For a person who seems so dreamy and otherworldly, he certainly seems to find himself or place himself at the center of very worldly affairs, both personal and otherwise."

"That was an awful ghastly tragedy for him and all of us regarding the Montes woman," said Gisele. "How is Adam handling it?"

"Not well, I'm afraid," said Chaz.

CHAPTER 11

Saturday, June 20, 1987

THE DC-8 ARRIVED at 8:00 a.m. from Khartoum. It had sufficient remaining fuel to continue on to the airfield in Ghana, where it would be refueled for the return flight to Sudan. The men wrestled the heavy boarding and freight ladders into place and began the process of loading the plane and readying their own personal equipment. By noon, all was completed and the plane was ready to depart as soon as the men boarded. Instead the men were given a midday meal in the mess tent and instructed to dismantle the entire battalion headquarters. They were told to place the folded tents and other material in piles at the edge of the airfield to be taken away by others. This was completed by 2:30 p.m. and the men were told to be ready to board in one hour. At 3:30 p.m. everyone began boarding and the boarding ladders were pushed away from the plane when the process was completed at 4:00 p.m. With its reduced fuel load and limited freight, the DC-8 was well within its weight capacity even with somewhat more than one hundred of the men standing or sitting in the aisle and in the rear and forward galley areas. Major Vickers was seated in an aisle seat in the first row near Company A and his two associates were in aisle seats further back with Companies B and C. The men were very quiet. Many were clearly fearful, on their first flight in an airplane of any type. A few were airsick and the plane soon was filled with a sour smell. Major Vickers had carried a bullhorn aboard with him but, as it turned out, the public address system of the plane was operational. He stood in the front galley with the microphone which had been used by the lead flight attendant when the plane was engaged in regular passenger travel. Again he spoke slowly and simply, with many pauses to allow translation. And once again he and his two associates watched carefully to insure that everyone understood what the major was saying.

"Men, as I said earlier, this will be a short flight. We will be arriving in less than two hours at an airfield in Ghana."

He purposely did not mention that the airfield was located near the city of Kumasi. No doubt some of the men had friends or relatives in the area and Major Vickers did not wish the men to defect shortly after landing. Worse, some of the men might well refuse to perform the mission he was about to outline if any friends or relations happened to live close by the airport. Of course, it was possible that a few of the men might recognize their surroundings when they left the airplane. This was a risk which could not be avoided and, if it proved to be true, would have to be dealt with swiftly.

"We will be landing about 6:00 and our plane must be completely unloaded immediately. We will do this while other people we will meet on the ground are refueling the plane. By no later than 6:45 the plane must depart. Now I and my two associates are going to meet with your company and platoon leaders to discuss tomorrow's mission."

The 6:45 departure deadline certainly was true since the decision had been made not to install even temporary lighting.

If there were any delays during the critical unloading/refueling process, the DC-8 would be forced to remain overnight and depart at first light the next morning. Major Vickers wished very much to avoid this or any other distractions to their mission, which was to begin at sunrise. The tradeoff for the tight departure schedule was that, if all went well, the plane would arrive and depart in the hour between 6:00 and 7:00 p.m. when most people were indoors. Even if anyone took notice they would be unlikely to come out and check on the activity at the airfield until the next morning.

The DC-8 took a somewhat indirect route across southern Burkina and northern Ghana and then changed headings to the south along the western borders of Ghana with Burkina and then with the Ivory Coast. In this way the plane approached the airfield in Ghana from the northwest and avoided all large airports and their ground controllers. The plane landed at 6:02 and the unloading and refueling proceeded without a hitch. The DC-8 was in the air and heading back to Sudan by 6:50.

The watcher hired by the firm was preparing to leave the airfield outside Kumasi and return home for the night. Just as he was departing, he heard something unfamiliar. At first, it was just the sensation of sound, a kind of low rumble. He decided to wait and see what developed. The sound grew louder and he realized that it was a large jet and that it definitely was coming closer. Then it came into sight, flying out of the northwest. He watched it land and disgorge over three hundred armed men. He saw the unloading and refueling and then saw the now empty jet take off and disappear into the dusk. The news reached Emily Thelen in San Francisco about 1:30 in the afternoon, her time.

+ + +

The men from the DC-8 ate their MREs and then bedded down at various points around the airfield. They had been instructed on the plane to be as quiet as possible. Their mission would begin at sunrise.

+ + +

"Are we ready?" Max Spektor was in New York the previous afternoon with several of his senior managing directors.

"We are." answered one of them. "It's set to start early Sunday morning, Ghana time."

"Where are we with the press?"

"Our contacts are ready to alert the wire services and the networks, including CNN, the moment anything comes out of Ghana."

"We're going to need TV footage for the biggest impact," said Max.

"At first it will be local feeds to the networks and CNN. It should make the evening news shows tomorrow night and the newspapers will have it the following morning. If it's a big enough story, CNN will be on site in Ghana by the morning of the second day. That would be Monday."

"It better be a big story and it better have some staying power," said Max. "We don't want to start executing trades until Wednesday."

"Well, we know that's the tricky part. Our people in the Ghanaian military are going to be under pressure to get in there on the second day and shut it down," said one of the senior aides, looking to the others for support on this point. None was forthcoming.

"We're paying them a lot of money, plus the so-called spoils they demanded, to hold off until the third day," said Max harshly. "And we're paying Vickers and his boys a good sum to keep their men killing for three days."

"Max, I'm sure they'll both do the very best they can," answered one of the aides.

+ + +

Sunday, June 21, 1987

At 4:30 a.m., Major Vickers and his two associates roused the company commanders who in turn woke their platoon leaders. By 5:00 a.m. the men were eating their MREs. At the first hint of sun in the east, the men set out.

The mission outlined on the plane by Major Vickers and his men was as simple as it was barbaric. At 6:00 a.m. on the morning after their arrival on the DC-8, Major Vickers set the mission in motion. The airfield ran from west to east, which had required the DC-8 to make a change in heading near the end of its approach to land flying nearly due east. In accordance with Major Vickers' instructions, the men fell out and proceeded with the plan which had been practiced in detail several times at the airfield in Nigeria. The men were very familiar with the routine and by 7:00a.m. they were in place and had taken cover. In sum, there were two company sized units in single file forming about a one mile extension, to the west and east, of the northern edge of the airfield. Company B formed a line, again about a mile long, parallel with and about a mile south of the southern edge of the field. The men remained under cover and maintained silence until 9:00 a.m. In the two hours between 7:00 and 9:00 the various small villages and farms came to life as their inhabitants ate their morning meals and then went about their business for the day. Most of the activity here centered on agriculture. There were a few fairly large farms raising cocoa beans destined for export, but most of the farms were of small to medium size with crops grown for local consumption, often in the neighboring villages or farmhouses. By 9:00 most of the men and some of the women were in the fields tending the crops while most of the women and children remained in the huts which comprised the villages. At 9:15 a.m. the commanders of Companies A and C contacted their platoon leaders and ordered them to move out. The men of Company B remained in place in the picket line south of the airfield. Soon the muted sounds of small arms fire could be heard from the airfield, along with the dull thud of the grenade launchers followed in a moment by the distant explosion of grenades. The men of Companies A and C had been ordered to move south in a line from their original positions and to kill everything they encountered, including livestock. They had been instructed to move slowly and patiently and to conduct thorough searches of the areas they were traversing. They also were told to retain their ammunition clips for future use. The only orders were to kill everyone and everything. No orders had been issued regarding pillage, plunder and rape. Many of the men understood this as a license to engage in such activities. After about forty-five minutes, Major Vickers and his two associates began to hear scattered gunshots from the AK-47s of Company B arrayed in a line to the south. This was the sound of the men of Company B picking off survivors who were running from the onslaught of the other two companies. On two occasions, a lone woman and a woman with two children, ran across the airfield in full sight of Major Vickers and his two associates. These three men took no action other than point their fingers directing the women to the south. The killing proceeded at a deliberate pace until about noon. By this time, elements of Companies A and C were encountering the men of Company B still in their picket line south of the airfield. Radio contact was initiated to all platoon leaders instructing them to cease fire and take cover. At 1:00 p.m. the platoon leaders were ordered to begin to move in a northerly direction back toward the airfield. The three companies now were in a long line running east to west about a mile south of the airfield. Again, the men moved slowly and methodically killing everyone before them and searching carefully for any survivors trying to hide from the slaughter. The two platoons located at each end of the line advancing toward the airfield began to wheel toward the ends of the airfield. In this manner, anyone trying to escape to the east or west would be blocked and shot down. This wheeling maneuver also had been practiced repeatedly in Nigeria and was familiar to the men. Major Vickers and his two associates back at the airfield heard the assault weapons coming closer.

"Time to take cover," said Major Vickers, "These boys have their blood up and will be shooting at anything which moves, including us."

The men who had constructed the ladders used in disembarking from the DC-8 and unloading it also had constructed on the airfield a bunker in which Major Vickers and his men now took cover. The bunker was built of heavy timbers on four sides to a height of six feet with more timbers laid across the top. The entry at the north side of the bunker was essentially a tunnel of timbers with three right angle turns to prevent any stray rounds or shrapnel from entering on a direct line.

Major Vickers and his men remained in the bunker as the three companies slowly approached the airfield. By about 2:45 p.m. men began to reach the field and by 3:15 all three companies had returned to the areas in which they had eaten and slept the night before. While Major Vickers and his associates waited in the bunker, the three company commanders met with their platoon leaders who already had debriefed each of the squad leaders. At about 4:00 p.m., the three company commanders entered the bunker and took seats at a folding table which had been set up by the men who had built the bunker before the DC-8 arrived. Three light bulbs powered by a small gas generator outside the bunker hung over the table. The three company commanders took turns reporting to Major Vickers and his men on the day's mission.

"How many killed'?" asked Major Vickers.

Each of the company commanders replied in turn. Company A estimated about two hundred sixty killed by his men. Company C's estimated body count was about two hundred seventy. Finally the commander of company B advised a body count of about eighty-five who had tried to flee through his company's southerly picket line, plus another one hundred ten killed in the northerly return to the airfield.

"So a total of about seven hundred twenty-five," said Major Vickers. "Any casualties among your men?"

"A total for all three companies of fifteen killed and four injured," reported the commander of Company A. "Mostly gunshot wounds, but we had one man return from the fields and kill two men who were inside with his wife. He used a spade from the fields. Two of the injuries are minor but the other two are in pretty bad shape. We don't think they'll make it. Five of the deaths resulted when four men tried to desert and had to be killed. When the four deserters came under fire they returned fire and killed one of us."

Major Vickers knew that all of the gunshot victims in the three companies were almost certainly killed or wounded by friendly fire but he said nothing about this. Nor did he inquire as to the genders or ages of those killed by the three companies. Finally, he did not question body counts reported by the commanders even though an earlier survey by Spektor's men estimated a total population in the areas assaulted of about six hundred. Instead he addressed the commander of Company A, who apparently had been designated by the other two company commanders as the spokesman for all three commanders.

"Were all of the deserters killed or did one or two actually get away?"

"We killed all of them and no one escaped. We brought all the bodies back."

"Did your men leave all the other bodies in plain sight, as ordered?"

"Yes. Even those who had been hiding, we pulled out into the open after killing them."

"All right. Tonight we want all your men to come up to the area where the plane was unloaded. Start with first platoon Company A. We're going to issue four more MREs per soldier, plus another 800 rounds of ammunition. Also, we're issuing each company something new. Let's go out on the runway and we'll show you."

Major Vickers led the three company commanders out onto the tarmac in the area where the plane had been unloaded. He and his two associates went among the stacked MREs and ammunition boxes to a small tarpaulin which had been spread over some additional equipment. They removed the tarp to reveal three small piles which were not immediately identifiable.

Each of them picked up two items and brought them to a clear area of runway. They then went back and brought two more items apiece. One of the items carried by each man was a shell of some kind. They then proceeded to set up the weapons, which were three M224 60mm mortars. Each weapon had a narrow 40" long firing tube, a base plate and a bipod. Attached to the firing tube of each mortar was a sighting unit. All together the components for each weapon weighed a little under forty-seven pounds. The shells were 60 mm mortar shells designed to explode on impact. The units were gravity fed, which meant that the shells were dropped one at a time into the firing tube which had a firing pin at the bottom. The range of the shells depended on the angle at which the firing tube was mounted via the bipod to the baseplate which rested on the tarmac. Maximum range was slightly over two miles. Major Vickers had obtained the mortars on his own and even Max Spektor was unaware that he had them. They had been stolen from the U.S. military by friends of his still serving, in this case in the National Guard. He had gotten them in exchange for other favors he had bestowed on his friends. The cost of such mortars to the military, exclusive of shells, was about $7,000 apiece. This particular mortar, the M224, was newly developed to combine easy portability with increased range. Effectively, it allowed infantry units to carry their own light artillery along with them. Now Major Vickers picked up one of the shells. He reoriented one of the mortars so that the firing tube was positioned at its maximum range and pointing in a southerly direction toward the city of Kumasi. He dropped the shell into the tube and with a subdued "whump" the shell rocketed south. He stood motionless for about seven or eight seconds and then everyone heard the distant explosion of the shell.

"That shell landed in the middle of a fairly sizable village about two miles away. Tomorrow we want each company to take one of the mortars, plus thirty shells. After you have completed the mission we've already discussed, set up the mortars and target additional villages further out to the north. The land falls away slightly up there and you should be able to see the valleys with your binoculars. Spend about ninety minutes sighting in on these villages and shelling them. Then return to the airfield. Now go and make sure the perimeters are set up properly. And one other thing: Make sure that you and your men all wear their black shirts and that you and the other leaders wear your baseball hats tomorrow."

CHAPTER 12

Monday, June 22, 1987

BACK IN SAN Francisco, it was a dreary morning, the kind of day which inspired an old comedian to remark that the "coldest winter he ever spent was one summer in San Francisco." Emily had news from Ghana and now was with her husband in his office. Gisele also was present as was Adam, who had asked to be kept abreast of any developments involving Max Spektor.

"Something is happening in Ghana and we think it's Spektor," said Emily.

"Tell us," said Chaz.

"We've continued to watch the airfield near Kumasi and yesterday we heard that a large jet, probably a DC-8, had landed there and off loaded over three hundred armed men plus a quantity of equipment. The landing would have occurred Saturday evening Ghana time. Now we're hearing news that some kind of killing spree has occurred in the area of the airfield."

"News? You mean news from your watchers?" asked Gisele.

"No. This is actual radio and T.V. news. Accounts are sketchy, but the wire services are reporting possible deaths in the hundreds."

"How do you know it's Spektor?" asked Chaz. "When you identified the airfield earlier you said there was no evidence tying it to Spektor."

"We've heard from two sources, one at AP and one at CNN, that Spektor's people are pushing this story. They've been calling the news services and inquiring about the killings in Ghana, referring to them as a 'massacre.' Their pretext is that they have investments in Ghana and are trying to get more detail on what's happening. Yet the news people had heard nothing from their usual sources in Ghana."

"Still, couldn't they be legitimately concerned about their investments in Ghana?" asked Adam.

"The timing doesn't work. Think about it. Their inquiries are virtually concurrent with the actual timing of any massacre which may have been perpetrated by the men from the airplane. Spektor's people had to have advance notice and now they're trying to push the story in the international press. And it's working. Our source at CNN says crews are heading down to Ghana from Algeria as we speak. In a matter of hours this is going to be a major story."

"What are we doing about it?" asked Chaz.

"We've been having ongoing discussions with the Rawlins government about the disquieting reports floating around. Now I've spoken personally with his chief of staff. I related everything I just outlined to you. I also told him that the government absolutely, positively has to get in there and stop whatever is going on. Then, when we know more details we and the government must get out in front of the story and explain it as some kind of aberration which was quickly dealt with. If we can do all that, we might still be able to portray Ghana as an example of the new Africa, where stable, strong governments can stop occasional efforts to return to chaos."

"What do you think our chances are?" asked Gisele.

Emily shook her head. "Maybe 50-50. What we have going for us is that Rawlins and many of his men will profit if we prosper. And even more importantly, he and most of his men really are committed to a better Ghana."

On the second morning Major Vickers met again with the three company commanders, this time without his two associates. He reviewed the day's mission along with the added mortar barrage now planned for the afternoon. He checked that the men had reloaded their clips and were wearing their "uniform" black tee shirts and baseball caps. At the conclusion of his inspection, he handed a $100 bill to each of the company commanders.

"That $100 is just a down payment on what you'll be receiving if you choose to stay with us on future missions," said Major Vickers. "We'll be departing by air for a new location about 1700 hours. You can tell all your men that they will be receiving twenty dollars each after boarding the plane. When they arrive at the new destination in Ghana, they'll have the opportunity to go on their way or stay with us for an additional mission. Of course, each of the platoon and squad leaders will get a bonus also. Be sure to have your men back here at the airfield by no later than 1530 hours. We'll need at least an hour to get the plane loaded and the men on board for a 1700 take-off. Also, be sure to bring those mortars back with you. We'll need them on future missions."

"Yes, sir," responded the three commanders in unison.

+ + +

All three companies set out in a line moving in a northerly direction away from the airfield. Soon Major Vickers and his two associates heard sporadic gunshots which soon escalated into salvos of gunfire and grenades all along the line.

"Sounds like a lot of the men have switched to full auto today," said one of the associates of Major Vickers.

"I'm not surprised," said Major Vickers. "That means some of them will be low on ammunition when they return to the airfield this afternoon. Not a bad thing."

"No. We still have plenty of ammunition for tomorrow's action," said the other associate.

"We won't need any more ammunition. There's not going to be any action tomorrow. It will all be over by then."

Both associates looked at him quizzically.

"I've had radio contact from our friend in the Ghanaian military. Something has happened and he's under enormous pressure to end this operation today. Gentlemen, our transport has been brought out. It's time for us to depart."

The three men shouldered their personal packs and began walking to the south toward Kumasi. This meant that they were walking through yesterday's carnage. Every fifty or one hundred yards they came upon a body or a cluster of bodies lying in the open already beginning to decay, surrounded by hordes of flies. The single bodies usually were male while the clusters often were composed of women with one or more children. The men gazed at all of this dispassionately as they walked by. After about a mile and a quarter, there were no more bodies, dead or alive, only abandoned huts, farmhouses and villages. It was here that they found the white Range Rover which had been parked earlier that morning. As promised, the keys were tucked at the rear of the left front tire and hidden by leaves. Major Vickers and his men got into the Range Rover and drove into Kumasi. They drove directly to a prearranged meeting point with Major Vickers' friend in the Ghanaian military.

"They'll have returned to the airfield by 1530. Your men should be there ready to go well in advance," said Major Vickers.

"They will be. I don't know what happened but Rawlins is personally involved. This thing has to be shut down by the end of the day or it's my ass."

"That should be no problem for you. My men should be fairly low on ammunition with very few if any grenades left when they get back. Remember, they'll all be wearing black tee shirts and some of them will have on baseball caps. Kill the ones with the caps first. They're the leaders. There are three with gold caps. They should have at least $300 each on them."

"Excellent. Are the AKs the type 56 we discussed?"

"Yes, they are and the grenade launchers also are Chinese made. Also, you're going to find a bonus, probably very close to the company commanders—the ones with the gold caps. Each of them has a mortar. They're the new U.S. M224. We'll need to be paid extra for them."

"Fine. I'll give you $2,500 a piece."

"$12,000 for all three," said Major Vickers "and I'll arrange for delivery to you of sixty shells."

"Done. Are you heading out today?"

"We're going directly to the airport here in Kumasi. There's a small jet waiting for us. We'll leave the Range Rover there."

+ + +

Major Vickers' friend and his men in the Ghanaian military found only two mortars. All of Major Vickers' men were killed when they returned at 1530 hours to the airfield. It was a very straightforward, almost anticlimactic exercise. As soon as Major Vickers' men reached the airfield, they were surrounded by armored personnel carriers and shot down. Some of them, those with ammunition, returned fire but they were no match for the .50 caliber machine guns mounted on the personnel carriers and the superior numbers of the Ghanaian military force, all of whom were dressed in light colored khaki blouses to differentiate them from Major Vickers' men. When the men were dead, the Ghanaian forces moved in and efficiently stripped the men of their assault rifles and anything else of value on their persons. The weapons and two of the M224 mortars were loaded into a separate civilian truck which quickly drove off. The black shirts were stripped off the men and burned. CNN showed up with its cameras when the bodies were being buried in a large pit dug by a bulldozer which had been trucked in just behind the Ghanaian soldiers. The cameras duly recorded rather grisly footage but by that time the bodies strewn in the countryside surrounding the airfield had been removed. Major Vicker's friend was unable to locate the missing mortar, nor could he find much money on one of the corpses wearing a gold baseball cap. He later adjusted his payment to Major Vickers to account for the missing money and mortar.

The solution to the minor mystery of the missing mortar would not have surprised Major Vickers. One of the company commanders, the one who had acted as spokesman for his fellow commanders, had hurried back that morning after departing the airfield and had seen Major Vickers and his two associates march off to the south. This commander, whose name was Aboute, then rejoined his men and carried out the day's mission, including the mortar attacks on the villages to the north. When four mortar shells were left, he ordered his men to return to the airfield. He told them he would rejoin them after taking the mortar farther north and shelling a large village which he had spotted with his binoculars, just out of range. He gave his gold baseball cap to one of the platoon leaders to wear until he returned to the airfield. He then chose one man to go with him and help carry the mortar and shells. This man called himself Jerry, no doubt in honor of Ghanaian President Jerry John Rawlins. Aboute had watched over the last two days as Jerry fired his assault rifle into the air, into the ground, into trees, into anything at all other than the Ghanaian farm families. In two days Jerry had killed or injured no one at all nor had he taken part in the raping and looting. When Jerry and Aboute had moved north about half a mile, they came to a road. Here Aboute took off his pack and removed a tarp from it. He carefully wrapped the mortar, shells and the two AK-47s that he and Jerry carried and then hid the tarp and its contents just off the road. He removed his black tee shirt, tore a strip from it and tied it to a small tree near where the tarp was hidden. He gave the remainder of the black shirt to Jerry and told him to bury it along with his own black shirt, some distance off the road. Each man then donned another shirt from the packs they carried and walked off in a westerly direction along the road.

CHAPTER 13

<u>Wednesday, June 24, 1987</u>

MAXIM SPEKTOR WAS in Manhattan with his head trader.

"How did we do?"

"Well, we made money," answered the trader with a small smile.

"I expect so. The question is how much money?"

The trader hesitated a moment and then said "Just under two and a half million dollars. A hundred percent return on our investment."

Max Spektor showed no reaction other than a very small tic at the corner of his left eye. "Thank you. Please leave me now," said Max Spektor.

Max Spektor was deeply disappointed. He had expected to make at least ten and perhaps as much as fifteen million dollars, much of it at the expense of the Thelens. Max knew that in due course, his people would explain to him in great detail how the plan had gone awry and how only their quick thinking and fine execution salvaged any profit at all. But he already knew the real reasons the operation had failed and knew also that he had only himself to blame. First, he never should have entertained the notion put forth by Casque that collaboration with the Thelens was feasible, even though their cooperation was to be extorted via their son. Cooperation and collaboration implied trust in another party and trust of anyone other than himself simply could not be justified. Second, he had been guilty of small thinking. He should have realized that hundreds of deaths in a place like Africa would never penetrate the consciousness of western society for any appreciable length of time. He should have set out to cause thousands of deaths during an ongoing crisis. He would find ways to make this happen.

As often occurred in times of stress or crisis, memories of that day in 1943 on the Danube returned unbidden to Max. He had kept his bargain with the SS Sturmbannfuhrer. When the captain and his wife reached port with the resistance cargo they were towing, the Germans were waiting. They watched as the cargo was unloaded onto trucks and they allowed the trucks to drive off to the designated meeting place with the resistance forces. As the trucks were being unloaded, the Germans attacked. Seventeen resistance fighters were killed and the cargo confiscated. The Sturmbannfuhrer, his sergeant and four soldiers had remained at the river. When the unloading of the barges was complete, and the trucks had driven away, they boarded the Princess Elena. They took the captain and his wife and Max to the customs office. There, the Sturmbannfuhrer had engaged in some perfunctory questioning of the captain and his wife, both of whom denied any knowledge that the cargo was contraband. The Sturmbannfuhrer seemed uninterested in their answers and after a few minutes he directed the captain, his wife and Max to step out behind the building. The other five soldiers followed. The Sturmbannfuhrer placed the captain and his wife against the back wall of the customs office and instructed Max to stand about six feet away, next to the sergeant. The Sturmbannfuhrer removed his sidearm from its holster.

"You said you wanted the boat, didn't you?" said the Sturmbannfuhrer to Max.

Max kept his eyes on the ground in front of him and nodded.

"Speak up boy and look at us!"

Max raised his eyes to the Sturmbannfuhrer and to the captain and his wife. All three were standing in a small group near the wall.

"Yes," said Max.

"Well, here we are then. The boat is down at the dock, ready to go," said the Sturmbannfuhrer gesturing carelessly with his pistol. "But do you still want it?"

Max had lowered his eyes and now said nothing.

"Look at us, boy! I'll make it simple. The captain or the boat?"

Max remained silent.

"Answer me!"

Max stared at the Sturmbannfuhrer and said, "The boat."

The Sturmbannfuhrer smiled and shot the captain in the head. Elena gasped and then turned slowly toward Max. The light had left her eyes.

"Oh, Max," she said.

The Sturmbannfuhrer shot her in the head also.

As always when these memories returned to him, Max Spektor had the same thought.

I did not betray them. I did not kill them. They were dead already.

The Sturmbannfuhrer kept his bargain and Max kept his. He piloted the tugboat to the next port and found a man working on the wharves there who was willing to serve as mate on the tugboat. His first task was to paint over "Princess Elena" on the stern and replace it with the new name of the tugboat, "Reliance," a name which Max always prefaced in his own mind with the word "Self." Max worked for the Germans on two additional occasions, each time to entrap members of the Resistance. Then, when the tides of war shifted in 1944, he switched his allegiance to the Americans.

Wednesday, July 1, 1987

In San Francisco Chaz, Emily and Adam Thelen were sharing a lunch together at the Pacific Union Club. Gisele was in New York.

"Two times in one year at the PU Club," said Chaz to Adam. "That has to be a record for you."

"Yes, I suppose it is," answered Adam. "A lot of my old values seem to be in a state of flux. Also, my sense of humor I guess. I know you're simply engaging in banter."

"That's OK, really," said Emily. "I'm your mother and I say it's OK. You've been through a lot. How are you doing?"

"Serious answer?" said Adam.

"Of course," said Chaz and Emily in unison.

"I'm not doing well. I caused Lorena's death. I also caused the death of my own unborn child, your grandchild. I think a lot about the bridge."

"My God Adam," said Emily. "Surely you're not still thinking about suicide."

"No, I'm not," answered Adam. "I learned the hard way, the moment I left the railing, that my self-destruction was not the answer or solution to anything. If ever I have heard God's voice speaking, it was at that moment. No, I'm not going to kill myself. It's just very, very difficult to wake up each morning and face another day. I know it sounds like self-pity to say that but it's true."

"It's not self-pity in the least," said Chaz. "It's simply reality. Lorena is dead and so is the child."

Here Chaz Thelen began to weep. He was forced to pause in order to compose himself. Both Adam and Emily looked stricken. Adam was the first to speak.

"Dad, I'm sorry, so very sorry."

"Do not be sorry for me and do not claim any guilt for Lorena's death or that of the child. For a person in your position, your conduct with Lorena was irresponsible and was likely to cause her sorrow and grief. But in no way should it have caused her death or the death of anyone else. That responsibility lies elsewhere. We know in whom it resides."

"I know that's all true Dad, but that's a rational argument and reason just doesn't penetrate my consciousness. I want to see Max Spektor suffer. I want to see him dead. It's almost an obsession."

"My dear, dear son," said Emily. "It's still very early. You know that. You know the workings of grief better than any of us."

"Yes, I know the process. I've studied it. I've taught it and I've written about it. And now I'm going to Poland to study and write a great deal more about it. The people I'll be meeting, Holocaust survivors and their families, have experienced grief immeasurably greater than mine. My solace, if it exists, will be found among these people. If I can give them even the tiniest bit of comfort and succor, so much the better."

"When do you leave?" asked Emily.

"I'm wrapping up loose ends here right now. My travel arrangements aren't made yet, but I should be leaving sometime in the middle of August."

"Where will you be?" asked Chaz.

"I'll be living in quarters at Ignatianum and will be an adjunct professor at the Jagiellonian University. I'll have no classes there during the first semester and at most one or two starting in the second semester next year. For the first few months, my primary duties will be interviews with the survivors and their children and grandchildren. I'll start in and around Krakow but then travel further afield in Poland and Eastern Europe. Finally, I'll be traveling to Italy and Germany. It seems strange initially, but less so when you think about it. Quite a number of the survivors or their children returned there after the war."

By now, lunch had ended and the table had been cleared. Adam thanked his father and mother for lunch and excused himself in order to return to the University and continue his preparations for departure. When he had left, Chaz spoke.

"How badly did we get hurt?"

"A million four. It could have, probably should have, been much worse. We were lucky."

"Less than a million and a half dollars. I did expect quite a bit more."

"Ironically enough, we have Max Spektor to thank. If he hadn't tried to suborn me, we would have been fat, dumb and happy until the atrocities occurred around Kumasi. We wouldn't have been able to react until the damage had continued for a longer period and then festered in the markets. Thanks to Max's error, we were all over it on day one. I was in direct communication with Rawlins and his people as soon as the killing started. It didn't take much to persuade them that swift and decisive action was absolutely necessary."

"It looked to me as if the press coverage actually helped our cause," said Chaz.

"Yes. That was another stroke of good fortune. CNN actually got footage of Spektor's men, over three hundred of them, being bulldozed into a makeshift pit grave. Plus, they had firsthand accounts, although no actual film footage, of the carnage visited upon the surrounding countryside. That bastard Spektor killed at least a thousand people plus the slaughter of his own men. CNN was going to go with the atrocity story and, of course, they did report it. But the main theme of the story which reached the international press was communicated by Rawlins' people. Their message was twofold: 'The atrocities were clearly, incontrovertibly over and the reason they were over was because of the quick and efficient intervention of the government.'"

"And you were able to push this same theme in the markets," said Chaz.

"I certainly was, since it was the same message I gave to Rawlins and his people at the very beginning. After a brief period of uncertainty, which is when we suffered our losses, the realization spread that this actually was the story of growing stability in Ghana. We've actually made back some of our losses now that our bonds and the currency have stabilized."

"Are we positive it really was Spektor?" asked Chaz.

"No doubt whatever. I talked with two of the CNN people personally. The government forces wouldn't allow them to film it, but they witnessed the burning of the black tee shirts. They were the same Houston Rockets shirts which Spektor bought for next to nothing. It was him all right and it also shows that he had cooperation in the Ghanaian military. There also was the truckload of weapons."

"Weapons?" asked Chaz.

"At the same time the Ghanaian forces were stripping the corpses and burning the shirts, they also were collecting all of the AK-47s and loading them on an unmarked truck which quickly left the scene. In addition to the assault rifles, there also were other interesting items loaded into the truck."

"Like what?"

"Two M224 mortars. These are U.S. military weapons and they were only developed two or three years ago so they haven't even reached NATO forces yet. We don't know how Spektor procured them, but it doesn't really matter. The point is that Spektor cut a deal with people inside the Ghana military to kill his own men after they had wreaked horror on the countryside. And at least part of the payment was made in the form of weapons used by Spektor's slaughtered men."

"Does Rawlins know about this?"

"You bet he does. I told him all about it. He said, to use his own words, that he would 'take steps'."

"So maybe the government isn't as stable as the markets now think," said Chaz with a chuckle.

"Well, maybe we are guilty of some selective reporting," said Emily. "None of us is perfect."

"That's very true," said Chaz, "but we are infinitely more so than is Max Spektor. And, I want to tell you something which I already mentioned to Gisele. Never in my life, until now, have I allowed personal friendships or animosities to color my business behavior. With Max Spektor, if the opportunity presents itself, I and the firm are going to make an exception. I trust that you concur."

"Without a doubt," said Emily, "and I'll go one step further. I tell you here and now that such an opportunity certainly will arise."

CHAPTER 14

Thursday, August 27, 1987

WHEN HE HAD departed San Francisco en route to Krakow, Adam Thelen had not traveled directly. Instead, he had stopped in New York to meet with his half-brother, Theodore, ostensibly to say good-bye prior to his sojourn to Poland. He had known, however, that he also sought his half-brother's advice and counsel. Theodore Thelen, S.J. now was fifty-two years old and the Father-President of Fordham University. When Adam had attended Fordham and the Fordham Law School in the 70s, his half-brother had been a professor of history and later Dean of Men. During Adam's years at Fordham, the two men had forged a wary familiarity which gradually evolved into a genuine friendship. The wariness was the normal and appropriate caution which springs from an awareness of the possibility of at least perceived favoritism or nepotism. Caution also flowed from the fact that they shared the same father but not the same mother. Over time, these concerns had dissipated, to be replaced by mutual affection and respect. Now Adam looked forward to seeing his half-brother again; he also wished to mine his half-brother's vast knowledge of the workings of the Society of Jesus. Their private joke was that Theodore Thelen was privy to knowledge of all things Jesuitical.

"Theo," said Adam as he entered the Office of the President.

"Adam," he said rising from behind his desk and embracing his half-brother.

"It's good to see you," they said virtually in tandem, followed by mutual laughter. They took seats on two sofas arranged in an "L" shape on the two sides of a coffee table.

"How are you?" asked Theo. "This latest venture you've chosen is fairly astounding—almost a return to the missionary roots of the Order."

"In a way, it is. Yet, not surprisingly, some of my motives are not very selfless."

"How so?"

Adam hesitated a moment staring sightlessly out the expansive window of his half-brother's second floor office before continuing.

"Well, let me bring you up to date," said Adam. "But first I must ask you to suspend disbelief and also to suspend, at least temporarily, the censure I so richly deserve."

"I hardly think either suspension will be necessary, but please proceed."

Adam recounted the events of the preceding year, omitting nothing, softening nothing. He watched his half-brother's quizzical smile fade into a mask of sobriety. As he told of Lorena and of her death and that of her unborn child, his half-brother's face softened and his eyes became moist. As the tale of the attempted suicide of Adam and the subsequent deaths of Father Kung and the Weasel unfolded, Theo Thelen's jaw did, indeed, drop slightly in shock.

"My God, Adam. Suicide?"

"Yes, I know. It is a terrible sin. Perhaps the worst."

"That is not at all what I mean. Are you all right?"

"I am, Theo. I knew it was a ghastly mistake the moment I left the bridge."

"Thank God for your diving career. I doubt you'd have survived without that training."

"Probably not. I recall thinking, knowing actually, that I was going to die but I was determined to make a graceful entry into whatever eternity had in store for me."

"Adam. I want to come back to this and make sure you really are all right. First, however, regarding your unchaste activities, I have very little in the way of censure and what little I could muster would be hypocritical in the extreme. I could tell you a couple of stories…" he said with a faint smile, "but I won't. What censure l will offer is directed at the Church. A vow of chastity is problematic at best and especially so for the Jesuit Order. Our mindset is not that of the monastery."

"I happen to agree with you," said Adam. "But that does not excuse my conduct."

"Ha! You were a victim of seduction, albeit a very willing victim. The real tragedy lies in Lorena's death and of her— your—child. Our father must be heartbroken."

"He is. I had never seen him so full of rage as when he learned of their deaths. He and our mothers seem to believe that this man Spektor is involved and at least indirectly responsible. I think Dad will not rest until justice is done."

"That's the other thing I must discuss with you. I heard about what is being characterized as the suicide of Father Kung."

"That's the official ruling of the SFPD as to the cause of death. We have Mike Burke to thank for that. Had he not been there that night I would be dead and it probably would have looked like a double murder. Can you imagine the scandal for the Church and the Order? And even after Mike saved me from the Weasel, I would have been charged with manslaughter at the least, but for his extremely quick thinking and actions."

"That's all true and I need to meet Mike Burke."

"That shouldn't be difficult now that he's working for the firm. I will be surprised if Dad doesn't dispatch him here for a visit."

"I look forward to it. Now back to Father Kung. As you would expect, his death, because it was reported as a suicide, caused quite a stir within the Order. But it went beyond that. You likely are unaware since the Society of Jesus does not speak of it, but the Order takes these things very seriously and it has the means and resources to launch an investigation much broader in scope than even the police investigation. I happen to know that such an investigation was undertaken."

"And?" said Adam.

"And you are home free. I've see the investigative report and there is nothing linking you and Father Kung other than the dinner you shared with him, which was deemed innocuous. Your story to the police was accepted at face value by our investigators."

"Forgive me for asking, but how are you privy to the report?"

"That's a story for another time, but I will say that my involvement in such matters dates to the time of your matriculation here at Fordham, although you had no connection whatever to the matters at hand then. Suffice to say, I am now part of this rather clandestine investigative branch of the Order, which reports directly to the Father-General."

"I am duly impressed, although still somewhat puzzled," said Adam.

"Your puzzlement will have to continue unassuaged. But, there are a couple of additional items you should know. First, Father Kung was involved in some shady dealings and this was not the first time. As our father suspects, his most recent activities as well as some earlier relationships in his native Prague point to financially motivated transactions. The investigation is ongoing, but Spektor's name has not surfaced yet. Nor until just now did we know of any connection between the Weasel, who we knew as Ezra Casque, and Father Kung. We did know of the Weasel's status as an employee of Maxim Spektor and we also knew of his disappearance."

"I hope my story doesn't put you in the uncomfortable position of knowing too much with no good explanation of the source of your knowledge."

"Yes, there is that and I'm going to have to think through that issue. But the other thing you must know is that there is no indication whatever that Lorena Montes ever spoke with Father Kung or was counseled by him. I'm thinking that Father Kung initially targeted you because he knew who your father and mother were. I'm guessing he and this Weasel fellow had you followed and thus discovered your relationship with Lorena Montes. Then it would have been fairly easy to keep tabs on her movements, including her visit to whoever confirmed her pregnancy, probably some clinic. Then Father Kung put two and two together and confronted you. You unwittingly confirmed his hypothesis."

"Your investigation confirms that Kung finally spoke truthfully just before he died. He said that Lorena never approached him but that he had contacted her and told her that he knew all about the affair and the baby."

I should have known she'd never have spoken to him. But that meant that the bastard had arranged Lorena's death, just on the off-chance that I had mentioned his name to her. I'm glad I killed him.

"Adam, there is something missing here. I need to think more about it. Can you stay in town two or three days?"

"I don't need to be in Krakow for a week, so that should be no problem."

"Ah yes, Krakow. I need to speak with you about Krakow, also. But that will have to wait until our next meeting. Why don't you stay here on campus? We have plenty of room until the fall semester starts. Come by here about six tomorrow evening and I'll treat you to dinner in the Big Apple. Wear civilian clothes and we'll be able to enjoy our meal under the radar."

Friday, August 28, 1987

When Adam presented himself at his half-brother's office the next evening, he was asked to wait a few moments while a conference call was concluded. At about 6:10 his half-brother emerged from his office dressed in a button down blue shirt and a sport coat. Adam was similarly attired. They took a taxi down from the Bronx into Manhattan and arrived at a well known Italian restaurant in the East 80s. They had spoken of nothing of consequence in the cab. When they were seated and each had ordered a pre-dinner cocktail, Theo Thelen spoke.

"That conference call was with our father and Mike Burke. I told them that you and I had spoken and also alluded rather vaguely to an in-house investigation which the Order was conducting. I indicated that I had some fairly minor questions which were better explored outside the Order's inquiry and asked for their help. Of course, they readily agreed."

"What kind of questions?" asked Adam.

"Adam," said Theo while looking at him levelly, "I can't understand why either Father Kung or Ezra Casque would kill Lorena. She had left campus without having spoken with you and they believed you would be dead in very short order. Why kill her when there was no connection between her and them?"

Adam had asked himself the same question earlier in the day and had himself been tempted to call Mike Burke and bounce it off him. Ultimately he had concluded that Father Kung was simply an exemplar of the evil which walked the earth, willing to commit the vilest of acts at the slightest provocation. He said as much to his half-brother.

"I suppose that could be true Adam, but it just doesn't add up for me. A killing like this requires effort and money and there always is some degree of risk. I just can't see these people acting in a truly gratuitous fashion. In any event, Mike Burke is going to check into a couple of things and report back. Please stay a couple of days until we hear from him."

"Not a problem. I have some legal research in connection with my project in Poland and other parts of Eastern Europe. I can do it in the law library at my alma mater here in town. Plus, I want to catch up with Bradley, maybe have lunch with him tomorrow. By the way, you said you wanted to discuss my planned work in Krakow."

"I do but it's rather a delicate question. I hope you won't take offense."

"Ask away. What could be offensive between us?"

"Well, not surprisingly it once again involves the Order. I suspect you noticed that your request to be transferred to Poland was approved in a rather expeditious manner. You said you wanted to interview Holocaust survivors and also to help John Paul II however possible in his efforts to free his beloved homeland from the depredations of the communists."

"I did notice, and I thought it was just good luck. Was I mistaken?"

"No, you made your own luck when you determined that John Paul II was a special Pope and that you wanted to assist him."

Here Theo Thelen paused as if to collect his thoughts and determine how best to articulate what he had to say to his half-brother.

"Theo, for heaven's sake, please cut the drama and just spit it out. What am I getting into here?"

"Well, the Order sees merit in your Holocaust interviews and even greater merit in your desire to assist the Pope in whatever ways possible. You know that the Pope visited Poland twice early in his papacy, in 1979 and again in 1983. He also was there just a couple of months ago in June. During the first two visits, he was relatively restrained in his comments, but he made a major impression on the Polish Communist Party. The Pope is enormously popular in his home country and whenever he goes there the crowds are huge and the international press coverage is equally intense. In 1979, he was measured in his words, but he gave thirty-two sermons while in Poland and the message always was the same: human dignity and the right to religious freedom. The communists view him as their most powerful enemy and are scared to death of him. We, the Order that is, believe that the assassination attempt in 1981 flowed directly from the 1979 visit to Poland and subsequent pastoral visits elsewhere. Then, last June, John Paul upped the ante. His words, while not confrontational, were more direct. And it wasn't just Poland where his message resonated. All of the Eastern Bloc countries are listening as, indeed, is the rest of the world."

"Theo, what you say is true. The Pope truly is God's messenger and he is spreading His word fearlessly. But I've done my homework and I know all of what you are reciting. Please complete your circuitous journey to whatever point it is that you are trying to deliver."

"We think the Pope is in danger."

"Of course he is in danger. Whoever tries to change the established order of things always is in danger. The assassination attempt in 1981 proves that and it almost was successful. Many believe he would have died absent God's intervention. Then, his very public forgiveness of his would be assassin was simply inspired. It established this Pope as someone to be reckoned with, someone very special. But again, what can I do?"

"The Pope is coming to the U.S. He will be here on September 10th and he'll tour the country for ten days. One of his stops will be in San Francisco."

"And I'll be in Krakow."

"Actually not. The Father General has arranged for you to join the Pope's entourage when he lands on the 10th. You may, or may not, actually meet the Pope, but he will be aware of your presence and also of your planned activities in Poland and Eastern Europe. You will accompany the Pope throughout his U.S. tour. Then you will proceed to Krakow and begin your work. Your future colleagues at the Ignatianum are aware that your arrival has been somewhat delayed."

"The Society finally has lost its collective mind."

"Perhaps. But more likely not," said Theo Thelen. "Why don't we plan on meeting in my office at 10 o'clock, the day after tomorrow to hear what Mike Burke may have discovered?"

Saturday, August 29, 1987

Unlike the majority of investment banks, which were located in lower Manhattan, the offices of Stein Brothers, Singer and Thelen were in midtown near Rockefeller Center on Sixth Avenue, or as it now was known, Avenue of the Americas. This midtown location was due largely to the preference of Bradley Thelen who, at forty-five, was the younger of Adam's two half brothers. Bradley loved the concentration of cultural sites surrounding his office, including the theater district, Museum of Modern Art, Carnegie Hall and Lincoln Center. In addition, during periods of mild weather it was a pleasant two-mile stroll between the offices and his home in the venerable Dakota Apartments. Bradley was gay and this fact was well known within the family and to those closest to him. But with everyone else he kept his sexual preferences firmly in the closet and often was seen at high profile social events with a lady on his arm.

Now Adam and Bradley were sharing lunch at the Ginger Man, which was a restaurant about halfway between the Fordham law library and the Dakota Apartments.

"This is good," said Adam as he munched on his hamburger.

"Workmanlike at best," said Bradley. "This place is merely a prelude or postlude to the opera or ballet or concert. The food is only serviceable."

"You sound like an elitist, and by the way, I saw your picture again in the society pages – nice looking date."

"She is," said Bradley, "and also very discreet. She helps me maintain the façade, which is an increasingly heavy burden."

"Why do it? Why not just, 'come out', as they say?"

"For business reasons, it's better to be straight. Plus…"

"Plus what?"

"Adam, I know you and Theo think it's wrong – against the teachings of the church – to be gay."

"Did you choose to be gay, any more than I chose to be straight?"

"No, you're right about that. I arrived the way I am and became aware of it at an early age. But you did choose to be celibate whereas I did not."

"Ha! I'm sure you've heard from Dad about my celibacy."

"I have and it's a very sad story. But the point is you now are resolved once again to be celibate. I and the man I love are not so resolved."

"Look Brad, if you want my thoughts, I believe your committed relationship is every bit as praiseworthy as my sporadic celibacy."

"But how do you square this with the Church's teachings?"

"I cannot," said Adam, "and I won't even try. All I know is that it is not my place to judge you or others in similar situations."

CHAPTER 15

Sunday, August 30, 1987

THIRTY-SIX HOURS LATER Adam Thelen was walking across the Fordham campus in the Bronx toward his half-brother's office. It was a lovely late summer day with none of the oppressive heat typical of New York in August. His research at the law school the previous day had gone well and Adam should have been in reasonably good spirits. But he was not. The dinner discussion with Theo two nights earlier had brought back the images of Lorena in a flaming car and with them the gnawing self-loathing and the searing rage he felt toward Maxim Spektor, who likely had been in Manhattan yesterday, not too distant from Fordham Law School. Adam felt an urgent need to choke the life out of him, but he knew this was only an extension of the resurgent desire to destroy himself. In addition to all this, there were the Machiavellian maneuverings of the Order, the full meaning of which were beginning to penetrate his consciousness. Thus, when Adam Thelen arrived at his half-brother's office, he was in a genuinely foul state of mind.

"Adam. Good morning."

"Good morning, Theo,"

"You seem fairly subdued this morning."

"I am Theo. Best not to pursue it further."

"Well, we have fifteen minutes until our father and Mike Burke are scheduled to call. I suspect that your mood flows at least in part from the rather abrupt change in schedule arranged for you by the Father-General."

"It does Theo and, simply put, I'm not going to do what the Order wishes."

"I'm surprised Adam. You plan to decline the opportunity to accompany the Pope on his tour of the U.S.?"

"No, No. I'll be the obedient servant and will do precisely as directed by the Order. I'll be in Miami with the papal greeting party and will accompany him on every leg of his trip. Then I'll be off to Krakow."

"Then I don't see the problem," said Theo.

"Theo, please don't play the fool. The Order wants me there as a spy, not on the Pope so much as his closest advisors. And if I can curry enough favor with the Pope to be somehow involved in his future visits to Poland, which are a certainty, so much the better. I will not betray His Holiness's trust by spying on him or on the people he chooses to be close to him."

"Adam, it's true that the Order will do everything in its power to protect the Pope. And it's also true that we don't always agree with the directions and strategies urged on the Pope by some of the cardinals and others who advise him. But you're sadly mistaken if you think that any Pope and most especially this Pope can be easily manipulated. John Paul II has chosen his advisors with care, even those with whom we disagree. He listens to all viewpoints. He prays. And then he makes his own decisions on how to act and what to say. Finally, please forgive me for suggesting that you are being nothing short of grandiose if you believe that anything you are allowed to see or hear during the Pope's visit is not already known by the Order."

In the silence which ensued, Adam considered his half-brother's words and also his own rage filled and not always rational state of mind. He realized that he was unjustifiably attributing to the Order the same kind of evil conspiratorial practices in which Maxim Spektor indulged. He saw that he was not thinking clearly, and that he was being naive in the extreme. When he spoke again both his tone and expression had softened considerably.

"Theo you're right. I'm just a junior priest who has acted stupidly and caused several deaths. Now I'm casting frantically about in search of someone other than myself to blame, I'm sorry for my rant..."

Now it was Theo's turn to be silent. He arose from the sofa on which he was seated and paced about the room for a moment or two before addressing his half-brother.

"Adam, it's true that your emotions are running rampant, but not without reason. You've been through some terrible events and if you were fully yourself, your training would make clear to you that such traumas have consequences, sometimes long term consequences. Consider the Holocaust survivors and their descendants whom you plan to interview. Would you expect them to have fully recovered from their psychic wounds, even after all the intervening years?"

"No of course not, but those are far different situations."

"Perhaps in degree, but not in kind. Adam, I urge you in the strongest terms possible, to use this tour with the Pope to explore your own inner turmoil and come to grips with it. If you hope to be of any use to Holocaust survivors, let alone the Pope, you must do this."

"You're right of course and I will follow your guidance. I apologize again for acting like such a fool."

"You're certainly no fool. If you were, the Order would not be sending you to Krakow, let alone arranging for your participation, however peripheral, in the Papal tour." After a pause he added, "And your instincts regarding the Order's motives may not be quite as mistaken as I made them out to be. Certainly, no one expects you to spy on anyone. But the Order is subtle and devious and possessed of extraordinarily long perspective. If I had to guess, I would say that the Order is placing a bet that you stand a decent chance of becoming a confidante of the Pontiff at some point in the future."

"Theo, now it's your turn to get a grip."

At that point the phone rang and was answered in the outer office. In a moment, the door opened and the executive assistant to the Father-President announced that his father and Mike were on the line. Theodore Thelen thanked his assistant and activated the speaker phone.

"Hello Father. It's good to speak with you," said Theo.

"Likewise, Theo. I'm here with Mike Burke, who wishes to report on his trip to Nevada."

"And Adam is here with me."

"Hello Dad. Hello Mike," said Adam.

"I have to say," said Chaz Thelen, "that this is a highly unusual event. Never did I expect to be on a conference call with my two priestly sons participating."

"Enjoy it Dad. It's likely to be the last time it happens," said Adam.

"I wouldn't be too sure about that. But, let's get started Mike."

"Hello Adam. And hello to you Father Thelen," said Mike,

"Mike, this is a family conference. Please call me Theo."

"Of course, thank you. Well then, after your call two days ago I gave this matter some thought before setting out for Nevada. I agree with your interpretation of the events and it does seem unlikely that they would kill her, especially in such a flamboyant manner. I'm sorry Adam."

"Not necessary," said Adam. "I understand what you're saying. Please proceed."

"Two days ago I made arrangements by telephone with the Winnemucca police to meet with them yesterday at 11:00 a.m. Winnemucca is located in north central Nevada, basically in the middle of nowhere, except that I-80 goes right through town. It's almost a six hour drive from San Francisco so I left at 5:00 a.m. The two officers who had worked the case were there at 11:00 even though one of them was supposed to be off duty yesterday. I spent about an hour discussing the case with them and then another hour with them over lunch. I'm convinced that both of them are honest and competent cops with nothing to hide. Based on the evidence, I would have reached the same conclusion that they did. Lorena Montes died in a single car accident when the vehicle burst into flames after rolling twice and ending on its roof in the desert. There was no evidence of any foul play, and also no reason that the car should have left the road just at the one point where there was a small hill which caused the car to roll and then ignite. Had she left the road a hundred yards sooner or later the car simply would have come to a stop in the sand, perhaps damaging the car but almost certainly causing no personal injury. These officers chalked it up to bad luck. They figured she just fell asleep at the wheel, which is not an uncommon experience out there in the desert."

"How did they make the identification," asked Adam, trying to preempt discussion of the charred body.

"Well, as the newspapers in Winnemucca reported, they used dental records. And that's really the only somewhat unusual aspect of the case, at least in Winnemucca, that I discovered."

"How so?" said Adam.

"As you can imagine, the car was destroyed, but its California plates were legible, and California DMV was able to confirm the next morning that the car was registered to Lorena. So the presumption was that she was driving the car. Still, better evidence was needed to make a conclusive ID in the event of death. As soon as the address on the car registration was known, it was an easy matter to trace Lorena back to the University and from there to get contact information for her parents. The accident took place about midnight and was reported in the two morning papers but, obviously, with no ID. The parents' phone number was obtained about noon the next day and a call was made from Winnemucca to Spain shortly thereafter. The mother was the one they got hold of first and according to the two officers, she was naturally grief stricken. The fairly unusual detail is that she and her husband, who quickly became involved, were also extremely efficient. Lorena's dental records were faxed to the parents from a dentist in San Francisco that same afternoon and the parents faxed the records plus instructions for shipping the body back to Spain. The records and instructions were received in Winnemucca that evening, about eighteen hours after the accident."

"Is this unusual?" asked Theo.

"In my experience, yes, it is. Normally it takes at least two or three days for a conclusive ID of a decomposed or burned body. But the parents' efficiency is not unheard of and it's likely that one of the parents, the father probably, just wanted to bring a terrible situation to a close as soon as possible."

"So there's really nothing out of line which should be investigated further," said Adam.

"Not according to the investigating officers. These two cops had no reason at all to be suspicious. The dental records were a match to the victim so that was that. But, since I was passing through Reno, which has the closest international airport, I decided to stop there on my way home. The body was flown from there to Spain and I wanted to see if anything unusual happened there. When I left Winnemucca, I called ahead to a friend of mine on the Reno force and he called the airport on my behalf. When I arrived there, they were very cooperative."

"And was anything out of the ordinary?" asked Chaz.

"Nothing at all regarding the shipment of the body. It was transported from Winnemucca three days after the crash and loaded on a commercial flight the day after it arrived in Reno."

"So that's it then," said Adam.

"Well, maybe," answered Mike. "Since I was there I asked to check flights in and out of Reno around the time of the accident. What I found were the usual commercial flights plus some private flights to destinations within the U.S. There was one flight that was a little out of the ordinary. A Gulfstream 2 flew in the evening of the car crash. It arrived about 9:00 p.m. which was approximately three hours before the crash. The two pilots arranged for immediate refueling and about midnight a car arrived and parked near the G2. A single person left the car and boarded the jet. It departed at midnight, the same time the car was crashing in the desert"

"Is any of this unusual?" asked Chaz. "There must be high rollers flying into and out of Reno all the time."

"According to airport personnel, not many. Virtually all of the high rollers who can afford a G2 go to Las Vegas."

"Did the G2 pilots file a flight plan?" asked Chaz.

"Yes. They're required to do so."

"Where were they headed?"

"Geneva, Switzerland."

"And did they arrive there?" asked Chaz.

"There's no reason to think otherwise, but I suppose I could check."

"Do you think that would be appropriate?" asked Adam.

"Not really," replied Mike. "But there are two more items which I think do deserve some further investigation."

"What are they?" asked Chaz.

"First, I made a note of the tail number of the G2. I'd like to check into the ownership and home field of the plane. Secondly, I'd like to locate Lorena's dentist in San Francisco and have a short discussion with him."

"What do you think boys?" said Chaz.

Theo and Adam looked at each other and shrugged.

"We think both of those inquiries would be useful," said Theo.

"I concur," said Chaz.

CHAPTER 16

<u>**Thursday, September 10, 1987**</u>

THE 1987 PAPAL visit to the U.S. began when John Paul II and his entourage landed in Miami. The first to greet him was President Ronald Reagan who stated that "Americans of every kind and degree of belief will wish Your Holiness well, responding to your moral leadership." The contrast between Ronald Reagan, the preeminent leader of the western world, and the communist leaders of the east could not have been starker.

President Reagan embraced the Pope and his moral teachings without reservation while Eastern Bloc Communist leaders, including General Jaruzelski of Poland, rejected religion in favor of an all-powerful state. Worse, President Reagan asserted that the Pope's essential message of personal freedom and dignity as basic God-given individual rights transcended religious teachings, thus imbuing the Pope with legitimate moral and political leadership. This was anathema to the communists and was a portent of the massive social changes which were to ensue.

Also present to greet the Pope was Father Adam Thelen, S.J. When the plane landed and the Pope descended to meet the waiting President, all the cameras followed him. As the Pope and President stood, and then walked, in conversation, all eyes were on them. The papal entourage descended behind him to the tarmac with little notice from anyone. Adam Thelen's eyes also were on the Pope and he was somewhat surprised to be greeted by a man approaching from his side.

"Father Thelen?"

"Yes, I am."

"Hello. My name is Tobias Alessi, Monsignor Tobias Alessi. I'm part of the Pope's traveling party and I understand you will be joining us. I want to welcome you and guide you through the labyrinth of players involved in this tour."

"Thank you and welcome to the United States. But, how were you able to recognize me so quickly?"

"How many 6'2" 200 pound blue eyed priests do you see here on the tarmac?"

"Ah. You're right of course..."

"Besides, you have that certain Jesuitical bearing about you—an amused arrogance."

"Do I now? Should I be offended?"

"Not at all," said Monsignor Alessi. "It was meant as a compliment. The Jesuits deservedly have a reputation for seeing things clearly and getting things done in the world."

"Thank you, I guess," said Adam, nonplussed at having been so incisively sized-up and categorized.

"Our car is number five in the line over there," said Monsignor Alessi gesturing toward a long column of limousine and tour cars. "Shall we begin to move in that direction?"

"By all means," said Adam.

+ + +

While Adam and Monsignor Alessi were introducing themselves, Pope John Paul II and President Ronald Reagan had proceeded to the terminal and stopped to allow a few more photos. They then entered the terminal and were whisked a short distance to a non-denominational airport chapel. They entered the chapel, which had been rearranged for a private conversation between the Pope and the President. For the first time on American soil, agents of the Secret Service and of the Swiss Guards took up their posts together. Once they were alone, the Pope and the President smiled at each other and then, spontaneously, embraced. They sat in two armchairs facing each other.

"Mr. President, your speech at the Brandenburg Gate in June was excellent, a perfect lead-in to my trip to Poland only two days later," said the Pope.

"That was part of the plan we discussed in May, was it not, Holy Father?"

"Yes, of course, but the words resonated far more than I had dared to hope. 'Across Europe, this will fall. For it cannot withstand faith; it cannot withstand truth. This wall cannot withstand freedom'."

"Your Holiness, your recall is quite accurate. Thank you. Several of my advisors counseled me quite strongly to delete that passage. Too confrontational, too adversarial, they said."

"Yes, I have the same problem with the Vatican hierarchy. You would not believe the difficulty in preparing the homilies I will deliver during this trip. I plan to depart from the approved text and speak from the heart on a few occasions. This will cause great consternation, of course."

"I'm sure it will, Holy Father, but the damage will have been done. I and the people of America will have heard you, as will those in Eastern Europe, friend and foe alike."

"They will indeed, Mr. President, just as they did in Poland when I echoed the sentiment of your speech at the Brandenburg

Gate. Again, some of my people were aghast that we had challenged General Jaruzelski on his own soil, as if it were not my soil also."

"Well done, Holy Father! I truly believe we are on the cusp of prevailing. Is there any other assistance we in the United States can provide to you?"

"Since our first meeting in 1982, the U. S. has been extremely generous with money and counsel. Your Vice President has been especially helpful. He is a good man."

"Yes, he is and the knowledge he gained during his time spent as CIA Director has been most useful. He speaks highly of your Vatican Bank and assures me that it has used the money we have provided most efficiently and effectively. The Vice President has confided to me that he wishes our CIA was half as secretive as your bank."

"A two-edged sword, Mr. President. Sometimes I fear abuses flowing from that very secrecy, but that is a story for another time. For now, it is true that we have made good use of your gifts against our common foes. As it happens, we have a new asset, as your Vice President calls them, joining us this very day. A young Jesuit from San Francisco was among those on the tarmac to greet me. He will join us on the tour and I will take the opportunity to interview him. Then he will proceed to Krakow where he will reside indefinitely. I anticipate that he will be traveling frequently throughout Europe on various missions, all funded in part by your country's generous donations. We thank you Mr. President and we share your optimism about the defeat of totalitarianism. God bless you, Ronald."

"And you, Karol," said the President.

They rose and embraced again.

"Until we meet again."

+ + +

The fifth car in line was a black Lincoln Town Car. Its driver stood beside the car. When the two priests approached the Town Car, the driver greeted them and opened one and then the other rear door. The driver then entered the car and started the engine.

"You two are the only ones assigned to this car. We can leave whenever you wish," said the driver.

"No one leaves until the Pope completes his private meeting with President Reagan," said Monsignor Alessi while peering through the windshield. "It should be quite soon. They're only scheduled to be together for ten or fifteen minutes. As soon as the Pope departs we'll follow him to the hotel." Turning to Adam, Monsignor Alessi continued. "The Pope will take about an hour to refresh himself and then proceed to the stadium for his first Mass and homily. You can attend the Mass if you wish but I suggest not. There will be an early dinner at the hotel attended by several people who wish to meet you. If you're agreeable, I will accompany you to dinner and introduce you."

"Of course, I appreciate your guidance. I also appreciate your excellent English. I detect virtually no accent. Were you born here in the U.S.?"

"Not at all. I was born in Calabria but my father moved us shortly after my birth to join his siblings in Umbria in the family business. I grew up not too far from Rome. I'm afraid my English is a product of the Wharton School. I received my MBA there four years ago and I'm told I sound like a native born Philadelphian. Happily, when I speak Italian, no one mistakes me for an American."

+ + +

Shortly thereafter, the Pope entered his car, a regular limousine rather than the famous "Popemobile" and the column of cars moved off. All of the hotel check-in procedures had been completed in advance allowing the large traveling party to pick up keys and proceed directly to their rooms. The luggage had been off loaded from the plane and taken directly to the hotel and thence to each person's room. Adam Thelen carried his own single suitcase. He had shipped several packing crates of personal property several weeks before. They awaited him in Krakow.

At the rate I'm going, I may never arrive there. Who knows what further diversions await me?

Monsignor Alessi instructed Adam to relax in one of the lobby chairs while he joined the queue picking up keys. He returned about five minutes later.

"I've got our keys and we happen to be next door neighbors on the fourth floor. Do you need help with your luggage?"

"No, I'm fine. Let's go on up."

"OK, the elevators are this way I think."

The elevator was crowded, mostly with members of the Pope's party. Conversations in several languages were occurring. Adam and Monsignor Alessi exited on the fourth floor.

"Our early dinner is here tonight at 6:00. The restaurant is in a separate wing right over the water. Why don't you join me in my room about 5:30 and we'll go down together. Dress is informal but with this group, that doesn't mean civilian clothes. Your everyday priest outfit will be fine."

"All right. See you at 5:30," answered Adam.

+ + +

At 5:30 Adam knocked on Monsignor Alessi's door and was greeted by him.

"Father Thelen. Come in. We have a few minutes before dinner. We could go down to the bar or spend a little time here. What do you prefer?"

"Let's stay here. Maybe you can give me a few more details about the Pope's tour."

"Fine, Father. Would you care for something from the mini-bar?"

"No, thank you. And please call me Adam if you feel comfortable doing so."

"I do, but only if you call me Tobias. It's probably appropriate, since we're going to be seeing a lot of each other. I'm part of the Secretariat of State—the section for dealing with civil governments. I do have other duties but you are one of my major responsibilities."

"I'm sorry to be a burden."

"Not a burden at all. When your Order requested that you be allowed to join the U.S. tour, it came to the desk of my boss, Cardinal Martino. He simply approved the request and mentioned it to the Pope. We're honored to have you with us and I look forward to being your guide."

"So, what do I have to look forward to?"

"Personally, I want to know more about your plans in Poland. There's a lot going on there and I'm involved in some of it. But, basically, I've been told to make sure you meet a lot of people. So let's go downstairs and start."

+ + +

The restaurant was located not just on, but over, the water via a cantilevered dining area with wraparound windows. Joining Adam Thelen and Tobias Alessi were two priests, another monsignor and an auxiliary bishop. All four were working within one of the eight congregations or, like Tobias, the Secretariat of State. One of the priests, for example, a black man from Sierra Leone, was a functionary of the Congregation of the Evangelization of Peoples, which directed all of the church's missionary work around the globe. The conversation was brisk, if not scintillating, and everyone showed a great interest in Adam and his planned work in Poland and Eastern Europe. Wine was served with dinner and everyone had either an after dinner drink or coffee. By nine, everyone had returned to their respective rooms. Adam Thelen and Tobias Alessi lingered in the lounge, each with a final drink.

"Well, what did you think?"

"All very good people, all very well versed on my plans and all very solicitous of my welfare. I think they looked at me as some kind of stranger about to enter a strange land. Or, maybe already in a strange land."

"Perhaps not a strange land, but the Vatican is, to use a very overworked word, unique."

"Thank you for the introductions and also for papering over the awkward moments. I feel badly, though, about missing the Pope's Mass and homily."

"Ah, I'm glad you reminded me. Here is a copy of the homily which John Paul II delivered. Tomorrow morning you also will receive a VCR of the entire Mass."

"Your people are nothing if not efficient. But for the rest of the tour, I'd like to attend the Masses in person."

"Certainly, Adam. Tomorrow we're off to Columbia, South Carolina. You need to be in the lobby ready to go by 7:30."

"I'll be there. But I have one other request."

"Name it."

"I think you'll be able to accommodate me. What I'd like is to have a copy of each homily in both English and Polish."

"Ha! That I can do. You'll have the Polish version when I see you in the lobby tomorrow."

Adam quickly fell into a daily routine as the Pope and his retinue visited a new city each day. After Columbia, it was New Orleans, then San Antonio, Texas, followed by Phoenix, where Mass was celebrated in the Arizona State University Stadium. Each day was travel and a Mass celebrated or concelebrated by the Pope, including a homily delivered by him. Each homily was tailored to the particular city in which it was delivered but the themes were unchanged—human freedom and dignity as rights of all men, especially the poor, the oppressed, the dispossessed, immigrants and refugees. Each homily also referenced one of the quasi mysteries of the Catholic Church—the individual identity of each member remaining intact and yet merging into the unity of the community, called the Body of Christ, which comprises the Church's faithful. Travel and Masses were punctuated with a lunch or dinner, sometimes both, with Tobias and three or four new members of the entourage. The meals quickly blurred, with each new attendee exhibiting deep interest in Adam and promising to help however possible with his work in Poland. After Phoenix came Los Angeles and a very welcome two days in one city. The first day was a Mass for the faithful and a variation of the homily directed at the diverse population of Southern California. The second day in Los Angeles marked a definite departure from the usual Mass and homily. This day was a mass concelebrated with and attended by all the cardinals, archbishops and bishops of the United States. The homily was a very straightforward call to the bishops, with scriptural references, reminding them that the unity of the faithful required unity among the bishops, a not too subtle reminder that the Pope was the ultimate arbiter on matters of faith and morals.

CHAPTER 17

Thursday, September 17, 1987

THE NEXT DAY the papal entourage stopped briefly in Monterey, California. From Monterey the Pope traveled a few miles south to the historic Carmel Mission founded in the 18th century by Junipero Serra. The homily again emphasized the same themes as the Pope said, "And much to be envied are those who can give their lives for something greater than themselves in loving service to others." Later in the day Adam found himself back in San Francisco, which also was to be a two day stopover. At midday on Thursday, the Pope celebrated Mass at Candlestick Park, the home of the major league baseball Giants and of the National Football League Forty-Niners. Adam was in attendance and at the conclusion of Mass was part of the motorcade returning to the hotel in San Francisco. Their hotel was on Nob Hill and Adam's room overlooked the Pacific Union Club. As Adam gazed out the window, memories of the past year came flooding back to him. After a moment or two, he turned from the window and sat in a nearby chair staring sightlessly at the wall. Finally, he went into the bathroom, splashed water on his face, and turned toward the desk, resolved to work on a concurrent reading of the English and Polish versions of the latest homily. At that moment came a knock on his door.

"Adam. You have an appointment."

"Tobias, I'm not in a fit state for another meet and greet. Can you possibly make excuses for my absence?"

"I'm afraid not Adam. This is a command performance and I'd advise you to get yourself into a proper state of mind. I'll be back to fetch you in fifteen minutes."

What now? I feel as if I'm on a giant roller coaster which now has dropped me off right back where I began.

Adam stripped and jumped into the shower. When Tobias returned to lead him to the next group of Vatican dwellers, he was presentable and had suppressed the troubling memories triggered by the P.U. Club. When they entered the elevator it began to move upward rather than down to the restaurants and common rooms. Adam raised his eyebrows.

"Penthouse Suite," said Tobias.

"Who is it this time?" asked Adam. "Your boss?"

"You might say that" answered Tobias.

"Tobias, why the mystery...?"

At that the elevator reached the top floor and Tobias placed a finger to his lips signaling silence. The elevator opened directly into the parlor of a suite. In the parlor was a man wearing the distinctive clothing of a cardinal of the church.

"Father Thelen," said the man while extending his hand, "I am Cardinal Martino."

"Your eminence, I am honored to meet you," said Adam.

"And I you," he said, smiling, "Please take a seat. I will return in a moment."

Cardinal Martino knocked on the door to the next room then opened it and entered the room, closing the door behind him.

"Tobias, for heaven's sake, what is going on?"

Tobias just smiled and shook his head. At that moment the door opened and Cardinal Martino reappeared. He gestured to both men. They arose and followed him into the adjoining room. Seated at a desk and clothed in white was John Paul II.

Idiot! You knew there was at least a decent chance you'd have a brief greeting from the Pope sometime during the tour. You should have guessed from all Tobias's cloak and dagger antics on the way up. Thank God I showered and cleared my head.

John Paul rose smiling and with his right hand extended.

"Father Thelen, I am pleased to see you," said the Pope in English. "And you also Tobias. Thank you for taking good care of Father Thelen."

"Your Holiness," said Adam kneeling with the intent of kissing the Pope's ring.

"No, No. Arise please Father. No need of that here in private," said the Pope, taking Adam's right hand in both of his and shaking it.

"I know Tobias has introduced you to at least two dozen people. It must be a blur."

"He has, your Holiness and he also has been most gracious in helping me to keep them distinct."

"Tobias is very talented in that regard. I knew he would be as good a guide for you as he and Cardinal Martino are at guiding me through the shoals of foreign policy. Speaking of which, Cardinal, you and I have a meeting scheduled in about forty-five minutes. Tobias, I ask that you also return then with the Cardinal."

"We will both return in forty-five minutes," said Cardinal Martino as he and Tobias turned to leave the suite.

"Your Holiness, I am deeply honored to have met you," said Adam as he turned to accompany Cardinal Martino and Tobias from the room.

"No, no," said John Paul, laughing. "You can't escape so easily. Please be seated and let us have a private conversation."

Both of the departing men looked back with broad smiles as they closed the door behind them. Dumbstruck, Adam seated himself upon the sofa which John Paul indicated. The Pope sat in an upholstered chair and pulled it closer to Adam. The Pope's laughter had ceased but a smile still lingered on his lips and around his eyes.

"I meant what I said about your unenviable position coming into this milieu and meeting dozens of new people all at once. It truly must be a blur."

"In a way it is," said Adam. "But, as I said, Tobias really has been a great help. I'm keeping notes of each person I meet at the various lunches and dinners and then I review them with Tobias. He corrects errors and expands on my rather cryptic observations."

"The notes are an excellent idea in the event you happen to meet some of these people again. But tell me, how are they treating you at these lunches and dinners?"

"They are uniformly gracious and solicitous of my needs, Your Holiness. They never fail to offer to assist me in any way possible. I have no doubt of their sincerity."

"That is good, Father. No doubt you have many questions for them also. Are they forthcoming in their responses?"

Adam hesitated for an instant before answering, "They answer all of my queries, Your Holiness."

"Father, may I call you Adam? It seems appropriate here in this private conversation."

"Of course, Your Holiness."

"Fine. Then I will do so, provided you can find a way to be comfortable addressing me as Karol. It is after all my given name. Failing that, simply call me Father."

"Your Holiness..."

"Please, I ask you to, as you say, humor me. I want to have a completely candid and open conversation with you and undue formality is a hindrance."

"All right..." said Adam.

"Excellent!" said the Pope. "Now back to your previous lunches and dinners. I noticed that you hesitated momentarily before answering my question about the responses you received to your questions."

"Well, to be perfectly candid, all of them seemed much more comfortable asking about me rather than answering questions about themselves and their functions within the Vatican. Their answers were not non-responsive, but they invariably were general in nature and not particularly enlightening."

The Pope nodded and said, "They're afraid of you."

"Afraid of me, Your Holi... Father? Why would they find anything to fear in me?"

"You're an outsider. They fear that you may try to change the established order of things. That always is frightening to an entrenched bureaucracy."

"But...I have no authority. Even if I had in mind certain changes, I lack the power necessary to make them."

"Look at it from their perspective. You suddenly are invited to join this tour. Everyone knows that you would not be here unless I allowed it. And then, of course, there is the Jesuit cachet. There are many who fear that I meddle too much in political matters in my native Poland and elsewhere in Eastern Europe. They also fear that the Jesuits are complicit in these meddlings."

"I...know nothing of such things," said Adam.

"No. As yet you do not. But you do begin to feel what it is to be an outsider in a two-thousand-year-old institution."

The Pope paused for a moment before continuing.

"I also was an outsider when I first came here and then again when the conclave elected me as a compromise Pontiff. As you know, I am the first non-Italian Pope since Adrian VI, almost five hundred years ago. In some ways, I still am an outsider even after almost ten years. You would not believe how many people must approve all of my homilies. Nor would you believe the discomfiture if I deviate even slightly from the text. But, enough of my struggles. I want to know more about you. I hope you will be more open and candid with me than others have been with you."

"Certainly, Your Holiness. What do you wish to know?"

"Please Adam, save the honorifics for a more public setting."

All right. . . . Father. Please ask me anything and I will answer as fully as I am able."

"I already know your curriculum vitae to date. I also have had conversations with certain leaders of your Order, including your General. Really, there are only two questions."

"What are they?" asked Adam.

"First, why did you ask to leave San Francisco, this very beautiful city where we find ourselves today? You were progressing well at the University and seemed happy. Also, your family resides here. Then suddenly, you ask to go elsewhere."

Now what? I cannot lie or even be evasive with the Pope.

"Father, I asked to leave San Francisco for personal reasons. I will share with you every detail of my reasons if you wish me to do so."

John Paul paused for almost a half minute before responding to Adam. He appeared during this period to be lost in his own thoughts, transported to another time, another place. Finally, he blinked and returned his gaze to Adam, a faint smile on his face.

"No Adam, I need no details. Our journeys—all of them— are personal, yet they are taken also in the company of the community which surrounds us. I have details in my own life and have no need to know details in yours. But, I can see that you are troubled. Do you go to Poland—to Krakow—to escape your personal reasons, or perhaps to try to atone for something?"

"No. I have much to atone for but I do not go to Poland for this reason. I knew I must leave San Francisco, but I had no idea where I should go. Then, one morning I awoke with an epiphany and I knew that I must go to Poland to help. I go to help Holocaust survivors and their descendants but also—if it is possible—to help you. I hope you will believe me when I say that I cannot explain how this knowledge came to me."

"Of course I believe you, Adam. Your knowledge came to you from the Holy Spirit, who is directing you to go to Krakow. But tell me, do you also know how it is that you might help?"

"As to the Holocaust survivors and their children and grandchildren I do know. At least I know how I hope to help. Since you've reviewed my c.v., you know that I have both a law degree and a PH.D in clinical psychology. I was teaching psychology in the doctoral program at the University and I've been interested for some time in the relationship between law and psychology, for instance the question of whether a psychological diagnosis is sufficient to disprove legal capacity to commit a crime. I've also been active in researching anxiety disorders, especially one called Post Traumatic Stress Disorder, which first was included in the DSM only a few years ago."

"Adam, please slow down. Also, please tell me what is the DSM to which you refer."

"Oh, Father, I apologize for rushing and also for the jargon. DSM is the acronym for Diagnostic and Statistical Manual of Mental Disorders published by the American Psychiatric Association. It's updated regularly and a revision of DSM-III is due out later this year. I had some limited role in changes to diagnostic criteria for anxiety disorders, especially PTSD which is the acronym for Post Traumatic Stress Disorder. My theory, stated concisely, is that children and other family members of trauma sufferers can suffer severe adverse effects from a trauma they did not directly experience. It's hard to conceive of a trauma more devastating than the Holocaust and Auschwitz/ Birkenau is only a short distance from Krakow. DSM-IV won't be published for several years but I am a member of the work group for anxiety disorders. I see this as an opportunity to help the Holocaust survivors and their family members and also to help shape better diagnoses and treatment going forward."

"This all is admirable, Adam, and it answers another part of my second question—Why Poland, and what do you plan to do there? But how do you propose to help me in my struggles in Poland?"

"Father, I cannot answer that because I do not know. I may be guilty of hubris for even mentioning it."

"Not at all, Adam. You know, by the inspiration of the Holy Spirit, that you are going there to help me, but you don't know precisely how. I suggest that you leave the 'how' in my hands."

"Yes, Father. I will do so."

"It is clear to me that you have been called to Poland—to my dear Krakow. I suggest that you go now."

"Father, I will leave immediately after the conclusion of the tour."

"No Adam, go now. You have no need to hear another homily or two from me. Besides, you will be given copies of my final two homilies here in North America in English," said the Pope with a smile, "and in Polish."

"I will leave immediately, Father."

"First, make arrangements to see your mother and father here in San Francisco and to say good-bye, again, to them. Also, stop in New York and provide your brother with a complete synopsis of our talk here today. Omit nothing."

"Yes, Father."

"I will expect you to give me regular updates of your activities in Poland. Let us say one per month. I will want them in writing and they should be delivered to Tobias. As soon as you are able, I will expect the reports to be written in Polish."

"Yes, Father."

"Where will you be living in Krakow?"

"I will be living at the Jesuit school there, Father, and studying at the Jagiellonian University."

"Ah yes. Ignatianum and Jagiellonian. Very good. At Jagiellonian see Father Pilsudski. He will help you in many ways. I am in regular contact with him."

"I will, Father."

"Go, Adam. Now you may kneel."

Adam rose from the sofa and knelt on the carpet. John Paul II also rose and placed his hand upon Adam's head.

"In nomine patri et fili et spiritu sancti. Now arise and go. Go in peace."

Adam Thelen returned to his room with his mind and spirit in turmoil. Rather than try to bring order to his thoughts and emotions, he decided to follow John Paul's directions. He called his father and arranged a meeting with him and with his mother the following morning in the Transamerica pyramid, which was within walking distance of the hotel. He then called his half-brother in New York and left a message that he would be passing through New York and wished to meet with him, probably two days hence. Then, knowing that Tobias was meeting with John Paul and Cardinal Martino, he called his room and left a message suggesting that the two of them with no other guests dine together that evening. Finally, he reclined on the bed and tried to think of nothing at all. He was awakened some time later by the ringing of the telephone. He was momentarily dazed and could not remember where he was, let alone where the ringing phone was located. When he found it and picked up the receiver he heard Tobias's voice.

"I've made reservations for 7:00 o'clock. We're going down the street to the Huntington, away from prying eyes and ears. I'll come by your room about 6:45."

"OK. I'll be ready."

His inclination was to return to the bed but he resisted that impulse. Instead he removed his clothing and took yet another shower, his third of the day. He then dressed himself in civilian clothes and removed a small bottle of red wine, a California Cabernet, from the mini-bar. He poured the contents into a wine glass and sat in a chair near the window. Looking out he could see the upper stories of the Huntington Hotel where he and Tobias would be sharing dinner. Strangely enough, after the day's events, his first thought was of Lorena. If only she were with him now. He would cancel dinner with Tobias, order room service and spend the evening and night with her, thinking only of her, seeing only her, feeling only her. But she was not with him and the familiar ache in his chest returned to confirm this reality. Adam felt unutterably sad and alone. Predictably, his next thought was of Max Spektor and the anger and—yes—the hatred he felt toward the man immediately was alight inside Adam. After a moment, he was able to purge his mind of these thoughts of Lorena and Spektor and to focus on his audience with John Paul II. After several minutes of reflection he realized that he was happy, very happy indeed, to have crystal clear directions and blessings from the Pope and, apparently, from the Holy Spirit. When Tobias came to get him, his mind and heart and spirit were tranquil, more at peace than they had been in over a year. As they walked down California Street to the Huntington Hotel, the Pacific Union Club was on their right, across the street. Adam looked in that direction and, although memories of Lorena and of Spektor recurred, he experienced no anger or bitterness.

Perhaps the Holy Spirit is nudging me away from hate and toward love.

When they reached the Huntington, they turned into the lobby and then proceeded to The Big Four Restaurant named in memory of the four robber barons, Huntington, Stanford, Hopkins and Crocker. The place was dimly lit, with rich wood paneling and booths, a perfect retreat from all the buzz of the papal tour.

"Tobias, why didn't you allow me to prepare for a half hour audience with the Pope? A little advance notice would have been quite useful."

Adam was smiling but there was an unmistakable sobriety underlying his question.

"Adam, neither I nor the Cardinal had any idea this would occur. When John Paul saw the Cardinal this morning he mentioned that he wanted to meet you before the tour concluded and asked that we bring you by his suite. We, like you, thought it would be a quick greeting and that you'd be leaving with me. We were just as surprised as you when he sent us away and asked you to stay. And even now I am shocked, literally that the audience lasted so long."

"Come on, Tobias. This brings to mind a phrase I've heard my own father use about having smoke blown into a certain part of one's anatomy. I too am a little surprised, and greatly honored, that the Pope would spend a half hour with me. But, surely that's not something so unusual as to shock you."

"Adam, 'shock' indeed is the proper word. The Pope simply does not conduct private audiences, except with his very old friends from the Rodzina days. Take today for instance. . ."

"Wait. What is Rodzina?" asked Adam.

"Friends from the old days in Poland, right after he became a priest. Kind of a fellowship really—kayaking, skiing, long conversations lasting into the night. He meets with these old friends, even one on one, and everyone knows it's just that: old friends, not business."

"Business?"

"Yes, business. As I was saying, take today's meeting among the Pope, Cardinal Martino and me. I was there really only as a witness to the business transacted between the Pope and Cardinal Martino. In this case, it happened to concern Poland and General Jaruzelski, but it doesn't matter. Everyone knows that the meeting took place and they also know that the substance of the meeting will be reported to everyone at the weekly gathering of the heads of the various Congregations. Had there been a private meeting between the Pope and Cardinal Martino and then nothing was mentioned at the weekly meeting, there would be consternation. As with any entrenched bureaucracy there are rivalries, infighting, jealousies, even outright paranoia. It's even worse here in the Vatican."

"I see that," said Adam. "But how does an innocent meeting with a very junior priest qualify as 'shocking'?"

"Adam, come on. You're playing in the big leagues now. It's common knowledge that your General – your *Jesuit* General—placed you on this tour with the concurrence of the Pope. Now you have a private audience, the contents of which will not be divulged. There will be shock and dismay."

"I see it all clearly now. And to think I was about to tell you everything," said Adam, laughing.

Tobias joined in the laughter and the two men lapsed into small talk over the cocktails they had ordered. This continued for some time as their first courses arrived, were finished and then taken away.

Finally, Tobias could stand it no longer.

"So what did you and the Pontiff discuss?"

"Ha! I thought you'd never ask."

Both men again joined in laughter and Adam then told Tobias everything that had transpired during the audience.

"So we're going to be correspondents," said Tobias.

"Yes, we are, at least once a month and I suspect more often than that. I certainly hope you will let me know any reactions which occur relative to my reports. I also hope you will correct any errors in my Polish."

"I will keep you fully apprised of reactions and also include newsworthy developments around the Vatican. As to correcting your Polish, you're on your own. I struggle with the language, especially the pronunciation. Luckily most secular and religious diplomacy is conducted in English."

"Any other comment?"

"I think you have to accept in your own mind that this audience with the Pope concerning his home country really is extraordinary. You can be as blasé as you like but it really is special."

"I'll keep that in mind. Anything else?"

"Well, I have to admit that I have some difficulty with the concept of personal guidance from the Holy Spirit. But if John Paul says it happened to you, then I believe it."

The two men walked back to the hotel and parted with a warm handshake and embrace.

CHAPTER 18

Friday, September 18, 1987

THE NEXT MORNING, Adam rose early and packed his bag. He was scheduled to meet his mother and father at ten o'clock and his plan was to pack, check out and leave his bag with the bellman. Then, following his meeting he would walk back, retrieve his bag and take a taxi out to SFO for his flight to New York. Everything went according to his design until he arrived at his father's office. For starters, in addition to his father and mother, both Gisele and Mike Burke were waiting in the conference room. While he very much enjoyed seeing them and saying goodbye, they all had myriad questions about the papal tour. Then, when they learned of the previous day's audience with the Pope, the questions only intensified. Finally, he had to call a halt in order not to miss his flight. He promised to give Theo a full accounting of the tour and audience when they met; Theo in turn could pass the information on to all four of them.

"All right Adam," said Chaz. "That's what we'll do. We wish you Godspeed and in this case we mean it literally. At least let Mike drive you to the airport. He has some information he can deliver on the way."

"Yes, let's do that," said Mike. "I'm parked in the garage across the street."

Adam made his farewells and he and Mike set off. After they had stopped at the Fairmont, retrieved his bag and were on the way to the airport, Adam spoke.

"I really appreciate the ride, Mike. We were starting to run short of time."

"It's the least that an old cabbie can do."

"So what's the information you need to pass on?"

"More like non-information really. Do you remember the leads I was following regarding Lorena's dentist and the G2's tail number?"

"Yes, I do. What did you find out?"

"That's just it. Nothing, or at least nothing yet. The dentist faxed the dental records to Lorena's parents and then mailed the original records to them. End of story. The only odd thing was that the parents were very insistent about receiving all the original records immediately. They wired him $500 to send the fax and the next day air package with the originals."

"I guess that's a little odd, but bereaved parents sometimes do strange things," said Adam.

"I agree. Still, a bit of an anomaly."

"What about the tail number?"

"Anomaly number two. The tail number belongs to a two engine Cessna with a home airfield in Oklahoma City. The tail number does not belong to the G2 and that was either a simple record keeping error or was done intentionally. Either way, it's a dead end. We can't determine the G2's home field or ownership."

"What do you think?" asked Adam.

"I think two anomalies are at least one too many. I'm going to keep checking but first I'll have to figure out a new angle."

"Mike, as usual I can't thank you enough. Call me regularly please."

Adam arrived at his gate with twenty minutes to spare. The flight was uneventful and arrived on-time at JFK at 10:00 p.m. New York time. He took a cab to Fordham University in the Bronx where he'd made arrangements with Theo to stay in a dorm room that night. Due to a touch of jet lag, he didn't awake until 8:00 a.m. but this was not a problem. He was scheduled to have lunch with Theo and then cab back to JFK the next morning for his flight to Krakow.

Saturday, September 19, 1987

Adam met Theo in his office and they walked just off campus to a small restaurant.

"This place is only OK, but it has the advantage of being close to campus. You don't want to wander around some parts of the Bronx even at high noon."

"This is fine, Theo. The main thing is seeing you before I left. In fact, the Pope specifically instructed me to stop and relate to you everything we discussed. 'Omit nothing' he said."

"Did he now? That really is quite noteworthy."

"Yes. You're not the first person who's told me that. I keep hearing words like 'shocking', 'extraordinary' and now 'noteworthy.'"

"I certainly want to hear about the audience. In fact, why don't you tell me everything, starting with Miami."

Adam proceeded to do so, concluding with his rather inconclusive conversation with Mike Burke the previous day. When he had finished, Theo sat quietly for a moment and then spoke.

"Adam, how are you doing with that last topic—with Lorena?"

"I'm fine Theo, in the sense that I function well, at least as well as I'm able. I do have periods of sadness...and of anger."

"Anger?"

"Yes. I do have episodes of extreme anger at Max Spektor. I hold him responsible for Lorena's death. Then, when I return to a more rational state, I see that I am the one who caused her death. Max Spektor is just a proxy I use to deflect anger from myself."

"Adam, Max Spektor is an evil man but, as far as I can tell, Lorena's death was a tragic accident. Neither you nor Spektor was the agent of her death. My only counsel to you is not to dismiss these feelings you are experiencing. You'll have to find a way to work through them."

"You're right, Theo. One of the first things I plan to do in Krakow is to seek a confessor. Maybe this Father Pilsudski that the Pope mentioned can help in that regard."

"Perhaps so. But, let us return to the rest of what you told me. I must say that the people who have spoken to you about the papal audience are correct. It was extraordinary."

"Theo, don't you start on that theme."

"Adam, I need to speak by phone with the Father-General. When do you leave for Krakow?"

"Tomorrow at 10:00 from JFK. I should leave here by 7:00."

"All right. Let's go back right now and I'll try to contact the Father-General. I already have a dinner scheduled in Manhattan this evening. Why don't you come by my office at 5:30?"

+ + +

When Adam returned to Theo's office at 5:30 he found him in a somber and pensive frame of mind.

"Were you able to speak with the Father General?" asked Adam.

"I was. I spoke to him at length, first to relate what you told me and then later, after he had consulted with certain of his colleagues."

"And?"

"It is as I thought. You must act with caution during your time in Poland. You may be in danger."

"Come on, Theo. You've been reading too many Le Carre novels."

"Adam, I ask you to listen to me. And, please, try to curb your flippancy."

"All right, Theo. I'll try."

"You know that this Pope sometimes is called 'God's politician' for his resistance to communism. Yet, as Pope, his resistance has been non-confrontational. He gives homilies, but he does not urge the end of communism. What he does, over and over, is speak of rights of human freedom and dignity as being God-given to each person. Of course, this concept is despised by the communists who wish to subsume the individual into the collective and to posit the state as the all-powerful entity in place of God. This was the purpose of the just completed tour of the U.S., but it was not just for the opportunity to give more homilies. The centerpiece of the whole visit was the Pope's meeting with Ronald Reagan. These two men share more than simply the fact that they have survived assassination attempts. They are one in their resistance to totalitarian communism."

"I agree with all that, Theo, and I think the Pope succeeded in his goals."

"As do I. But, it's not enough for this Pope. It's never been enough. When he was a priest, bishop and even Cardinal in Poland, he was an activist—a pragmatic activist—but an activist nonetheless. Surely you know the story of the Nowa Huta church. For years this man Karol Wojtyla held Mass in an open field, regardless of the weather, and the people came. Finally, in 1977, the communists allowed a church to be constructed. He defeated the communists on this issue with his quiet, yet relentless pressure. It was unheard of. The communists fear this Pope and many say that the assassination attempt was their doing."

"I know the story and I agree. This Pope is a hero."

"Well, some in the Vatican hierarchy do not agree. They see him as a loose cannon and they seek to restrict his activism at every turn. They even tried, unsuccessfully, to quash the whole idea of the U.S. tour."

"I'm not surprised. The Pope made some allusions to being an outsider and causing turmoil, as I told you. But that's the way of bureaucracies. I can do nothing about that."

"I think you're wrong, and that's where the danger arises. This Pope wants to do more. He *is* doing more but I am not at liberty right now to give you details. Suffice to say, your audience with him was a means of speaking to you, but also of speaking with our Father-General. The Pope was being very literal when he told you to leave the question of your assistance in his hands. He will be giving you direction and I suspect that it will be through your friend Monsignor Alessi. I suggest you somehow alert him to this in your first report."

"Theo, I'll certainly keep all this in mind but I'm not going to skulk around Poland and elsewhere like some sort of a spy."

"Nor should you. That's the beauty of your Holocaust studies. You have a perfectly good reason to move freely and frequently throughout the Eastern Bloc and the remainder of Europe."

"OK Theo, Thank you for all this information. I guess."

"There's one more thing you should know"

"Dare I ask?"

"Father Pilsudski is an old and good friend of the Pope. He also is a close associate of the Father General."

My God. What have I gotten myself into?

At the same time Adam and Theo were conversing, Max Spektor was in his office just a few miles south in Midtown Manhattan. With him was his son George, who was almost precisely the same age as Adam. George had attended his father's alma mater, Columbia, and had earned both his undergraduate and M.B.A. degrees there. He had joined his father's firm four years earlier.

"George, you may be right. Why kill hundreds or even thousands when one well-timed and executed assassination can produce even more profit?"

"Finally, Dad, you see the light. All this cowboy shit, like Ghana, is not only risky and expensive, it's also uneconomical. We didn't come near to making enough in Ghana to justify the exposure. We're just goddamn lucky it didn't blow up in our faces, especially with that Thelen clan of assholes meddling in our business."

"Ah, yes, the Thelens. There's definitely a score to settle with them."

"Just wait, Dad. You know they'll come into your sights. Probably sooner rather than later. For now, let's focus on finding our next opportunity. This time we'll do it with a scalpel rather than a meat axe."

CHAPTER 19

Sunday, September 20, 1987

ADAM THELEN AROSE at 6:00 a.m. By 7:30 he was in a taxi heading to JFK and from there, finally, to Krakow, Poland, via Warsaw. As soon as he was airborne, the sense of tranquility and peace he had briefly experienced following his audience with the Pope returned to Adam. The sadness, regret and anger flowing from the events in San Francisco, now almost four months ago, did not leave him but they did recede into a separate compartment of his subconscious mind. At the front of his consciousness were the directions and blessing which he had received from John Paul II. He decided to work through the final two homilies delivered by the Pope after he departed San Francisco. These were delivered to the workers in Detroit, Michigan and, in a twist surprising even for the Pope, to the indigenous peoples of Canada's Northwest Territories, thousands of whom gathered in Fort Simpson to hear John Paul. Adam has been given English and Polish versions by Tobias at the dinner they had shared during the papal tour's final evening in San Francisco. Now he set himself the task of reading the homilies line by line. His goal was twofold. He wanted to see the Pope's themes, the God-given rights of all to peace, freedom, justice and dignity, articulated for his audiences in Detroit and Fort Simpson. He also sought to use the exercise to better his Polish. He was determined to deliver his first monthly report to John Paul in Polish, no matter how rudimentary. More than ever before in his life, he felt that he was in God's hands. Two hours before landing, Adam watched the light fade from the sky. He closed his eyes and contemplated Poland and where God might lead him during his time there. He arrived in Warsaw about midnight and took a cab to a rather drab but clean and reasonably priced hotel between the Central Train Station and the Palace of Culture and Science.

Monday, September 21, 1987

Adam Thelen awoke at 7:30 refreshed and eager to be on his way to Krakow. In short order he had checked out of his hotel, walked the short distance to the train station, an exceedingly gloomy building, and purchased his ticket. Trains to Krakow, a trip of two and a half hours, departed hourly and he had twenty minutes to spare. He went directly to the indicated platform where the train was waiting and boarded. After locating his compartment and seat, he settled himself and devoted the rest of his time prior to departure to a close observation of the Polish people who passed by. They appeared to him to be purposeful yet always on guard. They did not seem to make eye contact with their fellow travelers nor did they exchange any but the most perfunctory of pleasantries. Two or three minutes before the scheduled departure a man entered his compartment and sat down. He said nothing, only bestowing on Adam the briefest of nods, before turning his attention to a newspaper and later in the trip, a book. He did not speak to Adam during the journey nor did he look at him again. After departure, Adam spent some time looking out the window, but was not rewarded for his efforts. The suburbs and outlying areas of Warsaw appeared just as drab as the area surrounding the train station and, indeed, not much more inviting than the hulk of the Central Train Station. The smaller towns through which the train passed had much the same appearance and Adam soon joined his compartment mate in reading. When the train was within about a half hour of its destination, Adam's excitement began to mount. Although the scenery also grew more inviting, Adam ascribed his excitement to his own eagerness to reach, finally, his intended destination. But apparently this excitement was at least minimally contagious. Even his taciturn fellow passenger put down his book and began to peer out the window. Once, when a child waved at the passing train, Adam thought he detected the shadow of a smile on the man's face.

As the train pulled into Krakow Glowny Station, Adam could scarcely contain his burgeoning excitement. Before the train came to a halt, he had his bag in hand and was striding down the aisle to the nearest exit from the train. He exited the instant the train stopped and proceeded to the arrival hall and thence, at street level, to a more welcoming main terminal. He was torn whether to explore the terminal or the adjoining group of market stalls. Finally, he entered the main terminal, took a few steps away from the entrance and simply stood and watched for a few moments. It seemed to him that the people were more engaged and outgoing than in Warsaw. He noticed a few people glance his way and one man gave him a friendly smile. Adam was wearing his priest's collar and he wondered if the interest, and the smile, were due to that fact. In any event, he was heartened and felt welcomed to his new home. When he exited the main terminal after a few minutes of people watching, a row of taxis awaited him. Instead of entering the first in line, he decided to walk to the main square. He purposely walked west from the main terminal so that he could enter the city walls, dating from the 13th century, through the fortress from the same era known as the Barbican, and then through Florian Gate. Between the Barbican and Florian gate, he traversed Planty Park, which encircles Old Town Krakow. This park was created in the 19th century when the town elders determined to build it over the ruins of the City walls and the filled in moat which in earlier times had been crossed via a bridge from the Barbican to Florian Gate. Adam was strolling slowly and enjoying the sights. About ten minutes after he left the train terminal, and shortly after exiting Planty Park, he saw several hotels. Impulsively, he decided to spend his first night in Krakow anonymously in one of these hotels rather than at Ignatianum. After all the attention he received during the papal tour, he was not yet ready for more of the same. Briefly sizing up the hotels, he entered one which looked less grand than the others. He checked in and was shown to a functional and reasonably attractive room on the second floor with a view back toward Planty Park. After freshening up, he left his bag and returned to the small lobby. There he picked up a tourist map of the main square and surrounding area. In slow and simple English, he asked the desk clerk if he could recommend a nearby restaurant for lunch. After a few false starts the clerk was able to direct him to a place located back on Florian Street or as he quickly would learn in his accelerated language studies, *Ulica Florianska*. On his way to the restaurant he noted a large church called *Bazylika Mariacka* or St. Mary's Basilica. He decided to return to this church following lunch. The restaurant proved to be a *Bar Mleczny* or Milk Bar. These were communist subsidized restaurants where workers could purchase extremely inexpensive meals. Adam entered and was pointed to a table and given a menu in Polish. Almost immediately a woman approached to take his order. There was no English menu and clearly, English conversation was not an option. Quickly Adam scanned the menu and seeing a word he recognized ordered pierogi and, since he knew the word for beer, piwo, ordered one of those also. The pierogi proved to be very tasty but not at all what he expected. Adam thought they looked like ravioli but the tastes were quite different from what he knew. The beer, labeled Okocim, was full bodied and quite enjoyable. He'd eaten no breakfast and hadn't checked to see whether food was offered on the train, so he was quite hungry. He was heartened to discover that he found this workers' food to be quite palatable. He had changed some dollars to zloty before he left New York and was able to pay the very reasonable bill in local currency. Being unfamiliar with the customary tipping practices he left twelve zloty on top of the bill, representing about a 20% tip. This prompted the waitress to hurry after him as he was leaving to return two zloty. When he smiled and refused the money saying "Thank you" in Polish, *"Dzie kuje"* (Jehn-koo-yeh), she was flustered but obviously grateful.

When he returned to St. Mary's Basilica, it was about 1:15 in the afternoon on a weekday. Adam anticipated that the church would be sparsely populated, mostly by elderly ladies. When he entered the Basilica, he was surprised to see that it was about one-third full and that a complete cross-section of the population seemed to be represented. Adam had to remind himself that about four-fifths of the people of Poland were Roman Catholic and not merely nominally so. These men and women were practitioners of their faith. Upon entering, Adam found an empty pew and knelt. He focused his mind and, concentrating on the words of the prayer, said three Hail Mary's in thanksgiving of his arrival in Krakow. Then he sat back in the pew and marveled at the majestic carved Gothic altar depicting the death of Mary and her assumption into heaven by Jesus. He did not know it then but in his subsequent studies Adam would learn that the altar was carved over a twelve-year period in the fifteenth century by Veit Stoss, a German. With the hinged wings fully open, the altar towers overhead and is almost forty feet wide. As Adam gazed at the altar and then at the ceiling high above, with its blue firmament and twinkling gold stars, he realized how little he knew of his newly adopted city. He, a Catholic priest, had set for himself the daunting task of concurrently studying and ministering to the Jewish survivors of the most despicable acts of premeditated hatred of the twentieth century. Yet here he sat in a church, some version of which had occupied this site since the thirteenth century, and he knew next to nothing of its history. If he were to hope for even a modicum of success, he saw that he must immerse himself in the language, history, and culture of this country.

When he emerged from St. Mary's, it was about 2:00 in the afternoon. It was a warm day, but the sky was overcast as if rain were a possibility. Adam had studied his tourist map while he ate his lunch. There were literally dozens of places of interest and historical significance within less than one kilometer from where he stood. Yet there was only one place he knew he must go on this, his first day in Krakow. Instead of continuing south on the so-called Royal Mile culminating at the Wawel Cathedral overlooking the Vistula River, Adam turned left on Ulica Sienna and followed it to Planty Park where it jogged to the right and continued through the park to the intersection with Westerplatte Ring Road. Crossing Westerplatte the road became Starowislna, a busy thoroughfare running southwest away from the main square. Adam continued walking on this road for about fifteen minutes, eschewing the trains which passed him at regular intervals. At the intersection of Starowislna with

Miodowa, Adam turned right and then left through a park to Ulica Szeroka. He now was at the historic center of Kazimierz, Krakow's Jewish Quarter. During the twenty minutes or so it had taken Adam to reach Kazimierz from the main square of Krakow, the temperature had dropped and a steady drizzle of rain now was falling. Adam was wearing a light jacket and he now zipped it up. Ostensibly, this was to combat the drizzle but he also wished to conceal his Roman collar. He proceeded a short distance to the Old Synagogue, dating from the fifteenth century. He paid the modest fee and accepted a yarmulke from the young attendant. Placing the skull cap on his head, he entered the synagogue and began studying its many displays of Jewish life and culture. At the end of an hour he felt he had at least a basic overview of the Jewish community which comprised fully one-quarter of the population of Krakow as it existed prior to the devastation wrought during World War II. Leaving the Old Synagogue, Adam made his way back to Miodowa, and turned east across Starowisina and continued under the railway bridge. He replaced the yarmulke and entered the New Cemetery, where Jews of Kazimierz who died after 1800 are buried. Desecrated and vandalized by the Nazis during World War II, Adam could see that the process of restoration was underway but still a very long way from completion. Some headstones had been replaced in their original location but many others could not be properly relocated. The rain now was light but steady. Adam looked to his right at the Holocaust monument constructed of broken headstones, then allowed his gaze to sweep across the large and overgrown expanses of mostly unrestored gravesites. Adam did not proceed further into the cemetery. Instead, he slowly sank to his hands and knees and kissed the ground. He knew that, had there been anyone in the vicinity to see him, this action likely would have been viewed as a presumptuous and pretentious imitation of John Paul's gesture upon first returning as Pope to his beloved Poland. Adam knew that this was not the case. He knew that this country, this place, was where he was meant to be at this moment.

Adam departed the New Cemetery, retraced his steps to Starowislna and caught a train back to the main market square and his hotel. He had dinner at another nearby restaurant, somewhat more upscale than the milk bar where he had dined at lunch. After dinner, he suddenly was quite tired and therefore retired early and went directly to sleep. Almost immediately, it seemed, he was wide awake, the result of jet lag. The bedside clock indicated 12:30 a.m. He arose, drank half a glass of water and paced about the room. No noise whatever came from outside the room, even though it was a Monday night.

These Poles are not party animals, apparently. Such frivolity probably is not encouraged by the communists.

He lay back down on the bed and resigned himself to a restless and fretful night. Inevitably, his thoughts turned to Lorena and the child.

My God, a child dead even before it is born.

The deep sadness which he could neither deflect nor diffuse engulfed him and the familiar ache blossomed in his chest. Then the now predictable cycle continued with rage and hatred toward Max Spektor seeming to suffuse his entire being. Finally, he fell into a fitful sleep punctuated by jagged dreams of violence and loss.

CHAPTER 20

Tuesday. September 22, 1987

WHEN ADAM AWOKE he felt as if he had been
bludgeoned. The room was full of light and now
there was noise from outside. It was a fine fall morning and
droves of people were in the market square. Looking at his
bedside clock, he realized it was nearly a fine fall afternoon. The
clock said 11:00 a.m. Rising sluggishly, he made his way to the
bathroom. After showering, Adam quickly packed his bag and
checked out with apologies for his late departure. He walked
east across the main square and continued in the same direction
on Kopernika across Westerplatte and then under the railway to
#26 Kopernika. Adam had arrived at his new home, the Jesuit
University of Philosophy and Education, universally known by
its common name, "Ignatianum." The common name referred
to the twin jubilees, once again fast approaching, celebrated by
Jesuits around the world. These would mark in 1991 the four
hundred fiftieth anniversary of the founding of the Society of
Jesus and, in 1990 the five hundredth birthday of the Order's
founder, St. Ignatius Loyola. Adam entered a small lobby area
with an unobtrusive front desk. No one was at the desk. Adam
placed his bag on the floor and looked about him. Presently

a young man, perhaps twenty, came into one of the hallways behind the desk. This man looked in Adam's direction and seeing his Roman collar appeared to straighten his posture. He hurried in Adam's direction. As he approached, he spoke in Polish.

"Father, may I help you?"

"Hello, I am Adam Thelen," he answered in English.

The young man paused and appeared to switch gears.

"You are Father Thelen. Father Stan has been waiting. I will bring him. Please wait."

The young man sped back down the same corridor and disappeared into a door on the right. About three minutes later he reappeared with a priest appearing to be not much older than he but substantially taller and thinner with light reddish hair and a prominent nose. The younger man returned to Adam and, gesturing at the slightly older priest, said in English, "Father Thelen, this is Father Stanislaw. I will leave you now."

Hello, Father Thelen. I am Stanislaw Matejko but everyone calls me Father Stan," he said in English with his hand extended. "I am very pleased to see you. We were becoming worried. We had expected you more than two weeks ago."

"I joined the papal tour in Miami at the last minute at the direction of the Father-General. His staff assured me that you would be notified of my delayed arrival. I am very sorry to have caused you concern."

"We were told you were delayed but not the reason. We assumed, wrongly, that it would be a matter of days. No matter. You are here now and we welcome you."

"Thank you, Father, I am very happy to be here."

"You must be quite tired after your long trip. We had planned to greet you with a party at which you could meet everyone. It probably would be best to have that welcoming party before dinner tomorrow evening."

"That would be fine, Father. It was a long trip," said Adam, omitting the fact that he had arrived a day earlier.

"Father let me show you to your quarters. I would be honored to share dinner with you this evening. But, please feel free to decide otherwise, if you wish."

Adam knew that he would be wide awake at the dinner hour due to the combination of jet lag and his very late awakening this morning.

"Dinner with you this evening would be wonderful. However, please allow me to take you out somewhere. I'm very anxious to become familiar with the area. Please pick a restaurant you like."

"Excellent, Father Thelen. I will come by your quarters at 7:00. Now please follow me," said Father Stan while picking up Adam's bag.

Adam followed Father Stan along a rather circuitous route which led to an unprepossessing door opening off a hallway. Father Stan opened the door into a very pleasant suite consisting of a bedroom, bathroom and a living/dining area adjoining a small kitchenette with a sink, an obviously brand new small refrigerator and a microwave. The two trunks he had shipped from San Francisco were in the apartment but had not been opened. Adam saw another door and walked toward it.

"That opens into the courtyard, which I believe you will find very pleasant."

Adam opened the door into what was indeed a meticulously landscaped courtyard with a small fountain and a grove of linden trees at its center.

"Father Stan, this is a beautiful place! Looking at this building one wouldn't suspect that such a lovely place lies inside."

"Yes, I know. Our facade is quite plain. I think you'll discover this in many of the newer buildings in Krakow. Nowa Huta is an excellent example. The communists tend to build drab structures but we Poles manage to make the interiors warm and inviting."

"You've certainly succeeded here. I look forward to living here. Thank you!"

"You're welcome, in every sense of the word. Please begin to make yourself at home. I'll return at 7:00."

After Father Stan had gone, Adam opened both of the trunks which had been shipped from San Francisco. Rather than beginning to unpack, however, he went out into the courtyard and sat on a bench contemplating the fountain and surrounding linden trees. After a few moments he drifted into thoughts of the past year, clearly the most tumultuous of his life. Again, he thanked God for the highly improbable chain of events which had brought him to this new and strange place.

+ + +

At 7:00 he was casually dressed and quite wide awake when Father Stan knocked on his door.

"Good evening Father Thelen. Ready to go?"

"Yes, I am but please call me Adam."

"Let's make it Father Adam, if you're comfortable with that. I think it's almost inevitable that's how the students will address you and you may as well become accustomed to it."

"That's fine. Father Adam it is."

"Then let's be off. I've made reservations at a classic restaurant which is one of my favorites, although it's more Hungarian than Polish cuisine. You're very lucky it's open this evening. With the food rationing it can only open three days a week. Now — it's Tuesday, Thursday and Saturday."

"Sounds good to me."

"It's about a kilometer away. Shall we walk? It's a fine evening."

They retraced the route Adam had taken earlier in the day back toward the main square. After they crossed Westerplatte, Father Stan took a series of streets jogging in a generally southerly direction. As they walked, Father Stan described the various landmarks they were passing, including St. Mary's Basilica which Adam had visited the previous day. A little further south, he pointed out St. Francis Basilica.

"I highly recommend a thorough exploration of St. Francis, especially given your interest in the Holocaust. There is a fine painting of St. Maksymilian Kolbe, the priest who traded his own life at Auschwitz to save another."

"I will put St. Francis Basilica at the top of my list," said Adam. "But, how did you learn of my interest in the Holocaust?"

"We were told only that you would be interviewing Holocaust survivors and their descendants. I'm actually very curious, if you're willing to share more details."

"Certainly. We can talk over dinner about my plans. What else were you told about me?"

"Only that you wish to become fluent in Polish at the earliest opportunity. But, here we are."

They had reached the intersection of Grodzka and Poselska and on their right was the entrance to a restaurant called Balaton. They walked in and Father Stan immediately was greeted by name and shown to a table set for two. Before they had settled themselves, a waiter appeared and, with a smile, placed a glass in front of each of them. Adam thought that it was a relatively small water glass until Father Stan took his glass and extended it toward Adam.

"*Na zdrowie!* Cheers! Welcome to Krakow."

"Nah-DRO-veh!" said Adam, doing his best to imitate Father Stan phonetically.

Father Stan tossed back the entire glass and Adam was about to do the same when some instinct made him pause. He took a modest sip and was glad he had hesitated. It was vodka, and a rather fiery one at that. Father Stan laughed.

"Consider that your first language lesson. You did very well for a newcomer. Next time insert a hint of 'z' at the beginning of the second syllable. Also, both the 'i' and the 'e' at the end are sounded separately. All in all though, very good!"

"Thank you," said Adam, "for the compliment, for the language lesson and for the vodka."

"Well the first vodka is on the house, for us at least, but you're welcome for the other two."

"Tell me Father Stan, how you came to speak English so fluently. You sound like a native of the U.S."

"They sent me to Loyola University in Chicago very soon after I was ordained, which was only three years ago. I was told I had one year to learn to speak and write English as well as any North American. I returned a year ago mission accomplished. It turns out that I have a moderate facility with languages, even a relatively difficult one like English. I do still have difficulty with the idioms though."

"Father Stan, it seems to me that you're hiding your light under a bushel."

"Pardon me, Father," said Father Stan with a puzzled look.

"That's an idiom meaning that you're being too modest," said Adam with a laugh. "Your facility with English is much more than 'moderate,' especially after only one year. It seems that all the young European Jesuits I meet have learned English in the U.S."

Adam then told him about Tobias Alessi and his similar although longer experience at the Wharton School. This naturally led to questions about the papal tour. When Adam briefly outlined his audience with the Pope, Father Stan could not contain his amazement.

"Father Adam, that's..."

"I know. I know. Extraordinary. That's what everyone says."

"But it is. It truly is!"

"I suppose so. I think it happened because the Pope has a lot he wants to accomplish here in his homeland and I'm just a resource who may prove useful at some point. Which reminds me that John Paul directed me to contact a Father Pilsudski. Apparently, he teaches at the Jagiellonian University. Do you know him?"

Father Stan instantly was very sober. His response was guarded.

"Of course, everyone knows Father Pilsudski, at least they know of his existence. I'm not aware of anyone who actually knows him in the sense of being his friend or even being familiar with him. What did the Pope say about him?"

"If recall correctly, he said that I should see him and that he could help me. The Pope also said that he was in regular contact with Father Pilsudski."

"That is very strange. I know of no one who is in regular contact with Father Pilsudski and I've asked quite a few people. I at least know what he looks like, which is more than anyone else I've asked. Apparently, no one has ever seen a photo of him."

"Perhaps they have seen no photos, but how can they avoid seeing him if he teaches at the Jagiellonian University?"

"He is listed as a faculty member and the listing indicates that he has an office there. But no one has ever heard of him teaching a class. I can tell you, however, that he does use his office, at least occasionally."

"How so?"

"I was walking down the hallway one day and I saw him emerge. His office is at the end of a side hallway and there's an outside staircase next to his door. He looked back at me and then disappeared down the stairs."

"It sounds like an out of the way office. What were you doing there?"

"What is 'out of the way'?"

"Ah! Another idiom. It means remote or secluded."

"Thank you! I very much enjoy learning nuances of English. Yes, his office is remote and secluded and I was merely passing by, not loitering as you seem to be implying."

"Not at all, Father," said Adam with a smile. "I merely was inquiring. You seem to be the resident authority on the mysterious Father Pilsudski."

"Well, perhaps my interest in him is somewhat more than average. I do know something else about him that I'll wager no one else does."

"What is that?"

"I know where he lives," said Father Stan.

"How can that be, if no one else even knows what he looks like?"

"I followed him one evening, from this very restaurant. Just as I was leaving I saw him walking on the other side of the street."

"And?"

"And I followed him, taking care to stay well behind him so as not to be noticed."

"Where did he lead you?"

"Right to where he lives, #11 Kanonicza, not far from here. I returned the next day and looked around in the daylight. It's similar to his office, set back in an alley with exits to both Kanonicza and, at the rear, Grodzka. Out of the way, as you would say, and with more than one way in and out."

"Thank you, Father Stan. You've made my task easy. I'll do as the Pope directed and go there tomorrow to meet Father Pilsudski."

"Please Father, do not do that. He may well conclude that I told you the location of his apartment."

"Why would he reach such a conclusion, Father Stan? I thought you were undetected when you followed Father Pilsudski."

"That is true. I was stealthy but…"

At that moment the waiter returned to take their orders.

"I know what you want Father Stan — the wild boar stew — plus of course another of these," he said, gesturing to the empty vodka glass and then turning toward Adam.

The waiter was speaking Polish and Adam asked Father Stan to tell him that he would have the same, except that he wished to substitute red wine in place of the vodka.

"An excellent choice, Father Adam," said Father Stan. "We will have wild boar stew for two and my friend would like a bottle of the Bull's Blood."

Before Adam could demur and indicate that a single glass of wine would suffice, the waiter gave them a broad smile and departed.

"A fine choice! As you can see, I have the stew whenever I come here."

"I'm happy to take your guidance, although I don't know what I'll do with a full bottle of the rather ominously named Bull's Blood."

"I think you'll like it. The one they serve here still is made with the Kadarka grape blended with cabernet franc and merlot. It's very good and if you have trouble finishing the bottle I certainly will help you."

"Thank you, Father Stan. I appreciate that. But, we were talking about Father Pilsudski and how to get in touch with him, when the waiter arrived."

Again, Father Stan was serious and thoughtful.

"I fear I have said too much. This man is not to be taken lightly."

"Your secrets are safe with me Father. However, the Pope specifically instructed me to contact Father Pilsudski. What do you propose I do, ignore the Pope's directive?"

"No. You must obey the Pontiff. But please do not be frivolous about this. I am very serious when I say that he is a dangerous man. People do not contact him. If you are to see him at the direction of the Pope, then Father Pilsudski already is aware of your presence. He will contact you. I beg you. Please do nothing. Most especially, do not make inquiries about Father Pilsudski. Many people, even some of our fellow priests, collaborate with the communists. You do not wish to attract their attention, particularly so soon after your arrival here."

Adam recalled his half-brother cautioning him to suspend his flippancy and be aware that he was entering into danger. Now a second person, this one with apparent local knowledge, was warning him that the danger was real and that he should not be cavalier.

"All right Father Stan, I hear you and I am taking you seriously. I will do nothing impulsive or foolish. Do you know anything else about the man?"

"I know nothing else save rumor and hearsay, the details of which are even more ominous."

"You'd better tell me the rumors also, or at least a summary of them. One of our English sayings is similar to an idiom, but really more of an aphorism: 'Forewarned is forearmed!' But you'd better wait. Here comes our food."

The waiter brought their wild boar stew in a pot with a ladle and two bowls which he placed upon the dishes already set in front of them. He also had a bottle of vodka with which he refilled Father Stan's glass. Finally, he placed a wine glass in front of Adam, opened the bottle of Bull's Blood and poured a little into the wine glass. Adam tasted it and declared it to be very good, which it was—a fairly simple but quite enjoyable wine. With another smile, the waiter was gone again.

"Father Stan, let's finish with Father Pilsudski and then move on to lighter topics. What are the rumors?"

"The details vary but the substance is the same. One hears that Father Pilsudski was in the Polish Army—a major — and a communist. He is said to have been a member of General Jaruzelski's staff, and a rather nasty one, responsible for executing enforcement actions, as they call them. People got hurt or worse, simply disappeared. Then sometime in the late 60s, he came into contact with John Paul, who was Cardinal Wojtyla at that time. No one is very clear how he met Karol Wojtyla but shortly thereafter he is said to have resigned from the army. After some time in a seminary, some say a very short time, he was ordained a priest. That much, at least, is historically correct. Cardinal Wojtyla ordained him personally. Now one hears that he is just as nasty as before, still working secretly except now it's for the Pope. Others claim he really is a double agent who still reports to his old communist bosses. Still others hold that at some point after his ordination he was accepted into our Order and now is a fellow Jesuit. As I said, it's all rumor and innuendo."

"And I'm supposed to meet this mythical creature."

"Yes, you are, and if the Pope has directed you, I am certain that you will."

Adam and Father Stan finished their meal discussing lighter topics and as promised Father Stan finished more than half of the Bull's Blood, preceded by two more vodkas brought to him by the waiter, who kept a close eye on his glass. Father Stan also promised to help Adam in his study of Polish and, if Adam wished to work with him, in preparing his early monthly reports, in Polish, to Monsignor Alessi.

Saturday and Sunday, September 26-27, 1987

Adam spent the weekend unpacking the trunks and familiarizing himself with the layout of Ignatianum. He dined in the refectory each evening and Father Stan introduced him to the staff, teachers and administration of the school. On Sunday morning, he arose at 5:00 and said his first Mass on Polish soil in the school chapel. Just as he began the Offertory, he was surprised to see a rather shapeless man in overalls enter the chapel and kneel in a pew. The man had flowing white hair and a rather wispy beard. He wore very dark round wire rim spectacles and he walked very slowly with his head down as if peering at the floor in front of him. At the Communion, the man walked slowly up to the altar.

"The Body of Christ," intoned Adam.

"Amen," whispered the man as he received the host onto his large and calloused hand.

When Adam turned toward the chapel and gave the traditional injunction, "Go in peace to love and serve the Lord," the man had gone. Adam mentioned this incident to Father Stan at dinner on Sunday.

"Oh, that was Stepan. He comes in on the weekends to do maintenance, mostly on the boilers. He stays on Saturday and Sunday nights in one of the attic rooms. it's strange, though. I never saw him attend Mass before."

September 28-October 12, 1987

The next two weeks were frenetic. Adam met with the Jesuits at Ignatianum and agreed to share in some rudimentary duties at the school. Ignatianum was in the process of expanding its curriculum to include masters programs pitched at laymen, some of them to be taught in English. Now, however it remained largely a seminary for the training of future priests. Most of the students were the equivalent in the U.S. of high school juniors and seniors or college underclassmen.

Adam's duties seemed to him to be something akin to a hall monitor or resident assistant-at-large, available to give advice and counsel as needed. Adam also spent much time at the Jagiellonian University, referred to in casual conversation as "UJ." He met many more people than he could hope to remember but, as he did during all the introductions on the Papal tour, he kept copious notes of each introduction, scrupulously recording each evening all the people he had met that day, along with whatever personal details he could recall. During this time, he gathered a basic understanding of the long and distinguished history of UJ, which dates from its creation by King Kazimierz the Great in 1364.

Adam had a particular interest in Kazimierz the Great, who established Poland, especially Krakow, as a safe haven for Jews in the 14th century — a time when other nations were deporting them. The original name of the university was simply Krakow Academy. Adam learned that the name "Jagiellonian" was applied to the university in 1817 to commemorate the beginning of the Jagiellonian dynasty resulting from the late 14th century alliance of Poland and neighboring Lithuania after King Kazimierz died without a legitimate male heir.

During this period, Adam and the administration of UJ came to a consensus as to his role there, at least through the summer of 1988. Adam would immerse himself in the study of the Polish language and, with one exception, would neither teach nor take any other classes. He would be free to travel as required for his studies of Holocaust victims and their descendants. The only exception involved Adam's agreement to act as an adjunct professor in the Faculty of Law and Administration and, as such, to give lectures on U. S. Law for the School of Foreign Law. He was assured that these lectures could be flexibly scheduled around his travel and his language studies. Adam was pleased with these arrangements which were the product of multitudinous discussions over ten days.

Adam was very busy during this time but he also was mindful of his need to contact Father Pilsudski. Finally, when all the details were hammered out and then blessed by the President of UJ, Adam's schedule became more predictable if no less rigorous. He was studying Polish five hours a day, six days a week at UJ, supplemented most evenings by another hour with Father Stan. At the end of two weeks in Krakow, Adam had heard nothing from Father Pilsudski. Notwithstanding Father Stan's warnings, Adam decided to act. With Father Stan's reluctant assistance, he located Father Pilsudski's unmarked office and went there alone one morning about 10:00. Taking care that the adjoining hallway was deserted, he knocked on Father Pilsudski's door. After all he had heard, his first reaction was one of relief when there was no answer. Yet it was imperative that he meet this man in order to comply with the Pope's explicit instructions.

He took one of his cards, crossed out the old address in San Francisco and wrote on the back the single word "Ignatianum." He slid the card under Father Pilsudski's office door, turned and walked away. Another week passed, during which Adam submerged himself in the study of Polish. There had been no hint of contact with Father Pilsudski, even though he visited his office again and then, with more than a little trepidation, walked to his residence at #11 Kanonicza and knocked on that door, again with no response.

Helped by Father Stan, he had prepared and forwarded the first of his monthly dispatches, in Polish, to his friend Tobias Alessi, who in turn would deliver it to John Paul II. He had detailed all that had transpired since Tobias and Adam had parted in San Francisco a month earlier, with two notable omissions: He said nothing of his conversation with Mike Burke concerning Lorena's final days and, at Father Stan's insistence, he had made no mention of his unsuccessful efforts to contact Father Pilsudski.

CHAPTER 21

Monday, October 19, 1987

ANOTHER WEEK HAD passed with no word from Father Pilsudski. Adam now felt he had no choice other than to take more direct action. He was debating in his own mind whether to speak with the President of UJ or, through Tobias, ask for more guidance from the Pope. He was inclining toward the former if for no other reason than the fact that the University President could be reached without delay. During his brief lunch break one day at UJ, he had decided to speak with the University President the following day. Walking back to Ignatianum, Adam was glad that Father Stan was not available that evening for his supplemental language lesson; he needed a break from Polish and was looking forward to a relaxing evening alone in his apartment. When he reached Ignatianum and let himself in, no one was about. Walking back to his apartment, the halls were deserted. As he opened the door to his rooms, Adam already had removed his coat and was in the process of unfastening his Roman collar. As he stood in the threshold with the door still open, he saw a man seated at the small dining table. Adam hesitated, unsure whether to retreat and seek assistance.

"Come in Father and close the door."

The man had spoken in English, but with a very noticeable Polish accent. After debating for another instant, Adam entered the room and allowed the door to shut behind him. He placed his coat on the small sofa and completed the removal of his collar. He then sat in a chair across the small table from the man.

"I am Father Pilsudski. Do you speak Polish?"

"Not yet. I think in another five or six weeks I will be reasonably conversant."

"That is good. I'm sure Karol instructed you to report to him in Polish. For now, you and I will speak English, but slowly and simply, please."

"The Pope did make that request and I have honored it in my first report, with some help from others."

"Father Stan, I assume. I hope you said nothing of a sensitive nature."

"The first report contained only a routine description of the month since I left San Francisco."

"Good. Father Stan is, I think, a good man with good intentions. But he is what you would call simple... perhaps foolish."

While Father Pilsudski was speaking, Adam was examining him closely. He appeared to be about forty years old, somewhat shorter than Adam but as heavy and stronger. He had very short grey hair and piercing blue eyes and was wearing a light black nylon jacket zipped all the way up to his collar. He exuded a sense of barely suppressed power and of... danger, as Father Stan had stated. Adam knew of a certainty that Father Pilsudski easily would prevail in any physical confrontation between them, notwithstanding his own knowledge of martial arts.

"Father Stan was astute enough to advise me to wait for contact from you. Also astute enough to know who you are and to discover where you live."

"Ha! You prove my point. First he loiters outside my office and then he tries to follow me from Balaton. Is he not aware that he is 6'4" high and weighs 170 pounds? Or that he has red hair and a nose like a potato? Or, finally, that he was drunk and was attempting to follow me in broad daylight? The man is a fool, just as I thought. As for thinking that I live at #11 Kanonicza, well, I had hoped that leading him there might solve a very serious problem for Ignatianum."

"What do you mean about Ignatianum?"

"I cannot concern myself with that now. We have much more pressing business which is why the Pope told you to see me."

"Yes, he did. I was beginning to wonder whether we ever would meet."

"At least Father Stan was correct in telling you to wait for me to make contact. Now please tell me everything you and the Pope discussed, in as much detail as possible."

Adam thought for a moment about telling Father Pilsudski that he needed a lesson in civility, but quickly discarded that idea as pointless. Instead, he related to Father Pilsudski every detail of his audience with John Paul II. He could remember it as if he had just left the Pope's suite in San Francisco. When he had finished, Father Pilsudski's demeanor appeared to soften for a moment.

"How is the Pope? How did he appear to you?"

Adam paused for a moment before responding. He thought back to the audience, remembering not John Paul's words but his expressions, his body language, his overall appearance.

"Physically, he seems very strong. I saw no continuing effect of the assassination attempt. He is very purposeful—driven even—in completing his mission, and he has a very clear sense of what that mission is. He seemed frustrated at the obstacles thrown up by the bureaucracy which surrounds him and at the slow progress toward his goal."

"What do you think he sees as his goal?"

"His homilies say clearly that he wants dignity and freedom for all men. He sees these as God given rights. His homilies don't say it, but I believe he especially wants these rights for the people of his beloved Poland. He wants to cause the removal of the forces that deny these rights."

"He is a good man, maybe the only one I know. God has made him a powerful man, powerful enough to gain rights for his people."

Father Pilsudski paused then, and Adam could see him return to the present, to the issue at hand. Suddenly, Adam knew that *he* was the issue. Father Pilsudski was going to examine him mercilessly, to determine whether he was a potentially useful resource or just another well intentioned simple fool.

"You told the Pope that you were coming to Krakow to study Jews who survived the Holocaust as well as their families and descendants."

"Yes."

"There are no Jews in Krakow. The Nazis shipped them to Birkenau or one of the other camps and killed most of them. Those that survived and returned were deported by the communists in the '60s and '70s, many to Israel but also to other countries all over Europe. Some even went to the U.S. There are less than one thousand Jews in all of Poland. Why come here to study Jews?"

"What you say is true. Jews today live elsewhere. But there are two good reasons for coming to Poland, especially to Krakow. First is the history. Until World War II, Krakow was a haven for Jews from all over Europe since the 14th century. On the day I arrived here, I walked to Kazimierz and visited the Old Synagogue and the New Cemetery. I've been back to Kazimierz twice since then and as soon as I'm reasonably fluent in spoken Polish, I'll be there frequently, as well as at Auschwitz. And that's the second reason: Many Jews, thousands of them, travel here, not to live, but to revisit their culture and their ancestors. I will meet them and talk to them. Then I will travel to interview some of them, wherever they may live in Europe or Israel or even the U.S."

Adam realized that his mission had overcome him and that he had become unduly voluble, perhaps even strident. He stopped and bowed his head, gathering himself.

"That is a good and true answer," said Father Pilsudski, "As for the travel, when do you think that will start?"

"Probably early in the new year — 1988."

"That is good. That may be useful," said Father Pilsudski but with a note of doubt.

"But?"

"What do you mean, 'But'?" said Father Pilsudski.

"There was uncertainty in your voice — skepticism."

"Father, I do not know you. But I have dealt with some Americans in the past. They are not soft, but they tend to think that everyone is like them, wanting freedom and democracy. They cannot see that some people — many people—hate such ideas and will do anything to stop them from spreading. Americans are. . . what is the word?"

"Idealistic?"

"Yes! They are idealistic! They forget that their enemies are dangerous. They tend to believe promises which we, here, know are just empty words."

"You seem to be saying that Americans are not only idealistic but also credulous and naive."

"Yes. Those are the words. Not all Americans, but some. Your President now — Reagan — may be different. I know Karol — the Pope — believes that this is so."

"You're saying that I may not recognize the danger I would be in if I work with you—that I may get hurt."

"Yes. You would be in danger and if you do not take the danger seriously, you will be hurt. You might be hurt anyway."

"Is that your concern, that I—literally an innocent abroad as you see it—may be hurt?"

"I said I don't know you, so I don't know how you will act. But, my real concern is not for you. It is for the harm that you could do to our larger goals which are, by the way, the goals of the Pope and of your President."

"I appreciate your candor and honesty. I agree fully with what you say. The goals are more important than any individual. Still, I told the Pope that I would help him in any way I could and I meant what I said. He said to leave that in his hands and then he told me to see you. I guess it's now in your hands."

"Yes. I will watch and I will talk to people. If you are needed, you will hear from me."

"All right, Father. Is there anything else I can tell you?"

"No. I am glad we met. Please send my affection and respect to the Pope in your next report. Also, you may tell him of our meeting but, you must refer to me simply as his friend, with no mention of my name. Also, you are not to divulge any of our discussions regarding goals and how to achieve them to Father Stan or to anyone else. If necessary, write the report in English."

"I will do as you say, Father Pilsudski."

"Thank you. I will go now."

Father Pilsudski stood and Adam could see that he was about 5'10" and two hundred pounds. His body was wide and flat with no evident bulges. He smiled faintly at Adam and

202

then left via the door into the courtyard. Adam wondered how Father Pilsudski would exit the premises of Ignatianum; he had walked the entire perimeter of the courtyard and it appeared to open only into the private apartments which faced onto it. He did not, however, make any attempt to see the direction Father Pilsudski had taken. Rather, he sat on his sofa and pondered what had just occurred.

CHAPTER 22

Tuesday, October 20, 1987—Wednesday, November 11, 1987

T HE NEXT EVENING after dinner, Father Stan came to Adam's apartment for their usual supplemental language lesson. Their custom now was to conduct all conversation in Polish, with English used only to correct or clarify. However, Adam now addressed Father Stan in English.

"I met with Father Pilsudski yesterday evening."

"Ah! I told you he would find you! Where did you meet?" responded Father Stan in Polish.

"In this discussion of Father Pilsudski, we must speak English. Your English still is far better than my Polish and on this topic there can be no misunderstandings."

"All right, Father Adam, we shall speak English. Now, please tell me where Father Pilsudski found you."

"Here."

"Here at the school?" asked Father Stan incredulously.

"Here in this room. I returned from UJ last evening and he was seated right where you are now."

At this Father Stan stood up as if touched with an electric prod. He looked at the chair in which he had been seated and then took another.

"I told you the man is frightening. He is like smoke!"

"Frightening, yes, but not like smoke. He is a man in the too, too solid flesh,"

"What did he say?"

"Father Stan, I cannot relate to you or anyone else, save the Pope, most of what we discussed. He was very clear about that. There is, however, one part of our discussion that I believe I can share with you."

The prior evening after Father Pilsudski had departed, Adam had reviewed their entire conversation and parsed precisely his prohibition against speaking with others, with the exception of the Pope. He finally had concluded that one portion of the discussion could be told to Father Stan.

"What is it that you can tell me?"

"Well, first I must apologize. Father Pilsudski implied that you were somewhat… naive. I'm afraid that, in an effort to defend you, I mentioned that you were astute enough to learn where he lived."

"Oh, no…"

"Wait a moment, Father Stan. He did finally acknowledge that you were wise to counsel me to wait for Father Pilsudski to make contact. However, he was not overly impressed with your skills at following him."

Adam then related what Father Pilsudski had said, omitting only his comment about Father Stan's nose. Father Stan listened and then looked crestfallen.

"I guess I did look like a fool."

"Perhaps so, but that is not what I want to share with you. Father Pilsudski made a rather strange comment about #11

Kanonicza. Then when I asked him about it, he refused to elaborate. He would only say that he couldn't allow such matters to distract him from more important issues."

"What did he say about #11 Kanonicza?"

"He said that he had hoped by leading you there to solve a very serious problem for Ignatianum."

"What kind of problem?"

"He said nothing more and insisted on speaking of other matters which I cannot divulge."

"What could he mean?"

"I don't know Father Stan. I was hoping you might have some idea."

"Well… I'm not sure, but I think I know a way to find out."

"Father Stan, I want you to promise me not to do anything foolhardy. Also, if you discover anything, you must come to me and let us discuss what, if anything should be done."

"Yes, I can promise those things. In any event, what I'm thinking will take some time."

Saturday and Sunday, October 31—November 1, 1987

Adam spent the weekend composing his second monthly report to John Paul via Tobias. After relating all of note which had occurred during the preceding month, except his meeting with Father Pilsudski, he gave the report to Father Stan for correction and clarification of Adam's steadily improving Polish. Next, Adam painstakingly prepared an addendum in the form of a postscript to his friend Monsignor Tobias Alessi. After three hours of work, with many false starts, changes and corrections, the addendum finally was complete:

P.S. Tobias, please mention to the Holy Father
that I was able to meet with his friend. We had the
opportunity to spend forty minutes together and
to discuss several topics. He showed great interest
in my plans to work with Holocaust survivors and
their families. He indicated that he might have
some ideas on this topic to share with me when
next we meet. He sends his respect and affection
to the Holy Father.

When Father Stan returned the body of the report, Adam
made the suggested changes, added the addendum and posted
the report to Tobias.

Max Spektor and his son George were dining at La
Grenouille. It had been a relatively slow day at the midtown
office, probably because this particular Wednesday happened to
be Veterans' Day. Max had staged a mini-scene with the *maitre
d'* upon entering but not because he had any valid complaints.
Rather, he felt the need to assert himself vis-a-vis the *maitre d'*
and, as an added benefit, to be noticed by the other patrons.
With any luck at all the small contretemps would be reported to
one of the society columnists and would appear in the Thursday
papers. When they finally were seated, Max had made a great
show of perusing the wine list but then had ordered the same
Bordeaux as always. He also ordered his customary entree,
rognon de watt moutarde. His son looked on with an expression of
bemused distaste while all of this was transpiring. Still, he could
not quibble with the quality of the food, or the service for that
matter, at this restaurant. Their entrees now were before them.

"I read your analysis of prospective targets," said Max.

"What did you think?"

"In general I liked it, although I think most of your African and South American candidates may be premature. These are third world countries now and some of them may achieve second world status in five or ten years. Brazil may be a possibility but they're probably going to self-destruct with outlandish inflation without any help from us. Besides, we're not the only people who can see that. No arbitrage there. The Philippines look good, plus I like two or three of the Eastern Bloc countries."

"As it happens, I agree with you about Africa and South America, although perhaps for different reasons. The markets there are just too small, especially the options markets. It's just too hard to take any sizable position without moving prices. Don't write off Africa though. I have some ideas for the future— commodities based ideas—which don't depend on destabilizing governments."

"What do you think about the Philippines?" asked Max.

"I like it and I have some specific ideas. We've got a couple of decent contacts in the government, although both are such slime bags, it's hard to be sure they won't double deal us. I'd like to go over there, make a couple more contacts and explore things further."

"Go for it," said Max.

"I also agree that the best opportunities right now are Eastern Europe. Things are moving fast there what with Reagan and that mackerel snapper Pope working together against the commies. Now they've got Gorbachev, who seems to be a spineless sack, leading Russia. Czechoslovakia is interesting as is Poland. There's an added advantage to Poland. There, all the progress is focused on one man: Lech Walesa. The guy is a firebrand and has charisma but he's only a steel mill electrician with no real education. He might be easy to manipulate, but even if he's not, he's still a very attractive target. If something were to happen to him, their perceived economic progress would go in the toilet. That's assuming, of course, that the Prez and the Pope succeed in the overthrow of communism in Poland and Gorbachev keeps the Red Army on the sidelines. Could be an opportunity for a very nice score."

"OK then, go ahead and spend a couple of months developing resources and strategies with the emphasis on the Philippines, Czechoslovakia and Poland," said Max. "For now, let's keep this between the two of us, at least insofar as possible."

"Yes. We have to assume that the Thelen clan, those fucking assholes, are still out there trying to meddle in our business."

CHAPTER 23

November 16-30, 1987

On Monday the 16th, Adam received a note from his friend Tobias:

> Adam,
>
> As requested, I gave your report including the post script to John Paul. He said to tell you he's happy you were able to meet with his friend. The Pope already had heard about the meeting from his friend. The Pope asked me to pass on to you his support of your work with Holocaust survivors and his assurance that his friend will have some good ideas which will help both you and the Pope.
>
> Respectively,
> Tobias
>
> P.S. The Pope also mentioned that your Polish is improving but is still uneven. He said the body of the report was much better written than the addendum.

Hmm. In addition to being a good and holy and powerful man, this Pope also has a rather droll sense of humor.

A week later, on Monday the 23rd, Adam returned to his apartment after leaving early that morning and spending a very long day at UJ. A folded sheet of plain paper, on which was printed the words "Father Adam" was on the small dining table where he and Father Pilsudski had been seated during their earlier discussion. Adam unfolded the paper and read:

Please open an account with Bank BPH, Kazimierz branch. Tell them that you anticipate receiving regular wire transfers of charitable donations supporting your work with Holocaust victims. You may advise that you anticipate receipt of the Zloty equivalent of $5,000 (U.S.) per month. Banks wiring the funds will be located in Italy and Germany. Explain that you anticipate the need to write checks, make occasional wire transfers to other banks in Poland and that you also will be making cash withdrawals, usually in Zloty but that conversions to other European currencies occasionally will be required. On November 30, leave a note on your table with account and routing numbers.

The note was unsigned but was, of course, from Father Pilsudski.

On Tuesday the 24th Adam opened the account. The branch manager seemed very pleased to hear that he was a Catholic priest planning to engage in charitable activities benefitting Jews throughout Europe. He was at least as pleased to hear of the anticipated amounts of the wire transfers.

On Thursday the 26th, Thanksgiving Day in the U.S., Adam made separate calls to Theo and Bradley in New York and to his mother and father in San Francisco. Both calls were made with the intent of exchanging Thanksgiving greetings and catching up on family affairs. With his half-brothers that was in fact the extent of their conversation. On the call to San Francisco, however, his mother and father, together on a speaker phone, had more to discuss than a simple update and exchange of pleasantries.

"We have more news, Adam—news with sinister overtones," said Chaz Thelen.

My God, I hope it's not his health.

"What is it, Dad?"

"I'll let your mother tell you. She's the one who's been working on it."

"Adam, I think you know that, after the Ghana affair, we've continued our efforts to monitor the activities of Max Spektor and his firm."

"Yes, I am aware of that, Mom."

"Well, we've heard from two separate sources within Poland, one an analyst and the other a journalist, that Max's son George has been making inquiries."

"What kind of inquiries?"

"They could be completely appropriate questions about the potential for economic progress in Poland. The Spektor firm does, after all, make investments and some of them are in developing countries."

"So, these inquiries could be innocuous."

"They could be but, in both instances, George Spektor's interest was focused on Lech Walesa."

"Again, that could be in the normal course of business. Walesa is the most visible foe of the Communist regime."

"True, Adam, and that's the extent of what we've heard. If it were anyone other than the Spektor's I wouldn't be concerned, but this raised red flags for your father and me, and for Gisele also. We're listening for more information."

"I think you're right to be concerned, Mom. Max Spektor is no good and I seriously doubt that, in the case of his son, the apple fell far from the tree. Max Spektor could mate with Mother Teresa and still produce an evil spawn."

"Interesting imagery, Adam," said his father, "especially about a colleague in the Church."

"I'm sorry, Dad and Mom, but I feel rather strongly about this man Max Spektor."

On the Morning of Saturday the 28th, Father Stan knocked on Adam's door. When Adam answered, it was obvious to him that Father Stan was badly shaken. His complexion was ashen and he seemed torn between fury and extreme sadness.

"Father Stan, come in. What is it?" said Adam in Polish.

Father Stan said nothing, seeming literally unable to speak. Instead, he removed a thick envelope from the inside pocket of his jacket and handed it to Adam. He opened the envelope and saw that it contained perhaps two dozen photographs. He motioned Father Stan to the table and they both sat down. As Adam began to examine the photos, he saw immediately that the entry to #11 Kanonicza was shown in each photo and that one of the priests from Ignatianum also was in every photo.

"This is Father Edmond."

Taking a deep breath, Father Stan was able to answer. "Yes it is."

"And these are students here, some of the younger ones if I'm not mistaken."

"Yes, they are. Two different students appear in these photos and they are fifteen and sixteen respectively."

"Father Stan…"

"Look at all the photos Adam, but please prepare yourself for the last six."

Adam looked at each of the photos carefully. All but the final six frames appeared to be taken from a vantage point somewhat above the door to #11 Kanonicza and the resolution was very good. Adam surmised that they were shot with a telephoto lens. The last six were interior shots, also high resolution, and apparently shot inside #11 Kanonicza. As Adam perused each photo, he felt his jaw tighten and an enormous fury begin to build within him. When he had examined the last photo, he looked at Father Stan.

"I promised to show you whatever I discovered. Now I'm going to confront Father Edmond."

"No, you are not," said Adam. "You will do no such thing."

"What? You want this. . . monster to get away with these unspeakable acts?"

"Not at all, Father Stan. But if you care about these boys, the last thing you will do is confront Father Edmond. We must deal with Father Edmond immediately so that he cannot come in contact again with these boys. When that is accomplished, we must counsel these boys separately. Their identities must not become known and they must come to understand that they have done nothing wrong. If you confront Father Edmond now and all of this becomes public, the lives of these boys will be ruined and there will be a serious risk of suicide. Think about it for a minute. Not long ago here in Poland homosexuals or people who engaged in homosexual activity, no matter whether under coercion, were consigned with Jews and Gypsies to the death camps. Obviously, the Nazis did that. But, are you absolutely confident that all such attitudes have disappeared here in Poland and elsewhere?"

"I guess you're right, Father Adam. But we must do something and it has to be done right now."

"Yes, we must. I'll make a phone call in just a moment. First, tell me how you obtained these photos."

"One of my brothers is in the surveillance business, usually in the employ of the communists. He's everything that I'm not. Average height and weight, nondescript hair color, normal nose, methodical—average in every way and able to blend in. He took the exterior shots from a second floor window forty yards away. Then, when it was obvious what was happening, it was an easy matter to gain entry when the apartment was empty and install a hidden camera in the bedroom."

"All right. I'm going to make that call now."

On Sunday the 29th two men appeared without fanfare and met briefly in Adam's apartment with Adam and Father Stan. After about ten minutes of discussion the two men departed with the photos and proceeded to Father Edmond's rooms. About three hours later, in mid-afternoon, Father Edmond left Ignatianum with a single suitcase.

Shortly thereafter, the two men returned to Adam's apartment. Father Stan was there with Adam. With the two men were the rector and principal of Ignatianum, Father Jakub. He appeared shaken but resolute. The two men said nothing.

"These two men have shown me the photos and explained how they were obtained. They also have given me signed and witnessed resignations from Father Edmond, one from Ignatianum and from the Society of Jesus and the second from the priesthood. He left here about an hour ago with a few of his belongings. We will forward the rest if he supplies us with his new address."

"But... he was allowed simply to walk away?" said Father Stan.

"Yes. I understand what you are asking and I have no answer," said Father Jakub while looking at the two men, who remained silent.

"Father Stan, I assure you that other steps are being taken," said Adam. "I think we can be confident that Father Edmond will not engage in more predatory activity."

"But..."

"Father Stan, I suggest we concentrate on the boys," said Father Jakub. "There are three of them according to these two men. One of them was not photographed, but Father Edmond provided these men with his name. I will see each of these boys and begin the healing process. They also will see Father Adam until he determines that they have dealt with their trauma as well as possible. Thereafter, we will arrange private counseling as and when needed."

At this point, the two men shook hands with each of the priests and departed Ignatianum, again with a complete absence of ceremony. When they had gone, Father Stan spoke.

"Father Adam, how did you arrange this?"

"I called my brother—half-brother really—who also is a member of the Order. He in turn called the Father-General. A member of his staff contacted these two men yesterday in Rome, where they reside."

"You mentioned other steps regarding Father Edmond," said Father Jakub. "Can you elaborate?"

"I cannot, at least at this time. I ask each of you for your trust and forbearance."

"As you wish, Father. I will contact each of the boys tomorrow and begin the process of healing. I thank each of you for discovering and then terminating these despicable acts."

That evening, rather than preparing a note containing the banking information requested by Father Pilsudski, Adam instead slid a note under the door of an attic room at Ignatianum. The note contained no salutation.

"I have the account and routing numbers but it is imperative that I see you. I will be in my rooms all day next Saturday, December 5th."

Saturday, December 5, 1987

At 5:30 in the evening, when most of the priests were gathering in the refectory, Stepan knocked on Adam's door.

"Come in Father Pilsudski," said Adam in Polish.

The man entered Adam's rooms and took a seat at the table. The flowing white hair, wispy beard and formless clothing were the same as Adam recalled in the chapel during his first Mass at Ignatianum. Once the man entered Adam's apartment, however, the bent posture and shuffling gait disappeared.

"Tell me how you discovered my...small deceit," said Father Pilsudski, also in Polish.

"Later," said Adam. "First, as you would say, we have more pressing business. I have opened the account as you requested. Here are the account and routing numbers."

"Thank you," said Father Pilsudski as he perused the sheet of paper given to him by Adam.

"Where will the money be coming from and how will it be used?"

"As should be obvious to you, it will be wired into Italian and German banks by the Institute of Religious Works, better known as the Vatican Bank. You then will use the money for your Holocaust studies and also, on occasion, for other purposes as directed by the Pope through me. Do you have a problem with that?"

Even with his "Stepan" disguise, Father Pilsudski's gaze was steady and unwavering; Adam greatly desired more detail as to the Pope's directions, but he knew with everything else which had to be discussed that evening that this was not the time.

"I have no problem with that."

"Thank you. Now please tell me how you discovered me."

"We have two more items to discuss before I get into that."

Adam then told him of his Thanksgiving Day conversation with his mother and father regarding the Spektors, and provided a brief summary of their activities in Nigeria and Ghana. He did not relate the earlier actions of Max Spektor in San Francisco.

"This is excellent intelligence. Please thank your mother and father and assure them that we will be watchful. But, Father Adam, this Max Spektor seems to arouse in you a rather visceral reaction."

Adam felt himself coloring and cursed his lack of control. Somewhere in the prehistoric precincts of his brain he knew that he hated Max Spektor.

"Yes, the man is rather distasteful," said Adam. "But now, let me ask you something. Did you intend to allow Father Edmond to molest these boys indefinitely?"

"Ah! I noticed that he was absent today when I arrived. Have you dealt with him?"

"Yes, he is gone from here, no thanks to you," said Adam.

"I disagree. Neither you nor Father Stan would suspect a thing even now, had I not led you to Kanonicza St."

"That's true, but even you had no faith in Father Stan, or me for that matter."

"Not so. After I mentioned the problem to you, I thought the chances were 50-50 that something good would happen. Now it has happened and apparently in a discreet fashion. Congratulations!"

"Yes. Father Edmond has gone and now we are left to deal with the wreckage of the innocent boys. This could have ended months ago."

Adam could feel his anger rising and with it the impulse to attack Father Pilsudski physically notwithstanding his earlier rational conclusion that any physical confrontation would be a losing proposition.

"This is what I had in mind when I spoke to you earlier about Americans. You would put at risk our goals — which would benefit all of Poland — for the sake of three boys. I took a chance even mentioning Kanonicza St. to you, especially with that fool Father Stan involved. Had this scandal become public, the communists would have used it — to the severe detriment of the Pope and of his goals and the goals of your President."

"All right, enough of this. We could dispute this all night. Please return to your boilers."

"I will but, before I leave, I ask you again to tell me how you discovered me. Obviously, I was careless and I do not wish to repeat my mistake."

"It was pretty simple. So simple that Father Stan could have done it. The initial clue was your hand, into which I placed the sacred host. The hand was far too strong and healthy to be attached to an old, bent man like Stepan. I learned from Father Stan about Stepan's attic room. Then, on Monday morning, I followed you, although I really didn't have to. As soon as you left here, you turned straight north toward the railway station, only a quarter mile away. I knew where you were going so I took a parallel street to the same destination. With you walking at Stepan's pace, I had plenty of time to arrive before you. I saw you enter the lavatory as Stepan and then emerge shortly thereafter as Father Pilsudski."

"Thank you. I look forward to working with you. Also, you may tell Father Stan that I no longer consider him a fool."

"There is one other item before you leave. Father Edmond is away from here and has resigned from the priesthood. But he is a free man and the only thing preventing him from further predatory acts is his belief that he is under continuing surveillance."

"Yes, I see your point. I will see to it that he *is* under surveillance —obvious, overt, albeit irregular, surveillance that he will be unable to overlook. If that is not enough to keep him away from young boys, then further action will be taken. I can assure you that he will not molest again, at least here in Poland."

Father Pilsudski arose and departed. As he approached the door, his head fell to his chest so that he was looking at his feet and his stride shortened to that of an old man.

Wednesday, December 9, 1987

"You no longer are a fool," said Adam.

"Why thank you Father Adam. To what do I owe this substantial elevation?"

Adam and Father Stan were in the refectory of Ignatianum just before the dinner hour. They were awaiting Father Jakub who was to join them shortly.

"Father Stan, it is not I who elevate you. Rather, it is the estimable Father Pilsudski. It is he who told me last Saturday that I should so advise you. Apparently, he was duly impressed by your successful discovery of Father Edmond's depredations. What, by the way is Father Pilsudski's first name?"

Despite himself, Father Stan found that he was elated by his unexpected promotion by the otherworldly Father Pilsudski. Simultaneously, however, he could feel himself beginning to color and he knew what that meant.

"Why Father Stan, you are positively beaming. I shall have to report this to Father Pilsudski when next we meet."

"You shall do no such thing. Besides, I am not beaming. I've just come in from the rather unseasonable sunshine and it has caused me to color."

"Ah, thank you for correcting my mistaken perception. I thought you were blushing with pride at Father Pilsudski's compliment."

"Not at all. And, to answer your question, no one knows Father Pilsudski's first name. It's part of his mystique. He is simply Father Pilsudski."

"It wouldn't be Stephen or some derivative thereof would it?" asked Adam.

"I told you. No one knows. Why would you think Stephen, in any event?"

"No reason. Just a hunch. But, enough of this jollity. Here comes Father Jakub."

Father Jakub joined them at the small corner table. He looked from Adam to Father Stan and back again and a smile formed at the corners of his mouth and eyes.

"Why the merriment? Have I just missed a good joke or am I the butt of one?"

"Neither, Father Jakub and certainly not the latter. We are simply exulting at the unusually fine December weather," said Father Stan.

"It is delightful, isn't it?"

The three priests engaged in small talk until their meals were served to them. Father Jakub's demeanor then became serious.

"I've now seen all three boys separately and, if it is possible, I am pleasantly surprised. What do you think Father Adam?"

"I believe you are right in your initial reaction and for that we are very fortunate. We also have Father Stan to thank for his very efficient sleuthing."

"Indeed, you are correct in that. We do thank you, Father."

Father Stan, barely recovered from his earlier bout of blushing, was overcome again.

"I did very little really."

"Nonsense, Father. These boys have much for which to thank you," said Father Jakub.

"That is true Father Stan," said Adam. One of the boys — the one who was not pictured in any of the photos — had only been taken by Father Edmond to #11 Kanonicza on one occasion, on the pretext of a field trip and extra study outing.

Apparently, this was Father Edmond's way of causing the boys to accompany him. This boy was not molested. The first trip was designed to instill a sense of comfort and trust. I think he will be fine."

"What of the other two?" asked Father Stan.

"Sadly, as the photos showed, they were molested repeatedly. Ongoing counseling will be necessary. The good news is that both boys visibly brightened when they learned that none of the other boys knew anything of their experiences and that we planned to keep it that way. I think, ultimately, that they'll be OK, but it will take time."

"However long it takes, we shall be there for them," said Father Jakub.

"I have some good news on another front," said Adam.

The two other priests looked at him expectantly and he proceeded to relate his conversation with Father Pilsudski concerning the ongoing surveillance of Father Edmond.

"That is good news Father. But tell me, how is it that you, a newcomer to Krakow, not only knows Father Pilsudski but have access to him? I am a native of Krakow and all I know of Father Pilsudski I have heard second and third hand," said Father Jakub.

"Father, I can only say that he was referred to me during a brief audience I had with the Pope during the recent papal tour of the U.S. More accurately, the Pope referred me to him. My first meeting with him occurred only after he presented himself to me."

"Extraordinary," said Father Jakub.

CHAPTER 24

Friday, December 18, 1987

"WHAT HAS IT been—five or six weeks since we last dined together?" asked Max Spektor of his son.

"I recall that it was Veteran's Day and that you made a scene at La Grenouille, so it's been a little over five weeks. Why no scene tonight? You've been remarkably civilized thus far," said George Spektor.

"The night is young, but you needn't worry. This whole place is a scene. That's why people come here."

Max and George Spektor were dining at the Russian Tea Room, a restaurant noted for its high celebrity to commoner ratio, as well as superb Russian fare. Caviar of the finest grades was a virtual staple; indeed, the Spektor's, father and son, were sharing an order of blinis with red caviar and sour cream, although George was not exhibiting much interest.

"George, the red caviar seems not to hold much attraction for you. Have you forgotten your Ukrainian heritage? Perhaps I ought to resume calling you by your true given name, Giorgei."

"Dad, you can peddle that Ukrainian bullshit to others, but please not to me. My name is George and I have not forgotten my true heritage."

"I can see that you are your usual bubbly self this evening. So on to business. Any progress on our prospective targets of opportunity?"

"Nothing of note on the Philippines or Czechoslovakia, but we have had several discussions within Poland. It seems that Lech Walesa is just as he appears: a man who believes in the rights of workers and sees the Solidarity movement as the best way to procure those rights. The man is making progress too. Solidarity was founded in late 1980 by Walesa and one of his buddies and was outlawed in 1982 by General Jaruzelski. Last year, though, the general granted amnesty to Solidarity members and started the so-called Roundtable Negotiations. It looks as if the commies are searching for a way to coexist with Solidarity. Of course, when they say coexist, they really mean co-opt. Word is, the reds are trying to bring some of the tamer Solidarity types into a coalition government which would still be run by the commies."

"Interesting stuff, but what about Walesa? Surely he must be driven by self-interest."

"As far as we can see, he's the real deal. An idealist—not in it for himself at all."

"Then he's no good to us is he?" asked Max. "That is, unless something unfortunate befalls him at a time that happens to be opportune for us."

"Yes, that's true. But I'm also thinking of an additional angle—something you might like, since it involves the media."

"Tell me."

"Well, I'm thinking that Solidarity might actually succeed sometime in the next few years. Reagan is pushing it and he seems to be working in tandem with the Polish Pope. Every time one of them says something, the other one echoes it. And, when we talk to people, there's a lot of chatter about monetary aid flowing into Poland for the benefit of Solidarity. I wouldn't be surprised if the U.S. or the Vatican was supplying it. Maybe both. Then there's Gorbachev. As usual, he seems to be sitting on his ass doing nothing."

"OK. Let's assume that at some point they do succeed. What's your idea?"

"Solidarity is popular in the U.S. and it gets a lot of ink. What if you became a visible supporter of the cause, with a little help from our friends in the media? You could become the hero of the working man and the enemy of communism. Maybe later you could be seen as the capitalist who saves the working man from the excesses of capitalism."

"I like it."

"I thought you might," said George. "Looking out a little further, there may be an additional benefit."

"Tell me."

"Africa already is unstable. There are all sorts of new rulers coming into power and most of them are the opposite of Lech Walesa—they're only in it for themselves. For instance, there's this new guy in Zimbabwe which was Rhodesia until recently."

"So, more of the same. Find a crook and try to work with him until he stabs us in the back."

"Yes, but I think I see a new twist. If we develop your image as the protector of the oppressed and poverty-stricken, we could set up an aid organization and receive donations—big ones."

"Sounds good so far."

"I think it could get better. There are all sorts of acronyms for these organizations but NGO—non-governmental organization—is the most common. The beauty of the thing is that they are virtually unregulated and unaudited. We could declare broad and wonderful sounding charitable goals for the poor people in Africa and use the money over there any way we want. Plus, the media loves to publicize how bad things are over there. Our operations could be externally funded at no cost *and* you'd look like a hero."

"How would we use the money?"

"The opportunities are endless. Just the natural resources—diamonds, copper, cobalt—you name it."

"I like it. Let's start in with the media right away. As of now, I'm a Solidarity supporter. Have a Merry Christmas Giorgei!"

"Fuck Christmas. And my name is George."

Wednesday, January 5, 1988

George Spektor lay staring at the ceiling of his bedroom on the upper east side.

There's got to be a better way. My father is losing it. His pathetic adventure in Ghana proved that. A thousand deaths...and no one noticed. We barely recovered our investment. Actually, he's lost it already. Still, he could be useful as a tool to manipulate the media. Lord knows they love to be manipulated—always mewling about the plight of the poor—especially the third world poor. As if their plight is the fault of anyone other than themselves. It could be perfect. Dad, the tool to manipulate the media fools who in turn manipulate the brain-dead public.

<u>Monday, January 25, 1988</u>

Vernon Walters was the embodiment of the term "public servant." Born during World War I, a life-long bachelor and having no education beyond the equivalent of high school, he enlisted in the U.S. Army in 1941. He retired as a Lieutenant General. During his military career he became fluent in five languages and served as an interpreter for three presidents. From 1972 until 1976 he was Deputy Director of the Central Intelligence Agency under Richard Nixon. Ronald Reagan appointed him to the post of Ambassador-at-large and he served in this capacity until 1985. During this period he traveled between Washington D.C. and the Vatican carrying messages from President Reagan and returning with replies from the Pope. He developed a warm relationship with John Paul at least in part due to his fluency in their *lingua franca*, Italian. In addition to messages, he also brought satchels of cash which were deposited in the Vatican Bank and dispersed in accordance with the Pope's directions to various foes of communism. Much of this cash found its way to Poland via courier or wire transfer and was used to fund the logistical needs of Solidarity. Due to the nature of many of the messages he carried, Mr. Walters also developed a good working relationship with functionaries within the Secretariat of State including Cardinal Martino and, starting in 1984, Monsignor Alessi. In 1985, President Reagan appointed Mr. Walters U.S. Ambassador to the United Nations and in 1988 he continued to serve in this capacity. Nonetheless, the President called on him once again to visit the Pope and to renew what by then had become a friendship.

"Your Holiness, the President wishes to deploy mid-range missiles in Europe."

"What does he wish of me in this matter?"

"Holy Father, the President knows you are a man of peace but that you do not seek peace, along with freedom for all your people, through force. He knows that you would have all nations lay down their weapons and live in harmony under God."

"Yes, this is true. In some cases, my methods are not his."

"He knows this and asks only that you remain silent when these weapons are deployed. The President believes that victory over the communists is near and that these weapons will further encourage Mr. Gorbachev to keep his Red Army at home when freedom begins to prevail in East Germany, Poland and elsewhere in the Eastern Bloc. He needs your silence as tacit assent to these missiles. He believes that they never will be utilized."

"Please brief the Secretariat of State on this matter. I anticipated something of the sort when you made this appointment to see me. Cardinal Martino is waiting for you now. How long do you plan to remain in Rome?"

"My schedule is flexible, given the gravity of this situation."

"You shall have our answer in two days' time. I look forward to seeing you then."

Two days later, Vernon Walters was meeting with John Paul in his chambers. It was 11:00 a.m.

"I shall remain silent when the missile installation is announced," said John Paul.

"Thank you, your Holiness. The President will be extremely pleased to hear of your forbearance."

"Please tell the President that my silence does not constitute my approval, tacit or otherwise, of the missiles. I understand from my advisors that this is an example of what is called projection of power. In other words, the presence of the missiles is meant to discourage the communists from responding with force should freedom gain a foothold in Poland and elsewhere. I shall remain silent because I respect the President's confidence that this display of force will preclude any actual application of force by either the U.S. and its allies or the communist bloc."

"Holy Father, you are very wise in your analysis of this situation. I shall relate every detail of your position to the President."

"My wisdom, if such it is, flows from the Holy Spirit. We have completed our business. Now Vernon, will you share lunch with me so that we may discuss happier matters. Cardinal Martino and Monsignor Alessi will be joining us. I have instructed them not to talk shop and I am quite confident that they will ignore my counsel utterly."

"I would be honored to join you, Holy Father."

CHAPTER 25

Tuesday, February 9, 1988

ADAM THELEN'S LAST update to Monsignor Alessi had been forwarded in mid-January. Adam had felt confident enough in his Polish to write it in its entirety by himself, with no assistance from Father Stan. Feeling somewhat immodest, he had mentioned this fact to his friend Tobias Alessi. He also had mentioned his efforts, thus far fruitless, to meet with Holocaust families visiting Kazimierz. It was true that winter was not the high season for tourists anywhere in Poland. Yet there had been some visitors to the synagogues and cemeteries and Adam had made efforts to contact them. Through the good offices of one of the rabbis, he had spoken with three families, who had listened respectfully and promised to consider more in-depth interviews in the future. Thus far there had been no further follow-up from any of the families and Adam's frustration no doubt had been evident between the lines of his update. Today Adam had picked up two pieces of mail when he returned to Ignatianum. One was from his father and the other envelope bore the now familiar handwriting of Tobias Alessi. After entering his rooms, Adam first opened his father's letter and scanned it. He saw that the letter was a brief summary of family events and developments at the firm, including a reference to how well Mike Burke had settled into his new job. The letter was typewritten and beneath his father's scrawled "Love. Dad" was a postscript in his father's handwriting: "Adam—Suggest you call me at the office sometime during the next week."

Next Adam opened the letter from Tobias and read through it carefully.

January 29, 1988

Dear Adam:

The Pope notes with pleasure your increasing fluency in Polish and congratulates you. He indicated that, assuming your oral abilities mirror your proficiency in the written language, you should have no difficulty communicating with any native speaker of Polish. He counsels patience in your efforts to meet with the families of Holocaust victims and survivors. He asked that I emphasize that your labors, while primarily secular in nature, cannot fail to be seen also as cooperation and collaboration between Catholicism and Judaism. What you are attempting goes beyond even the very ambitious goal of ecumenism, which is, of course, worldwide Christian unity. Thus, there will be hesitance and reticence on the part of those you hope to interview. You are asking Jews to share their most private and painful experiences and emotions not just with an academic possessing excellent credentials in the field of psychology, but also with a Catholic priest! This will require a very high degree of trust, the creation of which will be difficult and time consuming. The Pontiff concluded his discussion with me by stating that he is developing some additional thoughts and ideas which may assist you, and that you should expect to hear more from him in the future.

Your friend, Tobias

Sunday, February 14, 1988

As had become his custom, Adam Thelen arose at 5:00 a.m. and twenty minutes later was in the school chapel performing his Sunday Mass. He enjoyed both the silence and the solitude afforded him at this early hour before others were up and about. No one had attended his Mass since "Stepan" had done so on Adam's first Sunday at Ignatianum. Adam was surprised therefore when he turned and raised the host to see Stepan there once again this Sunday. And, just as he had that first Sunday, Stepan came forward and received communion. However, instead of responding simply "Amen" after Adam had recited "The Body of Christ" Stepan appended a whispered question.

"May I meet you in your rooms this afternoon at 4:00?"

"Yes," answered Adam in the same whispered tone.

At 4:00, Adam was in his rooms practicing spoken Polish, comparing his diction and accent to the voice emanating from a small cassette player. When he heard the knock on his door, he arose and opened it with the cassette continuing to play. "Stepan" stepped inside and closed the door behind him. He

carried a small toolbox which he placed on the dining table and then took his accustomed chair.

"I applaud you, and no doubt the Pope does also, on your diligence in learning our language."

"Thank you, Father Pilsudski. I appreciate your compliment," said Adam as he stopped the cassette player.

"Should anyone ask, I am here to correct a minor blockage in the plumbing of your sink."

"Don't worry Father. I shall do nothing to compromise your cover. Now, please, to what do I owe the pleasure of your company?"

"To the Pope, of course. He asks that I communicate two items to you."

"And they are...?"

"The first involves your bank account. It should contain the zloty equivalent of $10,000 by now."

"That is correct. The bank manager is very pleased with my business."

"As well he should be. The Pope wishes you to withdraw $6,000 in cash and take it to this man in Gdansk. Delivery can be made at any time during the next ten days."

As Father Pilsudski said this, he pushed a sheet of paper across the table. On it was a name followed by an address in Gdansk.

"I certainly will do as the Pope requests. I can leave this coming Thursday afternoon on an overnight train and arrive in Gdansk the following day. However, this may cause some curiosity here at Ignatianum and at UJ, since I have no particular reason to go to Gdansk and February is not the optimal time for a vacation on the Baltic Sea."

"I have given that some thought and I believe I have a solution. Curiosity, after all, is not something we wish to encourage."

"I agree. So, what is your solution?"

Father Pilsudski pushed another sheet of paper across the table. On this page were two names, one male and one female, each with the same surname, and a single address.

"These are the names of family members of a Jew who survived the Holocaust but now, sadly, is dead, as is his wife. They have been told of your impending trip to Gdansk and are willing to be interviewed by you."

Adam took the sheet of paper and studied it. His eyes widened as he read the common surname of the man and woman.

"Mr. and Mrs. Pilsudski. Do I have you to thank for arranging this interview?"

"You do, but they are not Mr. and Mrs. Neither of them ever has married. They are my brother and sister. Both are several years older than I."

"So, you are . . ."

"Jewish. Yes, I am. And then communist and now Catholic. All other questions will be answered in due course by my brother and sister. I have assured them that your motives are pure and that your work may benefit Jews. I can assure you that they will be open and forthright with you."

"I am... stunned. I thank you."

"It is possible that you will hear more than you bargained for. You may be more than merely stunned. I shall be interested in the conclusions you draw from your discussions with them. Now, the Pope has a second mission for you."

"Yes?"

"He directs you to travel to Israel and to celebrate Easter there. You are to arrive at least three days prior to Easter

Sunday. On the Friday prior to Easter, April 1 of your calendar, Passover commences. You will be attending a Seder. You'll be at a communal Seder rather than one of the multitude of family Seders which will be held in homes throughout Israel. This particular Seder will be led by the chief Sephardi rabbi, Mordechai Eliyahu who, along with the chief Ashkenazi rabbi, is the co-leader of the Rabbinate of Israel."

"I don't know where to begin. I am honored. . ."

"You can begin by studying all things relating to Passover and to the Passover Seder. The Book of Exodus might be a good starting point."

"I will start immediately."

"Excellent. Next week, after your return from Gdansk, I have arranged for you to meet with Rabbi Malina at the Old Synagogue. He will assist you in your preparations."

"Father Pilsudski... Thank you."

"Do not thank me. I do this for the Pope and he is the one you should thank. He does this to speed the process of gaining Holocaust interviews. In addition, if you perform well and make favorable impressions on the rabbis and other Jews you will meet in Israel, you will be helping the Holy Father in ways which will become clear in due course."

"I will make the best effort possible to justify the Holy Father's faith in me. Regarding the Pontiff's first request, is there anything further that you can tell me of the man to whom I am to deliver $6,000?"

"Only that he is an associate of Lech Walesa, that he will be most pleased to receive the money and that it will be well used."

Tuesday, February 16, 1988

"Dad, how are you?"

"Adam. Thank you for calling. I am excellent this morning and everyone else also is fine as far as I know. How about you?"

"I'm fine Dad. I'm off to Gdansk on Thursday."

"Let's see now. Gdansk is what I knew as Danzig during the War, isn't it? The seaport on the Baltic which was held by the Germans?"

"That's the one Dad. Now that it's back in Polish hands, It's Gdansk again."

"We bombed the hell out of that place when the Germans held it, but I'm sure it must be fully restored by now."

"I'm told that it not only is restored, but that the Old Town was rebuilt just as it was, with all the period details replicated. I'm looking forward to seeing it."

"What takes you over there at this time of year? I have heard that the Baltic Coast is delightful in the summer, but February can be a little harsh."

"I've been referred by a colleague here in Krakow to a Jewish brother and sister whose parents somehow survived the War. I'm told they're willing to be interviewed."

"That's very good news, Adam. But, it's a bit strange that you call me with news of an impending trip to Gdansk."

"How so, Dad?"

"Well, Gdansk is the birthplace of the Solidarity movement isn't it?"

"Yes, it is. Lech Walesa worked at the shipyard there as an electrician. Now he's back there again since the communists granted amnesty to Solidarity members. There's even talk that free or at least somewhat free elections may be allowed sometime soon. But what's strange about me going there?"

"Nothing strange at all. The interviews are a wonderful development. What's odd is that our good friend — you know to whom I'm referring — suddenly has become an ardent supporter of Solidarity. There have been two or three newspaper articles about him and his newfound affection for the working man."

"Knowing our friend, the articles have to be plants and there has to be an ulterior motive."

"You're probably right. But your mother and I felt you ought to know. I've saved the clippings and will enclose them along with my next letter."

"I appreciate the update and the clippings. I have an associate over here who also will be quite interested in this news. In fact, I... ah... I'll be doing him a favor while I'm in Gdansk."

"A favor. What kind of favor?"

"Well... let's just leave it at that for now."

"All right, Adam. But there's one other item of news — actually two. The first is on the same topic. Our friend's son is becoming more active in the business. While our friend is becoming a compassionate media darling, his son is having multiple conversations in Poland and in other parts of the world."

"What kind of conversations?"

"As usual, we're having difficulty gathering accurate details. We're getting a lot of chaff and conflicting reports. But, based on our experience in Ghana, we have to assume sinister implications."

"I agree with that, Dad," said Adam as he felt the old anger begin to kindle. "What's the second item?"

"Happier news, for you at least. Your mother is planning to visit you. She wants to see where you are, and also to check with some of our sources regarding these conversations of our friend's son."

"That is good news Dad. Why don't you join her?"

"Not this time. I'm not as enamored of international travel as I used to be. Besides, someone has to stay home and run the shop."

"Dad, you have plenty of people for that and I'd love to see you."

"Maybe next time Adam. It sounds as if you may be there for some time and I understand that Krakow is a beautiful and historic city."

"It is Dad. You will enjoy it. When is Mom planning to come?"

"No firm dates yet, but she's been talking about Easter."

"Easter could be a problem Dad. Ask her if she could make it a week or so later."

"I'm sure that she could do that. As I say, she hasn't made firm plans yet. I'm glad I checked with you. What do you have scheduled for Easter?"

"It's not my schedule Dad. It's a schedule that John Paul II has arranged for me." Adam then related the Pope's directive, relayed to him by Father Pilsudski, that Adam attend a Passover Seder to be led by Rabbi Mordechai Eliyaha in Israel.

"Adam, yet again you surprise me. This Pope seems to have plans for you."

"Not at all, Dad. It's just that he is trying to help me gain the trust of Jewish families so that they become willing to agree to interviews with me."

"No doubt, Adam. But since your audience with the Pope in San Francisco, I've instructed my clipping service to broaden the publications it scans on my behalf and to forward anything to do with John Paul II. I think even you would be surprised at the number of initiatives this Pope is undertaking. And, increased rapprochement between Catholicism and Judaism is one of them. I suspect that you are meant to aid in this effort. You'd better be on good behavior," he said with a laugh.

"No joke there, Dad. I've already been told by the Pope's emissary that I need to learn all I can about Passover and the Passover Seder, so that I may acquit myself well. My lessons with the local rabbi in Kazimierz begin as soon as I return from Gdansk."

"My knowledge of Judaism is woefully lacking. I know Passover is the celebration of the Exodus flight from Egypt. The Seder is a dinner at the beginning of Passover, isn't it?"

"All correct Dad. The Seder usually is celebrated in Israel on the night before the first day of Passover and there are multitudes of them, almost all of them family affairs. The main purpose is to celebrate the Jews' escape from slavery in Egypt, as told in Exodus, but also to tell the children the story, so they know how important this is to them even now when people all over the world are still oppressed or in bondage. It's a beautiful ceremony, solemn yet joyous. I'm sure I'm going to study not just the Torah, but also the Talmud, Kabbalah and some of the commentaries."

"Ah, thank you. I've been trying to remember where I had heard Mordechai Eliyahu's name and your mention of the Talmud jogged my memory. Rabbi Eliyahu has visited the Rebbe, Rabbi Menachem Schneerson in Brooklyn. Apparently, they have become friends."

"Thank you, Dad. That's good to know. Now on another topic, I've been meaning to ask you if Mike Burke has discovered anything further regarding the death of Lorena. He mentioned a couple of anomalies when he was driving me out to SFO the last time I was there."

"I'm sorry Adam. He's found nothing, but not for lack of trying. Everything was a dead end."

"I expected as much. Please pass on my thanks to him for all his efforts."

"I will Adam. And, Adam?"

"Yes, Dad?"

"Regarding that "favor" you're doing for someone in Gdansk?"

"Yes…"

"Please be careful. You're in a totalitarian country now with entirely different rules from those you're accustomed to in the U.S."

"Dad, I'm just a priest…"

"Yes, I know what you are. It's an excellent cover."

"Dad, you're being melodramatic."

"Please trust me on this, Adam, and be careful."

"OK, Dad. It's good to talk to you. Please pass on my greetings to everyone and be sure and tell Mom how much I'm looking forward to seeing her."

"I will Adam, and I'll also remind her to be careful."

CHAPTER 26

<u>Friday, February 18. 1988</u>

ADAM THELEN HAD boarded the train in Krakow the previous evening. He already had eaten and therefore had gone directly to his sleeping compartment. Just after midnight the train had arrived in Warsaw where three cars, including his, were shunted onto a siding.

At 6:00 a.m. a new train, including these three cars, was formed and moved north. It now was 2:30 in the afternoon and the train was about fifty miles southeast of Gdansk. Looking out the window, the marine influence of the Baltic Sea already was evident. The snow which had been much in evidence as soon as the sun had arisen was thinning and the temperature was rising into the 30s. As his proximity to Gdansk increased, so too did Adam Thelen's anxiety. He was carrying $6,000 in cash within a communist country to the representative of an organization which was an avowed enemy of the State. If he were traveling out of the country, his person and luggage certainly would be subject to search at the border, but searches of travelers within Poland also were not uncommon.

Yet searches were not his biggest concern. If a search by the communists discovered the cash, he could claim with some plausibility that the cash was destined to the brother and sister of Father Pilsudski, either as consideration for their cooperation or as a charitable offering for their suffering. But what if he was followed to his assignation at the address given him by Father Pilsudski with the Solidarity representative. He had memorized the address and then burnt the note and the only name on the note, "Ivan", clearly was a *nom de guerre*. None of that would matter if he were followed and caught in the act.

In the event Adam needn't have worried quite so much. When he arrived at his hotel in a taxi and checked in, the clerk handed him a typed telephone message:

> "Welcome to Gdansk! I look forward to meeting you and discussing your Holocaust project. Please meet me tomorrow morning at 10:00 a.m. in the library of the Law and Administration Building at Gdansk University.
>
> Ivan

Saturday, February 20, 1988

Following directions he had obtained the evening before at his hotel, Adam had found his way to Gdansk University in Aleksander Kleina and then to the Law and Administration building. It now was 9:50 a.m. and he was seated in the library reading the local newspaper. The newspaper was, of course, communist controlled and Adam thought it needed a motto printed on the front page: "All the News that Suits the Regime."

Maybe in a few years all this will change.

Adam's briefcase was on the chair next to him and he felt ill at ease. The briefcase contained assorted materials he would need for the interviews of the Pilsudski siblings beginning tomorrow morning. However, it also contained a manila envelope containing the zloty equivalent of $6,000 U.S. This was a large amount of currency and the envelope was one designed for legal size documents. Five or six other people were seated in the library and to Adam each of them seemed to be a Red Army operative waiting to pounce upon the obviously foreign priest in their midst. He couldn't imagine extracting the envelope from his briefcase and casually passing it to "Ivan."

"Hello Father. You must be Adam Thelen."

The man saying this and standing next to Adam's table was of average height and slender build but he spoke in such a stentorian tone that everyone in the library looked in their direction. He was dressed in stereotypical academic garb, complete with the mandatory tweed jacket.

"Oh sorry," the man said to Adam and then, looking around the room said, "Sorry" again.

The man extended his hand and Adam rose and shook it. They then seated themselves at the table. Adam fully expected one of the other men in the library to arrest both of them, but everyone had returned to reading.

"Hello," said the man in a quieter tone. "I am Ivan Tusk and I've just come from a lecture to a large classroom of students. I'm afraid I still was in my classroom mode when I first greeted you. In any event, I am pleased to meet you."

"Then...you teach here," said Adam.

"Oh yes. I've been a member of the faculty for several years." Then in an even softer tone, he continued. "You can be quite at ease here. You see, I am indeed very interested in hearing of your Holocaust project and our discussions can only be seen as academic in nature, because that is precisely what they are. So again, welcome to Gdansk. Now, please, tell me your plans. I understand you will be interviewing two people here in Gdansk."

"They are in Gdynia, actually," said Adam, "and I am meeting them tomorrow after 10:00 o'clock Mass at St. Michael Archangel."

"You'll love Gdynia. The seashore is right there and it's gorgeous, even at this time of year. Take the SKM train to Kosciuszki Square. It should take twenty-five minutes or so. If you arrive about fifteen minutes early, you can walk to the church. But, please, I am extremely anxious to hear of your project."

Adam paused to realign his thoughts away from the $6,000 envelope and toward his Holocaust project. Then, over a fifteen minute period, he outlined his plans punctuated by questions from Ivan Tusk. As always when he was placed in the position of explaining his project to an informed and interested party, he found himself circling back to the questions which he could not answer to his own satisfaction.

Why am I really here in Poland? Do I truly expect to help the Jewish people or the Pope or did I simply come here to escape the horror of what happened in San Francisco?

"You're certainly helping the Pope."

After a moment, Adam realized that Ivan Tusk had spoken.

"I'm sorry. I was lost in my thoughts for a moment. What did you say?"

"Yes, you did look rather distant. I said that you're certainly helping the Pope."

"I hope so."

"No need merely to hope. It's true that you're here to interview two people. But your primary business here is that of the Pope."

"That's true," said Adam thinking that now they had arrived at the real purpose of his trip to Gdansk.

"I have to say, however, if you will forgive my candor, that I am less certain how you will help Jews. No doubt you do see clearly how this will occur and I simply am insufficiently familiar with your plan."

"No. I too am uncertain how good will occur from my work with these people. When I expressed my doubts to the Pope, he said only that the Holy Spirit was guiding me."

"That is as good an explanation as any. After all, when Solidarity began eight years ago, no one could have predicted that it would even be in existence today, let alone still calling strikes to compel a more civil society. Sometimes one simply must have faith, which brings us to the purpose of our meeting. Do you have the money with you?"

"I do. It's in a large manila envelope in my briefcase. But, before we go further, is it possible for you to tell me how it will be used?"

"I can't give you precise details because I do not know them. In general, however, the money will be used for propaganda. This would be propaganda in the positive sense, as in the propagation of ideas — good ideas of individual freedom as opposed to communist ideas of statism, totalitarianism and subrogation of the individual. This money is spent on mundane items such as word processors, copy machines, and small printing presses. We follow the Pope's example. It has been literally a godsend to Solidarity."

"How so?"

"This Pope — our Pope — visits us regularly and his message is immutable. So too is the message of Solidarity. We, like John Paul II are relentless but never violent. The communists know how to deal with violent efforts to change. Hungary is but one example. Even now, eight years after Solidarity's founding, we remind ourselves that Soviet tanks were massed on our borders. Just one violent incident during the initial strikes would have been all the excuse the communists needed to invade. Solidarity would have died in its cradle."

Adam smiled to himself and as he did so, Ivan Tusk stopped speaking.

"I'm sorry. I must be boring you. This must seem like ancient history to a citizen of the United States."

"No. Quite the contrary. Your passion reminds me how special our freedoms are and how easy it is to take them for granted. Here the struggle is a daily reality and the danger always is immediate."

"Yes indeed. The slightest misstep and Gorbachev could be forced to send in troops. I have to remind myself every day to take inspiration from the younger generation — people like my nephew Donald. He had barely taken his degree in 1980, right here at this university, although in history rather than law. He was extremely active in the founding of Solidarity — practically a co-founder along with Lech. Now, however, he's already moving beyond Solidarity into the creation of a free market economy. He says we've already won — that the communists simply lack the ideas to prevail over ten million people with better ideas."

"I hope he's right," said Adam.

"As do I," said Ivan Tush. "Now, I have another class at noon, so let us proceed with our required tradecraft. After we part, please use the toilet on your way out. Leave the envelope under a layer of paper towels in the waste bin. I will tarry here for a few moments with some reading from my own briefcase and then also visit the toilet on the way to my next lecture."

Ivan Tush now rose from his chair and extended his hand once again. Speaking again at almost the same volume as when he initially entered the library, he addressed Adam.

"Father Thelen. I am extremely pleased to have become acquainted with you and I genuinely hope to see you again in the future. Good luck on your endeavors!"

"And the same to you in yours," Adam responded as he shook the man's hand.

Adam departed, stopping to visit the toilet as instructed by Ivan Tusk. He spent the remainder of the day exploring the newly restored yet historic Old Town of Gdansk and familiarizing himself with the nearest stop of the SKM train he would be taking to Gdynia in the morning.

CHAPTER 27

Sunday, February 21, 1988

ADAM HAD DECIDED the previous evening to arrive in Gdynia by 9:00 a.m. to allow time for a brief exploration of the city. Consequently, he was up at 6:30. After a small breakfast at the hotel, he set out for the train stop about a ten minute walk away. He was dressed in his standard priestly garb except for a heavier jacket over his black coat. It was a rather blustery day in the mid-30s. He carried his briefcase with the usual interview materials, including a small cassette recording device.

Gdynia, when he arrived at Kosciuszki Square, was every bit as beautiful as Ivan Tusk had represented. Adam strolled along the seashore admiring the sights and then made his way to St. Michael Archangel Church. He was glad to arrive twenty minutes before the 10:00 o'clock Mass and to watch everyone file in. At first, he tried to examine each new arrival and determine which ones might be Father Pilsudski's siblings. As 10:00 a.m. approached, however, the numbers became too great as a steady stream of faithful filed into the church. Poland was, indeed, a Catholic country.

The Mass began promptly at 10:00 and, of course, followed the liturgical tradition of two millennia, albeit with certain changes; the most notable was the use of the native language, Polish, as championed by Pope John XXIII. Adam let it wash over him, feeling a sense of comfort. Thus, he was caught unawares when the priest, following the Gospel, began his homily. Adam was drifting, allowing the familiarity of the Mass to dull the unfamiliarity, and discomfort, of being in a foreign land and about to undertake an endeavor filled with uncertainty. Suddenly, he sat bolt upright.

The priest was speaking the words of John Paul II, from his homilies during the U.S. tour, the same homilies to which Adam had paid rapt attention as he tried to relate the Pope's English to the Polish translation he held before him at the various sites at which the Pope had spoken. The Pope's themes were there in their entirety and in many cases the language was identical to the Polish translations which Adam had been given.

Individual freedom... individual dignity... God given rights... Never abandon the struggle.

Adam knew in that moment that the same homilies were being given throughout Poland, week after week, underlining and reinforcing the message of Solidarity.

Why have I not thought to go out into the Churches of Krakow, and of surrounding cities and villages, instead of staying within the insular confines of Ignatianum and UJ. The Pope's message and the message of Solidarity are one and the same!

When the Mass ended, Adam joined the throng exiting the church and then, as arranged with Father Pilsudski reentered the church and sat in the last pew, his Roman collar evident.

"Father Thelen."

Adam turned and saw a man and woman standing in the aisle. The man was a carbon copy of Father Pilsudski aged about ten years, but he'd never have taken the woman to be related to him. She appeared to be younger rather than older than Father Pilsudski. Her eyes were green and she had light colored hair. She was beautiful now and must have been stunningly so as a younger woman — a classic Slavic face, yet not.

"Yes I am. You must be Father Pilsudski's brother and sister."

"We are. I am Mick Pilsudski and this is my sister Trude," said the man.

"Thank you for seeing me," said Adam. "I am more grateful than you know to have the opportunity to speak with you."

"Father, we are at least as interested in speaking with you as you are in interviewing us."

Again the man, Mick Pilsudski, had spoken. Thus far Trude had said nothing but clearly she was watching Adam carefully and listening to every word he said.

"Please come with us, Father. Our apartment is nearby."

They walked for about five minutes before arriving at a three-story apartment building located two blocks from the Baltic Sea. The building appeared to be fairly new and well maintained. They entered the lobby of the building and then the elevator. Mick Pilsudski pressed the button for the third floor, and they began to ascend. Mick had made small talk during the five minute walk and pointed out some of the sights. Trude still had said nothing.

The apartment was modest yet well appointed with two bedrooms and two bathrooms. It was at the rear of the building with a view over another building to the sea. The kitchen, dining and living areas comprised one large room at the center of the apartment, with a bedroom on either side.

"This is lovely," said Adam, "and the view is enthralling. You must never tire of it."

"The view is striking. You're right in calling it enthralling. The light on the water constantly is changing. I find myself watching it for extended periods. But, please sit down. May we offer you anything. Tea perhaps. We also have pastry and fruit."

"A cup of tea would be wonderful," said Adam.

"Upon hearing Adam's request, Trude went to the kitchen and busied herself with the ritual of preparing tea, while Mick and Adam engaged in further small talk. After a few moments Trude emerged from the kitchen and placed a tray with three small mugs and a pot of tea on the low table between Adam's chair and the small sofa upon which Mick was seated. She then seated herself on the sofa next to her brother. When all three had taken a mug of tea — Adam's black, Mick's and Trude's with milk added from a small pitcher — Mick spoke.

"How do you wish to proceed, Father? We are available to you for the remainder of the day and we would be pleased if you would join us for an early dinner out. There's a decent café nearby which is open on Sunday evenings. Unfortunately, each of us will be working tomorrow but we assume you wish to take the train back to Gdansk following dinner anyway."

"That sounds like a good schedule, Mr. Pilsudski."

"Please call us by our given names, Father, and do tell us how you conduct these interviews."

"Well, there is no set pattern since you are the first people I have interviewed. If you are willing, I suggest you simply tell me the story of your lives, during World War II and in the years before and since. I'd like to take notes and ask questions as you speak. May I use this cassette recorder to make a record of our discussions to which I can refer later as needed?"

"The recorder is fine, Father," said Mick Pilsudski, who then paused to collect his thoughts. "Any account of our lives before, during and after World War II must begin with our father,

Tomasz. He was a Jew born in Gdansk in 1900. He grew up here in the tri-city and went to work in the shipyards when he was eighteen. After fifteen years helping to build ships he hadn't married but he had developed an urge to travel. So, in 1933, just as Hitler was coming to power in Germany, he signed on as a seaman on one of the newly commissioned ships leaving the Gdansk docks for the first time. He sailed around European and African ports for over three years and even got to the United States on two occasions, both times to Baltimore, Maryland. Then, early in 1936, his ship docked in Dublin, Ireland. By this time our father was second mate. So, when one of the seamen from his ship was injured in a barroom brawl, Father took him to a local hospital for treatment. There, in the emergency room, he met a young nurse who was assigned to suture the seaman's face. This was the woman he would marry and who would become our mother."

"Was this woman from Dublin or elsewhere in Ireland?"

"She was born and raised in Dublin and her name was Mary. She was twenty-four years old when Father met her and she was betrothed to another. No matter. When our father's ship sailed, he was not on it. He stayed in Dublin and courted our mother. The courtship lasted until October, but ultimately Father won our mother away from her betrothed husband. I'm sure you can imagine the tensions and hard feelings which arose when a Polish Jew proposed marriage to an Irish Catholic. We could spend the rest of this interview telling those stories. Suffice to say, they were married in Ireland after our father agreed that any children of the union would be raised as Catholics. They returned to Gdansk and our father was true to his word. I was born in late 1937 and Trude arrived in the summer of 1939."

"Both of us were raised as Catholics by our mother and our father was very supportive, even accompanying us to Mass on

Sunday. According to my mother those were happy years. But the Germans came in September of 1939 and the repression of Jews began in earnest. Our father felt that we would be much safer if he left and he was right. As you know, Judaism flows from the maternal side of a marital union and our mother was a practicing Catholic, as were we, although we were too young to know. Our father fled Gdansk and joined the Polish Armed Forces in the West. The Germans viewed us — my mother and sister and me that is — as Christians and as far as we know, never learned that our missing father was Jewish. Thus, we were not rounded up and sent to Jewish ghettoes and thence to the concentration camps. That's not to say that life was peaceful. Gdansk was being bombed to rubble by the Allies. That's why we moved out here to Gdynia, where the bombing was less severe. Things continued like this until 1943 when, we later learned, Father was captured by the Germans, who discovered he was Jewish. He was sent first to the Warsaw ghetto and then to Auschwitz Birkenau. He survived until the Russians liberated the camp in 1944. He made his way home and rejoined us. Physically, he recovered here with us and our mother became pregnant with our younger brother late in 1944. But, in other ways he could not recover. I remember that he would sit for hours and stare out to sea. Our mother later told us that he felt an enormous guilt at having survived when the vast majority at Birkenau died from the gas or from hard labor and starvation. Apparently, he was one of the Jews assigned to guide new arrivals into the gas chambers. The Germans systematically killed these so called guides every sixty days, so he would have died had not the Russian liberation intervened. In any event, he never recovered from the experience and he simply died when our mother was six months pregnant. Our brother was born in the summer of 1945. She raised us to the best of her ability until 1948 when she too died. The doctors said our father probably died of some kind of stroke, but they never were clear as to the cause of our mother's death."

"She died of grief, Michael, as well you know."

These were the first words spoken by Trude Pilsudski since Adam had met her at St. Michael Archangel Church. Having spoken these words she once again lapsed into silence.

"You may be right, Trude, but we'll never know for certain. But it is certain that we three surviving siblings were very fortunate indeed. We were placed in a Catholic orphanage and allowed to remain together. They educated us and then in the early 50's Trude and I began to take a more active role in the daily operation of the orphanage. We stayed there until 1955 when I was seventeen and was able to go to work in the shipyards as a common laborer. As soon as I could afford it, I took a small apartment near the orphanage. Trude and our little brother began to visit me regularly. Soon enough they were spending most of their non-school time there. As soon as we demonstrated our ability to function as a family unit the orphanage allowed them to move permanently into the apartment. Of course, both of them continued to help with the children. This was our situation until 1962, when our little brother joined the Army. He left us then not only in a physical sense but philosophically as well."

"What do you mean by 'philosophically'?" asked Adam.

"Well, he became a communist and as with everything he did, he threw himself into it. He proved himself to be both ambitious and intelligent. They educated him further and he became a commissioned officer in 1966. It was a dark time for Trude and me."

"How so?" asked Adam.

"Our little brother was a communist and there were no half measures for him. We saw very little of him but we heard of some of what he did. Thank God he met Cardinal Wojtyla, now our Polish Pope."

"When did that occur?"

Mick Pilsudski described his brother's meeting with Cardinal Wojtyla in 1975 as a fluke which occurred only because of the Cardinal's intercession. Major Pilsudski had attended one of Cardinal Wojtyla's Masses in Nowa Huta. He was there with some of his men to hear the Cardinal's message and then meet with his superiors to plot counter measures. The Cardinal noticed his presence and sent one of his priests with a discreet invitation to meet with the Cardinal in Krakow.

"Soon thereafter Major Pilsudski embarked on the journey which would transform him to Father Pilsudski."

"That's a wonderful story Mick and your earlier history as a family is extraordinary. The three of you were very fortunate not only to survive but to remain together in a relatively safe environment. It's quite clear that both your father and mother died as a direct and proximate result of the Holocaust. Can you tell me how that has affected your lives and that of Father Pilsudski? How do you live with the painful knowledge that some of the perpetrators of the Holocaust escaped and are alive even today?"

Mick, at least for a moment, was nonplussed. Trude, on the other hand merely looked thoughtful. To Adam's great surprise, Trude was the first to speak.

"We kill them," she said.

"Trude . . ."

"No Michael, it's all right. I've watched this man and listened carefully to him and I agree with Padraig. He is a good man, although an innocent."

Now it was Adam's turn to be nonplussed. He was flummoxed and had very little notion of what to say. Finally, he gave voice to the first question which had come to his mind while Trude was speaking.

"Who is Padraig?"

Mick and Trude looked at each other in puzzlement and Trude actually smiled.

"Padraig is our brother. I thought you knew him," said Mick.

"Padraig is Father Pilsudski's given name?"

"Yes, it is. Since we were being raised in the Catholic Church, Mother thought that we should have good Irish names. I am Michael, as you have heard, although I'm usually called Mick. Trude is really Trudy. And Padraig is...Padraig, although some in the orphanage tried to call him Paddy. It did not go well for them. How is it that you do not know our brother's name?"

"No one knows his first name — at least no one that I have met. He is known simply as Father Pilsudski. Now that I think about it, I assume the Pope knows his full name but I never thought to ask him."

"You've met the Pope?" asked Mick.

Adam immediately regretted his mention of the Pope. He was concerned that his reference to John Paul would distract Mick and Trude from the central purpose of the interview. Worse, he feared that it could be construed by Mick and Trude as blatant name dropping on his part. He quickly described his audience with the Pope in San Francisco, making it sound like a routine encounter.

"I am merely a minor player trying to help the Pope achieve his greater goals. I'm positive that your brother is and will continue to be a far more important actor in the Pope's drama. Father Pilsudski certainly has made a very distinct impression on me. He is a very imposing figure. But please let us return to the interview. Trude, what did you mean when you said you kill them? Do you mean that you somehow bury your pain?"

"No Father, what I meant was what I said. We kill the perpetrators of the Holocaust. Before he died Father gave our mother a list of six names. He described to her what these six people did at Birkenau. He believed that better times were coming to Poland and that the six people on his list would be brought to justice."

Mick took a sip of tea while his sister was speaking and then continued. "Our mother gave the list to us shortly before she died. We were just children but we kept the list along with the memory of our parents. Of course, Padraig had no memory of his father and only a faint recall of his mother's touch. Trude and I reinforced our own memories and created new memories for Padraig by retelling the stories of our childhood. Some of those stories were of the horrors perpetrated at Birkenau by the beasts on our father's list. Father told our mother and she, with misgivings, told Trude and me shortly before she died. She simply could not live with the horror. First it took our father and then our mother."

Adam found himself thinking of Father Pilsudski — his father dead before his birth, his mother gone barely three years later. Then, as he was in his most formative years, learning why they died and hearing the stories retold over and over. In this new light, Father Pilsudski's furtive, mysterious and secretive ways were far more understandable.

"Those stories must have been difficult to tell and to hear for such a long time — more than a decade."

"The stories were difficult and they were told for almost fifteen years, until Padraig left," said Trude. "Of course, they were most difficult for Padraig. He rejected Catholicism as soon as he was able and declared himself to be Jewish, because that's what his father was and that's why his father and mother died. Then when he went into the army, he became a communist of the most brutal sort. Now he is a Catholic, a militant member of the Pope's army. I hope that he finds peace before he dies."

Trude's mention of "finding peace" struck a chord somewhere deep within Adam and he was tempted to abandon the interview and pursue this new emotion. But he suppressed this urge and returned his thoughts to Mick and Trude.

"All right. Trude, you say that you kill the perpetrators of the Holocaust. Am I to take this literally?"

"Please erase your recording back to my first statement and then turn the recorder off," said Trude.

Adam did as requested and then turned back to Trude.

"My statement is the literal truth. Father left us a list of six names, along with a brief description of each person. There were five men and one woman. All of them now are dead except one man, but he was the first, and worst, on Father's list. Padraig finds these people and then Mick and I travel to each person's locale, usually more than once, and learn all that we can of the person's habits, movements — everything. Then we make our plan. In each case, even the woman, I have been the hunter — the one who lures them and then entraps them. In all but one case the bait has been sex and that was true also with the woman. The one exception was a sociopath who saw me as merely another person he could destroy, yet another victim."

"So, you... kill them," said Adam.

"Father, I don't know how to be any more clear. Yes, we've killed five of the six and we continue to search for the last man. Do you wish to know the details of each killing?"

Adam paused and thought before answering. He was shocked and his thoughts were disorganized. Again, he was unsure what to say next.

"How, how do you reconcile this with your Catholicism?" he asked haltingly.

"We no longer are Catholics and, therefore, do not reconcile our actions with the tenets of Christianity," said Trude. "We both converted to Judaism in the late 50s. We met you at St. Michael Archangel but did not attend Mass. We much prefer the God of the Torah — a God of mercy, but also a God of power and one capable of anger. We are doubtful that Jesus would approve of us or what we have done."

"I don't know what to say…I am shocked," said Adam.

"You are shocked." said Trude coldly, almost mockingly.

"Trudy. . ." said Mick imploringly.

"No! I will speak. I am merely a nurse whereas you, according to our brother, are not only a priest but the holder of doctoral degrees in law and in psychology. So, I hope you understand that we have confronted our trauma and at least mitigated its effects. Otherwise, we would be eternally fearful that similarly unspeakable events would befall us, especially under this hateful communist regime. But what about you? Why are you, a Catholic priest, interviewing Jews one generation removed from the Holocaust?"

Adam again was discomfited, but he managed to suppress his emotions and to rally his thoughts.

"PTSD, that is Post Traumatic Stress Disorder, was only identified in 1980 after years of studying veterans of the Vietnam War. I am a member of the DSM Work Group for Anxiety Disorders, with which I suspect you are familiar. My theory, which I hope to validate by means of these interviews, is that family members of trauma victims can suffer severe adverse effects from a trauma they did not directly experience."

"Lucidly and concisely stated, Father" said Trude. "I am positive what you say is true. I am equally positive that it is not relevant to your presence here with us and other Holocaust victims. I ask again, what about you, Father — you personally?"

Of course, it's the old adage: "None so blind as they who will not see." I'm here studying myself and my own trauma.

As these thoughts coursed through Adam's mind, he also recalled Trude's reference to "finding peace." He tried to collect himself and failed utterly. He began to cry and continued to do so for fully two minutes before he was able to speak again. When he could speak he launched into a full and complete account of his experiences in San Francisco culminating in the killing of Father Kung.

"I see clearly now. I am here for myself— for my own search for peace. I may cause some incremental improvement in the treatment of Holocaust families less strong than you and Mick, but my primary motivation is pure self-interest. I am not only selfish but also narcissistic."

"You are neither selfish nor a narcissist," said Trude. "You are like us — a person who has experienced horror beyond one's own control. You are — again like us — seeking to deal with the horror as functionally as possible. Surely you are aware that many others who are similarly afflicted have reacted far less functionally, with predatory acts, substance abuse, debilitating depression and an array of related counterproductive activities."

"I am aware but... murder?"

"Mick, do you see Father Thelen's actions as murder?" asked Trude.

"No, I do not," said Mick, "although I do not presume to be an expert in this area."

"Nor do I but I claim no more expertise than you," said Trude. After a moment she continued. "We thank you. You are very gracious. Now, I think the interview is at an end and we probably needn't go out to dinner. I suspect each of us has much to contemplate this evening and for several evenings to come."

"You're right Trude. I need to be alone for a while. Please accept my thanks and please let us talk again," said Adam.

"We would welcome the opportunity to speak again with you. Do you not agree Mick?"

"I fully agree, if for no other reason than to speak further concerning Padraig. He is the one suffering the most pain."

"That is true," said Trude. "Perhaps you will find a way to bring some peace into his life."

"I will try Trude, but he is not easily approached."

"Both of us know that. We have tried and failed."

At this, Adam gathered his interview materials, made his farewells and was leaving the apartment when Trude spoke again.

"Adam, I wonder if you see the connection between your Holocaust studies and your other efforts, which Padraig has described to us, to help the Pope achieve his goals of personal freedom, dignity and justice. This is a topic which perhaps we can discuss more fully when next we meet."

Adam caught the evening train back to Gdansk and then took a taxi to his hotel. When he reached his room, he tried to consider all that had occurred but instead fell into a deep and dreamless sleep.

Monday, February 22, 1988

Adam caught the first train to Krakow and spent the day traversing Poland from the Northwest to the Southeast. He was oblivious to the scenery outside the window and negotiated the requisite change of trains in Warsaw like an automaton. When he arrived in Krakow late that night, he walked directly from the train station to Ignatianum and went to bed. He slept soundly and dreamt graphically. In truth, the dream likely occurred only two or three times during the night, but when Adam awoke in the morning he recalled it as an endless loop playing remorselessly. In the dream he saw a speeding car leave the road and become airborne after striking a small mound of sand. The car rose spiraling slowly and then gracefully descended, still spiraling, nose first into the sandy wasteland. It lay there for a moment, motionless except for the slowly rotating wheels, and appeared not to be badly damaged. The figure inside the car was clearly visible, attempting to open the door and escape. Finally, a small tendril of flame appeared and quickly blossomed to envelope the entire car along with its occupant still seeking fruitlessly to free herself.

CHAPTER 28

Tuesday – Thursday, February 23-25, 1988

WHEN ADAM AROSE in the morning, he went about his usual routines mindlessly with one exception. Before leaving Ignatianum and walking across Old Town to UJ, he slid a note under the door to "Stepan's" quarters.

"We should meet. I will be at your office at 10:00 a.m. on Wednesday, Thursday and Friday."

The note contained no salutation and no signature. Upon his arrival at UJ he walked up to Father Pilsudski's office and, after checking to insure the hallways were empty, slid a similar note under that door. He also tried the door but it was, as expected, locked.

On Wednesday and Thursday, precisely at 10:00 a.m., Adam walked to Father Pilsudski's office, checked the hallways, knocked on the door and tried the knob. On each occasion there was no response and the door remained locked.

Friday, February 26, 1988

On Friday morning as he approached Father Pilsudski's door, Adam saw that it was cracked open, with perhaps a quarter inch space between the door and the jamb. He pushed the door open and entered, softly closing the door behind him. The office was austere, almost ascetic, furnished only with a battered round table, two wooden chairs, a bookcase on one wall and a locked steel four drawer filing cabinet. Father Pilsudski was seated in one of the chairs with an open file on the table in front of him. As Adam entered Father Pilsudski closed the file and gestured for Adam to seat himself in the other chair.

"Your tradecraft is improving" said Father Pilsudski. "The note you left is admirably brief and lacking in identifying detail. Still, the safest meeting is no meeting at all and I see no need for this one. You would be well advised to allow me to arrange all future meetings, just as I have done in the past."

"That would be so, were I one of the agents you are running."

"Ah, so you think yourself somehow superior to a man like Ivan Tusk."

"Decidedly not. Ivan Tusk is a true patriot. As a Polish national, he is putting himself and his family at great peril should his activities be discovered. I am simply an idealistic Catholic priest from the United States. If I am discovered the worst that will occur is deportation and being used as a tool to embarrass either the Pope or the President, or both."

"You're right about all that. Still, there is no real justification for this meeting. I already know that the money transfer went smoothly. One of those men loitering in the library works for the movement. He saw you enter the toilet and then he went in and guarded the money until Ivan had picked it up. You probably thought he was a communist operative about to arrest you."

Adam smiled at Father Pilsudski's last comment but did not acknowledge that his speculation was true.

"Everything I said about Ivan Tusk's patriotism and his peril is true for you also, Father," said Adam.

"Don't worry about me, Father Thelen. Besides, we're well on our way to winning. In a year or two all of this cloak and dagger nonsense will be a relic of the past. In the Roundtable Discussions, there's been talk of free elections as early as next year, although the term 'free' always is relative with the communists."

"You sound like Donald Tusk. His uncle Ivan says that Donald already has moved beyond Solidarity and is directing his efforts toward the creation of a free and open economy in Poland."

"Donald Tusk is a rare combination of visionary and pragmatist. He took some extraordinary risks in 1980 when Solidarity was being formed and he also kept Lech focused on the big picture. Without Donald, Lech likely would have settled for much less. The communists never should have let him live. They couldn't simply kill Lech Walesa without widespread turmoil, but a young man just out of school like Donald Tusk could easily have disappeared. If I were still in the army at that time, he would have disappeared. Perhaps God does work in strange ways."

"God saw you as a useful addition to His army and, through His Pope, drafted you."

"A facile Play on words." said Father Pilsudski. "Amusing but not worth the risk of this meeting. If you're here to tell me of your meeting with my brother and sister, I've already heard from them also. As I suspected, Trude judged you worthy of trust and she and Mick confided in you. I hope you were able to advance your studies and that their secret will be safe with you."

"Their secret, which is yours as well, is safe and will remain so. And their story — your story also — was extremely valuable in broadening my understanding of the potential scope and impact of trauma. But, did they also relate to you the story which I shared with them?"

"No, they did not. They alluded to your story but said that only you could choose whether to tell it to me. Have we now finally reached the true purpose of our meeting here today?"

"We have indeed, Father Pilsudski."

Adam proceeded to relate to Father Pilsudski the entire story from the previous year culminating in the deaths of Father Kung and the Weasel and of Lorena and their unborn child. Unlike his story to Mick and Trude, which was fraught with emotion, this telling was calm and dispassionate. He felt himself to be an observer witnessing, as if for the first time, the initial and ongoing effect of these events on this fool known as Father Adam Thelen.

I am a selfish and craven creature seeking only surcease of his own suffering, heedless of the pain he has caused to others and of his own immorality.

When he finished the story he sat quietly pondering again how his actions had brought him here to Poland, supposedly to help others, but truly to anesthetize his own pain. The sound of Father Pilsudski's voice returned Adam to reality.

"That is a useful allegory and I suppose it justifies our meeting. You are not as great a naif as I thought."

"Hardly an allegory. Every word I spoke is the literal truth. These events actually occurred and I really killed a man."

"Oh, I understand that your story is true, yet it also is allegorical in that it can be taken as a symbolic representation of human conduct in times of extreme stress."

"Symbolic representation? I killed a real man made of real flesh and blood. I am a monster!"

"Really, Father, don't give yourself too much credit. You executed a man who had forfeited the right to continue living. May God, if He chooses, have mercy on his soul. More important were the actions of your friend Michael Burke who not only killed the other piece of slime but also had the presence of mind to save you from simply surrendering to the police. Had that occurred, I would not be enjoying your company here today. I very much would like to meet Mr. Burke."

"Stranger things have happened, Father. Perhaps you will have such an opportunity."

"I suppose you believe, since you now have a fuller understanding of the source of your anger at Father Kung, that you will not revisit a similar anger in the future."

"I believe, at least, that I'm through killing people."

At this, Father Pilsudski merely smiled. He arose from his chair and went to the wooden bookcase where he searched for a moment and then extracted two books. He returned to the table, seated himself and handed the books to Adam.

"I suggest you check the indexes of these two books and then read the parts of each dealing with the ritual of the Passover Seder. When do you meet with the Rabbi at the Old Synagogue?"

"I'll be meeting with him every day next week, not including Saturday, of course, for three hours each morning. By the way, I learned from my father that Rabbi Eliyahu and the Rebbe, Rabbi Menachem Schneerson of Brooklyn, are friends."

"That's good intelligence, Father. Your father seems to be very well informed. You also should know that it was the Rebbe who last year requested that communal public Seders be held throughout Israel."

"My father works quite hard to be informed. He also mentioned that one of John Paul's initiatives is to create greater harmony between Catholicism and Judaism. So, as usual with this Pope, my visit, if I'm able to make a good impression, could help both the Pope's agenda and my own Holocaust work."

"The Pope has many agendas and he no doubt realized your potential usefulness well before your audience with him in San Francisco. But, back to your father for a moment. Has he heard anything more about the Spektors?"

"Yes. Max Spektor has launched a media campaign to establish himself as a major supporter of Solidarity. Meanwhile, his son George is having clandestine discussions with people in Poland and other parts of the world."

"Can you tell me the names of the people in Poland with whom he is speaking?"

"Not at this point. But my mother is coming to Poland right after Easter partly to visit me and partly to check with some of her sources. What's certain is that Max and George Spektor have sinister intentions and all this favorable press about supporting Solidarity is just a front."

"Your mother is coming to Poland? To delve into the activities of the Spektors?"

"Don't sound so amazed. My mother, as well as my father's ex-wife, are principals in the investment banking firm. My mother already was instrumental in mitigating some of the damage from another of the Spektors' plots, this one in Ghana."

"This ex-wife—Is she the mother of your half-brother in New York, the one who helped you with Father Edmond?"

"Yes, she is. Theo is twenty-two years older than I."

"You have quite an unusual and accomplished family. I look forward to hearing whatever intelligence your mother is able to glean here in Poland, or elsewhere for that matter. Incidentally, since we're on the topic of Father Edmond, I should mention that you no longer need fear further predations on his part."

"How so?"

"He is dead. As promised, two of my people have kept him under irregular but very overt surveillance. Apparently, Father Edmond grew tired of this. He packed his few belongings and boarded a train headed for the Czech border. My men were in the same car with him and were prepared to let him go. As we discussed, I could only guarantee that he would not prey on children again in Poland. We did not undertake to follow him outside of Poland, so my men were prepared to see him across the border and make sure that he took up residence elsewhere. They then would have returned to Poland. But, at the last Polish town before the border, Father Edmond disembarked from the train. He had his bag with him and he walked out of town with my men following him. When they reached a deserted stretch of road, he set down his bag and removed a gun. He then advanced toward my men with the gun in his hand. We have no idea where he obtained it. In any event, my men drew their own guns and ordered him to stop and lay down his weapon. Instead, be began firing and my men had no choice but to kill him. They took his gun and also his wallet so that it would appear as a robbery. They left him at the side of the road and took the next train back into Poland."

"My God!" said Adam.

"Yes. It is shocking and very strange also. Father Edmond shot twice before my men killed him and both bullets were aimed well over their heads. They believe he simply wanted to die."

+ + +

That afternoon when he returned to Ignatianum, he asked Father Jakub and Father Stan to join him in town for dinner. They went to Balaton, the same restaurant to which Adam had been introduced by Father Stan. Food rationing in Krakow seemed to be easing somewhat and Balaton now was able to open four days a week. Adam waited until they had finished dinner and were enjoying the last of their wine. He then told them the story of Father Edmond's death. Both Father Jakub and Father Stan sat in somber silence. Finally, Father Jakub spoke.

"It seems clear that Father Edmond no longer could live with his guilt. Let us hope that he somehow made peace with God before his death. I shall pray for the salvation of his soul."

"As will both of us," said Adam.

"Yes, of course," said Father Stan. "But what of the students he preyed upon? Shall we tell them of Father Edmond's death?"

"I think we shall," said Father Jakub. "But let each of us consider how best to do that and then meet again before we take any action.

CHAPTER 29

Monday, February 29, 1988

"AND YOU SHALL tell your child on that day. It is because of what the Lord did for me when I came out of Egypt." Exodus 13:8

Adam had spent his first morning with Rabbi Malina at the Old Synagogue. Rabbi Malina appeared to be approximately seventy years of age. He had explained to Adam his parents' fortuitous decision to emigrate from Kazimierz in 1936 and resettle in Brooklyn.

"I was seventeen years old in 1936 and I did not want to leave here. In fact, I had decided to stay here and live with my uncle's family and continue my rabbinical education. Five days before my father and mother were to depart, my father came to me and begged me to reconsider. He described to me his ghastly premonition regarding Adolf Hitler and what he believed was in store for the Jews of eastern Europe. My father's conviction was so strong that I did reconsider. I went to Brooklyn and became a part of the Jewish community there, which proved to be at least as vibrant as the one here before the Germans came."

"What of the extended family you left behind?" asked Adam as gently as possible.

"All gone. Neither my parents nor I could locate a single survivor after the war. We received letters until mid-1940 and then — nothing. My parents became fairly successful in the United States but they refused to move from their original apartment in the hope that a letter would arrive or that someone would show up on their stoop. My father died in 1978 and still my mother stayed in that apartment. She died there three years ago. That's when I came back here."

"You must know the Rebbe if you grew up and became a rabbi in Brooklyn."

"I do know him! He's the one who nurtured my return here after my mother died. He wants very much to recreate the Jewish communities in Poland which were extinguished by the Holocaust. I'm not sure that ever will occur. Kazimierz certainly has rebounded and more Jewish tourists are coming every year but this simply is no longer a Jewish community. Perhaps your Holocaust studies will help."

Adam and the rabbi then had begun their study of Passover and of the Passover Seder during which the children of each family are asked the traditional question...

"Ma nishtanah ha lyla ha zeh mikkol hallaylot?"

("Why is this night different from all other nights?")

They had studied the basics of the Seder including the four cups, symbolizing the four expressions of God's deliverance in Exodus as well as the four matriarchs — Sarah, Rebeccah, Rachel and Leah — and the three matzot symbolizing the three patriarchs — Abraham, Isaac and Jacob. As the week progressed they would delve further into Haggadah, Mishnah and some of the Talmudic commentaries.

+ + +

Now it was 9:00 in the evening and Adam was calling Theo in the Bronx.

"Theo, am I catching you at a good time? Can you talk?"

"Adam, I have someone in my office but we're just concluding our conversation. Let me call you back in five minutes."

"That will be fine, Theo."

Adam spent the time considering the purpose of his call, which was to tell his half-brother of Father Edmond's death, and also pondering the question of how best to tell the three students. When the phone rang, he still had no good answer.

"Hello Theo. I apologize for interrupting what no doubt is a busy Monday afternoon."

"It is busy, Adam but not one of the supposedly urgent issues I'm deciding is of any import whatever. Your call is a welcome break. What's on your mind?"

"I wanted to tell you about Father Edmond."

Adam then repeated Father Pilsudski's account of Father Edmond's death including the impression of Father Pilsudski's men that Father Edmond wanted to be killed.

"Of course, I've told Father Stan and Father Jakub," said Adam, "and they are praying for his soul. As am I," added Adam almost as an afterthought. "We're also trying to figure out whether to tell the three boys and, if so, how best to do it."

"Yes, there is that," said Theo, "and I too will pray for Father Edmond's soul, but…"

"But what, Theo?"

"Well, Adam, I know it may sound heartless, but I believe Father Edmond's death may be for the best."

"How so, Theo?"

"I'm hearing more and more rumors concerning this type of child abuse. It's mostly among parish priests. I've heard nothing within the Order. With us, it's mostly women and alcohol."

"Hey, I'm one for two — not bad at all," said Adam.

"I'm glad to hear that you retain your roguish sense of humor. But this problem in the parishes and the parish schools is serious. It's bad enough that it seems to be happening. What's worse is that it's being suppressed. The bishops and cardinals are simply shuffling priests who fall under suspicion to another parish. At least we know Father Edmond will no longer prey on children and teenagers."

Friday, March 4, 1988

Once again George Spektor was in his bedroom. It was 3:00 a.m.

The old fart really is losing it. We form the NGO and give it a great name — Dignitas et Libertas — and the liberal jerk-offs love it. They think it really is about dignity and freedom. We collect almost a quarter million dollars in donations in the first six weeks and now Father Dearest is making noises that we really ought to spend the money in support of pipe dreams like Solidarity. Really the old fool is just enamored of the phony media image we're creating of him as Hero of the Downtrodden and Depressed. What a crock of shit. Cutting him out of the planning for the actual Solidarity gambit was the right decision.

CHAPTER 30

Monday, April 13, 1988

"**M**OM! OVER HERE."
Adam had ridden the train and then taken the short shuttle bus ride to the Balice Airport, about ten kilometers from the train station near Krakow's City Center. He had been waiting in the International Arrivals area for about twenty minutes for his mother to clear customs. Now she finally had emerged. She made her way to him and then they were hugging each other. Adam had been looking forward to his mother's visit but not until this moment did he realize how much he had missed her.

"Oh Adam, I'm so happy to see you! Are you well?"

"I'm very well Mom and I'm absolutely delighted to see you. Welcome to Krakow. How was your flight?"

"Not bad at all. I flew from San Francisco to New York two days ago and spent some time in the New York office. I took the red eye from New York last night and it left on time and arrived on time. You can't ask for much more than that."

It now was just after noon in Krakow. As they made their way to the luggage carousel. Adam again marveled at his degree

276

of happiness at seeing his mother for the first time in over six months.

"How many bags, mom?"

"Just one plus my carry-on, but it's a rather large one. Ah, we're in luck, there it is now," she said while pointing to one of the bags moving toward them on the carousel.

Adam moved a few feet along the carousel and lifted the bag onto the floor.

"I see what you mean," said Adam. "It is a weighty item. Thankfully, it has wheels."

"Adam, you must be respectful toward your mother," said Emily, laughing. "That bag has traveled all over the globe with me and it contains not one unnecessary item."

"Just kidding, Mom. It rolls right along. Let's see if it attracts any attention from the customs people."

When they approached the exit from the baggage area, a gimlet eyed officer did glare at the large bag suspiciously. Then he looked up and saw Adam in his Roman collar shepherding his mother toward the exit. He smiled and waved them through.

"We can take a taxi directly to your hotel, but it's just as easy to take a two minute ride on the shuttle bus over to the train platform. It looks like the bus is getting ready to depart. What do you think?"

"By all means, let's take the train. I'll be able to brag to your father how thrifty I was in Krakow."

After they boarded the train for the fifteen minute ride into Krakow's City Center, Adam suggested that his mother spend the afternoon in her hotel and then join him for dinner that evening.

"Adam, I'd rather not languish in the hotel this afternoon. The first rule of jet lag is to stay as active as possible until as close to normal bedtime wherever you are. I've already eaten on the plane. So, if you're available this afternoon, I'd rather do a quick tour of the sights and then share dinner."

"Sounds fine Mom. I'm free the rest of the day and all evening. Let's drop off your luggage at the hotel and get started."

"One more thing, Adam" said his mother.

"Yes? What is it Mom?"

"I'd like to meet with your Father Pilsudski as soon as possible."

"You? Meet with Father Pilsudski? Why ever would you wish to do that?"

"Two reasons, Adam. First, your father insists that I have someone both formidable and knowledgeable with me. Second, in this instance your father is correct, which is not always the case."

"What about Morris? I thought he traveled with you in situations like this."

"Morris is formidable but he does not possess the requisite local knowledge here in Poland. I'll be talking initially to bankers and journalists and then to others whose names come up in the initial discussions and who seem like promising leads."

"I see the problem. Things here are much different than in the U.S., especially for someone who's just entered Poland. It's almost impossible for someone like you or me to judge who might be collaborating with the communists. But Father Pilsudski..."

"What about him? I thought you had spoken to him several times and passed on our preliminary intelligence regarding Lech Walesa."

"I have, Mom and he has expressed great appreciation for what I've told him. But, the man is... evanescent."

"Evanescent? What do you mean?"

"Arranging a meeting with him usually takes at least several days. However, let's do this. I'll take you to your hotel, which is where I stayed my first night in Krakow. It's quite close to UJ—Jagiellonian University—where I study and teach and where Father Pilsudski has an office. I'll cab over there and place a note under his door. Then we'll have to hope that he visits his office and agrees to meet."

When they arrived at the train station, Adam proceeded with his mother to the first taxi in the queue and rode with her to the hotel where she was greeted by the bellman and then began the check-in process. Adam instructed the taxi driver to continue on to UJ. Upon arrival, he paid the driver and went to his own small office where he penned a note to Father Pilsudski:

"Imperative we meet tomorrow (Thursday) at 9:00 o'clock or as soon thereafter as you're able. I'll be there at nine and thereafter every hour."

Adam slipped this note under the door of Father Pilsudski's office and then returned directly to the hotel. His mother was waiting for him in the lobby.

I'm checked in and ready to go and, by the way, this hotel is an excellent choice on your part. They couldn't have been nicer to me. The manager came out and greeted me personally, and they gave me a corner suite overlooking the Park."

"That's Planty Park and it's on our itinerary this afternoon. First though, I'm taking you to St. Francis' Basilica. I know you are an aficionado of Art Nouveau and this basilica was redone after a fire in that style by various members of Mloda Polska."

"I'm reasonably familiar with that movement. Let's go! Do we need a taxi?"

"It's just across the Market Square. Let's walk and I'll point out some of the other sites of interest."

Adam and his mother spent a very pleasant afternoon in and around Old Town Krakow and then shared a casual Polish meal at a restaurant called Chimera which was open that night.

Adam left his mother at the hotel at about 8:00 and said that he would meet her there in the morning at 8:30.

Tuesday, April 14, 1988

Adam arrived punctually but his mother already was waiting in the lobby. She was chatting with the night manager who was still on duty and who had rudimentary English. Just as Adam entered his mother laughed and turned to Adam.

"He wants to know whether it's true that people in the United States can say whatever they want. What should I tell him?"

"Tell him it's legal but not always advisable," said Adam, laughing.

The night manager also laughed while Adam's mother excused herself and she and Adam left the hotel. It was a clear, crisp morning in the high 40s.

"This place is utterly enchanting. I asked for a 7:00 a.m. wake-up call. Instead the night manager sent one of the bellmen to knock on my door and deliver fresh fruit and pastry along with a pot of tea. I wish that some of the four star places I've stayed were half as thoughtful."

"That is very gracious of them and I can tell you that they're not doing it in hopes of a big tip. If they like you, they're genuinely solicitous of your well-being. They clearly have taken a liking to you."

"I'm very flattered. But, what's on our agenda this morning. Have you heard from Father Pilsudski?"

"One doesn't hear from him. Usually he simply appears. I should tell you that he is thought by many to be a dangerous man. Before he was a priest, he was a major in the Polish Army and is rumored to have been a kind of enforcer."

"Sounds fascinating. I look forward to meeting him."

Adam turned to look at his mother thinking she might be joking. He couldn't determine whether she was or was not.

Well, I've always heard that she can more than hold her own at the negotiating table.

"It's possible you'll get the opportunity to do so. My plan is for us to go to his office as soon as we arrive at UJ and see if he's in. If not, I'll show you around the University and we'll try his office again later."

"Father Pilsudski was not in when they tried his office at 9:00. Adam spent the next hour giving his mother a private tour of the Collegium Maius, including the famous Copernicus Room. Normally the Collegium Maius could be entered only via a public tour but Adam, as an adjunct professor, was able to gain entry prior to the first public tour at 10:00 a.m. They left the Collegium Maius shortly before 10:00 and returned to Father Pilsudski's office. Adam was happy to see that the adjoining hallways were still deserted. As they approached Father Pilsudski's door Adam saw that, as before, it was slightly ajar.

"He's here," Adam whispered to his mother. "Please wait here a moment while I speak with him. He doesn't like surprises at all and you definitely qualify as a surprise."

Adam quickly entered the office and left the door slightly open. His mother waited just outside.

"Father Thelen, this has got to stop. You simply cannot call for meetings based on some whim which overtakes you."

Adam tried to explain that his mother was with him and that she wished to ask for Father Pilsudski's assistance. He had spoken only a word or two when Father Pilsudski interrupted him.

"Well, you're here now so please sit down and tell me what's so important as to put us at risk of being seen together. First however, please fully close and lock the door."

At that moment, the door opened and Emily Thelen walked into Father Pilsudski's office. If looks were daggers, Adam would have been impaled on Father Pilsudski's glare.

"What...What?" he sputtered, initially unable to articulate his anger.

Adam, left with no other option now that his mother was in the room, simply introduced her.

"Father Pilsudski, this is my mother, Emily Thelen."

"Your mother..." said Father Pilsudski as his rage palpably evaporated. "This is your mother?"

"Yes, it is, Father. I believe I mentioned to you that she was coming to Poland. She needs your help."

"I'm honored to meet you, Father," said Emily, "and Adam is correct. I do need your help."

At this, Father Pilsudski leapt into action. He pulled out one of the chairs and offered it to Emily Thelen, who gracefully sat down. He motioned Adam to sit in the other chair and then extracted from the corner between the bookcase and filing cabinet a small stool upon which he sat.

"I'm sorry, Mrs. Thelen, to have forgotten my manners. I too am pleased to make your acquaintance. But I am puzzled how I possibly could be of assistance to you."

Emily Thelen succinctly explained to Father Pilsudski her plans to contact various people within Poland to discuss topics of a sensitive nature.

Father Pilsudski was seated on the stool with his elbows on the table. He made a steeple of his fingers and assumed a thoughtful pose for a moment.

"I see your problem but . . ."

Here it comes. A litany of the reasons helping my mother would compromise his own security and simply is not practicable.

"... I'm not available until tomorrow morning. Starting in the morning I could accompany you for three days wherever you go. Would that be satisfactory?"

"That would be perfect Father. This afternoon I'm meeting with a banker I've known for decades and trust implicitly. Adam can come with me to see him. But, where can we meet tomorrow morning?"

"A car will pick you up at your hotel. The driver will identify himself to you as Kevin. I will join you thereafter. Where are you staying?"

Adam's mother described the hotel Adam had arranged for her.

"Ah yes, the same hotel where Adam stayed on his first day in Krakow. An excellent choice. Kevin will be there at 8:30 if that suits you."

"8:30 is excellent. I look forward to seeing you."

Throughout this exchange between his mother and Father Pilsudski, Adam had been sitting as if stupefied. Now Father Pilsudski turned to him.

"Well, your mother and I are all set for the next three days. Anything else? Father Thelen?"

"Adam, Father Pilsudski is speaking to you. Are you all right?" asked his mother.

"Oh... Yes. I'm fine. Nothing else. I think you've handled everything. I... uh thank you."

"Then, Mrs. Thelen. I look forward to seeing you tomorrow. But, Father Thelen, there is one other item I should mention before you leave."

"What is it?" asked Adam warily.

"The feedback I'm hearing regarding your recent trip to Jerusalem is uniformly excellent. John Paul is especially pleased."

"Oh. Well... thank you," said Adam.

Father Pilsudski arose and shook Emily Thelen's hand as she and Adam departed and closed the office door behind them. They took the stairs directly down to the University commons outside the building.

"Adam, you made Father Pilsudski sound like some kind of sinister ogre. He's a delightful man and seems very eager to help. Also, I have been remiss or perhaps too focused on my own agenda. I want to hear all about your trip to Israel over dinner tonight."

Adam, still befuddled at the wholly unexpected turn of events, could only look at his mother and shake his head.

Adam and his mother met that afternoon with her contact in the banking industry who confirmed only that George Spektor, or people acting on his behalf, had indeed been making inquiries. One could interpret these inquiries as benign or otherwise depending on one's perception of the Spektors. The banker also provided Emily Thelen with the names of three other people she might wish to contact.

Adam and his mother were at Balaton, which was open on this drizzly Tuesday evening. Adam had just concluded the story of his first encounter with Father Stan and of the dinner they had shared at this restaurant on Adam's second night in Krakow.

"It sounds as if you've made a good and loyal friend in Father Stan. Now, please tell me about your trip to Israel," said Emily Thelen.

"It started with Father Pilsudski. He and the Pope have been associates — and friends — since the days when the Pope was Cardinal Wojtyla here in Krakow. He remains in regular contact with John Paul II and through Father Pilsudski the Holy Father instructed me to attend a communal Passover Seder in Jerusalem. The stated goal was to assist me in my studies of Holocaust victims but clearly I was also a small piece of the Pope's efforts to build harmony between Catholicism and Judaism. I spent a full month studying all aspects of the Passover — the Torah and Hagaddah, Talmudic Law, Kabbalah, the commentaries and much more. My mentor was the rabbi at the Old Synagogue in Kazimierz, which is only a few minutes from here. He came here from Brooklyn a few years ago and is an associate of the Rebbe—Rabbi Schneerson."

"Even I have heard of the Rebbe. He's well known all over New York."

"Not just in New York or even the U.S. The Rebbe is a major force throughout Judaism. He's the one who suggested to Rabbi Mordechai Eliyahu that communal Seders be held in every Israeli city and it was Rabbi Eliyahu who presided at the Seder I attended."

"And were you closely questioned on your Passover knowledge?"

"Not at all. I was introduced during dinner to at least a dozen rabbis and scores of lay Jews. They all knew that the Pope had sent me there and that anyone he sent would be well prepared. One of the more candid laymen said as much."

"We know your Pope wouldn't send us a nebbish," he said.

"A nebbish? What's that?"

"In our world it would translate as a fool, a boob or a loser."

"That's a good word and I'm going to add it to my lexicon. I see nebbishes all the time in my business," said Adam's mother.

"But, if they didn't ask about the Seder, what did you talk about?"

"Two themes really. The first, not surprisingly, involved various questions as to why I wanted to help Holocaust families and how I proposed to do so. The second was more surprising and much more secular than religious. These questions were from both lay people and rabbis. Typically, they would start with questions about the Pope and our President and how they were working together against communism. At first, I thought they were merely being polite and asking questions about two people I, as a U.S. Catholic, would know. Invariably, however they would link communist oppression in Eastern Europe with the existential threat of the Arab world which surrounds Israel on all sides. I came to realize that these Jews, both religious and secular, were looking to the future. They were inquiring whether Rome and Washington D.C. would be steadfast allies against secular threats. Increased religious harmony between Jews and Catholics could be a byproduct of such secular assurances; I already mentioned this in my last report to the Pope."

"But I thought after the Six Days War in '67 Israel's position in the Arab world was reasonably secure."

"That's our perspective in the West, but the Israelis have a differing outlook. They see millennia of diaspora followed by only four decades of statehood. They continue to view their existence as tenuous."

"But, in any event, you're reasonably conversant on these topics aren't you?" asked Emily.

"Happily, I am. I wrote a paper in a political science class many years ago on the creation of the Jewish state in 1947 and on how the Jewish leadership at that time and for three decades before made it all possible. I concluded then that David Ben-Gurion was a leader of genuinely biblical proportions. Also, of course, I am a bit player in the current drama of the Pope and President versus communism in the Eastern Bloc. So, I was able to converse intelligently with these people."

"Well your performance must have worked if Father Pilsudski already is receiving good feedback from Rome."

"Yes, I expect I'll hear more about that in my next communique from Rome. On a more selfish note, I'm already receiving inquiries from Holocaust families planning to visit Kazimierz later this year."

"I'm proud of you Adam," said his mother.

"I appreciate that, Mom, notwithstanding your rather clear bias in my favor."

CHAPTER 31

Wednesday, April 15 – Friday, April 17. 1988

EMILY THELEN DID not return to her hotel on Wednesday or Thursday night and Adam grew increasingly apprehensive. On Thursday morning and again Friday afternoon he checked Father Pilsudski's office in addition to visiting his mother's hotel, both to no avail. At 5:00 p.m. he was back at Ignatianum and still had heard nothing. He was considering a call to his father in San Francisco, where it was Friday morning when there was a knock on his door. It was the student assigned to the front desk announcing that his mother was in the lobby.

"Mom, are you OK? I was worried."

"Now you know how mothers the world over feel when their sons and daughters fail to return home at the appointed hour. In any event, why should you be worried? You knew I was in good hands for three days."

"Yes, but…"

"Adam, I had them drop me here knowing that you would be worried. Now I'm going to walk back to my hotel, where my bag has been delivered. I propose that you meet me there at 7:00 and we'll discuss everything over a farewell dinner."

Adam could only smile as he replied, "As you wish, Mom."

+ + +

"Adam, I still can't believe you portrayed Padraig as irascible and mysterious," Emily said over dinner that evening. "He was charming and completely open and his son is a wonderful young man."

Padraig?!? Son?!?

"You mean he told you his first name?"

"Of course he did. We were traveling together for three days. Were we supposed to call each other "Father" and "Mrs." the entire time?"

"No, no. Of course not. Uh… where did you meet his son?"

"I met Kevin at 8:30 on the first day when he picked me up in his father's car. He drove all three days and was with us the whole time. One thing 1 will grant you is that they definitely have the potential to be dangerous men. I'm virtually positive both of them were armed and they were very watchful everywhere we went."

"I see. Did… Padraig mention whether he has any other children?"

"He has only Kevin, whose mother died in childbirth. I assume that Father Pilsudski was married to her but he never actually confirmed that. Kevin is twenty-two so Padraig was quite young when he was born — barely twenty-one."

Adam was having difficulty digesting all of this. He resolved simply to file all this new information for future consideration and carry on with their last night together before his mother's departure in the morning. They were at Hawelka, only a stone's throw away from his mother's hotel. The restaurant was located right in the main square and was justly famous both for its main courses — beef tenderloin being the specialty of the house

— and for its desserts. His mother had ordered the beef and Adam the salmon.

"Did you discover anything of interest relative to the Spektors?"

"We learned for certain that George Spektor has had several phone discussions with people in Poland and that others in his employ have made inquiries in person. All of their questions focus on Lech Walesa but we discovered nothing proving categorically that the Spektors' intentions are evil. We also learned that Max Spektor is holding himself out as a great friend of Solidarity. Some monies from their new NGO—*Dignitas et Libertas*—actually have made it here in the form of donations to Solidarity and its supporters."

"NGO?" asked Adam.

"NGO is an acronym for non-governmental organization. They're typically created for charitable purposes and they are very loosely regulated with virtually no meaningful audits."

"Sounds like a perfect vehicle for abuse."

"That's what Padraig and I both believe, just as we believe that the Spektors are in this for their own interests rather than those of Solidarity."

"I certainly join you in those beliefs," said Adam, feeling the old anger and hatred begin to rekindle.

"Yes, but the problem is that we found no conclusive evidence. We cannot say precisely how, when, where or by whom something untoward might occur."

"I think you'll find that Father Pil . . . I mean Padraig, will be very helpful in that regard. He seems to have eyes and ears all over Poland."

"I certainly concur. We spent most of our time in and around Warsaw and talked to a total of eight people, five of whom were introduced to me by Padraig."

"So, you were staying in Warsaw the last two nights?"

"Yes, we were. Padraig and Kevin shared a room and I had a single. I have to say the hotel was a very out of the way location. It had no name and I doubt that I could find it again."

"I'm not surprised," said Adam with a smile.

The real Father Pilsudski resurfaces.

As if she had read his thoughts, Adam's mother then said, "That's the other item I should mention — Padraig's ability to be menacing. Everyone we spoke to, including my contacts, knew him. They were very cordial but also very careful. And it was eminently clear that none of our discussions would be passed on to anyone else."

"Did you do anything other than track down contacts for discussions?"

"We had about two hours of free time yesterday afternoon. Padraig and Kevin took me through the Royal Castle which was rebuilt after the war but contained original furnishings brought out of hiding after World War II. They showed me around Pilsudski Square, the name of which both Padraig and Kevin found rather amusing."

Amazing! Father Pilsudski has a life outside the shadows.

"Mom, I have to tell you that you've brightened my world. I didn't realize how much I've missed you."

"Thank you, Adam. It's been a wonderful visit, plus I think we've made real progress against the Spektors even though there was no smoking gun. But, before I leave, I have to ask you. How are you bearing the deaths of Lorena and . . . the infant?"

"Mom, I function well enough every day and I'm reasonably confident that this Holocaust pursuit, coupled with helping the Pope, will see me through. But, I have to admit that I sometimes vacillate between self-flagellation for causing these deaths and absolute hatred and detestation of Max Spektor."

"Adam, thank you for your honesty. I can only ask you to keep in mind that all of us at home love you."

"I will Mom. Thank you."

Monday, May 4, 1988

"Right place. Wrong time."

This was George Spektor addressing his father in the latter's New York office.

"Poland definitely is a plump target of opportunity for us. The face of Solidarity is Lech Walesa. In reality, there are many other important players in this drama but nobody outside of Poland knows anything about this supporting cast. Around the world, if you mention Poland people think of Lech Walesa and John Paul II."

"Can we work with this guy Walesa?" asked Max Spektor.

"If you ask whether he is corruptible, my discussions, both first and second hand, indicate you'd have a better chance suborning the Pope. Walesa is a fucking zealot. All he cares about is the success of Solidarity in gaining individual rights for his beloved workers."

"Well then, how can we profit in Poland?"

You god damned old fool! We can wait until Solidarity succeeds and the world views Poland as a rapidly developing and stable economy. Then we can arrange the assassination of Lech Walesa, the virtual embodiment of Solidarity in the eyes of the world.

Here George Spektor hesitated. He seriously considered sharing his thoughts with his father and seeking his feedback. But, after a moment's reflection, he did not.

"Dad, there also is the problem of timing as I said at the outset. It's too early to do anything in Poland. It's now clear to me that Solidarity *is* succeeding against communism with no small amount of help from the Pope and the Prez. Again, however, people outside of Poland can't see the imminence of success. Nobody is aware of the Roundtable Talks or of the concessions the communists already have made. Talking to people in Poland, I'm convinced that reasonably free elections are only a year or two away."

"OK. So, what do you recommend we do?"

"Your idea that we actually give some of the *Dignitas et Libertas* donations to Solidarity is a good one. By doing so, we can cement your reputation as a hero of the oppressed and also build real credibility in Poland with Walesa and the other leaders of Solidarity. After all, we can still use most of the donations for our own purposes. If we give him a few thousand dollars here and there it will be money well spent. And anyway, it's not like it's our own money."

Max Spektor had begun to smile the moment his son mentioned Max's new media image as a good and decent man seeking to lift up the oppressed. It was a genuine smile of happiness, an extreme rarity for Max Spektor.

"That's right son. Then, later on, I'm sure we'll find some way to profit."

George Spektor nodded his head in agreement.

Tuesday May 12, 1988

As he had mentioned to his mother, Adam had sent his monthly report to Rome shortly after returning from Israel. He now had in hand the reply from his friend Monsignor Tobias Alessi.

Adam,

The Pope has heard back from his friend Rabbi Eliyahu concerning your recent trip to Israel. Before he spoke with the rabbi, the Holy Father had read your report, which was quite useful to him and for which he thanks you. The short summary is that the Pope is well pleased with your visit and believes that your efforts will bear fruit relative to your Holocaust project. I'm sorry that I cannot provide details at this time. It's extremely busy here right now with many visitors scheduled, including an emissary from your President who will be here in Rome by the time you receive this.

Regards,
Tobias

But more details are what I crave!
Adam considered contacting Father Pilsudski and seeking more information from him, but he knew instinctively that this was a bad idea.

As open as he was with Mom, he will be just as opaque toward me. It time for me to concentrate on Holocaust families.

CHAPTER 32

Summer, 1988

JOHN PAUL II was correct in his assessment of the impact of Adam's visit to Israel on his Holocaust project. By the end of June, he had met with seven members of three separate Holocaust families, all of whom were visiting Krakow from other parts of Europe and spending time in Kazimierz and at Auschwitz. One of these people was a woman in her late 70s named Esther Katz whose husband had died in 1942 in the former Polish military base which the Nazis had converted to Auschwitz I. In short order the crematorium at this facility was unable to keep up with disposal of the ever increasing number of corpses and Auschwitz II (Birkenau) was constructed about two miles away. This woman had been visiting relatives in Riga when she received word of her husband's arrest and then, shortly thereafter, death. After the war, she was preparing to return to Krakow when the communist Jewish deportation program began. Instead of returning to Poland, she emigrated to Israel in 1949.

"We had planned to have children after the war was over. Then I never really thought about remarrying. When I was teaching at Hebrew University, I returned every three or four years. Then, when I retired in 1980 I decided to come every year. I heard of your project after your recent visit to Jerusalem. I spoke with my rabbi in Israel about you and also talked with Rabbi Malina in Kazimierz before I agreed to speak with you."

"Thank you for doing so, Mrs. Katz," said Adam. "I hope I can help in some small way."

"I don't seek help for myself. I've coped as well as I am able with what happened in 1942. But such a loss is life altering and nothing can change that. What I believe is that the real danger lies in trying to erase the memory and pretend it never happened. Worse yet, I've visited your country three times and I see Jewish children, whose parents try to protect them from any talk of the Holocaust. These Jews seem to think that the United States is the new normal world for Jews everywhere and that something like the Holocaust never can happen again. They need to visit Israel and see how it is beset on all sides. Even some of your political leaders who also are Jewish are like this. I hope a part of your message is that the pain and horror of the Holocaust is real and that it didn't magically disappear at the end of World War II."

By the end of the summer, Adam had interviewed, usually in Kazimierz but on one memorable occasion at Auschwitz Birkenau, fifteen individuals representing ten Holocaust families. Three of the interviewees were actual Holocaust survivors, although none had survived a concentration camp. Each had been between ten and fifteen years old in 1940 when their parents had sent them to "visit" relatives outside of Poland. These visits became permanent when their parents' prescience was proved tragically correct. In each case both parents had perished in the camps.

+ + +

The interview at Auschwitz Birkenau began at Kazimierz where Alma had requested that Adam accompany her to the camp, which was about two hours from Krakow. Alma was from Racine, Wisconsin and was twenty-six. She never before had been outside the United States. They had toured Auschwitz I with its exhibits of shoes, clothing, stuffed animals and hair – bushels and bushels of hair. Then they had transferred to Auschwitz Birkenau and toured the quarters and the "showers" and crematoria. Now they were on the receiving platform where all the Jews were separated as they exited the trains.

"I knew when I saw 'Sophie's Choice' a few years ago that I had to come," said Alma. "My father was watching the movie with me. He had never spoken of the Holocaust but, when Sophie was presented with the choice of which of her children to send to the right, he said, "There was no choice." I stopped the movie and asked what he meant.

After a moment's reflection he responded. "The German officer had only a second or two to direct the arrivals to his right or left. He sent my mother and sister to the right and me and my father to the left. I was thirteen. We had come from Vichy France after leaving Bavaria in 1938. We thought the officer was merely dividing us by gender. After we went to the huts and my father learned the truth – that those who went right entered directly into the "showers" – he simply quit. When he wouldn't join the work party the next day they shot him."

"That's how I learned about my grandmother and grandfather and aunt," said Alma. "And about my father who was always good and kind but damaged… damaged beyond repair."

Two of the other interviews were conducted in Poland but at some distance from Krakow, one in Poznan and another in Lublin. In each case Adam dutifully informed Father Pilsudski in advance of the planned trip and was duly instructed to deliver sums of cash to an individual designated by him. As in Gdansk, the transfers occurred without difficulty and Adam's comfort level with such activities increased accordingly.

In early September two events occurred in quick succession. First, one of the people he had interviewed in Krakow earlier in the summer sent him a postcard thanking Adam for his interest in Holocaust families and advising that one of his sons now was willing to be interviewed provided Adam was able to travel to Bialystok. The man he had interviewed during the summer had been separated from his wife by the Nazis. She had died late in the war at Auschwitz Birkenau while he had gone to another camp and had survived when it was liberated by the Russians. Following the war, the man had remarried; this son was the product of that second marriage. Neither the second wife nor the son was Jewish.

After some thought, Adam agreed to the interview notwithstanding the somewhat tenuous Holocaust connection. When Adam mentioned his planned trip to Father Pilsudski, he was not surprised to learn that he once again would be carrying cash for delivery in Bialystok.

The second event was the commencement of Adam's teaching duties at UJ. As agreed during his discussions the previous fall, Adam would be teaching, in English, a class in the Faculty of Law and Administration. It was to be entitled "Constitutional

Law in the U.S., a Model for Eastern Europe." The class would be attended by students from the United States and Europe and would meet on Tuesdays, Wednesdays, and Thursdays to allow the students to travel in Poland and elsewhere in the Eastern Bloc over long weekends. Incidentally, it would allow Adam to conduct interviews as needed and to deliver shipments of cash should Father Pilsudski deem it necessary.

Friday, September 26, 1988

Adam left Ignatianum and walked to the main train station a few blocks away. He carried a small suitcase along with a briefcase containing the materials he would need for the interview and the now customary manila envelope of cash. On this trip, however, the envelope contained $10,000 (U.S.) rather than the zloty equivalent. He arrived at the platform with about ten minutes to spare and boarded the 8:15 a.m. train to Warsaw. The train departed on time and Adam removed the first partial draft of the Holocaust paper he was writing for publication in the American Journal of Psychology. He began to edit and revise what he already had written.

When this process was completed after a little over an hour, he began an outline of an additional section. The train arrived in Warsaw at 10:45 and Adam disembarked and walked to the platform for the Bialystok train. He boarded this train and it departed at 11:20. The interview was scheduled for the next morning to accommodate the subject's work schedule, but the money transfer was to occur in the early evening today at a large but anonymous hotel about a mile from the small hotel near the train station where Adam was booked. Promptly at 6:20 he was to appear in the lobby of the hotel wearing his Roman collar and carrying the manila envelope folded inside the local newspaper. He was to seat himself on a chair near the entrance and begin to read a section of the newspaper. The remaining sections, with the manila envelope inside, were to be placed on the table between Adam and the next chair. At 6:30 a man dressed in a blue business suit and a rather garish green tie was to emerge from the elevator and sit in the chair on the other side of the table from Adam. Three minutes later Adam was to exit the hotel, leaving the newspaper, with the money inside, on the table. Adam looked forward to a quiet dinner alone after ridding himself of the cash, especially since he lacked even a flimsy reason to be carrying any U.S. dollars, let alone ten thousand of them.

The train was late into Bialystok, arriving a little before two o'clock. Adam was booked at the Hotel Turkus, an easy walk from the train station and a twenty minute walk or short taxi ride to the more upscale hotel where the money transfer was to occur. Adam checked into the Hotel Turkus and spent another two hours working on the Holocaust paper. A little before five o'clock he took a quick shower and prepared to set out for the handover of the cash. As usual, he chose to walk rather than hail one of the taxis outside his hotel. Also as usual, he left early and embarked on an indirect, almost circular route to his destination. He did this to orient himself with the Bialystok Ghetto, where 60,000 Jews from Bialystok, "The Jerusalem of Poland," were confined by the Nazis and then transported to Treblinka Concentration Camp starting in 1943. Adam planned to remain in Bialystok following the interview on Saturday and explore the Ghetto which was the site of a major uprising in August, 1943.

He especially wanted to gather more information concerning the 1,264 Jewish children removed from the Ghetto by order of Adolf Eichmann and transported first to Theresienstadt

Concentration Camp and then to Auschwitz Birkenau where they were gassed and burned on the eve of Yom Kippur in October 1943.

Now however, Adam was lost. It was 5:30 p.m. and, mindful of the precise scheduling of the money transfer, he had abandoned his orientation tour and focused all his efforts on locating the hotel in which he was to hand over the cash. The problem, Adam belatedly realized, was the fact that the streets and lanes were not straight. A street in which he was walking in a westerly direction could have him walking north after only one hundred yards or so. Also, he seemed to be in a sparsely populated area of abandoned industrial buildings with few pedestrians. Finally, after three or four minutes of increasing frustration, Adam saw a man approach him from the opposite direction. Just as Adam was about to ask directions of the man, he became aware of another man approaching from behind him. When Adam turned back to the first pedestrian, a gun had materialized in the man's hand.

"Let's do him right here," said the first man to his accomplice who had approached from behind.

"Right. There's not a soul around and there's an alley I passed just now. We'll put him in there. The money has got to be in the briefcase."

The men were speaking in rapid colloquial Polish and evidently believed Adam did not understand what they were saying. Now the second man turned to Adam and addressed him in English.

"Give me the briefcase."

The money was indeed in the briefcase but Adam saw no alternative to handing it over, given the gun which the first man was holding casually but with a steady and unwavering aim at Adam's chest. Adam also had noticed the alley a few yards back and recalled that it was only about eight feet wide with brick buildings on either side. Adam judged the man with the gun to be about 5'9" and one hundred fifty pounds. He also noted that the man was staying just outside Adam's reach. Adam looked back at the second man and, saying nothing, handed over the briefcase. The man opened it and quickly located the money.

"Yes, the money's here," he said in Polish to the first man. Then smiling at Adam he said in English while pointing toward the alley, "Please come with us."

Adam complied and the three men moved toward the alley. When they reached the opening to the alley, Adam turned to face the man with the gun, who held it in his right hand. The second man, still smiling, motioned to Adam to walk further into the alley. Adam turned to his right as if to obey but then, in a single fluid motion turned back rapidly to his left. As he turned he clamped his left hand on the right wrist of the man with the gun. He continued, turning, pulling the man's right arm so that the gun now was pointed to Adam's left. With his right hand Adam grasped the man just where the back of his head met his neck. Adam continued to pivot to the left and with the full force of his momentum drove the man's face into the brick wall. As the man's face crumpled against the wall, Adam heard two distinct cracking sounds and concurrently felt in his right hand the man's upper vertebrae separating. The man instantly was lifeless and his body inert.

As the man collapsed, Adam took the man's gun in his own left hand and turned to confront the other man. But he was not there, nor was the briefcase. Adam could hear the man's running footsteps as he retreated back the way he had come. Adam knew he had no hope of overtaking the man in this unfamiliar neighborhood and simply stood as if in a daze with a gun in his hand and a dead man at his feet. Suddenly, the sounds of the man's receding footsteps were punctuated by two soft pops, after which there was no sound at all.

Then, a moment later, Adam heard the sound of rapid footsteps coming toward him and then saw a man peer cautiously into the alley. The man, whom Adam had never seen before had a gun in his right hand and Adam's briefcase in the left. He stood and took in the tableau before him. When he saw that Adam apparently was unhurt, the man replaced his own gun in its holster and took the gun from Adam's hand and placed it in his pocket.

"Do you make a habit of wandering around strange cities before a scheduled money transfer?" asked the man, a faint smile upon his face.

"No, I..."

"Save it for later, Father," said the man as he bent over the crumpled form in the alley. "Jesus, you've killed him."

"I know... I..."

"Again, save it for your debriefing with Father Pilsudski. For now, here's your briefcase. You have just enough time to get to your meeting."

"But... I'm lost."

"My God, Father, if I didn't know better I'd think you were joking. Follow this lane about two hundred yards to a bigger street. Go left another two hundred yards to a major thoroughfare which will have fairly heavy traffic. Turn right and you'll see the hotel on the right. I'll have to stay here and clean up this mess so we'll just have to hope they don't have a second team."

"Thank you... Thank you," said Adam. "Is there anything I can do to help here?"

At this the man laughed. "Father, please just go. I think you've done quite enough here."

+ + +

There was no second team and the transfer of the cash was uneventful. Adam returned directly to his hotel. He thought about eating but could not. He went to his room and sat in the dark for about ten minutes. He then removed his clothes, carefully hung them in the armoire and went to bed.

Saturday, September 27, 1988

The next day, Adam arose early and prepared for the interview. He showered, shaved and dressed carefully in the Roman collar. He ordered and consumed a large breakfast at the cafe off the lobby of the Hotel Turkus. He obtained from the desk clerk precise directions, involving three different buses, to the home of the Holocaust survivor who had written to him. He set out early allowing himself plenty of time to arrive punctually. At no time did Adam think about any of the events of the preceding evening. He arrived about twenty minutes early and walked around the neighborhood before presenting himself at the home of the interviewee precisely at the appointed time. He conducted a thorough and professional interview which lasted for two hours and fifteen minutes. The substance of the interview was contained in one statement by the subject.

"You know, Father Thelen, it's very strange. I'm not Jewish nor is my mother or my sister. None of us suffered during the Holocaust and obviously, we never knew our father's first wife who died in a camp. And it's not like our father talks about the Holocaust. Quite the contrary. He never mentions it. When he told me he had spoken with you, I was shocked. Yet, not one day goes by that I do not think about the Holocaust, or read more about it or see one of the documentaries. I look at my father — at how he is — and I wonder what he was like — before. I see how he is with the communist oppression and the communists' own brand of anti-Semitism and I think about the thousands of others here in Poland, all over Europe really, who are going through the same thing. It's a haunting experience." After the interview, Adam retraced his path back to the hotel. He had a light meal and then returned to his room and went to bed.

Sunday, September 28, 1988

Adam arose and followed the same routine as the previous day except that he dressed in casual clothing. Following breakfast, he returned to the Bialystok Ghetto area, after first attending Mass at a nearby chapel. Again, he gave no conscious thought whatever to the events of Friday evening. Just as in Kazimierz, Adam found the former Jewish ghetto transformed with little to remind one of its heritage. He did find a small ramshackle building where volunteers were working to keep the memories alive. In this building was a photo of some of the 1,264 six to twelve-year-old Jewish children taken from the Ghetto in 1943 along with about two dozen adult overseers. He could not determine whether the photo was taken at Theresienstadt or Auschwitz Birkenau. It simply showed the children looking out through a barbed wire fence, some obviously hopeless but some with a residual light in their eyes.

+ + +

Adam boarded the train to Warsaw at 3:15 p.m. He was back in Krakow and in his bed by 9:00 p.m. At no time during his return trip did he think about Friday evening.

CHAPTER 33

Fall, 1988

IT WAS DURING this time that Adam Thelen made, if not a peace, then a truce with himself. In the preceding eighteen months he had killed two men and watched as another was killed by his friend, Mike Burke. And yet another was killed by Father Pilsudski's agent in Bialystok. In each case the dead men had behaved in a manner which courted death and their demise was at least arguably justifiable.

The fact remained that Adam, a priest in the service of God, had killed two men with his own hands. During this same period, he had chosen to have an extended love affair with a woman and the affair had resulted in the conception of a child. Now, that woman was dead because of her involvement with him and the unborn child also had perished, either in a fiery car crash or by means of an abortion. He never would have certain knowledge of the cause of the child's death.

Yet, interspersed among all this carnage, Adam had, he was certain, helped the Pope in his efforts to better mankind and had at least made a start in helping Holocaust victims and their families. He continued to work with the victims of Father

Edmond's depredations, although he also was involved, however indirectly, in Father Edmond's death.

Adam was unable to comprehend, let alone reconcile all of these conflicting threads and in the end he determined that he wouldn't even try to do so. Instead, he resolved simply to live each day as best he could in accordance with God's teachings.

✝ ✝ ✝

Even Father Pilsudski, no paragon of kindness and delicacy, seemed to sense the change in Adam. After Adam returned from Bialystok, Father Pilsudski made no immediate attempt to contact him and when he did make contact about three weeks later, it was to request that Adam arrange for a wire transfer from his bank, again in U.S. dollars.

"This money is going to Prague, but there's no need for you to deliver it. Here is the account and routing information your bank will need to send the money."

"All right. I will arrange the transfer tomorrow," said Adam.

"I heard about the incident in Bialystok."

"I had no doubt that you would. Thank you for sending a man to follow me. I know I exercised poor judgment in taking such a circuitous route in a strange city. I was trying to locate the Bialystok Ghetto area."

"Well, it's true that such wanderings were not advisable while you were carrying such a large amount of cash, especially U.S. dollars. But you acquitted yourself well. Where did you learn to disarm and disable so effectively?"

"I took martial arts classes while I was in San Francisco. Tae Kwando mostly and mainly to stay in shape. I did have some ability; I was due to receive my black belt in another three months or so when I left the city."

"Yes. You do...seem to have an affinity for self-defense. There were no adverse consequences in Bialystok, at least from the police. The man you met very briefly simply dragged the second of your two assailants, the one he shot, back into the alley. He put his own gun, which of course was not traceable, into the hand of the one you killed. I'm sure it didn't convince the police, but why should they care precisely how two obviously bad men had died."

"It sounds somehow familiar," said Adam.

"Ah, yes. I see what you mean. But this clumsy cover-up had none of the elegance of what took place in San Francisco, I'm sure it left the people who sent those two to kill you and take the money in a state of consternation, as am I. There will be no more money transfers until I determine what happened and take steps to prevent a recurrence."

During this period of uneasy truce with himself, Adam focused on preparation for his course in the Faculty of Law and Administration at UJ. This required a fair amount of effort on his part. He of course had taken constitutional law during the second of his three years at Fordham Law School and he still had his notes and outlines from that time. In addition, he had prevailed upon Fordham to prepare and forward to him twenty copies of a selection of the Supreme Court decisions appearing in the casebooks which Fordham currently was using in its constitutional law classes. Thus, he was well prepared to lecture on the U.S. legal system and by extension the English common law in which that system has its roots. But, Poland and other Eastern Bloc countries were not common law countries and never had been. Now, with the possibility of free elections and the first stirrings of a free economy, it was quite possible that the study of constitutional law in Poland would quickly move from an academic exercise to a pragmatic necessity. Discussions at UJ of this topic were ongoing and Adam's class was one of the results.

The class had begun in mid-September, shortly before Adam's weekend trip to Bialystok. Adam and the faculty at UJ had been pleasantly surprised. An initial class of perhaps half a dozen had been expected but the actual enrollment comprised eleven students, including six from Poland, four from other European countries and one from the U.S.

Meredith Adler was a New Yorker, born and bred, and raised in Islip in Nassau County Long Island. After high school, with an abundance of choices, she attended Vassar College on the outskirts of Poughkeepsie, where she was a history major with a minor in modern dance, becoming sufficiently adept in the latter discipline to audition successfully for the Vassar Repertory Dance Theater in her senior year. Upon graduation in 1967, Meredith was offered the opportunity to try out with the Martha Graham Dance Company. After some reflection she had opted to follow the advice of her father and mother, both Wall Street merger and acquisition attorneys, albeit in different firms, and attend law school. However, as *quid pro quo* for her cooperation, she extracted her parents' agreement to fund a year abroad accompanied by two of her Vassar classmates. Her parents readily agreed provided that Meredith confine herself to travel destinations they considered to be safe and secure for a U.S. citizen. Ultimately it was agreed that Meredith and her friends would explore Western Europe from a base in West Berlin. Thus, Meredith spent a year beginning in mid-summer 1967 living in a flat off Kurfursten Strasse. For the most part Meredith hewed to her parents' entreaties to confine her travels to "safe" places. However, her definition of "safe" did not always match that of her parents. For instance, since her Berlin flat was less than fifty miles from the Polish border, she twice ventured into Poland, first to Krakow with her friends for a three day stay. During this visit she felt an affinity with the Polish people, an affinity strengthened no doubt by the young Polish man from Poznan whom she met at a cafe. About a month later, Meredith boarded the train from Berlin to Poznan, Poland. This time she traveled alone and her planned two day stay was extended to four days. This trip to Poznan was repeated four more times during Meredith's year in West Berlin. Now, more than two decades later, Meredith Adler was enrolled in Adam's class.

Meredith Adler now was forty-three years old. She was 5'9" and weighed 132 pounds, precisely one pound more than she weighed when she graduated Vassar more than twenty years earlier. She had earned her JD degree from Columbia Law School in 1971 and worked as an associate at her mother's law firm for three and a half years, working the requisite 85-90 hour weeks. In 1975, as she was being considered for partner in the firm, she married an investment banker she had met while working on two of his deals. This man, Joseph Lewinski, was a partner in his very large and very white shoe investment banking house and was fifteen years older than Meredith. Meredith kept her own surname and, after no children were forthcoming, devoted herself to a life of charitable endeavors. She was wholly sincere in these charitable efforts but also not averse to combining personal pursuits with the pursuit of charitable dollars. On occasion these personal pursuits were of a sexual nature, since her marriage soon had settled into a kind of affectionate but not overly passionate arrangement. This Polish odyssey was no exception. She had heard about Solidarity from one of her husband's business associates at another financial firm. Her intent was to attend one semester of Adam Thelen's class and afford herself the opportunity to visit her former lover in Poznan, with whom she had maintained contact through the years since her time abroad.

As evidenced by her one pound weight gain over twenty plus years, Meredith Adler took very good care of her body and her efforts had been rewarded. She had natural blond hair, now tending toward an even lighter shade, which she usually wore swept straight back and gathered at the nape of her neck. This simple, almost severe style set off her green eyes and finely boned face.

In general, Meredith was pleased with her body. She long ago had come to terms with the two features of her person which had displeased her from adolescence, her feet and her breasts, both of which she felt were too large. Her feet were size 9 Bs and her breasts were, she believed, C cups on a B cup body. Her solution to these two perceived problems was to celebrate her feet and deemphasize her breasts. She lavished her feet with pedicures, elaborate but tasteful painted nails, foot massages, and other assorted spa treatments. Her feet never had tan lines and her sandals and shoes were chosen with utmost care. Her breasts, however, while not subjected to Victorian era strapping, never appeared in public while not encased in custom made bras and swimsuits which reduced them to the B cup appearance she felt her body deserved. In all, the effect was striking. Men looked at Meredith and then looked again. The irony of her breast deemphasis campaign was not lost on Meredith. Men tended to sense in her a repressed, smoldering sensuality. Many felt a duty to liberate her passions and Meredith long ago had learned to use this to her advantage, if she so chose.

After three weeks in Krakow, Meredith availed herself of the four-day weekend created by the Tuesday, Wednesday, Thursday class schedule. She traveled to Poznan to meet her lover from twenty years earlier. She took an early train and arrived in Poznan at noon. As arranged, she met Jacek for a late lunch. He now was fifty years old and still a good looking man, although certainly not as angular and sculpted as she recalled. It was evident from his looks and comments that he found Meredith to be just as attractive as twenty years earlier. During their sporadic correspondence, they had shared the major developments in their lives, and she knew that he was married with two teenaged children. The lunch was enjoyable and their pleasure in seeing each other again was genuine. He professed a willingness to rekindle their earlier relationship but his inchoate guilt was palpable. Meredith explained her reasons for being in Poland and said she was happily married with no desire to resuscitate their affair, although that had not necessarily been her intention when she boarded the train that morning. They parted with promises to stay in touch. Meredith took a room at a hotel and spent the remainder of that day and most of the next exploring Poznan. She departed Poznan late Saturday afternoon and reached her hotel in Krakow about midnight. During the return train trip, she resolved to complete the first semester of her course at UJ, which concluded in mid-December, and return to New York in time for Christmas.

Meredith did just as she resolved. The first semester ended on December 15 and she was on the plane home on the 16th. Yet she found herself continuing to think of her time in Krakow. The course itself was excellent — better in fact than she had expected. Also, she had learned much more about Solidarity and had seen the hope it gave the Polish people. When she first had heard about Solidarity at a fund raising luncheon sponsored by her husband's business acquaintance, she had been impressed by the cause but singularly unimpressed by her luncheon hosts. Now she had learned firsthand that Solidarity was a real force for good in Poland. Finally, as the 747 flew westward, Meredith's thoughts turned to the teacher of the course. Father Adam Thelen was knowledgeable and a fine teacher, but there was something more about him which she could not quite define just yet.

When the second semester began on January 24, 1989, Meredith Adler was in her accustomed seat in the front row. The other ten students from the first semester also had returned.

CHAPTER 34

Thursday, April 6, 1989

"T HE CLASS WILL be ending later this month and I wanted to thank you," said Meredith. She was in Adam's small office at UJ following the last class of the week which had ended ten minutes earlier.

"Thank you. I truly appreciate your compliment. You've been a wonderful student. I think some of your ideas could be useful to Solidarity if the rumors of free elections next year prove true. A new constitution may actually be drafted. What a great day for Poland that would be."

"Yes, it would. When I came here last fall I never thought I'd become such a believer in Solidarity. Just since I've been here I see new hope in the eyes of the people."

"That's true, and the hope is spreading across the entire Eastern Bloc. The real purpose of this course is to introduce concepts of individual freedom and dignity and justice to people who may be able to turn such ideas into reality if the opportunity arises."

"I can see that relative to the other people in our class. They are people of some influence here in Poland and in other European countries. I on the other hand am merely a dilettante

315

from a country which already enjoys individual freedom, even if it's all too often taken for granted in the U.S."

"Not at all. You're a gifted attorney who could be a real asset to Lech Walesa and his people if they ever have an opportunity to draft a new constitution. I could introduce you to some people in Gdansk."

Meredith was somewhat taken aback. She had come to thank Adam Thelen for teaching an excellent course, but she also had another agenda. She wanted to become better acquainted with Adam in the three weeks remaining before the semester ended. Now however, Adam had introduced a potential course of action which resonated within her.

"You know, Father Thelen, the idea of giving meaningful assistance to Solidarity does appeal to me. It's not as if I'm doing anything important in the U.S. And I must admit that when I first heard about Solidarity's goals at the Spektor's luncheon, something clicked inside me."

"You… know Max Spektor?" asked Adam.

"I've met both Max Spektor and his son George, but I can't say I know them well. My husband has had some business dealings with their firm."

"Have you… spoken directly with them about Solidarity?"

"I have. I was seated next to George Spektor at the fundraising luncheon for their NGO. I'd love to tell you all about it, but I have an appointment back at the hotel in fifteen minutes. Why don't you come by my rooms tomorrow afternoon and we can discuss it further?"

"I… would be happy to do so."

"Let's say 3:00. You can join me for my daily swim. I chose the Hotel Adlon because they have one of the few lap pools close to UJ. I know you were a swimmer at Fordham. Come up to Suite B on the third floor."

"That's fine. I'll look forward to seeing you then."

Max Spektor. This woman has information regarding Max Spektor.

Friday, April 7, 1989

"This is nothing short of exquisite," said Adam as he and Meredith got out of the pool. "I can't tell you how much I have missed swimming. We had a pool on campus in San Francisco and I worked out three times a week without fail," said Adam.

"I thought you were going to say you worked out religiously," said Meredith.

"Ha! That would be untrue. One of the beauties of a swimming workout is that one can maintain a serene absence of thought, religious or otherwise."

Unless, of course, the swimming workout follows a leap from the Golden Gate Bridge.

Adam and Meredith were in the swimming pool located in a separate building connected to the Hotel Adlon via a covered causeway. They had completed seventy laps of the twenty-five metre pool, for a total distance of just over a mile. The hotel was located about one half mile south of UJ very near the Wisla River. The pool was over forty years old but had been thoroughly renovated eight years earlier at the behest of General Jaruzelski's predecessor as head of the Polish Communist Party. The pool water was pumped directly from the Wisla, purified via filters and chemicals and then heated. Once a month the water was pumped back into the river and the pool was refilled.

"Yes, I agree that serenity is one byproduct of a good workout," responded Meredith, although her own mind had been occupied with thoughts of Adam's body as he flowed through the water alternating among the four strokes, with emphasis on his two main strokes from college days, freestyle and breaststroke.

"I'm sure you could negotiate a deal with the hotel to use the pool after I've returned to New York."

"I was thinking the same thing," said Adam. "I'll speak to management about it."

"I'm going to wrap up in a robe and go straight up to my rooms to shower. Please come up after you've showered and changed and we can discuss Solidarity and the Spektors."

"Fine. I'm going to swim five more cool down laps. I should be there in fifteen minutes."

On the way up to Meredith's rooms a certain sense of *deja vu* overtook Adam Thelen. Meredith Adler was an extremely attractive woman and her attractions were not lost on Adam. He had noted her very businesslike black swimsuit and, just as in the classroom, had felt that her quite proper attire masked, even suppressed, a passion just below the surface.

This is entirely different. It's not about flirtation or anything other than the collection of all available information regarding Max Spektor.

Adam arrived at the door to Meredith's suite concurrently with a waiter pushing a trolley on which was a bottle of Champagne in an ice bucket and two champagne flutes. There also was a selection of fruits, nuts and crackers and a very soft cheese appearing to be Brie or something similar. Adam's sense of *deja vu* became more pronounced. Meredith answered the door dressed in a robe. Her hair was wet and her feet with tastefully painted and decorated toenails, were bare. Adam was thankful he had chosen to wear a hooded sweatshirt, sweat pants and running shoes rather than his Roman collar.

"Excellent! Perfect timing! Please put it all right here on the table," said Meredith to the waiter.

The waiter did as requested and then discreetly withdrew.

"I thought we could celebrate, only slightly prematurely, the end of two very rewarding semesters of study. I've learned a lot and maybe, as you suggest, I can help turn concepts into reality here in Poland."

"Meredith, I'm positive you can do so if you choose to go in that direction and I'll be delighted to introduce you to some good people inside Solidarity."

"We'll talk about that and more. First, however, please open the champagne."

Adam took the bottle from the ice bucket, noting that it was a very nice Roederer, and removed the foil and wire. He twisted the cork out of the bottle with a soft pop. As he was performing this ritual Meredith had seated herself on the sofa with her legs under her and Adam couldn't avoid noticing that there was something different —something unrestrained — about her breasts. He carefully poured the champagne into the flutes which were heavy cut crystal. When he handed one of the flutes across the table to Meredith, she bent forward to take it, and Adam was treated to a very nice view of her breasts as the robe, already low cut, fell open somewhat. They were beautiful and much fuller than he would have guessed. He felt himself becoming aroused and quickly took a seat across the table from Meredith. He knew he was blushing slightly and when he looked at Meredith he saw her faintly amused look.

"I know I shouldn't be such a tease, Adam, so let me be candid with you. I'm neither promiscuous nor puritanical. During my thirteen year marriage, I've had a total of four lovers other than my husband. All of these affairs were with married men and they each ended by mutual consent and on good terms. Now, over the last six months, I have developed a strong attraction toward you. I hope you will choose to be my lover."

Adam wanted this woman, wanted to hold her, to be one with her. He was strongly aroused and knew of a certainty that his priestly vows would not cause him to refrain. He smiled and began to move toward Meredith. Then suddenly, he knew, just as certainly, that he could not do this. He moved back again, away from her.

"Meredith, I want you more than you know but I can't do this."

"Because you're a priest?"

"No. If that were the case, I'd be holding you right now. I want you very much and my vows wouldn't stop me."

"Yes, I can see that," said Meredith with a smile as she looked at Adam's crotch. "But why not then?"

"It's because I love someone else. I always will. I just now realized that. Another woman. She was carrying my child, but. . . she died last year."

"Another woman. You're turning me down because of a dead woman?" said Meredith, who then looked crestfallen. "I'm sorry Adam. I shouldn't have said that."

"No, it's all right. She is dead and I love her still. I always will."

"Well, I'll take solace that I was hot enough to defeat Mother Church, but not the other woman."

"Meredith, I'm sorry…"

"Don't be," said Meredith. "I suspect that, at least, we share a distaste for Max Spektor."

"We do, although my feelings go well beyond distaste," said Adam.

Meredith said nothing, only looked at Adam appraisingly.

"Character and commitment. I see precious little of either in my life, and certainly not in one man. Don't worry, I'll still help you against Max Spektor. Let me change into something more conducive to conversation, and then we can discuss the Spektors."

"That will be fine, Meredith, but..."

"But what, Adam?" said Meredith, smiling.

"I shouldn't mention this now, but your breasts look quite different than what I have seen in class or even in the pool today."

"Ah, yes. I normally keep my breasts under wraps, so to speak," said Meredith with an even broader smile. "Now, however, since it appears we're going to be on intimate terms, excepting the physical, it's only right that you see me as I am."

Meredith swung her legs from beneath her and stood directly in front of Adam. Slowly, she pulled the sash of the robe so that it fell open. She wore nothing beneath the robe. She stood like that for a moment smiling at Adam as he gazed at her perfect dancer's legs, her neatly trimmed blond pubic hair and her breasts, still partially covered by the robe. Then she shrugged the robe from her shoulders and let it fall to the floor. She stood fully unclothed before Adam and her smile now was sultry — almost smoky. With her hands she lifted her breasts slightly.

"They are larger than I would have chosen, so I usually emphasize other features."

Adam sat transfixed and speechless. Finally, he was able to croak a response.

"You - all of you - are so beautiful."

Meredith performed a slow and languid balletic pirouette of one and a half turns. She looked over her shoulder, picked up her robe and retreated into her bedroom. When she reemerged a moment later she wore a tee shirt, sans bra, and a pair of white fleece lined sweat pants with zippers at the ankles.

"Now let's talk about Max and George Spektor. But, while we are doing so, I think we should finish this lovely champagne and sample this Brie."

And so they did. Meredith told of her luncheon encounter with George Spektor and of feeling uneasy, almost sickened in his presence.

"I was positive that if he had me in his power he would hurt me."

Adam for his part told how Max Spektor and his associates had tried to use Lorena's pregnancy to coerce him into involving his mother in the murderous Ghana tragedy.

"Your lover's name was Lorena?" asked Meredith.

"Yes. Lorena Montes. She was from Seville."

"A beautiful name. I envy her. Not her death of course, but her time with you. She must have loved you as truly as you love her."

"Yes, I believe that is true. But I must tell you Meredith that although we are not lovers in the conventional sense, I feel as comfortable — as natural — being with you as if we were lovers."

"Platonic love, perhaps?"

"A love that transcends mere physicality? No, I think not. I never will forget your body nor how aroused I was. I would say more like courtly love — chivalric, secret, courteous in the extreme. C.S. Lewis called it a humble love."

"Hmm. That sounds about right I guess."

"Whether it is or isn't, I want you to be part of my life going forward and I want you to think about how you could help Solidarity. Let's talk about it more after class next Tuesday. In the meantime, there's someone here in Krakow I want you to meet. I'll see if I can arrange it."

Sunday, April 9, 1989

Adam again was in the chapel at 5:30 a.m. saying Mass. When he turned to display the Host, he was not particularly surprised to see "Stepan" in attendance. Shortly thereafter he stepped forward to take communion.

"The Body of Christ," said Adam.

"Amen," responded Father Pilsudski, who then turned to return to his pew.

"Wait." As Father Pilsudski turned back toward Adam, he continued, "There's a student from my class I'd like you to meet."

"Meredith Adler, I suppose."

"Yes," said Adam trying to hide his surprise.

"Send her to my office after your class on Tuesday. Let's say 2:30."

The man is an enigma.

CHAPTER 35

Tuesday, April 11, 1989

"I WAS ABLE to contact the man I mentioned last Friday. He's another priest whose name is Father Pilsudski and I can assure you he is a good man. But he can be strange, and intimidating."

Adam then explained how to locate Father Pilsudski's office and said her appointment was at 2:30.

+ + +

"I'm sure Father Thelen introduced me."

"He did, very briefly. He made you sound rather mysterious."

"Ha!" said Father Pilsudski with a laugh, "If either of us is a mystery, it is Adam. But, please tell me about yourself."

Meredith gave Father Pilsudski a brief but reasonably thorough biography of her life, including her time at Vassar and at Columbia Law School.

"So, you were a dancer," said Father Pilsudski.

Meredith had mentioned in passing her courses in modern dance. Now, to her surprise, this was his first question.

"Yes, Father I was. Vassar has an outstanding dance program."

"How good were you?"

Meredith was too surprised at the bluntness of Father Pilsudski's question to take offense.

"I was good enough to audition successfully for the Vassar Repertory Dance Theater. Also, good enough to be offered a tryout with the Martha Graham Dance Company. Sometimes I wonder if I made the right decision in choosing law school instead."

"Please forgive my impertinent questions. I have a... deep interest in dance. Also, please call me Padraig. Adam tells me you may have an interest in helping Solidarity and that you certainly have the ability to do so if you choose. I very much would like to discuss this with you in detail. As it happens however, a rather pressing problem has arisen and I must leave now to address it. May we dine together this evening?"

Again, Meredith was surprised and her first inclination was to decline. But Adam had assured her Father Pilsudski was a good man. And there *was* something mysterious about him. *Perhaps I have a thing for priests in Poland.*

"I would be delighted."

"Excellent. A car will call for you at your hotel at 7:00 o'clock. The driver's name is Willem and he will bring you to me."

+ + +

Meredith arrived in the lobby and found Willem waiting for her. He led her outside to the car and opened the rear door for her. The side windows were curtained and a nearly opaque mesh screen separated her from Willem. Meredith had to remind herself that Adam had assured her that Father

Pilsudski – Padraig –was a good man. The trip took about fifteen minutes and involved multiple turns. At one point she felt certain that the car had turned in a complete circle. When the car halted, Meredith had no idea where she was. Willem came around the car and opened her door. She found herself in front of a stone house, obviously very old but well cared for, which was surrounded by trees. No other buildings were in sight. Before all of this could fully register, a man dressed as a butler emerged from the house just as Willem drove off.

"Welcome, Mrs. Adler. Please come in. Father Pilsudski awaits you."

Meredith entered through a rustic wooden door and found that the building was just what it appeared to be — a very old stone farm house with a vaulted post and beam interior. To the left was a bedroom with a bathroom visible through the open door. Past the bedroom door a stone fireplace comprised the remainder of the wall separating the bedroom from the living area. In front of the hearth were two fairly small upholstered chairs separated by a small table with a lamp plugged into an outlet installed in the floor.

Beyond the two chairs along the rear wall was a refectory table with six wooden chairs and a chandelier mounted above. On the wall behind the table were cabinets and shelves, one of which held a rather sophisticated stereo system. The bedroom, living and dining rooms all appeared to be original, albeit well maintained areas of the old farmhouse. To the right, however, Meredith could see that the original wall had been removed. The space previously occupied by the original wall now was a wooden counter at bar height with two high chairs. Beyond the bar was a new, well equipped kitchen alcove about twelve feet square with appliances, cabinets and counters around the perimeter walls and an island with sink in the center of the room. The flat surfaces, including the island and bar top, were covered with grey stone unlike any Meredith had seen before. The butler who had greeted Meredith outside the farmhouse now had retreated into the kitchen and was engaged in chopping an assortment of herbs and vegetables on a wooden block atop the kitchen island.

Suddenly Father Pilsudski emerged from the bedroom to join her.

"Meredith, thank you for joining me. Friedrich and I have prepared a simple meal for you to be accompanied by equally straightforward wines. May I offer you a glass now while Friedrich puts the finishing touches on the meal?"

"That would be delightful, Father Pilsudski. Were you able to deal with the pressing problem you mentioned this afternoon?"

"To be truthful, it is rather a chronic problem which can be addressed periodically but never fully resolved. It actually involves the topic we started to discuss, which is Solidarity."

While he was talking, Father Pilsudski had opened a bottle of chilled white wine which he now brought into the seating area in front of the hearth in which a small fire was burning. He placed the bottle and two glasses on the small table and pulled the chairs around so that they were facing each other at an angle. He gestured to one of the chairs and Meredith sat down. When she seated herself, Meredith could see that the other side of the fireplace opened into the bedroom.

"Yes, I've been thinking of Solidarity and of Father Thelen's words quite a bit. But before we get into that, I want to ask you an impertinent question," said Meredith while looking around the room. "How can you, a priest, afford all of this — the car and driver, the secluded farmhouse, the butler?"

"A fair question I suppose," said Father Pilsudski, "and I have to admit that you are not the first to have posed it. Several other people have suggested that I have entered into a Faustian bargain. Superficially at least, it is a reasonable answer but I have faith that ultimately this will be proven false. But at this time, I cannot be any more forthcoming."

After a fairly lengthy pause, Meredith responded, "All right Father, I accept that, for now at least. So, back to Solidarity. What Adam said about helping did resonate with me, especially now that I've met some of the Polish people and seen the oppressive nature of the communist government. Father Thelen indicated that you might be able to introduce me to certain people. He mentioned one name — Ivan Tusk — but he cautioned me quite strongly not to repeat it to anyone but you."

"Ha! I'm glad to hear that Adam finally sees the reality of the communist regime here in Poland. Americans tend to come here and think they can say anything which comes into their heads without fear of retribution, just as in the U.S."

"I fear that you're correct. I thought he was being overly dramatic until I stopped to think about what he said."

At this moment Friedrich announced that dinner was ready to be served. Father Pilsudski and Meredith arose and moved to the refectory table which was set for two with one setting at the end of the table and the other at the side looking toward the fireplace and front door. Father Pilsudski seated Meredith on the side of the table and then opened a bottle of red wine. He brought it back to the table with two additional wine glasses and sat at the end of the table with Meredith on his right.

"This is a Spanish garnacha which should be a decent accompaniment for our meal of sausages, small potatoes and local vegetables."

Friedrich placed bowls containing the vegetables and herbed potatoes on the table along with a platter holding an assortment of sausages. He also brought a pitcher of water and two glasses which he added to the place settings and filled. He then bowed discreetly and exited by the front door of the farmhouse which appeared to be the only way in or out.

"I'm afraid we're on our own now," said Father Pilsudski with a laugh. "Please don't be concerned however. If any need should arise which I cannot meet, both Fredrich and Willem are less than two minutes away in another building and can be summoned by this," he said while gesturing toward a communication set which appeared to be of military origin.

"Should I be? Concerned, that is?" said Meredith, also smiling.

"No, no. I really am a priest of the Catholic Church, although I was married long ago, as I suspect Adam may have mentioned. My wife died in childbirth twenty-two years ago."

"No, he didn't and, in any event, I've met priests in the U.S. who seemed to take their vows of chastity with a grain of salt." Again, Meredith was smiling.

"I'm not surprised. As it happens, I too think that a lifetime of chastity is rather unrealistic, although I have submitted to it since I became a priest nine years ago. And, I'll tell you a small secret. The Pope also has intimated to me his belief that a breach of chastity can be forgiven even in a priest."

"You are acquainted personally with the Pope?"

"Yes, I am, as is Adam. I first met John Paul when he was a Cardinal here in Krakow. Adam had an audience with him during the Pope's 1987 tour of the U. S."

"He never has mentioned that during our two semesters of classes."

"Again, I'm not surprised. Adam can be quite private about some things and he also tends to be rather hard on himself. But I digress. I did not mention the Pope simply to impress you. Truly, His Holiness is intimately involved in the struggle against communists here in Poland. He's also involved elsewhere in the Eastern Bloc but one of his dearest wishes is for his beloved Polish people to achieve freedom and self-determination. If you choose to help Solidarity you must know that you will be siding not just with the people of Poland but also with the Pope and, indeed, the Catholic Church. Also, you must know, as Adam has learned, that joining the battle is not without risk — and danger."

The conversation about Solidarity continued throughout the shared meal. Meredith asked many very specific and probing questions concerning how she could assist Solidarity and what the risks could be. She also asked what Father Pilsudski thought of Solidarity's chances for success.

"Meredith, please do call me Padraig. I think we are now well enough acquainted to forego the formalities."

"I can do that… Padraig. But please do give me your honest answer as to whether Solidarity can succeed in wresting a modicum of freedom from the communists, who have been in power all over Eastern Europe for decades and who have the full might of the Red Army behind them if needed. We Americans are, after all, oriented toward winning. We don't mind big challenges and big risks but we don't often choose to align ourselves with hopeless causes."

"All right Meredith. My best estimate is that the risks are great but that Solidarity ultimately will succeed. In the ongoing Roundtable Talks the communists showed a willingness to hold free elections and as we speak they are occurring. Of course, they are insincere when they use the word "free." They have put up a slate of puppets who remain under control of the communists. If this succeeds they will put forth 'reforms' which really amount to a continuation of the status quo."

"But Padraig, such an outcome would not constitute true success."

"Of course not. But I think the Polish communists are making two fundamental miscalculations. First, they underestimate the depth of the discontent and the ability of the Polish people to see through their subterfuges. Secondly, they underestimate the power of your President, with the assistance of the Pope, in keeping Gorbachev and the Red Army on the sidelines. I think the current elections ultimately will lead to the ouster of the communists via truly free elections which could occur as early as next year."

"OK, that seems like a reasonable scenario, but it sounds like it could happen regardless of whether I choose to assist or not."

"True enough. But even if truly free elections occur next year as I just discussed, Poland will have to move forward very quickly with a new constitution and with the massive reforms which will be required to create a free market economy. This, especially in the drafting of a new constitution, is where your help will be needed and it won't be an easy task. Even if they lose the elections and the Red Army doesn't intercede, there are plenty of steps, some of them violent, which desperate local communists could employ to hold onto power."

By this time, the meal was drawing to a close. Father Pilsudski arose and fetched a bottle of vintage Port from one of the cabinets. He poured it and sat down again.

"I think we've had sufficient discussions of Solidarity for one evening. Let's talk about something more pleasurable. Please tell me about your extended visit here in Poland."

"I'm happy to do so. But first, I want to ask what may be a painful question. You mentioned earlier that your wife died in childbirth. Did your child survive?"

"Oh yes. Again, I assumed, wrongly, that Adam had told you all about that. Kevin now is twenty-two and he sometimes helps me in my... activities. For instance, he drove Adam's mother and me to various meetings here in Poland a few weeks ago."

"It's obvious that you loved your wife very much. Are you able to tell me about her?"

"I did love her. I still do in fact. We were, what do you say in America? Soulmates, I think. She was a Ukrainian. We married very young. She was only seventeen and I was nineteen."

"Such a sadness. Only three years together."

"Yes, it is sad. But at least we had those years. And it was her memory — and her example — that eventually brought me back to God, and to the Church. She was a dancer you know. That's why I was so interested in your own experiences with dance."

"A dancer! What kind of dance?"

"She was a member of the Ukrainian National Ballet which was a kind of extended audition for the Bolshoi. I'm positive she would have been chosen had she not become pregnant. Like you, however, she was educated in all types of modern dance. She taught me to dance, actually. We used to dance together often, although never in public. Rising young officers in the Polish Army were expected to be wed to communism. Being known as a dancer would not have helped my career," said Father Pilsudski, smiling as he thought back to the years with his wife.

"Oh Padraig, will you dance with me now?"

"Dance with you? Now? I... of course I will."

Father Pilsudski first moved the chairs and table to create a large open space in front of the fireplace, then went to the stereo equipment on the wall next to the refectory table and opened a deep drawer beneath the turntable. Meredith saw that it was full of LPs, perhaps a hundred of them.

"How about a waltz. I've got the Henry Mancini sound track from `Thornbirds'. I know the series was a big hit in the U.S."

"An excellent choice."

Meredith knew she had been conflicted when she dressed for dinner with Father Pilsudski. On one hand, he was intimidating; on the other, she was attracted to the mystery seeming to surround him. Consequently, the first garment she had donned was one of her rather Victorian brassieres. Next however, she put on a black lace camisole which she then covered with a severe white jacket which buttoned almost to her neck. She finished the outfit with a plain grey skirt, cut perhaps an inch or two shorter than usual, and wedge heeled pumps. As Father Pilsudski put on the 'Thornbirds' theme and listened to it for a moment ("Legend about a bird....") she saw something change — soften really — in him. He turned to Meredith and smiled as he held up his hands. Meredith moved easily into his arms and they began to move around the room. At first they both were somewhat mechanical in their movements. Then, as the music played, they began gliding around the floor with coordinated fluid steps, moving as one. When the music ended, they lowered their arms but did not step apart.

"Padraig, that was wonderful! You are a fine dancer."

"Thank you, Meredith, but I'm not nearly at your level. Would you. . . like to tango?"

"Of course I would. it was one of my favorite dances at Vassar."

"But..."

"But, what, Padraig?"

"Nothing. A silly thought just crossed my mind. It's nothing."

"Tell me, please."

"Well, you are a truly excellent dancer, as good as my wife was, I think."

"Yes?"

"You are technically near perfection, but I felt a certain… reserve."

At this, Meredith laughed aloud. A continuing critique during her time at Vassar, especially when she was part of the Vassar Repertory Theater, was that she was "technically proficient in all respects but sometimes lacking emotion." This was especially true in dances such as the tango and Paso Doble.

"What is it?" said Father Pilsudski, alarmed that he may have said something hurtful.

"You don't know how many times I heard that while I was at Vassar, and it was a valid critique. I had great difficulty shedding my reserve and becoming spontaneous."

After she said this, Father Pilsudski returned to the drawer of LPs. He thumbed through it for some time before extracting an LP.

"This album has a long cut which is a re-recording of an early Troilo, from 1938 I think, around the time that he began leading his own group."

"Anibal Troilo," said Meredith. "I am very familiar with him. His nickname was Pichuco'."

"This cut is 'Tinta Verde,'" said Father Pilsudski as he turned to put the record on the turntable.

"Wait," said Meredith and Father Pilsudski turned back to look at her quizzically.

"As he watched her, she stepped out of her shoes. Now, in her bare feet with rather exotic painted toenails, she was about an inch shorter than Father Pilsudski. He smiled and removed his own shoes, making them virtually equal in height. Father Pilsudski was about to turn back to the stereo when Meredith began to unbutton her jacket top. He watched as the black camisole came into view, first only a strip of black and then all of it as she removed the jacket and hung it on one of the chairs at the refectory table. Father Pilsudski gazed appreciatively for a long moment and then placed the record on the turntable and set it in motion. As he was about to place the needle on the proper cut Meredith spoke again.

"You said it was Troilo didn't you?"

"Yes, I did," said Father Pilsudski as he turned to look at her again.

Slowly, Meredith turned until her back was to Father Pilsudski. He watched as she reached behind and undid the hooks of the brassiere and then lowered the camisole enough to expose the bra. With her back still turned she allowed the straps to slide off her shoulders and down her arms. When the bra was in her hand and with her back still turned, Meredith reached behind her and hung it over her white jacket. She then readjusted her camisole so that her breasts were encased within the lace top. Finally, she turned to face Father Pilsudski. Her breasts, freed of their restraint, more than filled the top of the camisole and were clearly visible through the lace.

"So much for reserve," said Meredith.

Father Pilsudski stood looking at Meredith, first gazing at her feet and legs, then her breasts and finally into her eyes. Then without a word he placed the needle on the 'Tinta Verde' cut and took Meredith in his arms.

CHAPTER 36

Thursday, April 12, 1989

MEREDITH ADLER HAD missed class on Wednesday, the first time in two semesters. Adam wondered whether he should check into her absence, but then decided to do nothing.

She's in good hands.

When Meredith appeared in class on Thursday, Adam knew instantly what had happened. He was somewhat surprised to feel no anger or sense of outrage. He was even more surprised that his only emotion was happiness for both Meredith and Father Pilsudski. Meredith came to his office after class.

"We made love. First, we danced and then we made love that night and most of the next day. Padraig said to tell you. He said you'd know anyway, the moment you saw me."

"He was right but if you're waiting for me to condemn either of you, I'll have to disappoint you. After I saw you in class, all I felt was happiness for both of you."

"I'm going to go back to New York as scheduled at the end of the semester. I'll be back in June to begin work on a new constitution. Padraig is going to introduce me to Ivan Tusk and a few others."

"Meredith, I'm so happy for you," said Adam as he came around his desk and embraced her.

"When I get back to New York, I'm going to try to learn more about the Spektors."

"Be very careful Meredith," said Adam. "They are evil people."

Wednesday, May 17, 1989

Adam and Father Pilsudski were in the latter's office. They were supposed to be discussing a wire transfer from Adam's bank account. Instead, Father Pilsudski spoke on another topic.

"I know you condemn me and I accept your censure. I deserve it."

"Are you speaking of Meredith?" asked Adam.

"You know that I am," said Father Pilsudski.

"Perhaps some would condemn you and I suppose it is possible that you deserve it. But you'll hear none of that from me. From the moment I saw Meredith in class, I knew and all I felt was happiness — for both of you."

CHAPTER 37

<u>Tuesday, June 20, 1989</u>

MEREDITH HAD RETURNED to Krakow from New York and now was seated in Adam's office.

"George Spektor called and asked me to meet him for a drink. I joined him at a rather sleazy bar in the upper thirties. He tried to seduce me and I told him that I found him very attractive but that I was happily married. When I managed to get away from him I waited across the street. I followed him to a hotel in Chelsea and then watched from the corner of the lobby to see if anyone came to join him. Sure enough, a woman entered about ten minutes later. I got on the elevator with her. She went to room 405. I'm sure she was joining Spektor. She looked like someone from an escort service."

"Meredith, this man and his father are extremely dangerous. I know they have killed people in Africa and I strongly suspect they've done the same elsewhere. I beg you to stay away from them."

"I will Adam. I agree with you. It made me almost physically ill to say I found him attractive."

+ + +

Later that day when businesses were open in San Francisco, Adam called his father and related to him and to Mike Burke what Meredith had told him.

Summer, 1989 - Fall, 1991

Adam Thelen entered upon a period of peace. He had learned that what he felt toward Lorena was much more than a transitory sexual attraction. It was genuine love and it was forever. He was grateful to Meredith Adler for teaching him, however inadvertently, this lesson. During this time Adam continued to interview Holocaust families and to assist the Pope in his continuing campaign against communism, especially in Poland. Father Pilsudski had advised that the person responsible for the leak which had led to the attack on Adam in Bialystok had been discovered. ("We found him. He will not trouble us again.") Thus, Adam once again was delivering cash within Poland and occasionally in other countries.

In the summer of 1990, Adam completed his first in what would prove to be a series of articles about Post Traumatic Stress Disorder among members of Holocaust families. It was entitled "PTSD: Cascading Down the Generations." It was published in August, 1990 in *American Journal of Psychology*. This first article detailed Adam's interviews with one or more members of twelve Holocaust families, including the Pilsudski family.

Adam continued teaching his courses at the Faculty of Law and Administration at UJ and his work with the victims of Father Edmond's predations at Ignatianum, all of whom were progressing well. In sum, Adam was at peace with the knowledge that he was in some ways a weak man, but a man nonetheless willing and able with God's help to give aid and assistance to those fellow members of humankind who found themselves in need.

When the summer elections of 1989 failed to perpetuate communist rule and, indeed, led to the appointment in September of the first non-communist Prime Minister, Adam rejoiced along with the Polish people. When the Berlin Wall fell in November 1989 and formal reunification of East and West Germany occurred in November, 1990, he rejoiced with the people of the Eastern Bloc and of much of the rest of the world. When further genuinely free elections took place in Poland in 1990 and Lech Walesa became President of the Republic of Poland later that year, he rejoiced anew. When John Paul II visited Poland in 1991, he rejoiced once again. Finally, in August, 1991, during the Pope's second visit, when John Paul met personally with him and Father Pilsudski, Adam graciously accepted John Paul's thanks because he knew that he really had helped to the best of his ability in the massive effort to oust the communist oppressor from Poland.

This feeling of peace persisted when Meredith Adler moved permanently to Poland in the Fall of 1991. She and her husband had divorced quietly and amicably earlier in the year and Meredith now was working with Lech Walesa's government to craft a new constitution for Poland. This would prove to be a difficult undertaking and ultimately a constitution would not be enacted until after a new President succeeded Walesa in 1995. Still, the fact that work was underway on a constitution as well as a multitude of other major initiatives, including the creation of a true market economy, entry into the European Union and joinder of NATO, gave Adam a profound sense of solace.

Thursday, November 7, 1991

Adam was in his office at UJ following his class at the Faculty of Law and Administration when he received a phone call from the U.S. Adam's father and mother along with Mike Burke were on a speaker phone in San Francisco.

"This is a welcome surprise!" said Adam. "What causes all three of you to call?"

"Adam, it's always a pleasure to speak with you and to hear happiness in your voice," said Adam's father.

"I very much appreciate that," said Adam. "However, it sounds as if a big 'But' could be appended to that greeting."

"Very perceptive of you Adam. We do have news we wish to impart. I'll let your mother deliver it."

"Hi Adam."

"Hi Mom."

"I'll start by saying that what we have to say is not definitively bad news. In fact, it may be no news at all. As you know, we continue to monitor the activities of the Spektors and I'm happy to report that our methods have become more sophisticated. What we've discovered is an intense flurry of activity by the Spektor firm centering on the Polish economy. Specifically, they are shorting the Polish Zloty. We think they've invested at least ten million dollars in 'put' contracts."

"What does that mean?" asked Adam.

"In simple terms, the puts they have purchased give the Spektors the right to sell Zloty at what is called a strike price. The put contracts they are purchasing specify a strike price 10% below the current price. So, if the Zloty falls significantly below this strike price then the Spektors will make several million dollars. Of course, if the Zloty remains stable or at least doesn't fall by 10% or more then the put contracts will expire worthless and the Spektors will lose their investment."

"When do these put contracts expire?" asked Adam.

"Very good question, Adam. We'll make a financier of you yet," said his father.

"Don't count on it anytime soon, Dad," said Adam with a laugh.

"It is a good question Adam," said his mother, "and we probably wouldn't have called if these were common one year option contracts. But they're not. The Spektors started buying three month put contracts at the end of September and lately they've been buying 60 day contracts. If the Zloty doesn't fall by more than 10% by the end of the year, the Spektors lose ten million dollars. They're betting that something very bad is going to happen in the near term."

"That sounds ominous, Mom. What sort of event could cause the currency to move so dramatically?"

"It could be nothing other than normal market forces. The Zloty has appreciated quite a bit since Walesa became President. Also, there has been volatility lately, probably because they've hit some snags in achieving a market economy. Others are shorting but nothing so dramatic or short term as the Spektors."

"Thanks Mom and Dad. I'll pass this on to the appropriate people. Any other news on the Spektors?"

Now it was Mike Burke's turn to respond. "We've followed up on what you told us about George Spektor's Chelsea hotel apartment. The intelligence your friend provided to you is true. George seems to be using these rooms for sexual liaisons."

"Well, at least George has some normal impulses. That's more than I can say for his father," said Adam.

"Don't be too sure about that. We're continuing to explore exactly what goes on when George Spektor visits this hotel."

+ + +

Adam was able to contact Father Pilsudski on the following day and to share all of this information with him.

CHAPTER 38

Saturday, December 14, 1991

T O CELEBRATE THE first anniversary of the new Polish republic and, not so incidentally, Lech Walesa's accession to the presidency, a great circular canopy had been erected at the Gdansk shipyard. The canopy was designed to allow seating of twelve thousand people. Two days before the event, people from all over Poland were streaming into Gdansk and it was apparent that at least twenty thousand would be present for the celebration on Saturday evening. In addition, the celebration was to be televised throughout Poland and arrangements were being made for viewing in countless auditoriums, bars, and homes.

On Friday the decision had been made to eliminate all seating in Gdansk to allow a much larger standing audience. Concurrently, it was decided to shorten the celebration, given the fact that the entire audience would be standing. The agenda would include a series of brief speeches from individuals including Ivan Tusk's nephew Donald Tusk who had been instrumental in the founding and ultimate success of Solidarity. These speeches would be punctuated with interludes of music and singing led by invited performers and would include audience participation.

The program was to begin at 7:30 p.m and Lech Walesa was to address the crowd beginning at about 8:30 p.m and ending at 9:00 p.m. The celebration was to conclude with a massive fireworks display scheduled to last until approximately 10:00 p.m. Four dozen folding chairs were arranged in a circle around the podium for the seating of various dignitaries. Around the outer perimeter of the stage at intervals of six feet, security personnel were seated facing the audience. Each wore full military regalia. Among those seated on the stage were Father Padraig Pilsudski, as well as two U.S. Citizens: Meredith Adler, who now was part of Lech Walesa's informal cabinet and Max Spektor, head of the U.S. Foundation *Dignitas et Libertas,* which had made major donations to Solidarity.

The program began on schedule at 7:30 p.m and proceeded as planned until President Lech Walesa reached the crescendo of his speech just before 9:00 p.m. As he raised his arms and uttered the single word "Liberty!" several things happened concurrently. To underline and emphasize President Walesa's declaration of "Liberty!" the first spectacular display of fireworks detonated high above him, just on the edge of The Baltic Sea. Next a man leapt over the plywood barrier separating the audience from the stage and leveled a large automatic pistol at Lech Walesa. As he fired his weapon one of the security men immediately in front of him rose with his arms spread wide. The assassin's round caught him squarely in the chest hurling him backwards toward the seated dignitaries. Now several events occurred in quick succession. First, all lights went out as the master switch was pulled and no further fireworks were launched. Second, the voice of Lech Walesa calmly announced that there had been a power failure and asked that the crowd remain calm and orderly. Third, the two security personnel on either side of their comrade who had been shot pulled down their night vision goggles and shot the would-be assassin with silenced weapons. Next four members of the security detail descended from the stage and quickly carried the inert assassin down the corridor leading away from the stage. The man who had intercepted the assassin's bullet was wearing a bullet proof vest and was able to exit the stage with the assistance of two of his comrades. While these security personnel were moving down the corridor away from the stage, replacements from a reserve force were racing in the opposite direction toward the stage to assume the vacated positions. The lights now had been out for about ninety seconds and at this point President Walesa calmly announced that power would be restored within two minutes and that the fireworks display would commence immediately thereafter. President Walesa then was escorted down the darkened corridor away from the stage. As he reached his car and the caravan of security vehicles the lights came up and the fireworks began.

<u>Sunday, December 15, 1991</u>

At 2:00 p.m. President Walesa's assistant press liaison held a media briefing to address questions surrounding the somewhat unusual events at the previous night's celebration. The President's representative handed out press releases.

<u>Independence Anniversary Marred by Intruder</u>

At the conclusion of President Walesa's remarks during last night's celebration at the Gdansk Shipyard, a man leapt the barrier surrounding the stage and appeared to brandish a weapon. The man immediately was shot by members of the President's security detail. The man was transported to a nearby hospital and died there approximately two hours later. No other injuries resulted from this unfortunate incident and the celebration continued without further interruption. The man's identity now is known but is being withheld pending notification of members of his family.

Given that it was a Sunday afternoon, this press conference was sparsely attended and the follow-on questions from the press corps were rather desultory. The only additional information elicited by the questions was the press liaison's statement that the man had an extensive record of psychiatric disorders. The story received scant coverage in Monday's print, radio and television reports.

Monday, December 16, 1991

"How can you fuck up a simple assassination attempt?"

George Spektor was screaming at Leon Knoss whose assignment had been to create very visible and very bloody evidence of instability within Poland.

"The fucking Zloty never even blipped and now we're out ten million dollars. All you had to do was shoot up the stage. it would have been nice to hit Walesa but failing that your man could have shredded the audience, even dear old do-gooder Dad, who had no clue what was going on. But no! As the press release says, quite accurately, 'No other injuries resulted.'"

"There was a second man in the crowd on the other side of the stage with an automatic assault weapon. He was supposed to open fire after the initial sacrificial lamb had created a distraction. However, just before the lights went out he saw the security people put on their night vision equipment. Except for the three right in front of the first man, the other security people weren't distracted at all. Their attention stayed right on the crowd. It was as if they had advance notice and had planned precisely for such an assassination attempt. Our second man knew it was suicide to try to jump the barrier."

"Yes, the idea that they were warned, that they somehow had advance knowledge of our plans also has occurred to me. We know that Adam Thelen is in Poland. Was he in attendance at the Gdansk event?"

"No, he remained in Krakow. The only possible connection is this shadowy figure of Father Pilsudski who also spends most of his time in Krakow and who was in Gdansk on Sunday. He was on the stage as a matter of fact, as was your friend Meredith Adler."

"No, Meredith is just another idealist who's been bewitched by Lech Walesa and Solidarity, just like my father. Speaking of whom, I'm sure he'll be in to belabor me about betting against the Zloty. Be sure to maintain the story that we were betting on the fundamentals. The Zloty did appreciate a lot, probably too much over the last year, and it has been volatile. Let's try to unwind those put options and maybe cut our losses at least a little. Anyway, the ten million was mostly *Dignitas et Libertas* donations."

"Well, we can try, but the Zloty hasn't budged a bit. In fact, it opened a little higher this morning."

"Do the best you can. And let's start monitoring Adam Thelen's movements more closely. I can't shake the notion that he or his family is somehow involved in Sunday's debacle. Every time he's in the vicinity our plans seem to turn to shit."

Wednesday, December 18, 1991

"The man had no record of any psychiatric disorder but he did have a record of a recent cash deposit of $5,000 to his bank account. He kept babbling about the second man who was supposed to back him up and the security detail which supposedly was part of the plot. He was nothing more than an expendable distraction and he gave us nothing more before he died. I doubt he knew anything more than he told us."

This was Father Pilsudski addressing Adam back in Krakow.

"No mention of the Spektors then."

"Nothing at all. I'm sure this man had never heard the name. However, I believe they were behind the plot."

"Even though Max Spektor was on the stage with you and the second man was supposed to have had an assault rifle?"

"Yes, I've wondered about that. Max surely would have been in danger had the second man sprayed the stage. Maybe Max was willing to take the risk. It certainly will build his credibility as a patron of Solidarity."

"I guess we'll never know. Too bad the first man didn't live and provide more details, if he knew any," said Adam.

"Yes, that is too bad. What isn't bad at all however, is the fact that your parents' intelligence enabled us to prepare. You can tell them there's a good chance that they saved Lech Walesa's life in addition to protecting the financial stability of Poland."

"I will," said Adam.

"You also can tell them that the Spektors must suspect their involvement and yours as well. First the Ghana venture goes bad and now this. You've cost them a lot of money."

"I don't care a whit about their money. I wish Max Spektor had been killed on that stage by his own assassin," said Adam.

+ + +

"President Walesa called me a 'hero of the Republic' in his speech," said Max Spektor to his son.

"That's great Dad. We did give Solidarity a lot of money, almost half of the donations received by *Dignitas et Libertas.*"

"George, you know what we gave them was closer to 30% of what we received. Then you took most of the remainder and bet against the Zloty. How's that working out for us?"

"Dad you know it's not working out worth a shit. We're going to lose ten million dollars when the puts expire later this month. You should be happy it's almost all from *Dignitas et Libertas.*"

"Yes, I suppose so. But the fact that I was on the stage when that crazy man took a pot shot also helped my cred. They apologized profusely after the event, but I had to compliment them on the way they dispatched the guy."

"Yes, their response was remarkably efficient and well organized. What did they say about that?"

"They all but admitted that they had some kind of warning. I think they actually practiced certain parts of their reactions, such as the lights and the orchestrated remarks of the President immediately after it went dark."

It had to be those fucking Thelens.

George refrained from any further questions about the attempted assassination or comments about the Thelens. Better that his father concentrate on his own narcissistic view of himself as a hero, rather than develop suspicions about his son's involvement in the assassination.

"Anyway, Dad, we're starting to make good money in Zimbabwe. There's a lot of opportunity there and no competition or interference so far. I think we can expand our operations there dramatically."

CHAPTER 39

Friday, December 20, 1991

ADAM HAD JUST concluded a telephone conversation with his mother and father. He had passed on details of the assassination attempt and thanked them for the advance warning. He'd also fielded questions about his plans for the holidays.

"When are you coming to visit us?" asked his mother.

"I just don't know, Mom. When the Pope was here in August he instructed me to travel to Rome early next year and spend some time with Cardinal Martino and Monsignor Alessi at the Secretariat of State. Apparently, he has some mission in mind for me, but I don't know what it may be. In any event, I'm afraid I won't be home anytime soon.

"OK Adam," said Chaz Thelen. "We understand and we look forward to talking to you again on Christmas."

+ + +

"What the hell, George?" said Max Spektor. "I've now discovered that you were behind the attempt to assassinate Lech Walesa."

"Where did you hear that fable, Dad?"

"I heard it from one of your, and my, trusted lieutenants and you know perfectly well that it's true."

"OK, Dad, it's true. What of it?"

"I could have been shot by your man."

"Actually Dad, there were two men and they were carefully instructed to locate you on stage before the shooting began. Had they been successful in killing Walesa, we'd have made a lot of money."

"Yes, and I'd be even more famous as a Hero of Solidarity with all the world wide publicity. But you failed."

You senile old fuck. I wish they'd killed both you and Walesa.

1992

After the attempted assassination of Lech Walesa, Adam's sense of peace left him. At first, he tried to pretend he was still at peace and that the outrages perpetrated by the Spektors, father and son, were just one more manifestation of evil afoot on the world — but not something affecting him directly. But then he would think of Lorena and of their unborn child and the old rage would return anew. Finally, he adopted a strategy of distraction by staying so busy that he had no opportunity to think of the Spektors. He wrote and published two more articles on PTSD after visiting and interviewing another two dozen Holocaust families throughout Eastern and Western Europe. He visited the Vatican and met with Cardinal Martino and Monsignor Alessi as instructed by John Paul during his August 1991 visit to Krakow. The first visit was followed by a second and third and then by regular visits each quarter.

The discussions at the Secretariat of State were supplemented by meetings with Cardinal Paulo Ranieri and his staff at the

Vatican Bank. He met twice more with the Holy Father while in Rome. On each occasion John Paul questioned him closely about his progress with Holocaust families and his discussions at the Secretariat of State and Vatican Bank. The Pope was not, however, forthcoming concerning his plans, if any, for Adam's future work as a priest of the Society of Jesus.

During this year, Adam also redoubled his efforts at UJ. His Holocaust project was drawing to a close and he therefore agreed to teach additional classes, one on the federal district and appellate courts of the United States and the other in psychology, based on his studies of Post Traumatic Stress Disorder.

At the conclusion of the spring semester at UJ, in late May, Adam finally was able to return to the U.S. spending four days in New York with his half-brothers Bradley and Theo and then flying on to San Francisco for a ten day visit. In New York he received from Theo the tantalizing news that the Pope's representatives and those of the Father General of the Society of Jesus had discussed "something" concerning Adam's future role in the Order. Theo had heard no specifics regarding what this "something" might be. In San Francisco, in addition to catching up on a myriad of family issues, Adam heard from Mike Burke and from his parents details of the ongoing monitoring of Max and George Spektor. Adam's mother indicated that *Dignitas el Libertas* continued to make moderate donations to the Polish Republic, but that the focus of the charitable efforts of this NGO seemed to be shifting to Central Africa, with emphasis on Zimbabwe and its new President. Details were sketchy but surveillance was ongoing.

+ + +

With all this activity, Adam usually was able to suppress the extreme antipathy he felt toward Max and George Spektor. Adam knew from experience that quiet interludes or any periods of reflection would trigger this antipathy and the extreme rage which accompanied it. He therefore went to great lengths to avoid any such inactivity and reflection. Occasionally however, as when he borrowed Mike Burke's car in San Francisco for a visit to the University and caught a glimpse of Lorena's old apartment, his rage and vengefulness would be triggered unexpectedly and he would be shocked anew at the intensity of these feelings. In these instances, others might have sought counsel, either formal or informal, from others. Adam did not. He simply tamped down his rage, willing it to subside.

Saturday, March 27 – Friday, April 2 1993

Adam had flown into Rome on the preceding Saturday and then spent Monday through Thursday in his regular quarterly meetings at the Secretariat of State and the Vatican Bank. At the former he had been gratified to learn that the Pope had nominated Monsignor Alessi to become auxiliary Bishop of nearby Ovieto where he had spent much of his childhood. He also had noted a subtle but substantive change in the tenor of his involvement at the update meetings. In early 1992 he had been decidedly junior in stature and had been expected only to listen respectfully. In this latest round of discussions and updates, especially at the Vatican Bank, his input and opinion had been sought and, he thought, actually heard. He did not know what this may or may not portend and the contacts he had developed, especially his friend Monsignor, soon to be Bishop, Alessi had been notably unforthcoming. On Friday Adam had begun his trip back to Krakow, this time by train. He had traveled to Florence on Friday morning and met with one more Holocaust family member, this an elderly woman who had survived the camps.

Saturday, April 3, 1993

Now, on Saturday morning, he had boarded the train in Florence for the all day trip to Prague where he planned on Sunday to conclude his Holocaust study with one final interview. He would remain in Prague overnight and return to Krakow on Monday morning. As the train began to move, Adam's thoughts were of the woman he had interviewed the day before and the man who was to be the subject of his final Holocaust interview tomorrow afternoon in Prague. His gaze out the window across the boarding platform was unfocused — nearly sightless. Then on the periphery of his vision he saw a little girl of five or six years of age. Something about the girl caught his attention and his vision cleared. Now he was staring at the little girl in disbelief. She was Lorena in miniature. The train was moving faster now and Adam realized he could not exit. Desperately he looked about the platform for the mother of the little girl. Then there she was, and it was not Lorena. Not even close. The woman standing next to the miniature Lorena was somewhat stout, pleasant looking and obviously protective of the little girl as she placed her arm around her shoulders. As the train pulled away from Florence, Adam was devastated — his sense of loss bottomless. For a moment the little girl was his own daughter and now he realized that she was just a little girl — someone else's daughter. As his sense of loss deepened, tears welled in his eyes. And his rage at the Spektors ignited and was at once a white hot volcano erupting in his head.

CHAPTER 40

Tuesday, May 25, 1993

TWO MONTHS LATER Adam Thelen stepped off the elevator in Max Spektor's penthouse atop the Pierre Hotel just off Central Park in Manhattan. This was a benefit for the Democratic Party State Committee. Max's expansive penthouse was teeming with more than one hundred fifty people, many of them drawn from the Democratic leadership in Albany and New York City. The guest of honor was Mayor David Dinkins, the first black Mayor of New York City. He had beaten Rudolph Giuliani in the mayoral race in 1989 and now was seeking re-election to a second term. Again, his opponent was Mr. Giuliani.

Although this party was billed as a state committee fund raiser, in reality it was designed to raise money for Mayor Dinkins' re-election run. It was a fine late spring evening and the main drawing room with fourteen-foot ceilings was fully opened to the balcony which looked west over Central Park to the lights of upper Manhattan.

The official donation for entree to the party was $500 per person, but Adam, as a member of the clergy, was allowed in gratis. He was dressed in his standard black suit with clerical collar. Adam was in Manhattan as a member of one of the panels which comprised a two-day symposium entitled "Law and Forensic Psychology" at Fordham Law School. The symposium had garnered a fair amount of publicity, at least in part due to Adam's articles on his study of Holocaust victims and their descendants. His invitation to this gala flowed from that publicity plus Max Spektor's desire to gather more information on the Thelen family.

"Ah, you must be Father Thelen," said Max Spektor as Adam entered. I am pleased to make your acquaintance. I am Max Spektor."

"Hello, Mr. Spektor," said Adam, shaking the proffered hand. "I've heard a great deal about you."

"No doubt. No doubt," said Max Spektor. "Please come in and meet the other guests. I apologize that there are simply too many to introduce individually. I'll track you down later. I have something I'd like to show you."

As Adam entered the room, Spektor greeted another guest. Spektor was shorter and more slender than he had imagined, but with a large and imposing head. Adam began to circulate, smiling at anyone who made eye contact and briefly introducing himself. Because of the symposium publicity some people recognized his name and engaged him in conversation. A few were even familiar with his articles.

The large room had two bars plus waiters circulating with wine and champagne along with elaborate canapes and hors d'oeuvres. Adam had taken a glass of red wine, which turned out to be a very passable French burgundy, soon after entering. After about a half-hour of banter, including a passing introduction to the mayor, he made his way to one of the side tables laden with hors d'oeuvres. He hadn't eaten since an early lunch, so he took a small plate, fork and paper napkin and filled the plate with several items. Just as he turned away from the table, plate and wine glass in hand Max Spektor approached him, again.

"Father Thelen, as promised I have something I wish to show you. It's in my bedroom. Just go down the hall past the bathrooms and turn right. The doors are unlocked. Please go in and I'll join you in two or three minutes. Please take your food and wine. It will be easier to eat in there anyway."

Before Adam could respond, Max turned away toward a nearby group and said something which caused everyone to laugh. Adam considered the invitation for a moment and then moved off toward Max Spektor's bedroom.

What's the harm? The devil you know is much more manageable than the unknown. Besides, Mother and Father will be acutely interested in whatever intelligence I can glean.

He proceeded past the separate bathrooms on either side of the wide hallway, marked "Men" and "Women" for this event. He moved as if to enter the door marked "Men." Looking back, he noted that the hallway was empty for the moment and he glided past the door and into the hallway to the right. An imposing double door lay ahead of him.

Balancing his plate and wine glass in one hand, he opened one side of the door and entered the bedroom, which was softly lit. Placing his wine glass on a table near the door, he surveyed the room. It was richly furnished and obviously expensive art work hung on the walls, but taste and coherence were not in evidence. The room was perhaps twenty feet square with a smaller alcove to the left set up as a library and seating area. The bed was on the right wall and to its left was another double door, no doubt leading to the bathroom and dressing area. Straight ahead were large sliding doors opening onto another balcony. As he began to examine the room in more detail. Max Spektor entered.

"I see you found it, Father."

"Yes, I did. It's quite an imposing room."

"Well, appearances are important. But I believe actions are much more so. Please put down your food and come into the library for a moment."

Adam set down his plate and wine glass and followed Max Spektor into the library. Spektor took a large framed photo, perhaps 8" x 10", from one of the shelves and handed it to Adam. The photo showed Lech Walesa on a dais with about thirty other men and a few women.

"That's Lech Walesa in the center of the picture. Look closely at the second person from the left in the photo." Adam did so and could see that it was Max Spektor.

About as far away from Walesa as possible, which made sense based on the information Mike Burke and his operatives had uncovered.

"I am partially obscured, but you can see that the person is me."

"Yes, I can see that," said Adam.

I also can see Father Pilsudski standing next to Meredith Adler on the right side of the photo, glaring across the stage at you, Max Spektor. Father Pilsudski will not be pleased to learn of the existence of this photo with him in it.

"That photo was taken only a moment or two before the attempt on Lech Walesa's life, an attempt which, happily, failed."

Adam said nothing while considering the certainty that the Spektors had been behind the attempt, even if that fact could not be proven in court. He felt his anger beginning to rise at the arrogance and sheer amorality of this man.

"I was and am a big supporter of Walesa and of Solidarity. Some say his survival was a matter of freakish luck, what with one of his security detail seeing the assassin and moving at the last second to take the bullet in Walesa's stead. I disagree.

Lech Walesa made his own luck by surrounding himself, in this case quite literally, with people whose loyalty was absolute. His planning, his own actions, saved his life. The man who took the bullet in his place was merely a victim."

Again, Adam said nothing, all his efforts concentrated on maintaining a placid external facade masking the rage building within. Spektor took the photo back from him and laid it flat on a table near the library shelves.

"It's a beautiful evening. Let's go out on the balcony and talk further," said Max Spektor. "Please bring your food."

Again, Adam obliged. Carrying his plate, he followed Spektor outside. It was, indeed, a beautiful evening. This balcony was located on the north side of the building with views up Park Avenue and, to the northwest, up the length of Central Park. All of the nearby buildings were significantly lower so that there was no impingement of the view. This also guaranteed the privacy of Max Spektor's penthouse.

"You know, speaking of victims, I feel rather strongly about this whole victimhood mania which seems to be sweeping the world. Take the Holocaust for example. I know you are studying this phenomenon and I've read your articles. I agree with your tentative conclusions that what happened reverberates down through succeeding generations. Still, the original victims were just that—victims. They allowed themselves to be exterminated like bugs. I was there you know, in Eastern Europe during World War II. I saw many people die and some would argue that I was complicit in some of the deaths. Nothing on the scale of the Holocaust of course. I would disagree in any event. But I'm rambling on. I must be boring you, Adam."

"Not at all Max. I am fascinated. Please continue," said Adam.

"I thought you might be interested. You're a survivor, not a victim. Just like me."

"How so?" asked Adam.

"Well, consider my time in the war. I always managed to take action, sometimes preemptive action, to insure that I lived, even if it meant that others must die. I would call those others who died victims only in the sense that they allowed their deaths to occur by their own inaction. They were passive, and they died. It's the same with the so-called victims of the Holocaust. They went like sheep to their deaths. I'm a believer you know—in God that is—like you. I see Hitler and his cronies as nothing more than God's agents here on earth. In the end, God gives each of us the means to live or die. Those who die— the victims—choose to die. Like Hitler I am merely God's agent when people die so that I may continue to live and prosper."

"Why are you telling me all of this?" asked Adam.

"Because you, like me, have chosen to live, and to prosper. I respect that. I share this with you because I want to work together with you in Poland. You've gained a lot of distinction there and have a great deal of influence. I propose that we cooperate in certain ventures, informally of course. I believe it could be enormously advantageous to both of us."

"Why would I be interested in such a proposal?"

"All right, let's get down to it. Let's recall San Francisco six years ago, specifically your colleague Father Kung and my associate Ezra Casque. I know what they had planned for you after you declined to cooperate. Yet Kung turns up dead and Casque simply disappears. I have no doubt that Casque is dead, just as I am certain that Kung did not commit suicide. I don't know how you did it, but I know that you were behind those deaths."

"Go on, please," said Adam.

"All right. Let's consider for a moment the girl, what was her name? Montes?"

"Yes, that's it," said Adam.

"We knew of your affair with her for two months at least. We even had people watching from outside her apartment. She was a tasty morsel and you chose to devour her. I don't blame you by the way. Priests have needs just like anyone else. Yet when she died—Oh, yes we investigated her death to insure that there were no loose ends—you went on with your life. She was just a smoking hunk of flesh who chose to die by associating with you. You also were merely God's agent here on earth."

"I see," said Adam, and at that moment the fork fell from his plate and clattered on the deck of the balcony.

Adam crouched down and carefully set his plate on the deck. However, instead of replacing his fork on the plate, he firmly grasped one of Max Spektor's ankles with each hand. Adam smoothly arose from the deck and, with all the power of his legs and torso, lifted Max Spektor's ankles to chest height and propelled his body over the four foot railing and into space. Being careful not to touch the railing, he looked over in time to see Spektor looking back at him with a puzzled look on his face.

"Ask God what He thinks of your agency here on earth," said Adam softly.

Adam watched as Max Spektor began to flail his arms and legs and then saw the body explode on the sidewalk far below. Adam felt a surreal tranquility. He also felt the spirit of Mike Burke by his side guiding him. He picked up his plate, fork and napkin and went inside using the napkin to close the balcony door behind him. He proceeded to the library where he carefully wiped all fingerprints from the photo of Lech Walesa and then replaced it upright on the shelf. He went to the bedroom door, opened it and used the napkins to wipe the knob which he had touched when entering the bedroom. Surveying the room, he saw no other evidence of his presence there.

He picked up his plate and fork along with the now empty wine glass and exited the room, using the napkin to open and close the door. Once in the hallway, he listened carefully for any activity in the hallway to the left leading to the bathrooms and then back to the main drawing room. Hearing nothing, he turned into the hallway, which was empty. He walked quickly to the men's room where he discarded the napkin and thoroughly washed his hands. He then took his plate, glass and fork and casually reentered the main drawing room. After depositing his plate, fork, and glass on a table set up for that purpose, he then obtained a fresh glass of wine from one of the bars and devoted himself to circulating about the room. He was careful to be relaxed, engaging and witty.

By the time the police arrived, he had been an active participant in four separate conversational groups totaling seventeen people. He was as shocked as anyone else to hear the news regarding their host and perhaps even more cooperative and responsive than most in answering questions from the police. By midnight, the police had everyone's contact information and the guests were allowed to leave, subject to further questioning in the future should the police deem this appropriate. Adam returned to his room at the Plaza, which was just a few blocks away at the southeast corner of Central Park. He went up to his room and decided to try to contact Mike Burke on his mobile phone. The new phone was about the size and weight of a brick but Adam knew Mike kept it close most of the time. It was only about 9:30 on the west coast. He dialed Mike's mobile number and heard him answer on the third ring.

"Adam, I've been trying to get in touch with you. I have news."

"Where are you?"

"I'm in New York also but I'm downtown with the peons at the Holiday Inn."

"You said you had news," said Adam.

"I do, but you first. Why are you calling at 12:30 in the morning?"

"I'm sorry. I thought you were on the west coast."

"Adam, the point is you called me at 12:30 in the morning your time. What's on your mind?"

"Well, Max Spektor is dead. I was at a big fundraising party at his penthouse. He was there working the crowd, and then the police came up and told us his body was on the sidewalk outside."

"Adam, I'm coming up there right now."

"No, Mike. I'm suddenly very tired. Let's have breakfast tomorrow about ten. Can you come here? I'll meet you downstairs."

"I'll be there tomorrow," said Mike.

"But you said you had news. What is it?"

"Tomorrow, Adam."

Wednesday, May 26, 1993

Adam awoke about 8:30 feeling refreshed and at peace. He showered, shaved and dressed casually. He was down in the lobby by 9:45, where he found Mike Burke already there waiting for him.

"I'm famished," said Adam. "Do you mind if we have breakfast right here?"

"That's fine, Adam."

They went into the Palm Court restaurant which was sparsely populated at this hour on a working day. Adam ordered a full breakfast while Mike ordered only a pot of tea and wheat toast.

"I already had breakfast. We serfs have to get up and work at a decent hour."

Adam's breakfast arrived almost immediately and he began to eat.

"I'm sorry. I've only had a few hors d'oeuvres and a couple of glasses of wine since noon yesterday. Anyway, I wanted to discuss a couple of things with you. Things that happened last night."

"That's fine, Adam. What things?"

Mike Burke was watching Adam closely. He saw his hands start to shake and tears begin to flow freely down his cheeks.

"Sorry Mike. No food."

Mike Burke kicked Adam under the table as hard as he could. Adam grabbed his leg and scowled. He tried to speak.

"Listen to me, Adam. I don't want you to say another thing. Just get a grip on yourself and finish your breakfast. Then we'll go for a walk in the park."

"But Mike. . ."

"Shut up! Just do as I say."

Adam finished his breakfast in silence and signed the tab to his room. Both Mike and Adam left the restaurant and crossed 59th St. into Central Park. They walked about three hundred yards in a northerly direction and then Mike directed Adam to a bench located a few feet off the main path.

"All right. Tell me what happened."

"I killed him."

"I gathered that much. Now I need to know precisely what happened. Every detail."

"I'm a serial killer..."

"Stop being melodramatic. That bastard deserved to die a hundred times over."

"Now you sound like him..."

"Adam. Stop it. Tell me, now, precisely what occurred."

Finally, Adam did tell him. It took more than thirty minutes, with Mike stopping him regularly to clarify something.

"Tell me again what you did when you returned to the main party."

"I told you. I talked to people. I was engaging."

"Yes, I heard that. But what was your demeanor?"

"Mike, I was as relaxed as if I had just come in from a croquet match. I was at peace. I must be some kind of monster!"

"Jesus, Adam. Knock it off. I'm sorry to be profane but you're the one with a doctoral degree in psychology. Can't you figure out what's going on here and what went on last night?

Adam stopped and thought. He started to speak and then lapsed into silence as he ran through everything again in his head.

Of course. I've been studying this type of phenomenon for five years yet I can't see what's happening to me.

"You're right of course, Mike. I can see it now."

"What about the police. How were you with them?"

"Completely normal. Shock, disbelief—just like everyone else. Then I made every effort to be cooperative. I can see myself clearly now. I don't think anyone would suspect me."

"That's not quite true, but we'll come back to that."

"The thing is, Mike, when I crouched down I had no other intention than to pick up my fork. Then this galvanic rage welled up inside me and he was gone in an instant. I can still see the puzzled look on his face."

"I think the fashionable term these days is temporary insanity due to irresistible impulse."

"But that's not all. I didn't feel we were alone."

"What? Someone else was there?"

"Not a person. Some being. Some force, and I don't know if it was good or evil. But you're right about irresistible impulse. That's one of the topics we'll be discussing at the symposium at Fordham."

"Well, we certainly don't want this to develop into a situation where you have to make such a plea. Based on what you've told me, I think the only additional questions you're likely to get from the police will arise if someone remembers Max Spektor approaching you and asking you to go to his bedroom."

"It was very brief, and I'm sure no one heard him. Of course, he could have said something to someone else."

"That's the other thing that I mentioned a few moments ago. I doubt that Spektor told anyone that he was planning to meet you in his bedroom. Even so, there is a group who will suspect you."

"Who would that be?"

"His business associates, including especially his son. Some of them will remember your involvement in the Ghana scheme six years ago. I very much doubt, for obvious reasons, that they'll go to the police with their suspicions. But they will suspect you. We'll have to give this aspect more thought. The other bad news is that neither his associates nor the police will have an easy time seeing this as a suicide. This is likely to continue as an open investigation. In any event, I think we've done everything we can do for now. I suggest you go back to the hotel and relax. When does this symposium begin?"

"Tomorrow at lunch over at Fordham. Then it runs through the evening of the following day."

"Are you going to be OK? You need to have your wits about you for the next few days."

"I'll be fine now. I'm just extremely happy you were here to work through this with me. But you said you had news. What is it?"

"Nothing all that important, Adam. Let's concentrate all our efforts on the problem at hand. I'm going to call your father and tell him about Spektor's death, but not your involvement, other than to say you were present at the fundraiser. I'll ask him if I can stay here for a few days and watch the fallout from Spektor's death. I'm sure he'll agree. I'll be available on the mobile number if you need me. In any event, let's get together after the symposium. How about lunch on Saturday?"

"That's fine Mike. I'll come down to your neighborhood. And Mike, thank you again."

Adam returned to his room and decided to lie down on the bed for a few moments.

<u>Thursday, May 27— Friday, May 28, 1993</u>

Adam awoke at 7:00 a.m. still in the casual clothing he had worn to breakfast the previous day. He arose, put on his running outfit and left the hotel. He ran a brisk four miles and then walked the final two miles back to the hotel. He showered and then ordered a room service breakfast of tea, cereal, and fruit. Finally, he dressed with care and set off to the symposium. It was another fine day and he chose to walk through the park over to 62nd St. and then west to the law school.

Over the next two days Adam performed quite creditably at the symposium, although he did come near to inappropriate laughter at one question which was posed, thankfully not to him, by an audience member. The audience member was respectful but essentially was asking whether insanity defenses such as irresistible impulse weren't simply additional examples of bogus psychology enabling attorneys to gain acquittals for their guilty clients.

+ + +

A message from the police awaited him when he returned to his hotel room following the conclusion of the symposium. The detective who left the message emphasized that it was routine. All that was needed was Adam's contact information after he checked out of the hotel. Adam immediately called back and provided the requested information to the night shift detective, who also stated that the request was purely routine. When Adam inquired as to the status of the case, the detective replied that it remained an open investigation.

Saturday, May 29, 1993

"Adam, over here," said Mike Burke with his arm raised in a corner booth at a deli about two blocks from his Holiday Inn.

"Hello Mike. How are you?"

"I'm good Adam. How about you? How was the symposium?"

"The symposium went well and my performance could best be described as inconspicuous."

"False modesty ill becomes you. My sources tell me that you performed quite well."

"And what sources might those be?"

"Your brother Bradley was in the audience the second day. He spoke to your father who in turn talked to me."

"No secrets in this family."

"I'm afraid not. But tell me, have you heard anything further from the police?"

Adam related the message he had received the evening before and his follow-up conversation with the night shift detective.

"That's good news Adam, and the confirmation that it's an ongoing investigation is no surprise. The papers haven't had much new information either. Max Spektor was quite well known, not so much for his presence in the financial arena as for his charitable activities. He should thank his P.R. Department."

"He would tell you that the credit is solely his and that anything his public relations people accomplished was due to his actions."

"You're right, but that's probably enough discussion of the late but unlamented Max Spektor. His son, George, seems to feel the same way. He's been very active and visible in establishing himself as the new leader of his father's firm."

"No surprise there either," said Adam.

"When do you go back to Krakow?"

"Tomorrow morning," answered Adam.

"Are you OK?"

"If you mean OK as in functional, the answer is yes," said Adam. "But I have to be honest. On two occasions in the past six years, in a blind rage, I've killed a man. On both occasions it happened immediately after a mention of Lorena. And, on both occasions I've been very lucky to escape consequences, at least legal consequences. It's extremely troubling, and I don't know what to do about it. Do you have any ideas?"

"I'm not too big on ideas. I'll stick to facts and I do have a couple of those which could help."

"OK, what are they?"

"First, keep in mind the suspicions which will continue to fester within the Spektor firm. My only advice for now is to stay alert at all times. Try to keep in mind that photo that Max showed you. These people are nothing if not spiteful and devious. For my part, I need to know more about George Spektor and I'll be doing some research."

"And the second thing?"

"The second thing, Adam, is that Lorena is alive."

Adam was dumbstruck, literally speechless. He looked at Mike, willing the words he had just spoken to be true.

"How. . . how do you know that, Mike?"

"I've just returned from Europe. I saw her, Adam, with my own eyes. She is alive."

"How did you find her?"

"It took a long time and it cost some money — your father's money — to confirm that she was alive and then to locate her."

"Tell me."

"You remember in '87, the two dead ends with the dentist and the tail number of the G-2. I said then that two anomalies were at least one too many for me, but that I didn't know where else to look."

"I remember, Mike."

"Well, I thought about it for two months and then I had an idea. I told you I was a little slow with ideas. I went back to Reno and researched other deaths which occurred at about the same time or a little before the car crash. I found several but one was intriguing. It was a girl, younger than Lorena — only eighteen — who was killed in another car crash five days before the one near Winnemucca. The funeral was over and she was awaiting cremation at a small Reno mortuary. This was where the money — at least some of it — was useful. I finally was able to persuade the young man whose responsibilities included carrying out the cremation that I was not out to expose him and that this was an opportunity for another payday. He was very cooperative after that, even giving us the name of the girl's dentist who sold her dental records. So, the girl in the car outside Winnemucca was this eighteen-year-old. Her cremation was just delayed somewhat."

"You discovered this in 1987. Why didn't you tell me?"

"Early 1988 actually. The reason we didn't tell you is that we couldn't find Lorena. We contacted the parents and it was a total stonewall. Only the mother would speak with us and all she would say was that the family was mourning its loss and could not talk to outsiders. We looked for years in Geneva and also in Spain. Nothing. Your dad made the call. He didn't want to get your hopes up until we had something definitive."

"How did you locate her?"

"It was the University. We checked back there regularly for any inquiries regarding her doctoral degree. Finally, we got a hit from a prospective employer checking her references. Adam, she's been married and divorced since '87. She kept her ex-husband's name. She's now Lorena Mateus."

"Where is she?"

"She's in Italy, Adam..."

"Wait. Let me guess. Florence."

"Adam! How did you know?"

"I thought I saw my daughter there about two months ago. She was the image of Lorena. But she was with a woman I'd never seen before. I convinced myself that it was just wishful thinking."

"She does have a daughter, Adam, about six years old. Her name is Caitlin. The woman you saw must have been her nanny."

+ + +

Adam Thelen departed for Poland the next morning. The symposium organizers had paid for a business class seat. As soon as the plane was airborne, he reclined his seat and closed his eyes.

Lorena is alive. And she has a daughter. Our daughter.

—End

The word paraclete occurs five times in the New Testament, all in the writings of John. "Paraclete" is derived from the Greek word "Parakletos". The translation of the word in English versions of the Bible is "Comforter" in the Gospel, and "Advocate" in the Epistle. [www.biblestudytools.com}

Hence, the title of Volume 2 of this series, Epiphany: The Paraclete.